Other books by Barbara Davies . . .

Bourn's Edge
Dee's Gentlemen and Other Stories
Frederica and the Viscountess
The Giulia Effect and Other Stories
Into the Yellow and Other Stories
Licensed to Spy
Rebeccah and the Highwayman

Christie
and the
Hellcat

Christie and the Hellcat

Barbara Davies

NuAnce
Books

Bedazzled Ink Publishing Company * Fairfield, California

978-1-960373-29-8 paperback

First published 2006
Second Edition 2013
Third Edition 2024

Cover art
by
Trish Ellis Art

Cover Design
by

Sapling
Studio

Nuance Books
a division of
Bedazzled Ink Publishing Company
Fairfield, California
http://www.bedazzledink.com/

In memory of Gareth,
without whose encouragement I would probably still be talking
about writing a story "some day."

ACKNOWLEDGEMENT

Christie and the Hellcat owes its genesis to Elmore Leonard's classic Western short story, *Three-Ten to Yuma*. Leonard's deputy protagonist is a farmer by occupation and he carries out his prisoner-escorting duties alone. I wondered what would happen in similar circumstances if the deputy were a woman, an ex-outlaw at that, and a civilian were willing to help her . . .

PART ONE

The Hellcat Gets Her Gal

Chapter 1

ZEE WIPED THE back of one gloved hand across her clammy forehead and resettled her hat. The mist was dampening everything it touched, but at least it was cool. They had left the sheltering pines of the mountains behind a while ago, and as the sun rose, so would the heat and the dust. Still, they should be in Contention before things got too bad.

Prescott slowed his horse to a trot, twisted in his saddle as much as his bound hands would allow, and looked back at her. His black eye was developing nicely, and the rope burns on his neck looked sore.

"My boys'll find you, you know." His voice carried on the still air.

"Yeah?"

"They'll figure out Hogan's a decoy and start looking for me elsewhere."

She shrugged. "Be too late then."

"Bisbee, Fairbank, Contention—"

She sensed he was looking for a reaction to each town named and steeled herself not to give it.

"—they'll stake them all out," he continued, "you can bet on it."

"Have to keep out of their way then, won't we?"

Prescott frowned at that and started to say something more.

She raised the sawed-off shotgun that had been resting across her saddle. "Keep moving."

He hesitated, and she gave the rope coiled round her saddle horn a pointed pat. His last escape attempt had ended painfully. She had roped him and dragged him from his saddle, almost throttling him in the process. With obvious reluctance, he kneed his gelding into a canter.

For a good long while after that, all was quiet except for the thud of hooves, the occasional nicker of horses, the creak of saddle leather, and the distant, melancholy cooing of mourning doves. Zee relaxed yet kept her senses alert for anything out of place. Prescott would reward handsomely the men who freed him; they wouldn't give a damn about killing a deputy.

She'd parted ways with Hogan just after midnight, hoping the gang hot on their trail would follow her boss and the spare horse instead of her and Prescott. She was hungry and tired now, and in need of a bath. Bluford Hayes should be able to take care of the food at least. Hogan had said the young man, whose house was close to the station depot, was the kind who'd be only too happy to help out a lawman in pursuit of his duties.

Lawman. She suppressed a grin. It was taking some getting used to, being on the right side of the law.

The trail brought them to a dried up riverbed, and the horses scrambled across it and up the other side in a noisy scatter of dust and pebbles.

Zee wiped the sweat from her upper lip. "Hold up," she called and waited until her prisoner pulled the gelding to a halt. She reached for her canteen, unstoppered it, and raised it to her lips. The water inside it was tepid, but it felt blessedly cool as it slid down her gullet.

"What about me?" croaked Prescott.

She took another careful swallow, poured some on her bandanna, retied it, and relished the coolness on the nape of her neck. Then she kneed her mare forward, bringing it alongside the gelding. Shotgun in one hand, canteen in the other, she leaned over. "Open wide."

He guzzled the water she trickled into his open mouth, losing only a little down the front of his striped silk shirt. After a couple of mouthfuls, she took the canteen back and moved out of range.

He looked round at her, water droplets sparkling in his beard. "Thanks, Hellcat."

"Don't call me that," she said, as she'd said a dozen times already. She stoppered the canteen then gestured with the shotgun. "Move."

They rode on in silence for a few more miles, the sun inching higher, the heat intensifying, until finally, through the shimmering haze, she saw the unmistakable outline of buildings in the distance. She pulled out the pocket watch Molly had given her and flicked open the case. They had made good time.

As they neared the outskirts of the little mining town, which, since the railroad's arrival, had expanded to both sides of the San Pedro River, Prescott turned to regard her once more, his gray eyes glittering.

"Contention," he said, with an air of satisfaction. "My boys'll be waiting outside the jail."

"Just as well we ain't going there, then." She gestured with the shotgun, and he turned the gelding toward the newer part of town.

As she rode along the rutted road, past houses made of clapboard, keeping the horses' speeds nice and easy so as not to attract attention, Zee pulled a slip of paper from her vest pocket and peered at Hogan's spidery scrawl.

Bluford Hayes.
Last house before the station depot.
White picket fence. Roses round the porch.

She snorted. *In Arizona?* But as they neared the rendezvous, she saw it was the literal truth. Still, if Hayes wanted to waste water on roses . . .

She urged Prescott past the cast-iron hitching post out front—two strange horses would only attract attention—and round to the enclosed back yard of the neat little house, where signs of a woman's presence were evident: hanging from a line were a pair of drawers, a petticoat (rainbow colored), and a button-to-the-neck gingham dress.

"It's not too late, Hellcat," said Prescott, as they came to a halt beside a woodpile and Zee dismounted and tethered the horses in a shady spot by the fence. She unbound his hands from the saddle horn, but not from each other, and dragged him out of the saddle.

"You can still let me go . . . Oof!"

"I can," she agreed. "But I ain't gonna."

She shoved him up the back steps to the porch, jammed the shotgun in his side, and rapped her knuckles against the wooden door.

"But Yuma . . . you can't send me back there." His voice cracked a little. "You of all people—"

"Yeah," she said. "Wearing a ball and chain ain't no picnic, that's for sure."

She raised her hand to knock again then heard sounds of movement from inside. *About time.*

The door opened.

Chapter 2

CHRISTIE HAD BEEN tidying away the bread-making things when she heard the knock at her back door. She tucked a wayward strand of hair behind one ear, shook the dust from her skirt hem, smoothed down her apron, and went to answer it.

When she saw the two figures waiting on her back doorstep, her first instinct was to slam and bolt the door, but she didn't.

The woman was very tall and shockingly, she was wearing men's clothes: a shabby black Stetson, check shirt, Levi's, boots, and a pair of well-worn guns at her hip. As for her companion, an overweight man who only came up to the woman's shoulder, one eye was swollen half shut and there were rope burns round his neck. Not only were his hands bound at the wrists, a shotgun was pressed against his ribs.

The woman tipped the broad brim of her hat. "Is this the Hayes place?"

Her eyes, Christie noticed, were a very pale blue—very striking against the deeply tanned face.

"Ma'am?"

She was staring, she realized. "I beg your pardon. Who wants to know?"

Belatedly she registered the metal star pinned to the tall woman's vest. A female sheriff? She had never heard of such a thing.

"I'm Deputy Brodie. And this," the woman dug her shotgun into the man's ribs, "is my prisoner, Ches Prescott."

"Oh." Christie gathered her wits. "Yes, this is the Hayes place. I'm Bluford's sister, Christie."

"Then could we get under cover, ma'am?" asked Brodie. "Someone might see us standing out here."

Christie stepped back and gestured. "Won't you come in?"

While Brodie and her prisoner stepped into the kitchen—the latter helped on his way by a sharp jab in the kidneys with the shotgun—Christie noticed the two horses cropping her flowers. They had clearly come a long way; their flanks were covered with alkali dust and sweat.

She gave her doomed flowers a mournful glance, then closed the door and went to join her guests.

Deputy Brodie was pulling out two of the four kitchen chairs and, even as Christie watched, she put a hand on Prescott's shoulder and sat him down on one—unnecessarily hard, it seemed to Christie. She turned the other wooden chair round, straddled it, and rested the shotgun barrel on its back.

"I'm afraid my brother was called away on business," said Christie, taking one of the remaining chairs.

Brodie frowned. "That puts me in a bind. Sheriff Hogan told me I could rely on Mr. Hayes to help me out of a fix."

"He did?" Christie hesitated. What would Blue want her to do? "Well, perhaps I can help."

"I'd be much obliged to you. We need to hole up here for a few hours. And for you to take care of the horses."

Christie blinked. "Won't you be needing them?"

"We're leaving on the afternoon train to Yuma."

"You hope." Prescott's interjection earned him a quelling glance from Brodie.

"I'll be back to pick them up in a couple of days," added Brodie.

Christie considered. "All right."

Brodie's frown smoothed. "Thank you." She took off her hat and placed it on the kitchen table. Her close-cropped hair was so black it was almost blue, and sweat had plastered it to her head.

"You look like you could use something cool," said Christie, rising.

"I surely could, Miss Hayes. The horses could use some water too."

The zinc sink was full—the water wagon had been by the day before—so Christie had no qualms about filling a couple of pails and carrying them out to the appreciative horses. (There was now no sign of her flowers, she noticed sadly.) She returned to the kitchen and fetched the jug of lemonade from the pantry.

Brodie pulled off her gloves, finger by finger, and began feeling in her shirt pocket for something. By the time Christie had poured three glasses of lemonade, Brodie had smoothed out a crumpled piece of paper and was holding it out to her.

"My authorization."

As Christie took it, Brodie's gaze flicked over her in what she could only describe as appraisal. She was used to men looking at her that way—Blue's friends often flirted with her—but this was another woman. It made her feel strange, hot yet cold at the same time.

Brodie pressed her glass of lemonade against her forehead before gulping it down. She put down the empty glass with a loud sigh. "That hit the spot."

The words on the paper swam and made no sense. Christie took a breath, regained her composure, and had started to read when a muffled exclamation made her look up. Prescott, his bound hands making it difficult to hold his glass, had spilled a good deal of the lemonade over himself.

Brodie reached over, took the glass from him, and set it out of his reach. "Wouldn't want you breaking this now, would we? Might come in handy to saw through those ropes."

She made no attempt to mop up the sticky liquid soaking his trousers. Christie frowned. Should she say something?

Maybe it would be better not to get involved. She took refuge in the closely written paper again.

The letter, from Cole Hogan, Sheriff of Cochise County, was straightforward enough. Its bearer, Deputy Brodie, was authorized to escort escaped felon Chester Prescott back to Yuma Territorial Prison. Members of the public were asked to render all assistance where possible.

"That seems in order," agreed Christie, handing it back.

Brodie folded the letter and tucked it in her pocket.

Christie turned her attention back to Prescott. Those marks on his neck . . . it was only right to help him, surely? "Can I get you anything for those burns?"

"Leave him be, Miss Hayes," said Brodie, before he could answer. "He ain't come by nothing he didn't earn." She rose from her chair and walked across to the kitchen window where she peered through the glass. After a moment, seeming satisfied with whatever it was she saw, she stalked back to her chair and straddled it once more.

"Deputy Brodie," said Christie. "I have a salve that will soothe those burns. It is only Christian to ease the poor man's suffering."

"Christian compassion don't come into it where the Hellcat is concerned."

Prescott's entry into the conversation startled Christie. She gaped at him, then his words registered. *The Hellcat?* She hadn't heard that name for . . . oh, it must be five years. Blue would have known all about it right off—he had collected Wanted posters for a while, the way boys do—but the details were muzzy in her mind.

"I'd welcome your kind attentions, Miss Hayes," continued Prescott. "And if there is anything I can do in return." He winked the eye that wasn't swollen. "Attractive young woman like yourself, no man to satisfy her needs . . ."

Her thoughts otherwise occupied, she barely heard him. Wasn't the Hellcat the woman bandit who had robbed the stage so often and so successfully that Wells Fargo had been on the verge of bankruptcy? She'd been caught in the end, of course . . . sent to Yuma Prison. What was her real name: Zee something or other? And why had Prescott mentioned her? *Oh, my Lord! It was Zee Brodie.*

A chair thudding over brought Christie back to her surroundings. Brodie was standing over Prescott, hands gripping his coat lapels, holding his face only inches from hers. "Keep a civil tongue in your head," she snarled, "or I'll gag you."

"See what I mean?" he managed. "Dangerous as a rattlesnake."

Brodie made a small sound of disgust, released him, then returned to the chair she had knocked over in her haste and righted it with one booted foot.

Christie's heart was pounding so hard she felt dizzy. An infamous outlaw sharing lemonade with her in her own house! She became aware that Brodie was studying her and fought to keep her breathing calm, her expression unchanged.

How in the world had the outlaw come by a deputy's badge and letter of authorization? Maybe she had killed the real deputy and taken his. Maybe, despite appearances, Prescott was not her prisoner but her accomplice. Maybe—her heart skipped a beat—they were planning to rob the Yuma train.

"Don't let this animal upset you, Miss Hayes." Brodie indicated Prescott. "He's just trying to stir things up enough so he can escape."

"I'm not upset," said Christie quickly.

Brodie clearly didn't believe her. "Then have I done something to offend you?"

"Of course not." Her mind was whirling, proposing and rejecting various scenarios. "Would anyone like breakfast?"

The abrupt change of subject made Brodie blink. "I could sure use a bite," she said, after a pause that seemed to stretch forever. She turned to Prescott who was looking balefully at her. "Him too . . . though he don't deserve it." She muttered the last part under her breath.

Glad of something to do, Christie crossed to the pantry and brought out ham, butter, and some rolls she had baked that morning. She fed fresh logs into the stove and put coffee on to brew. As she took down a skillet from its hook, she realized she had left the eggs in the pantry.

It was then that the idea came to her. The Hellcat didn't know she already had eggs. Maybe, just maybe, it would be excuse enough for her to get out of the house for a moment, to get help.

"I need to fetch some eggs from a neighbor," she blurted.

Brodie shrugged. "No need on our account, Miss Hayes."

"Ham without eggs? What would my brother say if he knew how I had fed my guests?" Already, Christie was untying her apron and fetching her sunbonnet and a little wicker basket. "It'll only take me a few minutes. I'll be right back."

Afraid that any minute Brodie would realize what she was up to and stop her, she headed for the back door. Placing her trembling hand on the handle, she opened the door. Then she stepped through, out into the morning sunshine . . . and freedom.

Chapter 3

ZEE CROSSED TO the window and watched Christie Hayes hurry out of the gate, tying the bonnet ribbons under her chin as she went. Prescott's insinuations had clearly upset her. She must have led a sheltered life up to now.

"You've got a dirty mouth," she told him.

"You're just mad because I upset your plans."

Zee scanned the kitchen, savoring the aromas of coffee, wood smoke, and freshly baked bread. "What plans would those be?"

He snorted. "A man would have to be blind not to see the way you were looking at her. She's your type, ain't she, Hellcat? Blonde. Nice figure." He gave her a knowing look. "Just like that little whore of yours at Madame Miller's—Molly Purple, wasn't it?"

"You talk too much." She eyed the scrubbed floorboards, the pans hanging gleaming on the wall. Christie Hayes was a conscientious housekeeper. She wondered if the brother appreciated the treasure that was his sister . . . and if Christie had a beau yet.

Prescott laughed. "What's the matter? Afraid you're losing your touch? From what I hear you sure liked to touch Molly—"

Anger impelled Zee across the kitchen. She lifted him bodily out his chair. "You don't hear too good, do you, Prescott?"

His bound hands scrabbled at the iron fingers gripping his throat; his face reddened, and his eyes began to bulge.

"You . . . talk . . . too . . . much." A shake accompanied each word.

The urge to save herself the trip to Yuma was strong. It would be so easy; and this miserable excuse for a human being deserved it. So what if some people disapproved? So what if Miss Hayes returned to find a dead body on her kitchen floor?

A vision of shocked green eyes came to her then. She blinked, swore under her breath, and released her grip.

Prescott slumped back into his chair, sucking in great lungfuls of air and, in between, calling her names that would have made even Molly blush.

Zee crossed to the window. *How long does it take to collect a few eggs?*

Her prisoner lapsed into painful silence at last, and for a while, there was only the crackle of logs burning in the stove and the ticking of a clock in the adjoining sitting room.

"What made you give it up?" Prescott's voice was a croak.

"It?"

"The excitement, the money, the pretty women falling over themselves to share their favors with an outlaw."

"I got caught." Zee gave him a sardonic smile.

He studied her. "But you miss it, don't you? You've still got that fire, that need."

"You're talking too much again." *It's true though. I do miss those things—especially since Molly died.*

"How does three hundred dollars sound?"

She turned to stare at him. "It sounds mighty fine."

"All you have to do is let me go."

She laughed quietly. "Not a chance."

"No?" He gave her an ingratiating smile. "C'mon, Hellcat. Think about it. You're gonna die of boredom as a lawman, and you know it. But someone with your skills," he eyed the guns at her hip, "could be a boon to me."

"You offering me a job with your outfit?"

"Interested?"

She shook her head. "Even if I *was* into gunning down innocents like that family you bushwhacked, like I said before: Not a chance."

"Damn shame." He shook his head in mock sorrow. "Because by the end of today, you're going to be dog meat. And all because you won't admit what you really want, who you really are."

"I ain't that person anymore, Prescott. I've changed."

A sound outside the back door made her turn. Then the door opened . . .

Christie Hayes stepped into the kitchen and pointedly ignored the gun aimed right at her. After a frozen moment Zee re-holstered her Colt.

"Sorry."

Christie shrugged, put down the basket of eggs, and untied her bonnet. "And I'm sorry it took me so long," she said.

"'S all right." Zee studied her and frowned. The air of nervousness about her had grown stronger. Zee glanced at Prescott's hands to check that they were still secure. Then she retied the holster thongs round her thighs, and slid her two revolvers out then back in, checking that nothing would snag when she drew. Finally, she pulled on her gloves.

Christie had put on her apron and was standing next to the huge stove. With a metallic clatter, she put the skillet on to heat and tossed in a lump of lard. Soon fat was sizzling and a delicious smell of bread toasting and ham and eggs frying began to waft round the kitchen.

Zee readied herself for what was to come.

Chapter 4

CHRISTIE TRIED TO control her trembling and focus on making breakfast.

It's going to be all right, she told herself over and over. *Rogers will take care of it.*

The Wells Fargo agent, who fortunately lived only a few doors down, had listened open-mouthed as she spilled out the information that the infamous Hellcat was at that very moment sitting in her kitchen, planning to rob the Yuma train. Then he closed his mouth with a snap, jutted his jaw, and stood up.

"You go right back home and keep her occupied. You hear?"

"Oh, but—"

"Now don't you worry your pretty little head about it, Miss Hayes. I'll get my rifle and be there before you know it." She could almost see the thoughts flashing through his head: the man who put this symbol of perverted womanhood back behind bars where she belonged would be famous. It would probably earn him a promotion too.

He placed his hands on Christie's shoulders, turned her round, and urged her none too gently back out the way she had come.

"Wait," she said. "If I'm going back, I must have eggs."

"In the coop out back," he told her. "Help yourself . . . but hurry." So she had.

She cracked the third egg on the side of the skillet and tipped its contents into the sizzling pan, trying not to think about the snippet of conversation she had overheard while she stood, gathering her courage, outside the kitchen door.

"I'm not that person anymore, Prescott," Brodie had said. "I've changed."

Suppose I've got it wrong? Christie thought suddenly. *Suppose* . . . She turned toward Brodie. "Deputy—" she began.

The tall woman arched an interrogative eyebrow, then blinked and swung round, hands reaching for her guns.

The crash of the back door slamming open made Christie drop the skillet. Sunlight silhouetted the Wells Fargo agent. She expected him to shout a warning and demand surrender, but instead his rifle muzzle flashed, then came the roar of gunfire. Clapping her hands over her ears, she fell to her knees and bowed her head.

There was a dull tearing sound. Then came a profanity, quick footsteps, a blow. Something thudded to the floor.

Ears still ringing, Christie looked up to see Brodie standing over a now prone Rogers. Her guns were holstered once more and a wisp of smoke curled up from the rifle in her gloved hands. Rogers' rifle.

"Don't shoot him!"

Brodie glanced across at her. "Wasn't going to." She pushed the back door shut and bolted it.

"Is he dead?" asked Christie.

"No." Brodie gestured at the rifle stock. "I hit him."

Movement made both their heads turn. Ches Prescott was making a break for it, heading for the sitting room door. In two strides, Brodie reached him. The rifle stock rose and fell. She dragged his now limp body into the center of the kitchen and rolled it under the table with her boot. A feeling of unreality stole over Christie.

Poc.

The faint dripping sound made her turn toward the zinc sink. Was there a leak?

"Why?" asked Brodie.

Poc.

It wasn't the sink.

Belatedly Christie registered the quiet question. She turned to ask for clarification, but her words died unspoken and she put a hand to her mouth. On the floorboards next to the outlaw's dust-covered boot was a widening red pool. What she had taken for the play of shadows on Brodie's left shoulder was a spreading stain.

Poc. Another droplet of blood rolled down the gloved left hand and hit the floor.

"You're hurt!" Christie got to her feet and started forward.

Brodie stepped back warily, her finger on the rifle's trigger.

Christie halted. "Don't be silly! Let me look at your wound."

Brodie shook her head. "I can take care of it myself . . . Why?" she repeated.

"Because two hands are better than one." Without waiting for the other woman's permission, Christie crossed to the dresser and pulled out the medicine chest. Her own boldness surprised her. *Why aren't I more afraid of her?*

Brodie gave an exaggerated sigh, then sank onto the chair recently vacated by Prescott. "Much obliged, I'm sure. But I meant: why did you set me up?" She nodded at the unconscious Rogers.

Christie busied herself with bandages and spirits of turpentine. "He was only supposed to capture you," she said stiffly. "His name's Rogers. He's the Contention agent for Wells Fargo."

Then she was standing beside Brodie, very conscious of her scent, a mixture of fresh sweat and horses and cordite that should have repelled yet was oddly enticing. She untied the red bandanna and undid enough shirt buttons to keep Brodie decent (*She's not even wearing a corset*) yet allow her to peel back the sodden check fabric from the shoulder.

The rawness of the bullet hole made her suck in her breath, but she steeled herself. *I've seen blood before. When Blue cut himself on those lethal dressmaking shears of his*. She reached for a swab and began to clean the wound.

Brodie hissed a curse, then flushed. "Sorry, Miss Hayes."

Nice manners. Christie peered round the other side of the shoulder and frowned. "No exit wound."

"Must've struck bone," said Brodie. "You'll have to dig it out." A faint groan from over by the door attracted her attention. "Wait a minute."

In spite of Christie's protests, she got to her feet and crossed to where the Wells Fargo agent lay. One-handed, she unbuckled his belt and slid it free of his trousers. Then she rolled him over on his substantial belly and tried to secure his hands with the belt . . . without success. She cursed under her breath and looked at Christie.

"Give me a hand."

"I don't know that I should. He was only trying to recapture an escaped prisoner."

Brodie blinked at her. "Is that why?" She gestured to the belt. "Come on, Miss Hayes. Before he comes round. Either that or I kill him. You don't want that on your conscience, do you?"

"Of course not." Reluctantly, Christie knelt next to her, looped the belt round Rogers' wrists, and pulled it tight. Brodie checked the result, grunted in satisfaction, and heaved him into a sitting position against the wall where he lapsed into unconsciousness again. Wearily, she returned to her chair and sat down with a groan.

"Just for the record," she muttered. "I ain't an escaped prisoner."

Christie's hand, which had been reaching for a fresh swab, froze. "You're the Hellcat, aren't you?"

"I was."

After a long pause, the hand continued its journey. Brodie flinched as Christie dabbed spirits of turpentine on her wound.

Clean enough, thought Christie. She took a knitting needle and some tweezers from the medicine chest, then fetched a bottle of whiskey from a cupboard. Brodie grabbed the bottle from her and helped herself to a long swig.

"Purely medicinal." Even white teeth flashed.

An indignant Christie snatched back the bottle and poured whiskey over the knitting needle and tweezers. "This is going to hurt."

"Let's get it over with, then." Brodie took a deep breath, let it out, and clenched her jaw.

Removing the rifle bullet was tougher than Christie had anticipated. She was able to locate it fairly quickly with the needle, but it had lodged in an awkward spot. Three times she thought she had it, only to find the tweezers sliding free. Eventually, her grip held, and with a horrid sucking sound and a gush of blood the bullet came out.

Clamping down on her nausea, she bathed and stitched the wound as best she could. By the time she'd finished—*Not a bad job, if I say so myself*—Brodie's tanned face was pale and beaded with sweat, and she was trembling.

Wordlessly, Christie gave her the whiskey bottle and went to rinse the blood off her hands.

"Thanks." Brodie tipped up the bottle and emptied it. Soon, to Christie's relief, some of her color returned.

"Something you should see." Brodie put down the bottle and fumbled in her shirt pocket.

Christie batted the still trembling fingers away. "Let me do it. What is it?"

"It" turned out to be a folded piece of paper, kept inside another sheet of paper for protection.

"Read it," instructed Brodie.

With a little shrug, Christie unfolded the paper and peered at the ornate script. There was a wax seal at the bottom—it looked like the Arizona Governor's stamp. As she read, a wave of shame washed over her, and her cheeks grew hot.

"Zerelda Brodie—that's you?"

"Yeah."

Christie looked up. "You were pardoned?" Her voice was barely audible.

"A year ago. By Governor Crossley himself." Brodie indicated the scribbled signature at the bottom.

Christie folded the pardon and handed it back to Brodie who stowed it away. "Isn't that unusual?"

"Reward for services rendered."

"What kind of services?"

"I'm afraid that's between me and the governor, Miss Hayes." Brodie shrugged, then winced and pressed a hand to her injured shoulder.

Christie shot her a concerned glance. The trembling seemed to have eased but Brodie was clearly in pain. "I've got some laudanum," she said. "Would you—?"

Brodie shook her head. "Best stay alert. That whiskey you gave me will have to do."

"At least let me put your arm in a sling." Christie began to sort through the medicine chest for a suitable piece of cloth. *Ah, that will do nicely.* She eased Brodie's arm into the sling, making sure the limb was fully supported.

"Miss Hayes." Brodie's tone was humorous. "Don't you think that'll slow down my quick-draw some?"

"Wear it for now at least." She tied the last knot behind Brodie's neck and stood back.

While Brodie gingerly tested the sling, Christie studied her. Brodie sensed her gaze and looked up, arching an eyebrow.

"I'm so sorry," said Christie at last. "I didn't know about the pardon." She glanced at the Wells Fargo agent. "He can't have known either."

"Well, ain't this sweet?" came a croak from under the table. "Seems like another one's fallen under your spell, Hellcat. Coulda sworn this one was respectable, too."

Brodie and Christie peered down at the groggy Prescott who was struggling to sit up—not easy with his hands bound together.

"Hope I didn't miss anything good." He winked, and Christie flushed, though she wasn't quite sure what he was implying.

"Keep a civil tongue in your head, Prescott," said Brodie, "or I'll brain you again." She helped him to his feet.

"What's this? An injured wing? I'll have to scale down my offer accordingly." He pretended to think. "How does one hundred and fifty dollars sound?"

"The answer's the same."

Christie was trying to follow the conversation and failing. "What does he mean?"

"Don't pay him any mind, Miss Hayes," said Brodie.

Once Prescott was sat firmly in his chair again, Brodie crossed to the window and stared out. She reached for her pocket watch, flipped open the lid, and glanced at it.

"What time's your train?" asked Christie.

"Just after four."

"They'll find us before then," said Prescott.

Brodie looked at him. "They already have."

Chapter 5

ZEE GLANCED OUT of the window again. Ed Tolliver, second in command of Prescott's new gang, was standing just outside the back gate, smoking a cigarette.

Maybe Rogers had told someone, or maybe someone had seen him hurrying along the street with his rifle, or maybe it was just the sound of gunfire that had attracted attention. Whatever, there was no doubt about it. Tolliver knew where Prescott was and had probably already sent a wire to his cronies in Bisbee and Fairbank.

She chewed her lip and considered her options. The horses tethered in the yard, especially Prescott's horse with its distinctive white blaze, were a dead giveaway. No point in gagging her prisoner, or in trying to hide.

Tolliver removed the cigarette and bellowed, "Hey, Ches. You in there?"

"Sure am," shouted Prescott. He threw Zee a triumphant glance. "Guess you won't be earning that one hundred and fifty dollars after all."

She shrugged, then wished she hadn't. This damned shoulder was going to cramp her style. Not that she was in form today, anyway, she reflected wryly. That Wells Fargo agent shouldn't have been able to wing her. But ever since she'd met the shapely Miss Hayes she'd been distracted, and her reactions were a fraction slower than they should have been.

Water under the bridge.

"Want me to smoke out the deputy?" yelled Tolliver. Zee's hand dropped to her gun butt. If Tolliver were to threaten Miss Hayes—

"No need," called back Prescott. "She'll have to come out eventually. You can get her down at the station." He grinned at Christie. "Can't repay your kind hospitality by burning the place down, can I?"

She gave him an uncertain look then joined Zee by the window, bringing the pleasant fragrance of lavender with her.

"What are you going to do, Deputy?"

"Have that breakfast you promised me."

"That wasn't what I meant."

"I know. But you heard Tolliver. They won't try anything until we leave. Might as well make my last hours good ones." She grinned.

But Christie looked distressed at her joke. "There must be something we can do. What about the town marshal?"

"Milligan?" Zee shook her head. "Best not. Be just as much trouble getting word to him as getting Prescott to the train . . . I'm not out of the running yet, Miss Hayes. This shoulder wound may slow me down some, but I still have a few tricks up my sleeve. After we've eaten, you can fetch me some wire."

"Wire?"

"It will even the odds some."

Christie opened her mouth to say something, paused, then closed it again. She returned to her stove and eyed the congealed eggs and ham, then threw away the eggs and went to fetch fresh ones from the pantry.

Zee took her seat at the table and waited, saliva gathering in her mouth as once more appetizing smells began wafting round the kitchen. When Christie placed a fork and plate of food in front of her, she reached for it, only to be told to wait while Christie cut up her food.

"I can manage," she said, drawing an exasperated, hands-on-hips stance from Christie, which in turn drew an amused snort from Prescott.

Zee sighed. "Go ahead then, if you must."

As Christie sliced the fried ham, egg, and toast into manageable pieces, Zee studied her, noticing the pinking her gaze brought to her cheeks. She suppressed a chuckle. *Yeah. A very sheltered life. It would sure be fun educating her . . . Damn! I'm getting distracted again.*

"There." Christie stepped aside.

Zee reached for her fork. "Thanks." While she ate, almost bolting her food in her hunger, Christie sliced Prescott's food too. Only after her guests had both been dealt with did she sit down to her own food.

Yeah. A treasure.

After they had finished eating and drunk their coffee, Zee reminded Christie of the wire, and she went in search of some. She came back holding out a spool.

Zee took it, pulled out the Colts one by one, and began carefully wiring back the triggers.

"Isn't that dangerous?" asked Christie.

"Yeah. But it means I can fan them." She didn't look up—the guns were loaded, and if she snagged a hammer on something . . . Gingerly, she resettled them in her holsters.

When she finally looked up, it was to find Christie gazing out of her kitchen window once more.

"Any change?"

"There are two men there now. Talking and smoking."

Zee nodded. "There'll be more."

"How many more?"

Zee glanced at Prescott. "How many?"

"That would be telling." Then he grinned. "Too many for you, Hellcat."

"I wouldn't bet on it."

Another check of her watch showed she had a couple of hours to kill. She would have liked a bath, but she didn't trust Prescott to behave himself once he was out of her sight. Then there was Rogers—he hadn't come round yet (she must have hit him harder than she meant to), and she didn't know how he was going to react.

An idea struck her. "Do you play cards, Miss Hayes?" Christie blinked at her in surprise. "Might as well occupy ourselves while we wait."

It was too much to expect Poker, but Zee anticipated a game of Gin Rummy at the very least. What she got was a choice of Artists, Musical Composers, or Shakespeare, apparently the latest thing in "educational" games. *Might have guessed.* Since she knew little about any of those topics, she let Christie choose.

Resigned to being thrashed, which she was, Zee decided to amuse herself by finding out more about Christie. Her initial questions, though innocent enough (When had Christie and her brother first come out West and why?) were met with stiff and to the point answers. But as Christie relaxed and began to ask questions of her own, conversation between them became easier and, inevitably, more personal.

At first, Prescott kept up a running and very sarcastic commentary, but he soon tired of this sport and set himself to dozing, his snores punctuating the shuffle and slap of the cards and the murmur of voices.

They had been playing for an hour when the conversation took an interesting turn. "Why do you wear men's clothes?" asked Christie, reshuffling the cards for another game.

"Because I want to. They're comfortable, practical—I don't ride side-saddle."

"Aren't people shocked?"

"Only those with narrow minds. You ain't shocked, are you?"

"Of course not." But her blush belied her words and made Zee grin.

She had discovered she liked the way Christie's cheeks pinked and the gentle confusion that overcame her whenever she wasn't sure whether to be astonished, outraged, or delighted, which, in Zee's company, was pretty often. It was entertaining, and, Zee admitted, arousing.

"Do you have a beau?" The question was out before she could stop it. *Ah well. No harm in asking, is there?*

Christie studied her cards before answering. "My brother wants me to marry Fred Younger. The Mill owner's son. He's quite handsome . . . though rather short."

Zee slapped down a card of her own. "What do you want?"

"I don't know."

"Haven't you kissed him yet?"

"What's that got to do with anything?"

Zee cocked her head. "A lot, I'd say. Don't you want to?"

Green eyes flashed. "I'm not a whore."

Zee blinked at her. "Wanting to kiss someone don't make you one." She pursed her lips. "So you've never kissed a man?"

"That's none of your business!"

"Which means you ain't." Zee decided to gamble. "Ever kissed a woman?"

"Really! I don't think this conversation is quite decent." The chair made a scraping noise as Christie stood up, waking Prescott in the process. "I will *not* be made the butt of your jokes."

"I ain't joking."

"Well, how would you feel if I asked you: 'Have you ever kissed a woman?'"

"Fine, thanks." Zee smirked. "The answer is: Yeah. Lots of times. I like kissing women. Very much."

At that, Christie let out a half shocked, half intrigued "Oh!" then beat a hasty retreat to the sitting room next door. The kitchen seemed empty without her.

"Trouble in paradise?" asked Prescott.

Zee resisted the urge to punch him. "Shut up."

For the next quarter of an hour, she paced and brooded. Then she stood by the sitting room door and called, "I'm sorry I teased you, Miss Hayes. If you come back, I promise not to do it any more."

At last a subdued Christie returned and they resumed their card game. This time, they kept to more impersonal topics, though Zee was sorely tempted to stray back onto dangerous territory by the glances Christie kept giving her whenever she thought she wasn't looking. Such behavior could have been considered provocative, but Zee realized that Christie was an innocent, unaware of the mixed signals she was sending.

I'd like to help her find out what she really feels, she thought. Then she chided herself for being a fool.

Rogers recovered consciousness, and Christie prepared dinner for four, serving chicken soup, salt pork and potatoes, rolls, and apple pie, which Zee enjoyed and said so, earning herself a smile. The hours passed pleasantly, until it drew near to the time the train was due to leave.

"Let me help you, Zee," said Christie—by this time the tension between them had eased and they were on first name terms.

Zee regarded her curiously. "It ain't your job."

"No, but I caused this." She indicated Zee's shoulder wound. "If I hadn't gone squealing for help to him—" She gestured at the now conscious Wells Fargo agent, who was still bound—partly because Zee didn't take kindly to being shot in the shoulder and partly because Rogers refused to believe her pardon was genuine. "If I had trusted you—"

"That's a lot of ifs," said Zee dryly.

"Please. Let me help," repeated Christie.

"How sweet," said Prescott. "And how loco."

Zee thought about the offer. The bullet wound had stacked the odds further against her. The triggers she had rigged would help, but pain could throw off her concentration and her bandaged shoulder would upset her balance. She couldn't risk Christie being injured, though, or—even worse—killed. She'd never forgive herself for that. She thought for a moment. Maybe there *was* a way.

"How are you at using a rifle?"

"Blue says I'm pretty good. On the trail here, I used to shoot game birds for the pot."

"All right, then," said Zee. "Here's what I want you to do."

Chapter 6

THE LOCOMOTIVE WHISTLED, two short blasts, and let out a rush of steam that made Christie jump. She bit her lip. In a few minutes the train would be leaving, bound for Benson and eventually Yuma. And if Zee didn't hurry up, it would be leaving without her.

Christie had left the house by the front door and, just in case any of Prescott's men were still watching, set off toward McClellan's General Store. Once out of sight, she'd doubled back toward the station, found herself a protected spot behind a rain barrel with a clear view of the train, the westbound platform, and, more importantly, the eight scruffy-looking men lounging there: Tolliver and his cronies, waiting to free their boss.

She checked her rifle for the umpteenth time, then settled back. Prescott's men had scared off law-abiding passengers, and those already on board the train had their faces pressed to the soot-streaked windows, trying to ascertain what was going on. As for the train dispatcher, he was hiding in his office.

The waiting men came alert, standing up then cocking their revolvers, rifles, and shotguns. Christie followed the direction of their intent gazes and saw Prescott and Zee heading toward the platform.

Zee had discarded her sling and was walking so close on her prisoner's heels he was her shield. "Atta girl," muttered Christie.

The waiting men melted back into the shadows. As Prescott neared the step up to the platform, he slowed and began to look about him. A jab of Zee's shotgun speeded him up again. She guided Prescott onto the platform, boots thudding on faded wooden boards, then halted as seven men, among them the one named Ed Tolliver, stepped out of the shadows.

As they fanned out in front of Zee, Christie gripped her rifle. Where was the eighth man?

She didn't have long to wait for an answer. A man in a ragged sombrero emerged behind Zee, his six-gun aimed straight at her back.

Aboard the train, passengers pointed.

Oh, my Lord!

"Call off your dogs, Prescott," said Zee, "or you're dead meat."

He shook his head and raised his voice. "Pay her no mind, boys. She's bluffing."

"No I ain't. Call 'em off. Last warning." Her murderous blue glare sent a chill down even Christie's spine.

Doubt flickered over Prescott's face. "All right," he said. "Ed, do as she—"

Tolliver aimed his shotgun at Prescott's plump belly and tightened his finger on the trigger.

Prescott gaped. "For God's sake, Ed!"

"Hit the dirt, Ches."

Prescott hesitated for only a moment, then he dropped to his hands and knees, exposing Zee. Simultaneously, Tolliver and the man in the sombrero fired and Christie's heart stopped . . . and started again. For Zee was no longer there. She had dropped and was rolling sideways across the platform, shotgun clasped in both hands.

Sombrero clutched at his breast and crumpled in a heap. A dismayed Tolliver sank first to one knee, then to both, and toppled forward onto his face.

They shot each other!

But six of the gang were still standing, and Zee was coming back to her feet, shotgun firing. The train whistle blew, two long mournful blasts this time, then a rush of steam enveloped Zee and the others, hiding them from view. Christie hissed in frustration. The steam cleared and she saw another of Prescott's men was down, screaming and clutching his belly. Zee had discarded her shotgun and now held a revolver.

With a screech and a clatter, the train's wheels began to turn. Slowly but surely, it began to pull out of the station.

"Hurry, Zee," muttered Christie.

Zee's instructions were clear in her memory. "Wait," she'd said, "until I'm out of bullets. Someone's bound to have the drop on me by then—take him out and give me a breathing space." She had pinned Christie with those striking blue eyes. "Think you can do that?"

Christie braced herself against the rain barrel and sighted along the rifle. She had told Zee she could, but now she wasn't so sure. Shooting men was different from shooting birds. Her mouth was dry. She swallowed.

Zee was aiming her gun with her right hand, and using her left to fan the hammer, in spite of her shoulder wound, the shots coming so fast there was barely space between them. Christie gaped as Zee took out three of Prescott's men as easily as shelling peas.

Then it came, the moment Christie had been dreading. Zee's hammer clicked on an empty chamber. As she threw down the useless gun and struggled to draw her remaining revolver, another of Prescott's men, a bristle-chinned cutthroat in a red bandanna, pointed his shotgun straight at her.

There was no time to think. Christie got him in her sights and pulled the trigger. Red Bandanna swayed and Christie held her breath. Then he crumpled and dropped to the platform.

Slowly but surely the train was gathering speed. Christie took an involuntary step forward. *She'll never make it.*

But her intervention had bought Zee precious time to draw her other Colt, and even as Christie watched, she gunned down the last of Prescott's men, holstered her weapon, and grabbed the still crouching gang leader by his arm. As the caboose came alongside the platform, she gave Prescott a mighty shove toward the steps, then leaped toward them herself, hands reaching. The tumbling figures disappeared from view, and the train rumbled off along the track.

Unable to believe it was over, Christie stumbled forward, barely aware of the onlookers emerging now the gun battle had passed. The man who had been gut shot was screaming, but she ignored him and let others go to his aid. She was too busy squinting at the disappearing train, hoping for a sign that Zee was all right.

A tall figure appeared on the caboose's rear platform, holding on to the rail. Christie shaded her eyes against the bright sunlight and saw a flash of even white teeth against tanned skin. Relief washed over her, and she waved her rifle in triumph. Zee removed her hat and waved it in reply.

As the distance between them widened, Christie's shoulders drooped. Then she remembered. *She's got to come back for her horses.* And found she was grinning from ear to ear.

"Miss Hayes," came a man's voice. She turned to find the stationmaster standing behind her. "Can you throw any light on all this?"

"In a minute, Mr. Carmichael. In a minute."

She watched the train shrink until it was only a smudge on the horizon, until it was nothing at all.

Chapter 7

ZEE FOUND HERSELF whistling as she strode along the rutted road from the station depot. She glanced down at the little burlap sack she was carrying and gave a snort of amusement.

You're going soft, Hellcat.

Even so, she kept on whistling, and it wasn't long before she reached the little clapboard house with the white picket fence and roses around the front porch.

A black stallion was tethered to the cast-iron hitching post out front, with no protection from the noonday sun. Its ears were laid flat back in annoyance and its neck was drooping. Zee frowned, and, careful not to spook the magnificent animal, approached him.

After dropping the sack, she unslung her canteen, unstoppered it, and poured tepid water into her cupped palm. At once, the horse began to drink.

"That better, boy?" She patted his hot neck with her free hand. A rough tongue licked her palm dry. The horse looked at her with mournful brown eyes and gave her a nudge. "Still thirsty? All right." His ears flicked toward her as she refilled her palm and held it out again. "I've got a few things to say to your owner, and that's a fact."

After the horse had finished drinking, Zee reslung the canteen over her shoulder, grabbed the sack, and pondered whether to use the front door. A glance down at her dusty boots decided her against it.

At the back porch, she stopped, feeling suddenly nervous. She polished the toes of each boot on the back of her Levi's, took off her Stetson, and ran a hand through sweat-slicked hair, then shook her head in disbelief.

You can face a gang of outlaws but you can't talk to one itty-bitty gal?

She took a deep breath then rapped her knuckles against the door. No reply. She knocked again, louder. She was hammering when the door at last jerked open, framing a scowling man with a bushy mustache.

"What's all the ruckus—?" He broke off as his gaze fell on the tin star pinned to her vest. "Deputy Brodie?"

"That's me." She studied his fair hair, saw eyes the same shade of green as Christie's. "Bluford Hayes?"

"The same."

She tucked her hat under her arm and held out a hand. He took it in a firm grasp and shook it.

"We expected you yesterday, Deputy."

"Sorry 'bout that. Something came up." A little matter of a riot. Some of the lowlifes in Yuma Prison had taken one of the guards hostage; Zee had helped rescue him—the irony of the situation did not escape her.

"Won't you come in? I'm sure you could use something to drink."

As she stepped into the familiar kitchen—as tidy as ever—her gaze roamed eagerly around it, but there was no sign of his sister. She hid her disappointment.

"You'll be wanting to know where your horses are," said Bluford, as he disappeared into the pantry and returned carrying a jug of lemonade. "They're over at Atkins Stables in Commercial Street. He's expecting you." He poured a glass and handed it to her.

She gulped down the cool, tart concoction, which tasted as good as she remembered. "How much will Atkins want paying?"

"No charge," said Bluford. When she made to protest, he interrupted her with an upraised hand. "Least I can do after what happened. Christie told me all about her little misunderstanding."

Zee put down her empty glass. "She did?" He had given her the opening she needed. "May I have a word with her?"

He frowned. "Well, right now I'm afraid she's in the parlor with her beau."

Something clicked into place. "That his horse out front?"

"As a matter of fact, it is."

"Needs watering," she said tersely. "Some shade would be good too."

"Oh, my Lord!" Bluford frowned, then the frown eased. "I know my sister was looking forward to seeing you again, Deputy, and since I'll have to interrupt them anyway to tell Younger about his horse . . . Let me take you in so you can pay your respects before you go."

"Much obliged." She reached for the burlap sack.

"One thing," he said, as he ushered her into the sitting room and from there toward another door. "I'd appreciate it if you didn't mention what happened when you were here."

Zee blinked at him in confusion.

"That Christie killed a man, I mean," he clarified. "Younger doesn't think that kind of thing is . . . well . . . ladylike."

Zee suppressed a snort but said merely, "I'll see what I can do."

He gave her a grateful smile, then reached for the doorknob. "Here we are."

THE PARLOR DOOR creaked open and Christie looked up, glad of the distraction. Fred had got onto his favorite topic—himself—and for the past half an hour had been droning on about the fine time he was sure to have and the excellent business contacts he was sure to make next week when he went to San Francisco.

With a start, she realized that Blue was not alone. Standing behind her brother in the doorway was a tall woman in men's clothing, a red bandanna at her throat, a well-worn gun belt at her waist. Her black hair was cropped short.

"Z—Deputy Brodie." Christie stood up, almost sending the occasional table flying.

Her gaze went to Zee's left shoulder. The bloodstain had gone from the check shirt, and the bullet hole had been neatly mended. She wondered if Zee had darned it herself, or if someone else had. The thought sent an irrational stab of jealousy through her.

"You've already met my sister, Christie," Blue was saying as he came further into the parlor, "and this is her beau, Fred Younger."

"Mr. Younger." Zee's gaze flickered over the bearded man still sitting on the sofa. Belatedly he got to his feet.

"Deputy," acknowledged Fred, moving closer to Christie.

Why did she have to arrive while Fred is here?

As Zee's gaze returned to Christie's face, her lips curved into a faint smile, and Christie felt her cheeks growing hot. Then Zee crossed the room toward her, threading her way between armchairs, sofas, tables, vases, and planters, her presence making the fashionable little front room seem suddenly cramped and overcrowded.

As though sensing a threat, Fred stiffened, but all Zee did, when she halted in front of Christie, was hold out a bulging brown sack.

Christie blinked at it, and Fred muttered something under his breath. A cool blue gaze flicked toward him, then dismissed him.

"It ain't much, Miss Hayes," drawled Zee, "but I'd be obliged if you'd take it. Reckon it's the least I can do, after what my horses did to your flowers."

"Thank you." Christie accepted the sack, wondering what in the world was in it, but resisting the urge to open it then and there. She could sense that Fred would rather she refused the gift, and wasn't sure whether to be flattered or offended. His behavior since Zee had entered the parlor put her in mind of a dog and its bone.

"Please sit down," she told Zee, indicating the upholstered armchair that had been their father's favorite.

"Er . . . erm." Blue cleared his throat and gave Zee a glance that halted her movement to sit down. She frowned and glanced back at Christie.

An arm took Christie's, and she turned in some surprise. "We mustn't keep the deputy any longer, dear," said Fred. "People are paying her good money for her time." He turned to Zee. "Isn't that right?"

The muscles in Zee's jaw clenched then relaxed. "It's a point of view."

"And I'm sure you've got a long ride ahead of you," chimed in Blue.

Christie raised an indignant eyebrow at her brother, but he shrugged and gave Fred a look. His meaning was clear.

Her rebellious streak surfaced. *Why should I say goodbye to this intriguing woman?* But even as she resolved to defy both Fred and her brother, she became aware that Zee had caught the nonverbal exchange and was putting on the broad-brimmed black hat that she had been fiddling with since she entered the parlor.

"I've a ways to go today," said Zee, her tone neutral. "So thanks all the same, Miss Hayes, but I'd best be making tracks." She tipped her hat, then headed for the door.

"Oh, but—"

"Now, now, my dear." Fred chuckled and patted her hand. "You can't keep a lawman from his duty."

She threw him a furious look. "Zee . . ." To her embarrassment, her voice cracked.

Zee turned at the parlor door and looked at Christie. "Yes, Miss Hayes?"

"At least tell me how your wound is."

That earned Christie a warm smile, which was a distinct relief after the frozen formality Zee had adopted. "It's mending fine, thanks for asking." But the relief was momentary, for Zee went on. "It's surely been a pleasure making your acquaintance, Miss Hayes."

Christie stared at her. *Don't go.* "You too, Deputy Brodie," she managed.

"Mr. Hayes?" Zee turned a suddenly harsh gaze on Christie's brother, who blinked. "Don't forget about the horse."

He blushed. "Oh . . . no, of course not."

She looked at Fred. "In my book, any man who treats his horse that bad deserves to be horsewhipped." Then she shrugged and gave a thin smile. "Of course, in *your* book," the emphasis was slight but it was there, "things may well be different."

Then with a final tip of her hat at Christie, she was gone.

Chapter 8

A SCOWLING ZEE headed toward Commercial Street, ignoring the apprehensive looks coming her way, her mind buzzing like a hornets' nest.

Turning up on her doorstep like that and expecting her to fall into my arms. What was I thinking? Courting a gal who probably don't even like me that way.

She turned left onto Commercial Street, located the sign that said "Atkins Horses" and strode toward it.

Just as well. What kind of life could I have given her? She's probably the type to want brats too.

She clamped down on her unruly thoughts and pushed open the stable door. After the heat and dust, the coolness and the familiar scent of hay and horses were soothing.

"Anyone here?" she called into the darkness.

An aproned boy, barely into his teens, appeared, clutching a pitchfork. "Ma'am?" He gaped up at her, then his gaze took in the tin star. "Deputy?"

"Name's Brodie. You have two horses for me? A black mare and a brown gelding with a white blaze on his nose?"

He nodded. "Sure do. Mr. Hayes said you'd be picking them up this week sometime. I'll get them for you right away."

"Take your time, son. I ain't going anywhere." She crossed to a hay bale, plucked a suitable wisp from it, perched on the bale, and began to chew.

Wouldn't have worked anyway. She'd have wanted everything steady and respectable, and I'd have gone loco. Zee sighed. *Sure would have been nice to steal a kiss or two from those pretty lips though.*

Hooves clopped nearer, pulling her from her reverie, and she got to her feet and waited for the boy.

"WHAT DID SHE give you?" asked Blue.

Christie looked up. "Pardon?"

She and her brother were alone in the parlor. Fred was in the back yard, watering his horse, and, from the sound of his cursing, making a mess of it. He hadn't taken Zee's parting shot well—in fact he would probably call her out, next time he saw her . . . if there ever *was* a next time. After all, Arizona was a huge territory, and since Zee hadn't mentioned where she was based . . .

The thought of not seeing Zee again brought an ache to Christie's chest.

"What was in the sack?" prompted Blue again.

"Oh." Christie had forgotten all about it. She rose and crossed to the table where the little burlap sack lay still unopened.

She untied the drawstring, then opened the neck and peered inside. Its contents looked unpromising. She reached in and pulled out a palm full of ancient, dusty looking seeds, brown bulbs, and wizened roots.

"Oh," she repeated, sorting through them with one finger. *Desert Lilies, Poppies, Marigolds, Verbena, and . . . what is that? Ah, yes, Penstemons, and . . .*

Blue was frowning at her.

"Flowers," she explained, holding out the treasure trove for his inspection. "She must have gotten them in Yuma."

He gave her a dubious look. "I dunno, Sis. Seems a lot of effort and a lot of water just to make a few flowers grow—"

"And worth every drop." Zee's thoughtfulness was threatening to bring a lump to Christie's throat, and she fought for control.

A sound in the doorway made her look up. A disheveled-looking Fred—he'd spilled water all over his new check trousers—was standing there. She poured Zee's gift back into the sack and put it down. He wouldn't appreciate what it meant to her, so no point in mentioning it.

He stopped beside Blue and whispered something. Her brother beamed, glanced at her, then nodded.

"I need to go to the store," he said. "I'm expecting a delivery of cloth this afternoon. You'll be all right on your own?"

Christie knew immediately that something was up . . . and she had a sinking feeling she also knew what it was. Zee's visit had been the catalyst, she supposed dully. Fred had suddenly realized that someone might steal Christie away from him.

Steal? she chided herself. *Don't exaggerate.* But as she pondered the question, she was shocked, and a little excited, to realize that if Zee *had* asked her to go with her, she would have seriously considered it. There was something magnetic about the deputy. *But that's all over now.*

"Christie." Fred came toward her and took her unresisting hand in his. "You and I have known each other for several months now."

Unable to speak, she nodded.

"I have spoken to your brother. He tells me he has no objections to our getting married. So now I'm asking you. Will you do me the honor of being my wife?"

If he had asked her that question an hour ago . . . But now . . . The room felt claustrophobic, lacking air. Giddiness overtook her.

"Are you all right?" Fred's voice came as though from a great distance.

"I don't feel—" Then his arms were around her, supporting her, helping her to a chair.

"You see, this is *exactly* why you need someone to take care of you, Christie. Let me be the one, my dear. Say yes."

Her giddiness was receding. As she stared at him, at the ridiculous Vandyke beard that he thought made him look so dashing, she felt a twinge of affection. Perhaps in time she could learn to love him. After all, what else was there?

"Yes, Fred," she murmured. "I will be your wife."

"My dear. My own." He pressed her hand to his lips.

IT WAS NIGHTFALL when Zee rode into Benson, tired, hungry for something other than beef jerky, and in need of a bath.

Main Street was already bustling with miners, cowboys, and railroad men, all spruced up the best they could manage, all looking for a good time. And since the rapidly growing town now boasted three saloons, a brothel, a gambling den, and a dancehall, the odds were they would find it.

She passed the Last Chance Saloon and headed toward the jail, where it was inevitable that some of the men would end up. As she came abreast of Angie's Palace, two of the scantily clad girls leaned over the balcony railing.

"Hey, Brodie," called the smaller one, Clubfoot Liz. "Glad to have you back."

"You ready for a little action?" called the other, known as Red Mary because (as Zee could testify) her hair was red all over.

She tipped her hat at the two whores and smiled. "Give me a chance to wash some of this trail dust off first, will you?"

"Sure thing, handsome," yelled Red Mary. "We'll tell Angie to get your room ready."

Zee nodded her thanks. Her arrangement with "Madam" Angie Tucker suited all concerned. Having a deputy on the premises quieted down some of the brothel's rowdier clients; and if it didn't, well, Zee was handy with her fists and guns. The tiny room that was hers came rent-free; anything else was meant to cost extra . . . but some of the girls were only too eager to supply their services to Zee gratis.

At the hitching post outside the jail—the only stone building in Benson—Zee pulled up and dismounted gratefully. A lamp was still burning in the office window. Hogan must be doing his paperwork.

She tethered her mare and looped the gelding's leading rein over the post. Then, pulling off her gloves as she went, she took the steps up two at a time and pushed open the door with a crash.

"Hogan," she called, as she strode inside then turned right into the office. "You in here, Hogan?"

The mustachioed man looked up from his perusal of *The Police Gazette* and smiled. "Brodie."

She perched on the corner of his battered old desk and grinned at him. "Did you miss me?"

"Only 'cause I wasn't aiming at you." Hogan's tone became serious. "So. Any trouble with Prescott?"

"No. He was enjoying all the comforts of prison last time I saw him."

"Good." He gestured at the darn in her shirt. "Who ventilated you?"

"Wells Fargo agent in Contention. Hadn't heard about the pardon."

Hogan stroked his mustache. "Dang! Feared that might happen one day. I'll have to send out another bulletin."

Zee shrugged. "I can handle it."

"I'd rather you didn't have to. It's bad enough the bad guys shooting at us without the good guys joining in."

"And I'd rather be waited on hand and foot by a pretty little green-eyed gal," she retorted, "but we don't all get what we want."

Hogan studied her. "Anyone I know?"

"No. Anyway, turns out she has a beau."

"You'll find the one some day, Brodie," he consoled.

"Like you did?"

Brown eyes twinkled at her. "I'm still hopeful."

"Me too."

Hogan stood up, stretched so extravagantly she was afraid he'd pop the buttons off his embroidered waistcoat, then reached across his desk to turn down the lamp. "I'm finished here." He glanced at her. "It's been quiet today. Granpappy Carpenter's in the cells—he got drunk and disorderly again—but that's it. I'll stable the horses. Go get some rest. You look beat."

"Thanks." She flashed him a cocky grin. "Got a bath and another little itch needs scratching first."

He raised an eyebrow. "Anyone ever told you you're a hound dog?"

She pretended to think. "Er . . . you just did."

"Danged right."

She followed him out of the office and waited while he closed and locked the door behind them.

"Enjoy yourself," he called, as he untethered the horses. "Think of me tonight, guarding a fierce desperado all on my lonesome."

"You'll be the *last* thing I'll be thinking of." With a wink, she set off toward Angie's Palace.

Hogan's voice carried to her on the cool night air. "Hound dog."

Chapter 9

CHRISTIE PACED UP and down the westbound platform, trying not to think about the last time she was here with Zee, and wondering how much longer Fred was going to be.

He had decided to personally (and unnecessarily, as far as she could tell) supervise the loading of the silver shipment from his father's Ore Mill, and had made her promise to wait for him before boarding. But the locomotive was making sounds of imminent departure, and if Fred didn't appear soon, she would board without him. She had an appointment of her own to keep, after all.

The sound of running footsteps made her turn. Her fiancé was dashing along the platform toward her, his face flushed.

"I beg your pardon, my dear," he said, as he drew near. "Those idiots—" He took her by the elbow and guided her up the steep steps and into the rail car. They had barely taken their places on the hard wooden benches when, with a deafening screech of brakes and whoosh of steam, the train lurched forward.

Through the grimy window, Christie watched Contention recede into the distance behind them. The San Pedro Valley gradient would be steep, but the view should be breathtaking—if clouds of cinder-streaked smoke and steam didn't obscure it.

A rustle of pages from beside her made her turn to find that Fred had got a copy of the *Tombstone Epitaph* from somewhere and was intent on reading it. He glanced at her and smiled. "Everything all right?"

She nodded and turned back to her window, knowing that everything was very far from all right but feeling helpless to do anything about it. A week of sleepless nights had left her weary, and that was before she contemplated the tiresome day ahead of her.

It was all Fred's fault. Nothing but the best would do for his bride-to-be. And since a Parisian seamstress had recently set up shop in Benson, that meant to Benson Christie must go. She had protested, of course. The price the seamstress was charging for a trousseau was obscene, and Christie could see nothing wrong with buying material from Blue's store and making the clothes and under things herself. She was quite a good needlewoman, and Blue stocked dress patterns. But Fred was having none of it.

"No offense, Hayes," Fred had said, "but that material really isn't of the quality I require. And those patterns—well!" He rolled his eyes. "Hardly the latest fashion." Her brother was wounded, she could see it in his eyes, but he said nothing.

Then Fred patted her hand. "No, Christie, I shall wire Madame Clemence in Benson and arrange for her to see you personally."

And so he had. Christie suppressed a yawn. Poor Blue was becoming quite concerned about her not sleeping, but she had waved him off, said it was nothing. How would he have reacted if he knew she was having nightmares about Zee?

Last night, for example, she had been hiding behind the rain barrel, rifle at the ready, watching Zee fan the hammer of her gun and take out three of Prescott's men. Then it had come, as she had known it would: the moment when Zee's gun clicked on an empty chamber and the man in the red bandanna pointed his shotgun straight at her.

As in real life, Christie had got Red Bandanna in her rifle's sights and pulled the trigger. But this time she had missed and the shotgun blast caught Zee full in the chest. Those compelling blue eyes had widened with shock, then, as though in slow motion, Zee had fallen to the platform and lain still, a glutinous pool of blood widening around her.

Christie had woken with her heart pounding and a cry of anguish on her lips. When Blue rushed in wondering what was wrong, she improvised quickly, claimed to have seen a spider. She wasn't sure he believed her though.

A rustle of newspaper pages turning brought her back to the here and now, and she glanced at her fiancé. He had wanted his snobbish sister Julia to accompany her to Benson and back, since he was staying on the train with the silver all the way to San Francisco. But Christie had shown him the loaded Derringer she kept in her drawstring bag, and reasoned that she was hardly likely to meet drunken riffraff in a Parisian seamstress's shop. Reluctantly he had agreed to let her return home alone.

At least she would be free of him while he was away. The way he insisted on treating her as though she was fragile had at first been flattering, but was becoming irritating. If only she felt the least bit fond of him. But the brief flash of affection she had felt when she accepted his proposal had not recurred. And whenever he kissed her—as he was entitled to do now they were officially betrothed—his lips awoke no response in her whatsoever.

She knew she had made a terrible mistake. But what could she do? Fred would be devastated if she backed out now, not to mention having grounds for breach of promise, and Blue . . . well, Blue would never say so, but she knew he was looking forward to seeing her settled in her own house, to being able to concentrate on his own prospects for future happiness—he had his eye on Jenny, the blacksmith's pretty daughter.

Fred turned and smiled at her. "Only a few hours to Benson, my dear," he said. "And it will be worth the effort for all those pretty new dresses."

Christie tried not to scream.

"WHY DO YOU always look so chipper and I feel so old," complained Hogan, as Zee came striding into his office.

"A healthy diet of wine, women, and song." She flung her Stetson at the hat rack and smirked when it plopped onto the hook.

"Ha! Don't let those Temperance Union biddies hear you. They'll be around here with their soap boxes, preaching the virtues of clean-living and teetotalism, before you can blink."

"After yesterday, I reckon they've written me off as a lost cause." She grinned, unrepentant, and perched on the corner of his desk. "So. What's on your mind?"

"I want you to mind the store." His gesture encompassed the curling Wanted posters and yellowing back copies of *The Police Gazette*.

She raised an eyebrow. "Going somewhere?"

"Heard some rumors—nothing substantial. The Cody Gang has been seen sniffing around the depot and railroad tracks."

Zee pursed her lips. "Think they know about the silver shipment?"

"That's my theory." Hogan rose, crossed to the rifle cabinet, unlocked it, and took out his Winchester '73 and some ammunition. "Anyway, thought I'd take a look-see, scout around a bit." He relocked the cabinet and began to load cartridges into the rifle's magazine.

"Anything in particular you want me to keep an eye on while you're gone?"

He shook his head. "It'll liven up tonight, always does on a Friday, but you can handle it; anyway I'll probably be back by then."

"Couldn't get much rowdier than it's been."

"Ain't that a fact."

It had been one of those weeks. Monday: she'd had to break up a fight between a Mexican and a Chinaman, former partners in a silver claim, who were attacking each other with pick-axes. Tuesday: Diamond Dust Kate had taken exception to something Clubfoot Liz said, and Zee had

had to soak the two of them with a pail of water before she could pry them apart. Wednesday: one gambler at the Golden Slipper had accused another of cheating. The accuser ended up dead; an innocent bystander was shot in the arm. And yesterday: members of the Temperance Union had marched into the Last Chance Saloon, singing "Rock of Ages" at the top of their lungs and smashing every glass and bottle in sight. Zee had grabbed the not so temperate ringleaders by the neck and bustle of their gowns and bodily thrown them out into the street, then advised the saloon owner to send them the bill for damages.

"All righty." Hogan grabbed his Stetson from the hat rack and crammed it on his head, then picked up the rifle and a full canteen and headed for the exit. In the doorway, he paused, turned, and nodded toward the comfortable chair he always reserved for himself. "Make yourself at home while I'm gone, Deputy."

"Thanks," said Zee, sitting down, crossing her ankles, and resting her boot heels on the desk. "I will."

BENSON LOOKED AS if it had started out like any other mining town, thought Christie, as she traipsed along Main Street looking for Madame Clemence's, but it was on its way up. Contention didn't have nearly as many stores or shops, and its hotel paled in comparison.

She could still feel Fred's wet kiss on her lips, his beard and mustache prickling her chin. At least, as they were in public, he hadn't tried to put his tongue in her mouth.

"I hope your trip is successful," she had said, meaning it, as they stood side by side at the bottom of the rail car's steps.

"It will be. Now remember, Christie, as my wife you will have a certain position to uphold, so let Madame Clemence do what she needs to. I wired her full instructions."

She sighed. "All right."

"Good. I'll see you in a week." Then he kissed her and bounded up the steps, and the porter closed the door behind him.

At the window, Fred raised his hand in farewell, and mouthed something that might have been "I love you." She threw him a weak smile and raised her gloved hand in reply. Then the locomotive whistled twice—a mournful sound in keeping with Christie's mood—and, with a great shudder and clatter, the train pulled away.

With a start, she realized she was passing by what was obviously a brothel and blushed at the sight of the whores lounging on the balcony in their petticoats. Unfortunately, averting her gaze caught their attention and gained her a barrage of whistles and comments for her trouble.

"What's the matter, honey? We got something you ain't seen before?"

"More like we've got something she wants."

Laughter. "Maybe she's just lost? You lost, sweetheart? Cute little thing like you? Why don't you come in? We'll soon put you right."

Cheeks burning and chin tucked in, she hurried onward, trying to ignore the comments wafting after her. Then she saw, on a recently painted store front, a sign proclaiming: "Direct from Paris: Henrietta Clemence, Seamstress to the Gentry."

She crossed to the glass-fronted door, turned the handle, and darted inside to the accompaniment of a bell jangling, then leaned back against the closed door in relief.

"Can I help you, Miss?" came a soft voice. The speaker was a girl with heavy eyebrows and a downtrodden expression.

"My name is Christie Hayes." Christie pulled the tattered remnants of her dignity round her like a cloak. "I have an appointment for a fitting . . . for my trousseau."

The girl brightened. "We've been expecting you. I'll just fetch Madame. One moment."

While the assistant hurried away into the interior, Christie turned and sneaked a glance through the door glass at the brothel. The "ladies" were now harassing another passerby, but far from being embarrassed or offended, the whiskery old gent had a grin plastered from ear to ear and seemed to be giving as good as he got. She sighed and turned back in time to see the assistant returning, and behind her, like a galleon in full sail, the seamstress herself.

"*Bienvenu*, Miss Hayes," said the matronly woman, swishing her full skirts. "I am Madame Clemence." She looked at her assistant. "And this is Jeanette. My measuring tapes, *s'il vous plaît*, Jeanette." She turned her attention back to Christie. "We have a lot to get through. Come upstairs to the fitting room and we shall begin."

One and a half hours later, Christie's back was aching from all the standing around while both Madame and Jeanette took their endless measurements. Fred had apparently given instructions that Christie should be provided with a complete new wardrobe from her under things up. Which meant she *absolument* must have: chemises, corset bodices, drawers, petticoats, nightgowns—edged with lace, of course, and monogrammed—a wedding dress (*naturellement*), a day dress, a tea gown, an evening dress, and a dinner gown . . .

Christie had held up her hand. "Please. This is far too much. May I not have just a few simple, easy to care for garments?"

A shocked Madame Clemence was having none of it though. If Christie wanted to be *très chic*, she must let Madame Clemence advise her. Reluctantly, Christie held her peace.

Next came the choice of designs and fabrics, which must match Christie's coloring. Madame was particularly taken with the color of her eyes and her hair, and thought she had just the thing, but she deplored Christie's unfashionable hairstyle. Had she never thought of wearing hairpieces? They were all the rage. Christie won the battle on *that* topic (*Oh là là*), but the war continued.

As the fitting progressed (though it seemed to Christie as if little progress was being made), and Jeanette adjusted and pinned according to Madame's directions, she learned Madame's opinions on the merits (or otherwise) of high necks versus low, puff sleeves versus leg of mutton, and wool versus silk brocade. Bustles, she was unsurprised to learn, since Madame was wearing one herself, were a must.

Muffled gunfire startled her. "What was that?"

"Miss Hayes, *s'il vous plaît*," chided Madame Clemence, preventing Christie from moving toward the window.

The shots, thought a frustrated Christie, sounded as though they had come from right outside. What was going on?

"We have far too much still to do," said Madame, "if you are going to catch your train home on time."

With a sigh, Christie resigned herself once more to the torture.

Chapter 10

ZEE STUDIED THE man lying face down in the dirt. Bill Gribble had been a fool, and vicious with it. Now he was a dead fool.

It had been a quiet morning, so Zee had pinned a note of her whereabouts to the jail door and returned to Angie's Palace, where she settled down to play poker with some of the girls not working. She had just been dealt a Full House, when they heard terrified screams.

Zee ran up the staircase flat out and reached the bedrooms in seconds. She kicked open Lazy Alice's door, and found Gribble, face red with rage, pistol-whipping the girl—too much beer had affected his prowess in bed, so, of course, he blamed the little whore.

She pulled the son-of-a-bitch off Alice and gave him a taste of his own medicine. But the weasely little man was so incensed at being pistol-whipped by a woman, he called Zee out.

She gave a mental shrug. Admittedly, she hadn't tried to dissuade him too hard, but she wasn't going to apologize for that. The memory of a battered and bleeding Alice cowering in the corner, unable to reach the Derringer all the girls kept in their bedside cabinets, was too fresh.

So . . . she had accepted Gribble's challenge, and they had taken their business out onto Main Street. With the inevitable outcome.

She reholstered her still smoking gun and turned the body over with the toe of her boot. *Straight through the heart. No need to call Doc Pellet.*

Squatting beside Gribble, she began going through his pockets. Three dollars. The town coffers would have to foot the rest of the undertaker's bill, since the bad-tempered miner had no relatives or friends, as far as she knew.

A grubby boy of about seven was gaping at her from the sidewalk.

"Hey, Brad," she called. He blushed. "Run and tell McGillivray there's another client needs measuring for a pine box, will you?"

Brad gave an eager nod and hared off down the street. Zee straightened, gave the body a last glance, and headed back to the brothel to check on Lazy Alice.

As she entered, the girls crowded round her, all wanting to either kiss her, slap her back, or shake her hand. On the bench by the door several of the brothel's regulars looked on, disgruntled at being kept waiting.

A sniffling Alice was receiving medical attention from Madam Angie herself. Zee went across to give the girl an encouraging pat on the shoulder.

"Thanks, Brodie," said Angie. "Gribble went too far."

"She gonna be all right?" Zee nodded at Alice.

"A little scarring, I expect. Nothing too bad though—you got to her in time."

As though to emphasize that life went on, someone turned on the player piano and started pumping its pedals, and Diamond Dust Kate struck a saucy pose and began to sing along to "The Girl I Left Behind Me."

Clubfoot Liz pressed a shot glass on Zee and winked at her. "Now, about that game of poker we were in the middle of."

Zee smiled, tossed back the whiskey, and followed Liz into the back room.

THE DOORBELL TINKLED and two fashionably dressed young women hurried into Madame Clemence's shop.

Christie eyed them, then returned to her perusal of *Godey's Lady's Book*. The seamstress had finished using her as a human pincushion a little while ago and had allowed her to get dressed and take a seat downstairs. She had never been so glad to sit down in her life. Madame was now sorting through beading and trimming swatches in the back of her shop.

"Disgraceful!" said one of the new arrivals to the other. "She shot him down like a dog."

"I know." Her friend's voice was full of pleased outrage.

Christie blinked. *She?*

"And you know where she is now, of course, don't you?" continued the first speaker. "Angie's Palace."

A little squeal. "My dear!"

"Isn't she too shocking for words? No wonder they call her Hellcat."

Christie put aside her magazine and stood up. She reached for her bonnet and with trembling hands tied the ribbons under her chin, then she grabbed her bag.

Madame Clemence's assistant appeared, looking as downtrodden as ever, and approached the two women. "How may I help you, ladies?"

"Well . . ." The taller of the two began a complicated saga about a ball she was going to attend in the near future.

"Excuse me, Jeanette." Christie's interruption earned her an indignant glance from the two women. "But will you please tell Madame that I must cut our appointment short." Her pulse was racing. *What am I doing?*

"I have . . . other business," she continued, "that requires my immediate attention."

"Oh but, Miss Hayes!" Jeanette looked dismayed. "I'm sure it will only take a few more—"

"You have already taken more than enough measurements, and made more than enough decisions about my trousseau than are surely necessary," said Christie as firmly as she was able. "If you'll send the account to Mr. Younger, as we agreed?" The girl nodded. "Then I'll say good day to you."

Then she escaped out of the gloomy store and onto the hot, dusty street under a cloudless blue sky.

As she hurried toward Angie's Palace, which, as she had feared, was the brothel from whose balcony those disreputable women had made fun of her earlier, she wondered if she had lost her mind—the impulse to see Zee was so overwhelming.

She crossed the street, careful to lift her hem clear of a patch of fresh sawdust stained red, then noticed the undertaker's wagon trundling away, with its shrouded cargo in the back, and realized what the sawdust's purpose was. Her sense of unreality increased, and she quickened her pace, fearing if she came to a halt now she might never be able to move again.

After all, she rationalized, *I must thank her for the flower bulbs.*

The brothel's gaudy swinging doors were straight in front of her. From the other side came muffled sounds of laughter, talk, and a piano playing "Oh, Susanna." She took a deep breath and pushed them open.

An overpowering mixture of musk and attar of roses hit her, and she gaped at the huge room with its glittering chandeliers, costly mirrors, ornate furniture, and embroidered wall hangings in every shade of red she could imagine.

Everywhere she looked, there were scantily clad women, standing, sitting, lounging. One was at a table, dealing cards, another, wearing only her petticoat, was sitting on a man's lap, stroking his whiskers and whispering in his ear.

The laughter and talk faltered, and a sea of eyes turned toward Christie. She gulped.

"Well, well, if it isn't Little Miss Lost," called the redhead who had teased Christie earlier, her voice barely audible above the manic tinkling of the piano, which, oddly, seemed to be playing itself.

It must be one of those new-fangled self-playing ones I've read about. Wonder what it's doing here?

The redhead stretched, then rose from her *chaise longue* and posed. "See something you like?"

Christie's reply died in her throat.

"Leave her alone," came a woman's commanding voice.

She turned to see who her rescuer was. A middle-aged woman wearing a splendid rose-colored Turkish costume and embroidered satin slippers (Madame Clemence would have had the vapors) was coming down a staircase toward her.

"She's not here to see *you*, Mary," continued the woman, her gaze pinning Christie like a butterfly. "Are you, dear?"

"N—No."

The woman halted in front of her. "Well, child? Why don't you tell me who you *have* come to see?" When Christie didn't reply, she continued, with a wink to the onlookers, "I don't bite. Well, not unless someone pays me to." The sally provoked a wave of merriment.

Christie's cheeks warmed. "Brodie," she croaked. "Deputy Zee Brodie. Is she here?"

"Ah." There was a wealth of meaning in the older woman's tone. "The good deputy does indeed stay here when she's in town. I take it you would like to see her, Miss—?"

"Hayes. Christie Hayes."

"Pleased to make your acquaintance, Miss Hayes. I'm Angie Tucker, the owner of this establishment." The madam glanced at the watching whores and gestured. "Fun's over, girls. Haven't you got anything better to do than sit gawking at this pretty young thing and speculating about our favorite deputy's love life?"

"No," came the chorus of grinning replies.

"No indeed." Smiling like the cat that had got the cream, Angie turned back to Christie, whose cheeks were now burning. "This way, Miss Hayes, if you please."

Chapter 11

THE POKER GAME was going Zee's way. She was still wearing her undershirt, Levi's, and socks, but Serena was down to her chemise and stockings, and Nellie the Fox and Rowdy Molly were both clad only in their drawers.

She cast an appreciative glance at their bare breasts then at her cards (three aces), and leaned back until her chair was balancing on its hind legs.

"Your bet," she told Molly, who shot her an aggrieved glance.

"You cheating again, Brodie?"

Zee smiled. "Who, me?"

Molly's *humph* was drowned by the sound of the door opening, and Zee glanced round to see who it was. Angie was standing in the doorway, and with her was—Her chair went over backward with a crash.

A rueful Zee got to her feet, rubbing the back of her head and trying to ignore the laughter coming her way.

"Christie?" She gazed at the blonde woman in the demure gingham dress and bonnet. "What are you doing here?" She moved toward Christie, took her elbow, and guided her back out the way she had come. "Did anyone see you come in?"

Something soft landed on her head and draped itself over her eyes, and she reached for it as Nellie called, "Don't forget your shirt, Deputy." Laughter and whistles followed her out into the corridor, and she stubbed her big toe on the doorjamb as she went.

"Damn!" she muttered, but didn't pause in her rush to get Christie away from all this depravity.

"I was in Benson," Christie said breathlessly, as she took the stairs Zee indicated. "So I thought I'd come and see you."

Zee guided her along the corridor to her bedroom, and with a relieved sigh bundled her in and closed the door behind them. She crossed to the window, drew the curtains so no one could see in, then turned to look at her.

"Are you loco? What about your reputation?"

Christie wrung her hands. "I know," she said. "But I *had* to come."

Zee blinked at that, then shook her head and, since there was no chair in her tiny box room, gestured at the bed. "What's done is done, I guess. Sit."

Christie sat down on the narrow bed. She set aside her little drawstring bag, then untied her bonnet and took it off.

Zee realized she was still carrying her shirt. *No point in putting it on now.* She flung it on the dresser. *Left my boots downstairs too.* She sat on the bed next to Christie.

An awkward silence followed. Christie was the first to break it.

"Thank you for the flower bulbs. They meant a lot to me."

"Hope they ain't all cactuses. One bulb looks much like another to me." Zee studied Christie, whose soft cheeks pinked under her scrutiny. "So, you had to come to Benson, huh? What for?"

"Fred insisted I visit that Parisian seamstress, Madame Clemence."

Zee laughed. "If she's Parisian, I'm Governor of Arizona." She wondered how Fred could insist, then it dawned on her. "For your trousseau?"

"Yes."

"You're gonna marry him?"

"Looks like it."

Something wasn't adding up. This sheltered young woman was about to be married, yet she had ventured all alone into a brothel just to find an ex-outlaw? "You don't sound very sure."

"I'm not. But it's the right thing to do."

"Says who?"

Zee's question got her an exasperated look. "Says everyone. He's the son of one of Contention's wealthiest families. His connections will be invaluable to Blue."

"Seems to me, there's something missing from this picture. Do you love him?"

Confused green eyes darted toward her then away again. "I . . . What *is* love?"

"Ask me something easy, why don't you?" Zee relaxed back onto the bed and clasped her hands behind her head. This time Christie's assessing gaze remained on her longer.

"Have you kissed him yet?"

"Back to that subject?" Christie blushed. "You seem obsessed with it."

Zee chuckled. "And why not?" she said. "Since it's so pleasurable."

"Is it?"

"I find it so. Don't you?"

Christie grimaced. "No," she admitted. She gave Zee a wistful glance. "I thought, when you kissed someone, it was supposed to feel wonderful. But when Fred kisses me . . ." She trailed off.

"Perhaps you ain't doing it right."

"What do you mean?"

Zee tossed a mental coin. *All right, here goes.* "Only one way to find out. You need another kiss to compare it to."

Christie gave her a look. "And just who's going to kiss me?"

"Thought I might give it a shot."

"You?" Christie licked her lips.

"Yeah."

The last time they had touched on the subject of Zee kissing women, Christie had fled. This time, if Zee was reading her right, the idea seemed to intrigue her. Perhaps it was the real reason Christie was here, though she might not be conscious of it. Encouraged, Zee unclasped her hands and sat up.

"When whatsisname—Fred?" She received a nod. "When he kisses you, does he take you in his arms like this?" She pulled a startled Christie onto her lap, ready to release her at once should she request it. She didn't.

"No."

Green eyes blinked at her from only inches away and the pulse point in the delicate neck was visibly pounding. Zee's own pulse was doing much the same.

"And does he hold you like this?" She eased Christie back and slipped an arm round her, making sure she was fully supported.

"Uh . . . no." Christie's breath was warm against her cheek. Still she made no protest.

"Then does he tease you, just a little? Like this?" Zee started placing butterfly kisses on Christie's neck, on her jaw, her earlobe—she pushed the fair hair out of the way—the corner of her mouth.

"N . . . uh." Christie's breathing had gone ragged and she was trembling.

"No, he don't, or no, you want me to stop?" Zee was enjoying herself and hoped it wasn't the latter.

"He . . . he doesn't."

Well, well!

"Then does he kiss you, like this?" She pressed her mouth to Christie's. At first Christie's lips felt cold and unyielding, then they warmed, became pliant, and, as Zee ran the tip of her tongue along first the lower lip, then the upper, they parted. She darted her tongue inside, tasting and touching teeth and sensitive skin.

Christie groaned. Zee pulled back at once. "Are you all right?"

No reply.

"Christie?"

"I'm . . . it's . . ." Christie closed her eyes, took a deep breath, then opened them and gave Zee a tremulous smile. "Sorry. I just wasn't expecting it to be so," she searched for the word, "intense."

Zee felt almost giddy with relief. "Ah." She pretended nonchalance. "So. Does Fred kiss you like that?"

"He doesn't even come close."

"Then that's where you're going wrong."

"Maybe." Soft lips curled in a speculative grin. "Could we try it again, Zee, so I can be sure?"

"Don't see why not."

Five minutes of leisurely and increasingly expert kissing later, Christie said, "You know, I'm really glad I came looking for you."

"Me too."

And five minutes after that, "But what are we going to do about Fred?"

"Don't worry, darlin'. We'll think of something."

Chapter 12

ZEE WAS UNBUTTONING Christie's dress when the knock came at the door.

"Go away," she growled. "I'm busy." The third button came free, and she peeled back the gingham.

Christie whimpered, and Zee smiled into dilated pupils.

"Easy, darlin'." She cupped a corseted breast. "I'll have you outta there in a tick."

The knock came again . . . louder.

"Brodie." It was Angie's voice; she didn't sound amused. "There are two men downstairs for you. They say they're here on sheriff's business. Oblige me by seeing to them at once . . . they're deterring our customers."

Zee dropped her chin onto her chest and groaned. Reluctantly, she withdrew her hand. "Hold that thought." She kissed Christie, then pulled back and rolled off the bed.

"Hold your horses, Angie." It was lucky she had kept her Levi's on. The check shirt was still on the dresser where she had flung it, and she reached for it. "I'll be right there."

She was still buttoning her shirt as she eased out of the room, careful to hide the interior and the half-undressed Christie from prying eyes . . . unnecessarily as it turned out. Angie had better things to do than wait around. Grumbling under her breath and settling her gun belt over her hips, Zee made her way along the corridor and down the stairs to the salon.

In other circumstances it would have made her laugh. The two men waiting with their backs to her beneath the chandelier could have been plague carriers judging by the distance separating them from the whores. Zee wasn't quite sure who despised whom more.

As the women glanced up at her and smiled, the men became aware of her too and turned.

"Deputy Brodie?" said the taller one, a fair-haired man with ears like jug handles. "We were just over at the jail looking for Sheriff Hogan. Saw your note directing us here. There's been a train robbery."

"You!" spat the other, a fashionably dressed young man with a Vandyke beard.

Zee blinked. "Afternoon, Mr. Younger." She wondered if Fred had any idea that his fiancée was upstairs in her bed. *Probably not.*

Both men smelled of sweat, and alkali dust had streaked their clothes and faces white. "Train robbery?" she asked. "What happened?"

"They were waiting for us at the water tank stop. About thirty miles northwest of here," said Jug Ears.

It sounded like Pantano, which strictly speaking was out of Cochise County jurisdiction. Zee gave a mental shrug. "Who were?"

"Six men on horseback. They had guns, rifles . . . threatened the passengers and crew. Told us if we tried anything . . ." He threw up his hands. "They uncoupled the locomotive and express car and left us stranded."

Zee nodded. "So how did you two get back here, Mr.—?"

"Comstock," he supplied. "Fortunately, there was a railroad pump car by the water tank. Mr. Younger here wanted to use it to pursue the locomotive, but the rest of us thought it would be more prudent to fetch help."

They were right. "Anyone hurt?"

"The engineer. They knocked him out. I couldn't say about the messenger. Locked himself inside the express car. Still inside, last I saw."

"Uh huh."

Christie's fiancé was regarding Zee's feet with disdain, and she glanced down. Her big toe was poking through the hole in her sock. "So who drove the locomotive?" she continued, ignoring him.

"One of the gang," said Comstock.

"Never mind all that," said Fred. "They've got my shipment of silver, and I want to know what are you going to do about it."

She ran a hand through her hair. "Well, first, I'm gonna get my boots."

He opened his mouth then closed it again.

"And, second, I'm gonna get me a horse and some guns and ammunition." She glanced at the two men. "If you want to rejoin your train, you'd better borrow some horses. Either that or," she glanced at their blistered palms, "take the pump car back out."

"Livery stable?" prompted Comstock at once.

She gave him an approving glance. "Out the front door. Turn left. Down the street a ways. Can't miss it. Tell Bradley he'll get his horses back, if I have to return 'em myself."

He tipped his hat. "Thanks, Deputy." He turned and made for the exit, the scantily clad whores parting ahead of him like the Red Sea. After an indecisive moment, Fred followed.

As the chatter, which had been subdued while strangers were present, resumed its normal volume, Zee headed for the back room and her boots. Had that game of strip poker taken place only an hour ago? She sighed and wondered what in tarnation she was going to say to a certain frustrated blonde.

CHRISTIE LEANED FURTHER out of the window and shaded her eyes. It was just possible, if she stood on tiptoe, to see the jail from here. A black horse, saddled and ready to go, was tethered to the hitching rail in front, but there was no sign yet of Zee.

When Zee had returned to her room and told Christie she was called away on sheriff's business, Christie had tried to hide her disappointment. Not very successfully. The feelings Zee's touch evoked in her were . . . well, overwhelming was the only word for it. She blushed at the memory and at how much she already craved more of the same.

Zee, who now had her boots on, she'd noticed, had grabbed her shabby Stetson, given Christie a bruising kiss, told her to take care, and left . . . only to return a moment later, hat in hands, an apologetic look on her face.

"Been taking it for granted you'll be here when I get back." Her tone was full of self-reproach. "Guess I should have asked you." She fiddled with her hat.

Christie opened her mouth to speak but Zee continued.

"I'll understand if you don't want to hang around. There won't be a train to Contention until the track's cleared, though, and the next stage don't leave till tomorrow afternoon. You can stay at the hotel overnight—"

She pressed two fingers to Zee's lips. "Of course I'll stay here and wait for you."

Those remarkable eyes pinned her. "Sure?"

Christie gave a half laugh, half sob. "I'm not sure of much of anything anymore. But I know I want to be with you." Needing to touch Zee, Christie reached up and reordered a strand of cropped black hair.

Zee gave her a brilliant smile and took the hand in her own. "Me too, darlin'." She kissed Christie's knuckles. Then her smile turned crooked. "Come to think of it, it might be better if you *did* stay at the hotel in any case. This room can get kinda noisy, if you know what I mean."

Christie didn't, but she had no intention of telling Zee that. "I'll stay here," she repeated.

Which had earned her a kiss that made her head spin, then Zee reluctantly released her and vanished out the door once more.

She sighed. There hadn't been much time for Zee to tell her what was going on. There had been a robbery, that much she knew. Fred's train, no less! He would be furious, and probably taking the theft of his father's silver shipment personally. Her fiancé always took things personally.

Christie craned her head toward the jail again, just in time to see two riders rein in outside it. One of the men, in a white shirt and check trousers, seemed vaguely familiar, but his hat obscured his face so she couldn't be sure. Then Zee bounded down the jail steps, her vest almost hidden under ammunition belts, clutching a shotgun and a rifle, which she shoved into saddle holsters. She mounted her horse and headed out. The two men fell in behind her.

As the riders approached Angie's Palace, the whores on the balcony below Zee's room began hooting and cheering. Christie hoped Zee would look up and see her, but just then a small boy on the other side of the street yelled at the deputy, who removed her hat and waved it at him, and the moment was lost. The smallest of the three riders, however, looked up at the whores then straight at Christie. She gaped at the familiar face with its neatly trimmed beard and mustache.

Oh, my Lord!

Hands pressed to suddenly hot cheeks, heart hammering, she reeled back from the window. *Did Fred see me? He must have done. Does he know this is a brothel? He'd have to be blind not to. Suppose he comes in and drags me back to Contention with him? Suppose he hurts Zee?*

Her thoughts in a whirl—seeing her fiancé had turned romantic fantasy into stark reality—she sat on the bed, deep in thought.

When she came back to her surroundings, the shadows had shifted. It was the noise that brought her back, a strange rhythmic creaking coming from the room on the right. *Boing . . . Creak . . . Boing . . . Creak . . .* She frowned. It sounded rather like . . . bedsprings.

"Oh . . . Ah."

The moaning brought Christie to her feet. Someone was in pain. She must fetch help. She was halfway to the door when she registered that it wasn't one voice she was hearing but two, a man and woman's.

How could they *both* be in pain, unless it wasn't pain of course, unless . . . *Oh!* Her cheeks warmed.

The noises were coming faster now and louder. Christie paced up and down, clapping her hands to her ears, trying to block out the moans and twanging, and failing.

Zee's words came back to her then. "This room can get kinda noisy, if you know what I mean." *I do now. Maybe I should have stayed at the hotel after all.*

But Christie had made her bed, now she must lie on it (she winced at the unfortunate aptness of the saying). She had told Zee she would wait for her, and she would. But not here, not listening to *this*.

Abruptly, the voices cried out and all sound ceased. She blinked and sat back down on the narrow bed. Perhaps it would be quiet now. Perhaps she could stay here and—

Boing . . . Creak . . . "Ah . . . Oh." This time the noises were coming from the room on the left.

Suppressing a scream, Christie stood, straightened her dress, and made for the door.

Chapter 13

ZEE GUIDED HER mare along the railroad track, keeping its pace to a steady trot. Her companions had wanted to gallop. She explained that getting to the stranded train was only the first hurdle; who knew how far she'd have to travel on after that?

For most of the trip from Benson, Fred had been unnaturally quiet. He was acting like a man who'd been hit over the head. Losing his silver had rocked him, she supposed. Conversation wasn't lacking though. Comstock liked the sound of his own voice, and it was no skin off her nose so she let him talk.

The jug-eared man was from 'Frisco, it emerged—an architect specializing in the Mediterranean style that was all the rage. He was relating anecdotes about some of his more colorful clients when Fred suddenly spoke.

"What was she doing in that place?"

Comstock fell silent, and a startled Zee turned in her saddle and looked at Fred. "She?" *I didn't think he knew.*

"My fiancée, Miss Christie Hayes. What was she doing in that . . . that den of iniquity?" His gaze became accusing. "Was she there with you?"

For a moment, she was tempted to get it all out in the open, to tell him Christie had chosen her over him. Once she did, though, Christie's break with Fred would be irreversible; Christie herself must make that decision.

Instead, she said evenly, "A gentleman wouldn't ask such a question. And I won't answer it."

"How would someone like *you* know what a gentleman would or wouldn't do?" A vein throbbed in Fred's forehead. "By God, if you've touched her, I'll—" Anger made him speechless, for which Zee was grateful.

She turned to face the front again, and almost instantly spotted the top of the water tank in the distance. Kicking her mare into a canter, she left the two men behind.

By the time they caught up with her, she had dismounted, tethered her horse to a door handle, and boarded the first railcar. The stranded passengers greeted her arrival with cries of joy and relief that soon turned to complaints and grievances.

"I was supposed to meet my mother in Tucson," said a man with muttonchop whiskers and a fancy waistcoat. "I'm going to be hours late."

"At least you'll be alive." She eased past him and headed for the far end of the car where a groggy figure in a railroad uniform, a bloody bandage round his head, sat huddled on a bench.

She stopped beside him and squatted. "You the engineer?"

He nodded weakly.

"How are you feeling?"

He eyed the tin star pinned to her vest. "Lousy headache, Deputy, but I can still drive a train, if that's what you're asking."

"It is. Feel up to a little horse ride?"

He groaned. "Do I have a choice?"

She considered. "Yeah, you do."

He sighed. "I'll come. Just don't let the sons-of-bitches who did this," he indicated his bandaged head, "near me again."

"I won't." She helped him to his feet, then steadied him until the color returned to his cheeks. "My name's Brodie."

"Olmsted."

She patted him on the shoulder then turned to address the passengers, who had gathered and were watching her, murmuring.

"Now listen up. Mr. Olmsted here is coming with me. He'll be driving your locomotive back and once it's reconnected, the train will be able to continue its journey to Tucson and points west. You'll be late some," she shot muttonchop whiskers a pointed glance, "but you'll get there."

A cheer greeted this announcement.

"What about my silver?" It was Fred, of course, who thankfully seemed to have regained control of his temper.

"And what about my government bonds?" asked a stout businessman in a top hat, stiff collar, and flat ascot tie.

"They're next on my list," she said.

She helped Olmsted step down from the train and mount the horse Comstock had ridden. Then she mounted her mare, and turned to reach for the reins of the gelding Fred had ridden . . . only to find the man himself climbing into the saddle once more.

She blinked. "Why don't you stay with the other passengers and let me do my job, Mr. Younger?"

"And let the Hellcat get her hands on my silver?" He curled his lip. "I don't think so."

Zee ground her teeth and wondered what in tarnation Christie had ever seen in Fred. If she refused, the damned fool was so obsessed with his silver, he'd find a way to follow the train robbers anyway. Probably get himself killed into the bargain . . . which would certainly solve the prior engagement problem. For a moment she was tempted, then her conscience got the better of her. At least with her around to protect him, he stood a chance.

"C'mon then, if you're coming." She kneed her horse into a trot, and the other two riders fell in alongside her.

They hadn't traveled far along the railroad track when Olmsted's curiosity got the better of him. "You're *the* Hellcat?"

"Was," she told him. "The governor granted me a full pardon. Want to see it?" The precious piece of paper went everywhere with her and was in her shirt pocket.

He studied her for a moment, then smiled and shook his head. "Guess I trust you, Deputy."

"Thanks." She meant it.

"Well I don't," said Fred. "And I'll be watching you every step of the way."

After that, they rode on in silence, the only sound the dull thud of hooves, the nicker of horses, and the distant call of a warbler.

It was mid afternoon, the sun a furnace in a cloudless blue sky. Considering his injury, Olmsted was bearing up well, but in his stiff collar, Fred looked uncomfortable. Zee pulled up her bandanna over her nose and mouth against the dust.

When the locomotive and express car came into view, a brown horse was tethered alongside it. Zee reached for her revolver, then relaxed when a familiar figure emerged from the deep shadows thrown by the car and strolled toward her.

"Hogan." She reined in her mount next to her boss and pulled down her bandanna.

He smiled up at her, brown eyes twinkling. "Took you long enough to get here."

"You too, you old coot." She slid out of the saddle and tethered her mare alongside his gelding. "Did you follow their tracks?" She reached for her canteen, poured some water into her palm, and let her mare drink.

He nodded. "Picked 'em up just outside Benson. Been trailing them all day." He grimaced. "They'd already got the heck out of here by the time I arrived though." He indicated some fresh and very deep wheel ruts. "Had a wagon waiting here, by the looks of it." He pointed to the many scuffed hoofprints. "Ten or twelve men. We're outnumbered and outgunned."

Zee flashed him a cocky grin. "Not outgunned."

He chuckled, then stopped as Fred and Olmsted rode up to join them. He tipped his hat. "Cole Hogan, Cochise County Sheriff. Glad you could join the search for the Cody Gang, gentlemen."

Fred gaped at him. "How do you know it's them?"

Hogan shrugged. "Recent sighting of them in these parts."

Zee helped Olmsted off his mount. He was obviously feeling well enough because he joked, "Now my rear end aches as much as my head."

"Mr. Olmsted here's the engineer," she told Hogan as she tethered the horse and gave it some water. "Mr. Younger is the son of the Contention Ore Mill owner whose silver they took." A thought struck her. "They *did* take it?"

Hogan nodded. "That, thirteen thousand dollars in government bonds, and ten thousand dollars in cash, according to the messenger's notebook."

Zee whistled. "Quite a haul!"

"Sheriff Hogan," said Fred. "I take it you're now in charge of this matter, so Deputy Brodie's services are no longer required?"

Hogan blinked at him then gave Zee a wry look. "I may be good, Mr. Younger, but even I can't take on a gang of a dozen armed men all by my lonesome." He turned to Zee, his expression suddenly somber. "They're killers."

She had noticed the express car's doors hanging off their hinges, their battered state indicative of crowbars and hammers. "The messenger?"

He nodded. "Pistol whipped him until he gave them the keys to the safes, then shot him through the head."

She sucked air between her teeth. "Sons-of-bitches didn't need to do that."

"No," agreed Hogan.

Olmsted had gone pale. "Poor Joe. He had a wife and two boys." He started toward the express car, but Hogan intercepted him.

"I wouldn't go in there," he said. "It ain't pretty and there's nothing you can do."

Zee urged Olmsted toward the locomotive instead. "Leave getting those who did this to Hogan and me," she told him. "Your job is to collect your passengers and get the train to Tucson." She stopped and studied him. "How's the head?"

"Hurts like blazes," he admitted. "Guess I'm in better condition than Joe though."

"Yeah." She helped him up onto the locomotive's foot plate then hopped up there with him. An overpowering smell of grease and soot greeted her; it was even hotter in the cab than it had been outside.

Olmsted crossed to a steam gauge and tapped it. "Not enough pressure," he said. He opened the firebox hatch and frowned at the cooling coals. "Needs feeding." A scoop was leaning beside the coal pile, and he reached for it.

"Let me." Zee took it from him.

While she shoveled coal into the firebox, he sat on the pull-down seat and watched her, from time to time examining the gauge. It was hot and sticky work, and Zee's hands were soon covered in coal dust.

She gave herself a rueful look. "Should have brought the fireman. He'd have been a damned sight more use than Younger is."

"He doesn't like you, does he?" said Olmsted.

"Understatement of the year."

The engineer checked the gauge again and made a satisfied noise. "Nearly there." He gave the whistle an experimental toot.

Zee jumped. "Hey, don't waste steam."

"Strong woman like you shouldn't mind doing a bit more shoveling."

She mock-scowled at him. "Good thing you're leaving soon, Olmsted."

He grinned, and she wiped sweat from her forehead with the back of one hand then leaned on the scoop handle while he checked the gauge again.

"That should do it," he said.

With relief, she stretched her overworked muscles and turned to go, then she stopped and held out her hand. "Pleasure meeting you, Mr. Olmsted."

"Likewise, Deputy." He shook her hand. "Good luck."

"Thanks."

Hogan, holding the reins of three horses, was waiting for her when she stepped off the plate. Fred was already mounted.

Her boss's lips twitched as he looked at Zee. "What happened to you?"

"Don't ask." She wiped her face and hands then retied the now sooty red bandanna round her neck.

"Are we going to stand here all day?" asked Fred.

Both Hogan and Zee ignored him. The mount Olmsted had ridden was surplus to requirements, so she looped its leading rein round her saddle horn. Putting her foot in the mare's stirrup, she mounted up.

A sudden *whoosh* of steam made everyone, including the horses, jump. Slowly at first, but gradually gaining speed, the locomotive began to reverse up the track, pushing the express car ahead of it. Olmsted's face appeared at the foot plate window, and he waved at them.

Zee waved back and watched the train recede into the distance for a few minutes, then she sighed and turned her horse to the north.

"Let's go catch us some killers."

Chapter 14

"HEY, GIRLIE. YOU'RE new here, ain't you?" A leathery old gent in a tobacco juice stained vest lurched toward Christie, and she recoiled from his whiskey breath. "Fancy going for a little ride upstairs?"

Her cheeks went hot. "I'm afraid you are under a misapp—"

"Leave her alone, Jack," said a little whore in red frilly petticoats. "She ain't on the menu."

Christie gave her rescuer, whose name she recalled was Clubfoot Liz, a grateful look.

"No?" The hopeful client's face fell.

"No. She's Deputy Brodie's."

His eyes widened, and he began backing away. "I never laid a finger on her, Liz." His gaze switched to Christie. "You can vouch fer that, can't you, little lady?"

He backed into a card table and sent it flying. Liz chortled as the players cursed and set about retrieving their jumbled cards.

Christie, meanwhile, was pondering the whore's words. "Deputy Brodie's?" She frowned, unsure whether to feel pleased or insulted.

Hazel eyes blinked at her. "That's what Angie told us. I'm Liz, by the way." Liz regarded her keenly. "*Ain't* you hers, then?"

Christie flushed. "I suppose I am. It's just . . . well . . . I'm not used to belonging to anyone except myself. My name's Christie. Christie Hayes."

"I know. We've been talking about you . . . Watch out for Red Mary." Liz pointed to the statuesque redheaded woman now talking to old Jack. "She don't like you."

"Why should she dislike me?" asked Christie. "I don't even know her."

"She wants Brodie all to herself, that's why." Liz laughed. "Ain't gonna happen though."

Red Mary nodded, took Jack's skinny arm, and set off upstairs to the bedrooms.

"Lot of us are crazy about the deputy," continued Liz. "Probably 'cause she treats us right." She turned back to Christie. "She treat you right, Miss Hayes?"

"Call me Christie, please." What did she mean by "right"? Chances were a whore would have a very skewed view of right and wrong. "May I ask you, Liz," she began, seeking to satisfy her curiosity, "how you came to be a . . ." She paused, searching for a term that wouldn't offend.

"Jane about Town? Horizontal Worker? Fallen Woman? Cyprian?" Liz laughed at Christie's expression. "You can't call us anything we ain't already heard, Christie. Whores we are and 'whore' you can call me. I ain't proud of it, but I ain't ashamed of it neither. This ain't back East. Out here, men gotta let off a little steam now and then. And whoring's better than killing, don't you think?"

Christie blinked. "I . . . er . . . I hadn't thought of it quite that way."

"Why would you?" Liz's voice held no resentment. "As to how or why . . . well, a girl's got to make a living."

She pointed to the buxom woman sitting at the player piano—a prototype given to Angie by its grateful inventor, Christie had learned—pumping its foot pedals, and singing along to the melody in a loud and surprisingly accomplished soprano. "That's Diamond Dust Kate."

The spangled garters must have been the source of her working name, decided Christie.

"Her no good husband," continued Liz, "used to sell her to his friends for a dollar, then drink the proceeds. She figured, since she was already whoring, she might as well do it proper. Left him, and took the kids to her sister's in Phoenix. Sends money home every month."

"How dreadful!"

Liz's gaze traveled on, settling on a lanky blonde in a plunging green dress that left little to the imagination. "Rowdy Molly's husband was a different matter. He gambled their money away then drank himself to death."

As the sad tales about the women's backgrounds continued (she suspected Liz was exaggerating, but there was undoubtedly some truth in them) Christie thanked God for her own good fortune. Though their parents had died of the cholera, Aunt Kathleen and Uncle Will had made sure she and her brother were well looked after until they were old enough to follow their dream and head out west. These poor women though . . . She became aware of Liz's gaze.

"It ain't such a bad life," said Liz. "'Specially when you work for Angie." She regarded the middle-aged woman in the garish Turkish trousers fondly. "She's fair and she looks after us when we're ill, and best of all she bars any man who hurts us."

Christie suppressed a shudder.

"Alice should have told Angie about Gribble." Liz's gaze had drifted to a mousy-haired little whore sitting in one corner talking with some of the other women. Her face was puffy and bruised, and if Christie didn't know better she would have said she'd been pistol-whipped.

"What do you mean?"

"He came near to hurting Alice on several occasions—he was a mean drunk—but she went with him all the same." Liz shrugged. "Still, Zee took care of him for what he did to her."

"Took care . . ." Christie trailed off as she remembered the red-stained sawdust in the street outside. *So that's what that was.*

"I've got to go to work now." Clubfoot Liz stood up and straightened her petticoats. "You'll be all right if you stay away from the benches." She pointed to the two benches packed with waiting clients and rolled her eyes. "Going to be a busy night." She turned to go. "Don't be afraid to slap 'em if they get too familiar. All right?"

Christie nodded and watched the little whore limp over to a bench, pick the youngest and cleanest of the men, and disappear upstairs.

"Good choice," came a voice from beside her. She turned to find Rowdy Molly standing there, a glass of apple juice in her hand. "Taking a break," she explained. "He's young and healthy," she continued, "and he ain't learned to despise us yet."

"Does that happen?"

"Sure. The respectable married ones are the worst. Reckon they'd throw us away when they've finished if they could." She took a gulp of apple juice. "Don't know what's worse—them or the thirty-second Charlies—"

Christie decided not ask.

"—or the great lovers." Molly gave a humorless laugh.

She couldn't resist. "Great lovers?"

The lanky woman nodded. "With them, you have to pretend you're having a good time too or their pride gets hurt. Of course," she gave Christie a sideways glance, "some actually *are* great lovers. Deputy Brodie for one. But I expect you've already discovered that." Her gaze was knowing.

"I . . . um . . . not yet . . . we . . . er . . ." Christie was sure that even the tips of her ears must be red.

Molly began to chuckle. "My, my. The deputy must be losing her grip. Either that, or," she gave Christie a speculative glance, "she's taking it slow 'cause you ain't been saddle broke yet."

Christie flushed. She still wasn't used to all this open talk about "relations," as her mother used to call it.

"After all, she can't risk tarnishing that famous reputation of hers," continued Molly.

"What reputation?"

"Don't you know?" Molly laughed and finished up her apple juice. "You'll find out soon enough. But in the meantime, think on this." She strolled away, and Christie had to strain to hear her next words above the hubbub. "Why do you think we give Brodie our services for free?"

Chapter 15

ZEE FOLLOWED THE wagon tracks for what seemed like hours. They led across desert and scrub, past saguaro cacti and palo verde trees, heading always toward the Rincon Mountains.

The heat was relentless, and she was forced to stop often to water her mare and to snatch the odd mouthful herself (that, plus some jerky from her saddlebag, had been her only sustenance since breakfast). Now, much to her relief, dusk was falling and the temperature dropping.

It was also getting difficult to see the trail. Fortunately, she no longer needed to. This was familiar territory; she knew where the train robbers were heading, and it wasn't far.

Zee pulled her horse to a halt. While she waited for Hogan to join her, she removed her hat and ran a hand through damp hair.

"Ain't nothing much out this way 'cept cactus," he grumbled, as he came up beside her.

"There's the old Spanish Mission." She put her hat back on and tried to ignore the fact that her undershirt was sticking to her in all the wrong places.

"Forgot about that." He nodded to himself. "Perfect place to hole up for the night."

Zee nodded and glanced back, wondering what was delaying Fred. From his drooping head, the figure in the distance was dozing; his horse had seized the opportunity to slow to a walk.

Hogan followed her gaze. "Not much love lost between you two."

"No."

"A leftover from your Hellcat days?"

She shook her head. "More recent. Remember that little green-eyed gal I told you about?"

Hogan stroked his mustache then nodded.

"She turned up in Benson today . . . looking for me." Zee smiled at the memory. "Found me too. We were just getting . . . reacquainted when news arrived about the robbery." She sighed.

"Danged bad timing," he agreed. "But what's that got to do with Younger?"

"He's her fiancé."

Hogan's guffaw made Fred's head jerk up. "Tarnation, Brodie." He wiped his eyes. "I said you were a hound dog, didn't I?"

She gave him a sour glance. "Keep it down, will you." She kneed her horse forward and the still chuckling Hogan fell in behind.

When the top of a ruined two-story bell tower finally came into view over the rise, as she knew it would, she reined in and dismounted. She grabbed her rifle from its saddle holster and crawled the rest of the way on her belly.

The compound was just as she remembered it, though ten years had knocked a few more holes in the adobe wall encircling the crumbling mission church and priest's living quarters. Two silhouettes were pacing up and down behind the wall.

Hogan crawled up beside her.

"They've posted lookouts," she whispered. "Two out front, probably more round the back. Don't think they've put one in the tower—it ain't safe."

"Why have we stopped?" came a loud voice from behind them. Zee twisted and saw Fred, still mounted, heading toward them. In a moment, he would be visible to the guards.

Cursing, she scrambled toward him and yanked him out of the saddle. He landed with a surprised squawk. She clapped a gloved hand over his mouth. "Behind that wall are ten maybe twelve killers. Got me?"

Zee could just make out the whites of Fred's eyes as he blinked at her then nodded. She released him and crawled back to her viewpoint.

"No reaction from the lookouts," whispered Hogan. "Guess they didn't notice anything."

"Just as well."

Fred crawled up awkwardly beside them. "Is my silver there?"

"Too early to tell," said Hogan. "It's going to get rough when we go in. You stay with the horses, Mr. Younger."

"It's my silver." Fred's voice grew louder. "And I have every right to—"

"Shut up," hissed Zee.

There was a moment's shocked silence. His next utterance was a determined whisper. "I'm going."

Hogan sighed. "If you must. But stay down, and keep quiet . . . and when the lead starts flying, find yourself a deep hole and stay in it."

"There's a corral out back," said Zee. "That's where the wagon will be." She sensed her boss looking at her. "Stayed here a time or two myself," she admitted.

Fred said something uncomplimentary under his breath. She ignored him.

"There'll most likely be extra lookouts posted round the wagon, to keep thieving hands off." She paused. "That's what I'd do anyway."

Hogan nodded. "I'll check it out."

"And I'll see where the rest of the gang are. My guess is the church . . . It's the only building that still has a halfway decent roof."

She set off, flitting from shrub to cactus whenever the lookouts' attention was engaged elsewhere and glancing round occasionally to check on the progress of her two companions.

A twig cracked beneath the sole of Fred's shoe, and he froze. For a tense moment, Zee wasn't sure if the lookouts had heard or not. When they didn't deviate from their routine, she released her breath.

"Younger's gonna get us all killed," she murmured to Hogan, when he joined her in the shadow of a bushy palo verde tree.

"What do you suggest? We tie him to his horse?"

"Don't tempt me."

Fred scuttled up to them, breathing hard.

"Stay here," she told him.

"But—"

"I said *stay here*." To Hogan, she muttered, "We'll reconnoiter, then meet back here in . . . quarter of an hour?" He nodded and wormed off into the darkness.

Zee took a breath, hefted her rifle into a more comfortable grip, then scuttled toward one of the larger gaps in the wall. She waited for the lookouts to pass, eased through, and headed past the priest's dilapidated living quarters, which as she had thought were unoccupied, toward the church.

Lantern light spilled out of the huge arched doorway, and from the interior came laughter and talk. She blinked in surprise. *Sounds like they've got women with them.*

A fat man in a black shirt appeared in the doorway, and Zee ducked deeper into the shadows. She watched him stretch, scratch his belly and stare up at the night sky. He rolled a cigarette and lit it. She schooled herself to patience. At last, the man threw down the butt and went back inside.

She crept to the now empty doorway and peered inside, then ducked back. The single glance had been enough. Quickly she headed back the way she had come, pausing until the lookouts had paced past, then arrowing toward the palo verde tree that was the rendezvous.

Hogan was waiting for her. There was no sign of Fred.

"Before you ask," he said. "I ain't got the faintest idea where Younger is. I've only just got back."

"Damn!" The moon was almost full, but even so, tracking Fred would be difficult; besides they were running out of time. "What did you find?"

"Twelve horses—two for the wagon. Three lookouts guarding the loot."

Zee pursed her lips. "Well, the rest of the gang is in the church. And it looks like they've settled in for the night. Got a nice fire going, and a couple of women cooking for them. Probably not all they do."

"Whores?" asked Hogan.

"That'd be my guess."

"Hm. All the comforts of home."

"So, what do you reckon?"

Before he could reply, a man's voice boomed out of the darkness. "If you don't want your dandified friend to get hurt, come out where I can see you." There was something oddly familiar about the voice, but Zee couldn't place it.

"Dang it!" hissed Hogan. "I knew he'd be trouble."

"I'm not joking," came the voice again. "You don't show yourselves sharpish, your friend here will be dog meat."

A dull thud was followed by Fred's panicky wail. "Don't hit me. Please . . . Hogan. Brodie. Do as he says."

"Sonofabitch!" said Zee. "He's just told them how many we are and who we are too." To her irritation, the identity of the voice's owner still eluded her.

"I've half a mind to let Younger take what's coming to him," said Hogan.

The missing piece slotted into place. "It's Tucson Pete." She chewed the inside of her lip then turned to face Hogan. "Do you trust me?"

"Do you need to ask?"

"Then unbuckle your gun belt and give it to me."

After a moment's hesitation, he did as she asked. She, meanwhile, was unpinning her tin star and tucking it in her vest pocket.

"Lord knows, Brodie, if you double-cross me . . ."

She ignored the grumbled threat, took the gun belt from Hogan, and looped it over her shoulder. "Turn around." He did so, and she stuck her rifle muzzle in his back.

"Mind the waistcoat. Cost me plenty."

"Quit moaning. If I don't do this, your fancy vest will get shot full of holes for sure."

"Might happen anyway."

"Might," she agreed. "But I'm betting not."

"Some bet!"

Her patience was at an end. "This is our only chance, Hogan. Now, move." She prodded him forward and stepped toward the voice.

Chapter 16

CHRISTIE HAD NEVER felt so superfluous. Every woman in Angie's Palace except her, it seemed, was occupied.

If they weren't "working" upstairs, they were singing along to the player piano (If she heard "Oh, Susanna" one more time, she was going to scream), or dancing (Nellie the Fox did a wonderful flamenco), or serving drinks, or dealing Lasconette or Monte or some of the other card games she had never heard of let alone played. It didn't help that, every time Christie was in earshot, Red Mary would wonder loudly and pointedly what on earth Brodie saw in such a "useless little chit" of a girl.

The fact that night had fallen and Zee still was not back wasn't helping Christie's mood either, nor was her worry about what Fred might decide to do.

"Cheer up. It might never happen." Rowdy Molly was smiling at her.

It already has.

"Oh, Susanna" started up again.

"That does it." Teeth gritted, Christie stamped over to the player piano and dragged Serena from the piano stool. As the startled whore's feet left the pedals, the music died, so did the chatter. Every head in the place swiveled to regard her.

"Hey!" yelled Red Mary. "Leave Serena alone. What do you think you're playing at?"

Christie tossed her head, smoothed her dress over her rump, and sat down. "I'm playing *this*." She pulled the lever that turned off the automatic mechanism, then flexed her fingers and positioned them over the keys.

She had played for her own family and for Fred, but the size and composition of this particular audience was daunting. At first, she fumbled the notes, but she soon got into her stride.

Her own repertoire was limited of course, and she'd discounted many pieces as being unsuitable, but that still left plenty of up-tempo numbers. She chose "Buffalo Gals." After a moment, one of the clients began to stamp his feet in time, and Diamond Dust Kate began to clap. Next, two of the girls began to dance together, laughing as they careered up and down the salon, whirling in and out of the card tables and round the *chaise longues* and sofas.

Our of the corner of her eye, Christie saw Angie come out of her office to see what was going on, smile benevolently, and disappear again.

Thank the Lord for that. She relaxed and began to enjoy herself.

At the end of "Buffalo Gals," she moved on to "Weevily Wheat," and after that to "Skip to my Lou." Then she took pity on the by now flagging dancers and slowed the tempo with "When the Swallows Homeward Fly." She had learned these tunes at her mother's knee, and she smiled sadly. Emily Hayes would never in a million years have pictured her daughter playing them under such circumstances and to such people.

Christie had been playing for half an hour when a hand on her shoulder made her look round. Angie was smiling down at her. "Time for a breather, Christie," she said. "You've earned it. Besides. It's supper time."

With a flourish, she ended her current tune and stood up. The girls (and some of the clients) crowded round her, offering congratulations and praise. Only Red Mary remained aloof, a sour expression spoiling her looks. Christie blushed and smiled and hoped Zee would be proud of her when she learned how successful her efforts to fit in had been.

Over supper—a cold collation of salt pork and potato salad, which was served at a much later hour than Christie was used to—she realized she had yet another skill to offer. The food was tasteless, and she resolved to give Angie's cook (a rather doleful woman named Hattie) a few tips regarding spices.

Some time later, when she was resting after playing the piano for another half hour (the women were quite giddy at the novelty of fresh tunes), she saw Lazy Alice putting pen to paper in a corner and went to offer her help. The little whore was barely literate and was struggling to write a letter to her mother. Christie was pleased to be able to offer suggestions and then write the final draft in her elegant hand.

The result brought a beaming smile to Alice's battered face. "Thank you, Miss Hayes."

Christie smiled in genuine pleasure. "You're very welcome."

Then, of course, other whores noticed and came to her with their own writing requests.

Chapter 17

"WE'RE COMING OUT," called Zee. "Don't shoot." Hogan moved out from behind the palo verde tree and she followed.

Moonlight illuminated a stark tableau: Fred was on his knees in the dirt, kept there by a tall man in shabby, fringed buckskins, who had twisted the prisoner's arm high up behind his back. More critical from Zee's point of view was the cocked six-gun he was holding to Fred's temple.

Buckskin laughed. "Well, if it ain't the Hellcat."

"Howdy, Pete," said Zee. "It's been a while. So you're working for the Cody brothers these days, huh?" She inclined her head toward Fred. "That ain't necessary. As you can see." She prodded Hogan with her rifle and he grunted.

"You expect me to believe you're turning outlaw again?" Pete's tone was skeptical. He jerked his prisoner's arm higher, and Fred whimpered. She pretended not to notice.

"Shipment of silver, thirteen thousand dollars in government bonds, and ten thousand dollars in cash. It's a powerful incentive. Figured you'd cut me in if I had me a bargaining tool."

Her old colleague raised an eyebrow. "And that would be?"

"Hostages and information." She gave him a slow smile. "The one ain't much use without the other."

Pete looked thoughtful. "Makes sense. But I ain't the boss of this outfit, Hellcat. You need to talk to John Cody."

She shrugged. "Then lead me to him."

After a moment that seemed to stretch for forever, Pete uncocked his gun and dragged Fred to his feet. "Come on, hero." His tone was sarcastic. "Let's go for a walk."

It was a strange procession that made its way inside the mission compound past the startled lookouts. Tucson Pete led the way, dragging Fred with him. Next came Hogan, and behind him, her rifle muzzle still jammed between his shoulder blades, came Zee. Boots crunched over dust and grit, then they were entering the arched doorway where earlier the fat man had smoked his cigarette.

She took in her surroundings quickly, noting that nothing much had changed since she had last used the church as a hiding place. Round the fire, in the spot where the altar used to be, lounged seven men and two sorry-looking women.

Zee found herself at the center of a circle of gun muzzles. She wasn't impressed. Their reaction times had been lousy. An opened beer barrel probably had something to do with that. Or maybe they were just lousy gunmen.

She smiled, knowing her bargaining power had just gone up, and allowed herself to be relieved of her rifle and two Colts. She still had a knife hidden in her boot, after all.

Tucson Pete sat Fred next to the fire with a thump, then turned to address a bear of a man with long grizzled hair and an unkempt beard. He had been watching events unfold with keen eyes, and was clearly the man in charge.

"Mr. Cody," said Pete, his tone respectful. "We got us a visitor." He gestured at Zee. "Hellcat meet John Cody."

"Howdy," said Zee.

The gang leader didn't reply. He blinked coldly at her then beckoned Pete over. Pete obliged, and the two men fell into muttered discussion, interspersed with occasional glances and gestures at Zee and Hogan.

At last, Cody turned to study her. "Pete thinks you're all right, Hellcat. But I need to know why I should even consider taking you on."

Zee smiled. "Because I can outshoot any man here . . . even Tucson Pete." The buckskin clad man acknowledged her remark with a wry nod. "And because I bring collateral."

Cody stroked his beard. "I'll admit, your guns could come in handy. As for the hostages . . . Well, Cole Hogan I can use. The next posse on our trail will think twice about an ambush if we have the Cochise County Sheriff with us. But as for the other one . . ." He gestured dismissively. "Might as well shoot him."

Fred squeaked in protest, and one of the gang cuffed him into silence.

"Ah, but that's where my information comes in handy," said Zee.

Cody tilted his head.

"That's Fred Younger." A blank look. "I know he don't look like much right now"—that was something of an understatement; Fred's once smart shirt and trousers were dust-streaked and torn—"but his Pa owns the Contention Ore Mill." Another blank look. She suppressed a sigh. "It was his shipment of silver you took." Cody's eyes began to gleam. "Very wealthy family, the Youngers," she said for good measure.

Cody turned to regard Fred, and Zee knew she had bought the man with the Vandyke beard a little time if nothing else.

"All right," said Cody. "That piece of information I can use." He turned back to her. "But I'm still not sure about you, Hellcat. I heard you'd got yourself a pardon, gone straight." He pursed his lips. "You expect me to believe you'd give all that up for money?"

"Frankly, Mr. Cody, I got bored. Ain't much excitement to be had locking up the town drunk night after night," she drawled. "And there are other things than money. Right now, for example, I've got an itch needs scratching, and," she gave the whores a lascivious grin, "I couldn't help noticing, you have just the ointment I need."

It took a moment for Cody to catch on, then he followed her gaze toward the women and began to chuckle. He turned to Tucson Pete. "You said the Hellcat liked the ladies, Pete. Looks like you were right."

He slapped his thigh then and roared with laughter. Some of his men joined in. "All right." Cody paused then nodded and held out one meaty hand.

Zee shook it, let him outgrip her, and pretended to shake the pain from her fingers.

Laughing again, Cody turned and called out, "Happy." A man with a doleful face looked up. "Fetch the Hellcat's horses and put them in the corral." He smiled at her, but it didn't quite reach his eyes. "Want to tell Happy where they are?"

There was no way out that she could see, so she gave the man directions. "Much obliged," she told Cody, playing along. She knew he planned to keep her horses for himself, and he knew she knew.

He nodded, then called out, "Frank." This time, the man who looked up appeared to be a younger version of Cody himself. "Tie up the prisoners and keep an eye on them."

Frank nodded and dragged a subdued Fred to the corner of the ruined church, where he roped him like a steer. Then he came back for Hogan, and did likewise—but not before Zee had exchanged a covert glance with her boss that promised this indignity would be only temporary.

Cody, in the meantime, had resumed his seat by the fire, and was beckoning Zee to join him. Obediently, she took her place beside him. He signaled to one of the women. "Get our latest recruit some coffee."

Zee accepted the tin cup full of black sludge and forced a smile. It was going to be a long night.

Chapter 18

A DEJECTED CHRISTIE placed the lamp on Zee's dresser, drew the curtains, and sat on the narrow bed. In the salon downstairs, surrounded by music and gaiety, and pestered by women wanting her to play the piano or write letters, she had been kept too busy to think. But now . . .

Half of them want Zee. Some are real beauties. Others are spirited, independent. All are worldly-wise . . . What in the world does she see in me?

The silence pressed in on her. At least it was better than those sordid noises. They'd probably start up again soon, and she could expect little sleep before dawn, when the whores stopped work.

It dawned on her that she had no night attire and would have to sleep in the clothes she was wearing. *Perfect!*

A knock at the door jarred her from her despondency. "Yes?"

"Christie." It was Madam Angie's voice. "May I come in?"

"Of course." Nervously, she stood and smoothed her dress.

The door opened and Angie came in. "Brodie said you'd need this." She held out a nightgown—plain but serviceable.

Christie exclaimed, both at the nightgown and at Zee's thoughtfulness. Then Angie held out something else.

She frowned at the wad of cotton wool. "I beg your pardon, but what—?"

"Pack some into your ears before you go to sleep."

Christie blinked. "Why should I wish to do such a thing?"

Angie gave her an arched look.

Then she had it. "Oh!" The tips of her ears felt as red as her cheeks.

"You really are delightful, my dear. Such an innocent!"

Angie's comments struck a nerve, and Christie flushed and turned away.

There was a long pause. "I'm sorry if I offended you." The madam sounded uncharacteristically chastened.

"It's not that." Christie sighed.

"No?"

"No. You just reminded me how impossible all this is." She sat on the bed and put her head in her hands.

"This?"

"Me and Zee. Red Mary is right."

The mattress sagged as Angie sat next to her. "Enlighten me, dear."

Suspecting ridicule, Christie glared at Angie, but found nothing but interest and sympathy in her gaze.

"As you so accurately detected," she began, slightly bitterly, "I am," she blushed, "inexperienced in the ways of the world."

Angie pulled a little clay pipe from the pocket of her Turkish jacket. "May I?" she asked.

"Er . . . Please do." Christie watched as Angie packed the pipe bowl with tobacco from a small pouch, lit it, and puffed to get it burning properly. "Red Mary asked what Zee can possibly see in a useless little chit like me. More and more, I'm wondering that same thing myself." She raised her hands then dropped them into her lap. "It was crazy of me to come. What was I thinking?"

A long silence followed and both women watched the fragrant clouds of smoke drift toward the ceiling.

"You followed your heart," said Angie at last. "You're here because not only does Brodie think you're special, you *are* special."

"That's the last thing I am."

Angie shook her head. "Not to Brodie. I think she sees something in you she hasn't seen in anyone since Molly."

"Rowdy Molly?"

Angie laughed. "No. Though Molly Hart *was* rowdy, by all accounts. Brodie's Molly went by the name of Molly Purple. Worked out of Madam Miller's place over in Tucson."

"Oh." Christie digested this new information.

"They were close for quite a while. Then Molly died of the cholera."

"Oh."

Angie gave her an appraising look. "She looked something like you: short, blonde, nice figure."

Christie's depression returned twofold. "So, you think that's why? Because I remind her of Molly Purple?"

"Lord save us, girl!" Angie shook her head in exasperation. "There's more to Brodie than *that*. And if you don't know that by now, then you certainly *don't* belong here."

Christie ducked her head in shame. "I do know," she admitted. "I just . . . forgot it for a little."

"When she came back here after that trip to Yuma," continued Angie, as though Christie hadn't spoken, "you were all she could talk about."

"Me?"

"The girls were mighty upset about it. Red Mary especially. They knew when she was bedding them it was you she was thinking of."

Christie let out a strangled gasp. Zee had been doing *that* and thinking of her while she did it? She felt quite faint.

"Brodie told us you already had a beau, though." Angie looked at her. "That correct?"

She nodded.

"When the deputy sees something she wants," continued Angie, "she pursues it relentlessly and takes it. That's her nature. That's what made the Hellcat so daunting." She regarded Christie thoughtfully. "She wanted you. Do you really think a little thing like your having a beau already stopped her?"

Christie wasn't sure what Angie was getting at. "I don't—"

"No." Angie puffed her pipe. "She stopped *herself*. She wanted you, but she considered what was best for you and let you go. Remarkable given her track record, don't you think?"

"Truly?"

"That's what I meant by special. Of course Brodie wants to bed you. You're a pretty girl, and the deputy's quite the one for the pretty girls." She smiled. "But she wants more than that." Her glance was stern. "Understand me?"

The lump in Christie's throat made it hard to speak so she nodded.

"If you don't want that too," Angie waved her pipe for emphasis, "then admit it now and leave. Go to the hotel—they have plenty of rooms." Christie opened her mouth to speak but Angie continued, "But don't lead Brodie on, then turn around and say it was all a big mistake. That would surely break her heart."

"I won't," managed Christie.

"Good. 'Cause the deputy may have a steel shell, but her heart is pure molasses." Angie gave her a conspiratorial wink. "Don't tell her I told you that, by the way." Her pipe finished, she got to her feet, stretched, and smiled at Christie. "I'm glad we had this little chat." She crossed to the door and opened it.

"So am I," said Christie, meaning it. "So am I."

Chapter 19

THOUGH JOHN CODY had accepted Zee as one of his gang, his men were much less welcoming. She could understand that; they had one more person to split the loot with, after all.

It wasn't all animosity though. She declined the beer the fat man in the black shirt offered her and for the umpteenth time turned down his leering invitation to "have a little fun." Spence was the gang leader's brother (there were four Cody brothers in all) and his attentions were growing tiresome, but she didn't want to offend anyone before she had to. She was relieved when he at last took the hint and disappeared with one of the whores instead.

The condition of the two women, Josie and Lola, appalled Zee, though she was at pains not to show it. Their cowed demeanor, the cuts and bruises on their faces, and the rips in their thin dresses showed they had been used frequently and brutally. And it wasn't over yet.

They had finished with the cooking and taken portions of lumpy stew out to the five lookouts, and now were performing their other duty. Every so often, one of the gang would grab one of the women by the arm, and take her off into one of the disused chapels that adjoined the main body of the church. Animal-like grunting noises would drift back to those by the fire. Not much later, the man would return, a satisfied grin on his face, and the bedraggled whore would slump back in her seat . . . until the next member of the gang felt the urge.

Zee turned her eyes back to the fire. She would have to rescue the whores too.

Tucson Pete had noticed the direction of Zee's gaze. "Don't remember you being so slow to sample the merchandise." Crooked teeth gleamed in the firelight.

She returned his grin. "You know me, Pete. I like to take my time, do a good job." She glanced at the men around her. "Wouldn't want to hold up the others none."

That brought a snigger from him, but she knew she couldn't put off going with a whore for much longer.

I need to talk to one of them anyway. Warn them to be ready.

She got to her feet and stretched. "Think I'll go get me a piece," she said to the world in general, and since Josie was currently "entertaining" she approached the little Mexican.

"Lola, ain't it? C'mon with me, darlin'." She reached down and took the other woman's arm. "You and me gonna have us a good time."

The whore stared up at her, her brown eyes very wide. Her reluctance to go with Zee was obvious to everyone and brought laughter and comment.

"Ain't never been with a woman before," called Pete, as she pulled Lola gently but firmly to her feet. "Reckon you'll be teaching her some new tricks."

Zee grinned at him and urged Lola away from the fire. "Better wish me luck, then, boys," she called back. "Got me a reputation to live up to, after all."

As they walked toward the chapel where Lola had been "working" on and off all night, Zee picked up a spare lantern. She could feel the tension radiating from the Mexican woman. "Don't be frightened," she whispered. "I'm not gonna hurt you."

Lola showed no sign she had heard. Once inside the ruined chapel—stars were visible through the huge holes in the roof—she led Zee toward the stained mattress that someone had thrown on the floor. Zee regarded it with distaste, then released her grip on the whore and put down the lantern.

Lola rubbed her arm and looked dully at her. She began to unbutton her dress.

"No." Zee put out a hand. "Just sit. I want to talk."

Lola gave her an uncomprehending look, then sighed. "Si. Talk first." She sat cross-legged on the mattress. Zee joined her there, adopting the same pose.

"Talk only," emphasized Zee.

"You not want me?"

"No."

Lola's face was easy to read. Confusion was followed by outrage. "I not good enough for you?"

"Of course you are. But I don't want to. You don't want to." Zee shrugged. "Simple as that."

"Si. Simple." Calculation was creeping into Lola's gaze and Zee hoped she hadn't misjudged her. If Lola were to tell anyone else . . .

"Here's the deal," she said. "I need the others to *think* I'm bedding you."

Lola cocked her head to one side. "What you do meantime? Steal loot maybe? Want all for yourself?"

"I'm not going anywhere, Lola. It's just too soon to make my move. Hogan and Younger could get hurt."

"They the men you came with?"

Zee nodded. "This badge," she pulled out the tin star she had pocketed earlier, "is real. I'm deputy for Cochise County."

Lola's eyes widened, then the calculation returned. "What about me?"

"How would you like to work in a properly run brothel?" asked Zee. "Where you don't have to bed anyone who hurts you."

A wistful look crossed the whore's face. "You not joking? This could happen? For Josie too?"

Zee nodded. "When this is over, I'll take you and Josie to meet Madam Angie. She'll give you a chance if I ask her to."

"You can promise this?"

Zee traced a cross over her heart with her forefinger. "And hope to die." She hoped she could keep her promise.

The silence stretched. "All right," said Lola at last.

Zee nodded. "All right then," she said. "But first we have to make this look good." She gestured at the mattress and gave Lola a wry grin. "My women always scream."

That got her an interested look. "Always?"

"Yeah . . . Think you can pretend?"

For the first time Lola smiled. "Si, Señorita. I pretend all the time."

Zee laughed.

Fifteen noisy (and at times hilarious) minutes later, Zee and Lola emerged from the ruined chapel and rejoined the rest of the gang. The glances that met them were envious. Lola went to sit with Josie while Zee resumed her own place by the fire.

"Sounds like you had a good time." Tucson Pete spat tobacco juice into the flames.

Spence Cody frowned at Lola, who was murmuring to her friend. "Better not have ruined her for the rest of us, Hellcat. Takes a while to break in a new whore."

Zee shrugged. "Don't usually get complaints." Aware of John Cody's gaze on her, she gave it a few minutes before yawning. "I'm beat. Think I'm gonna turn in."

Cody snorted. "Takes me that way too." He took out his pocket watch and squinted at it, then stood up and beckoned to Josie. "Gonna take my little bed warmer here," he gave her buttock a squeeze, "and get me some shut eye.

"George, Happy, Frank," he continued. "Relieve the boys guarding the wagon." The three men groaned but got to their feet. "Bud and Walter, you take over out front." He urged Josie toward the other chapel. "See you in the morning, boys."

"'Night, boss," came the chorus.

The shift change and Cody's departure seemed to be the signal for a general preparation for bed. Zee commandeered a spot near the fire, stretched out, and pretended to sleep for a while.

Her thoughts turned to Christie, as they had all day, and she wondered how the innocent young woman was faring. She hoped she hadn't changed her mind about waiting for her, or been picked on. Some of the whores could get a bit out of hand, and catfights were common. Nothing Zee could do about it now, though. And Angie would look out for Christie . . .

She pushed such thoughts away and concentrated on her surroundings. Though her eyes were closed, she was aware of every sound, every movement in the high ceilinged room and beyond. In the distance was the pacing of the lookouts, the occasional faint snatch of their conversation, the restless movements and nickers of the horses in the corral. Nearer, in the chapel, Cody's grunts as he took Josie had long ago changed to snores. The whore was almost certainly still in there with him.

Zee turned her attention to her immediate surroundings. In the corner, the man guarding the prisoners was sleeping heavily—a combination of too much beer and a belief that trussed men posed no threat. Fred was asleep, but an alert silence radiated from Hogan.

Around the fire near her, the relieved lookouts were asleep, tired by their long watch. Zee slit her eyes and let her pupils adjust to the dim light, then flexed her hands and reached for her boot. *Now or never.*

Knife in one hand, she came to her feet. She closed the gap between herself and the nearest sleeper. A hilt to the temple put him out for the count. Then she gave the same medicine to the two men near him. Her next target came groggily awake as she approached, sensing her presence or perhaps hearing the muffled thuds, but before he could raise the alarm she clapped a gloved hand over his mouth and knocked him out. The fifth man was still dreaming when she rendered him unconscious. Then she turned and headed toward the corner and the sleeping guard, who received the same treatment.

Now that she could do so at her leisure, she checked the identities of the unconscious men and frowned. Spence Cody was missing, so was Tucson Pete. Lola had disappeared too. Together or separate? Using the latrine or fornicating?

"Nice going, Brodie," murmured Hogan, as she crouched beside him and sliced through his bonds.

Fred stirred and opened his eyes. Before he could speak, Zee clapped a gloved hand over his mouth. "One word from you," she hissed, "and you're dead. Got that?"

His eyes bulged as he saw the razor sharp knife she was holding. He nodded and she released him.

Hogan had found his gun belt and was strapping it on. Zee handed him the knife.

"Think you can take out the lookouts with this?" He nodded. "Good luck." She clapped a hand on his shoulder.

"You too." He disappeared toward the arched doorway.

She found her own Colts, checked they were still loaded, and put them in her holsters. Fred had remained still as a statue throughout. "Stay here," she ordered, then glided toward the chapel and John Cody.

The bearlike gang leader was not only wide-awake but holding a gun to the terrified Josie's temple.

Damn!

"I was expecting you." His finger was resting lightly on the trigger.

Too lightly. She drew her Colts and fired in one movement. Her first shot hit the barrel of his gun, knocking it aside; her next took him between the eyes. He gazed at her in shocked surprise, then fell backwards.

Josie collapsed to the mattress in a sobbing heap and Zee spared a moment to check she was unharmed and give her a reassuring pat. Then something spooked her and she turned. A tall buckskinned figure stood in the doorway. He gave a snarl of anger.

She threw herself to one side. As the bullet smashed through the space she had just occupied, she was already coming back to her feet. Her bullet took Tucson Pete high in the chest and spun him round. Even as he fell, he was coughing up blood, and she knew his wound was fatal. She leaped over his thrashing body and headed back to the main part of the church, knowing the gunshots would have alerted the rest of the gang.

Something moved. She ducked back as a bullet ricocheted off the wall next to her. *Spence Cody. A rifle. Two paces to the left.*

She took a quick breath, then dove forward, rolling and getting off a quick shot at the fat man silhouetted against the fire's embers. He cried out in pain, clutched at his thigh, and fell over. Then she was on him, kicking the dropped rifle out of reach, grabbing his still holstered six-gun, and bashing him on the head with its butt.

How many more are there?

As she ran toward the corral, she came across two bodies and turned them over with the toe of her boot. George and Happy had had their throats cut; Hogan's work. She moved on. The next body she came to belonged to Frank Cody. Her knife was sticking out of his chest. She pulled it out, wiped the blade clean on his shirt, and returned it to her boot. Then she sighed at the carnage. These killers had deserved what they got, but she didn't have to like it.

Hogan appeared. "Get 'em all?"

"Mostly. Lola's still missing. What about you?"

"One of the lookouts out front got away."

"Damn! I hope he hasn't got her."

But when they found the remaining man—who turned out to be Walter, at seventeen, the youngest of the Cody brothers—he wasn't threatening Lola but rather cowering behind her skirts. Much to Zee's relief, the boy gave himself up without a fight.

"That the lot?" asked Hogan.

"Reckon so."

Chapter 20

CHRISTIE WAS IN the middle of her morning ablutions when a knock came at the door.

"They're back," came Rowdy Molly's voice. "Angie sent me to tell you Brodie's back."

Christie put down her washcloth and wrapped a towel round herself. She opened the door and looked at the grinning whore.

"Brodie and Hogan just rode in. With a wagonload of loot," Molly ticked off the points on her fingers, "and six prisoners. And seven bodies, face down over their own saddles. Oh, and two women."

"Is Zee all right?"

"Right as rain." Molly gave her a hug then laughed. "Only she could ride out into the middle of nowhere and come back with two gals on her arm."

Christie frowned.

"It's not like that, silly. They were the gang's whores." Molly sighed. "Looks like they had a rough time of it too. Zee's asked Angie if they can work here for a spell."

Christie didn't know whether to rush over to the jail or wait here. But after the doubts of last night, she needed to see Zee. And for all Molly's reassurances, only Zee's physical presence would convince her that she was safe and sound.

"I'll finish getting dressed and come down."

Molly nodded and left her to it.

Such was her hurry, Christie left off her corset—lacing it would take too long. She shrugged into her petticoats, pulled on her one and only dress, now sadly wrinkled, and buttoned it, slipped her feet into her shoes, and with a despairing glance at her reflection—her hair looked a mess—dashed down the corridor toward the stairs. She was crossing the salon toward the entrance when the doors slammed open and a familiar figure stood there.

Christie flung herself at Zee, who grinned and grabbed her and swung her round like a child. Then she was crushed in a welcome embrace that was anything but motherly.

She lost herself in the warm lips pressed against hers, relishing the sensation of affection, strength, and unrestrained sexuality . . . things she had never known she craved until this singular woman came crashing into her life without so much as a by your leave. As she returned the kiss with equal fervor, her doubts vanished like early morning mist, and she knew this was where she belonged, no matter where it led.

A need to breathe made them part at last, and they became aware of the gazes fixed on them—some mischievous, some admiring, some (in the case of Red Mary) envious.

A man's voice broke the mood. "Unnatural creatures!"

Christie flushed and turned. She had never seen Fred in such a state. He looked as though he had just been dragged for several miles behind Zee's horse. And as for that ugly scowl . . . How could she ever have thought him handsome?

"Your opinion ain't wanted, and neither are you, Younger." Zee snaked a protective arm round Christie's shoulder. "So if I were you, I'd vamoose and take care of that silver of yours."

He ignored her and addressed Christie. "Ever since that . . . that murdering harpy came on the scene, she's caused nothing but trouble. As for you," the venom in his gaze made Christie suck in her breath, "you disgust me. Thank God I found out your true nature before it was too late. You are not *fit* to be my wife, and I never want to see you again."

The arm around her tightened.

"Call *me* what you like, Younger," came Zee's deceptively relaxed drawl. "But have a care how you speak to my lady. She's got more spunk than you'll *ever* have. Your yellow streak damn near got us all killed today."

My lady. At the words a warm glow spread through Christie, banishing the fear Fred's presence had brought.

He flushed with rage. "If you were a man, I'd call you out."

Zee's grin was mirthless. "And if you were a man, I'd accept."

His indrawn breath echoed round the suddenly silent salon, and his face paled. Christie knew, with deadly certainty, that if she didn't intervene, her lover would kill her ex-fiancé . . . and all because of her.

"Go home, Fred," she urged. "She's faster than you and you know it. Go home before it's too late. There's nothing for you here."

Her words seemed to break him out of his trance. With a last attempt at dignity, he drew himself up to his full height (which since he was only a couple of inches taller than Christie was less than impressive), turned on his heel and left.

The entrance doors slamming was the signal for jeers and cheers. Then the player piano started up and the normal salon hubbub resumed.

Christie, who had almost collapsed in sheer relief at Fred's departure, felt Zee pulling her close, and pressed into her like a kitten seeking warmth.

"You all right, darlin'?"

"I think so." She gave a half-laugh half-sob.

"Sorry you had to go through that."

"Me too. But the silver lining is: *he* broke off our engagement, which means he has no grounds for breach of promise." Christie gazed up into Zee's face and drew her fingertip down one tanned cheek. "I'm free."

"I'm glad." Zee took her hand and kissed each knuckle in turn.

Catcalls greeted their antics.

"Leave 'em be, girls," came Madam Angie's voice above the din. "They've got some loving to catch up on, but they're going to take it up to the deputy's room." She turned a pointed gaze on Zee. "Aren't you?"

Zee laughed. "If you insist." She swept Christie up into strong arms and headed for the staircase, which she took two steps at a time.

Christie relaxed in the secure grip and enjoyed the ride. "You know," she said, after a few minutes, "you smell." She sniffed.

"Yeah?" Zee was carrying her along the corridor now. "Good smell or bad?" She shouldered open the door to her box room.

Christie considered the mixture of sweat, horses, wood smoke, and, rather oddly, coal dust, and the enticing, musky scent that she was beginning to learn was Zee herself. "Good."

"We *could* wait until after I've taken a nice, long bath." The suggestion clearly wasn't serious, and Christie *humphed* playfully.

With a groan of relief and muttered aside about "heavy blondes" that Christie would make her pay for later, Zee deposited her on the narrow bed, which gave a *boing* of protest.

Zee threw her Stetson onto the dresser, kicked off her boots, and began unbuckling her gun belt. Christie watched, her mouth going dry with anticipation, then realized she should be getting undressed too.

She unfastened her shoes and kicked them off, hearing a distant clatter. She had just begun to unbutton her dress when Zee, her undershirt and red flannel drawers revealing long tanned limbs, landed on the bed beside her, eliciting another *boing* from the bedsprings.

"Hands off," ordered Zee, "that's my job." And a few buttons later, "Mm. No corset."

"I didn't have time this morn—" Christie almost fainted as callused hands caressed her.

"Just the way I like 'em." Zee's mouth took over from her fingers while they dealt with the remaining buttons.

"Oh!" Christie gasped. "You know, Zee," she managed, as the delicious sucking sensation threatened to overwhelm her, "the girls told me quite a lot about you while you were gone. Uh!"

"Yeah?"

The last obstinate button came free and Christie's dress was lifted over her head. The air was suddenly cool on her skin, but the fire inside her was like a furnace.

"Yes . . . Oh! I found out why they don't charge you for their services." She couldn't help but writhe in pleasure as Zee applied her tongue to every inch of bare skin she could find.

"Mm?" Zee turned her attention to the rainbow-colored petticoats that were Christie's secret rebellion against conformity. They joined Christie's shoes in the corner of the room, and moments later, her drawers followed them. Then a warm hand found its way to the secret places Christie had allowed no one else to visit before.

She bucked as practiced fingers stroked her intimately. "Yes," she said, but if it was in answer to a question, or indeed what the question was, she could no longer say.

"You sure, darlin'?"

"Mmm."

And a little (and increasingly noisy) while later, Christie found to her delight that Zee's reputation was indeed well deserved, and her record as yet unbroken.

PART TWO

Stage to Phoenix

Chapter 1

THE STAGE, AND its six horses, was waiting in front of Tucson's Wells Fargo office on Main Street, its passengers' bags and cases piled high on the sidewalk. Two women, one an attractive blonde in a simple, green dress, the other a matron in a bustle, stood arguing beside its open door.

Zee closed the distance between them quickly, then halted next to Christie, whose cheeks were flushed.

"Here, darlin'. It was under the bed." She held out the reason for her tardiness. "Everything all right?" She took off her Stetson, ran a hand through her hair, and resettled the hat.

Christie took the necklace of turquoise beads that had been Zee's one-month anniversary gift to her and gave her a nod. "I was just explaining to Mrs. Grummond," she said, sounding annoyed, "that she cannot have your seat at the back of the stage."

"It's not *your* seat," objected the woman, whose massive bosom needed all the corseting it could get. "First come, first served."

"I *was* first," snapped Christie, her eyes flashing.

"That's as may be, but your friend wasn't." Mrs. Grummond's gaze flicked over Zee, her expression showing what she thought of women wearing men's clothes. Or maybe it was the guns.

Zee shrugged. "Would've been here," she said, ignoring the four sets of interested eyes staring out at her from inside the stagecoach, "but I had to go back to our hotel."

"Would have been doesn't count," stated Mrs. Grummond. As though that ended the matter, she prepared to board.

Fair or not, Zee had no intention of sitting on the middle seat, hanging onto a ceiling strap, all the way to Phoenix. She shot out a hand, blocking the matron's progress.

"Well, really!" said Mrs. Grummond. "Please let me pass."

During her Hellcat days, Zee had perfected a glare that would halt any man in his tracks. Well, it hadn't *just* been the icy look, she conceded—in the early days, her knuckles had been permanently skinned too. Now, she put that skill to good use. She narrowed her eyes, fingered the butt of one Colt, and waited.

Mrs. Grummond's florid complexion paled. "We-ell," she stammered. "Since she saved you a seat and . . . and she *did* get here f-first." She stood back.

"Knew you'd see it my way." Zee turned to the goggling Christie and gestured.

With a start, Christie collected herself and stepped up into the coach. Zee followed hard on her heels, eased herself into the rear seat next to Christie, and stared down the other passengers before assessing them.

The mountain of lard with the close-clipped whiskers sitting on the other side of Christie, mopping his sweating brow with a large handkerchief, must be a businessman, she decided—make that a banker. The young woman in the pink dress in the far corner—pretty enough, if you liked your women feather-brained, which Zee didn't—must be going to visit relatives. As for the man sitting next to her—if his blue uniform and insignia (a silver eagle with spread wings) hadn't given away his Army Colonel status, his ramrod-straight posture would have. Finally, there was the gaunt old man in black—his po-faced expression and long, narrow whiskers fairly screamed "preacher." Just her luck!

A thin-lipped Mrs. Grummond made herself as comfortable as was possible on the backless middle seat. Movement outside proved to be the driver emerging from inside the office with the green-painted iron shutters, and beginning to stow the luggage in the stage's trunk. Then a commotion announced the arrival of the last of the nine passengers.

A tall woman with a commanding air and a clean-shaven little man, both wearing Eastern garb, scrambled on board and squeezed themselves next to Mrs. Grummond.

"Sorry we're late," panted the woman. Her accent was unmistakably English, and Zee exchanged an interested glance with Christie. "We're not used to having to be up so early."

Six in the morning was hardly early, mused Zee. Not that she and Christie wouldn't have minded an hour or two more in bed themselves. Christie had revealed an aptitude for bed sports that was keeping Zee pleasurably occupied.

The door slammed shut, jarring her from her lascivious thoughts, and the stage rocked as the driver climbed onto the box. A few seconds later, a muffled "Hi!" was followed by the sound of a whip cracking, and the stage lurched forward.

The carriage bounced on its thoroughbraces, jolting Zee against Christie. At the thought of the torturous journey ahead, she almost groaned aloud. Not for the first time she wished the railroad link from Tucson to Phoenix had got beyond the planning stages.

A hand eased itself into hers, and she turned to regard an excited looking Christie. At once, all her disgruntlement vanished. No matter how hellish this journey turned out to be, Christie was with her . . . and that made all the difference.

CHRISTIE HAD DISCARDED any romantic ideas of stage travel she might once have entertained. They'd been traveling for a mere three hours and she felt as though she'd been in a rockslide. The jolting must be much worse for those on the middle seats though. She eyed Mrs. Grummond and tried not to smirk, then chided herself for being uncharitable.

Zee had drawn back the leather curtain and was staring out of the window. Christie rested her gaze on the strong profile silhouetted against the morning sunlight. Zee turned to smile at her. "Must be nearly time for a rest stop."

As if on cue, the stage began to slow. When it came to a halt, the groaning passengers stumbled out into what looked to Christie like the middle of nowhere—dry earth populated only by cacti—and set about restoring the circulation and feeling to their limbs. Matter-of-factly, the driver handed out several latrine spades and warned them all to be careful of scorpions and rattlers.

Zee was stretching methodically, and Christie copied her, feeling the stiffness ease somewhat. Zee circled behind her and with strong fingers began to ease the knots from her neck and shoulders. She almost groaned with relief, but became aware of the dubious looks coming their way. *Why are people always so quick to judge us?*

She wasn't aware she had sighed out loud until Zee murmured, "Ignore them. Who cares what they think?"

"I was thinking of Blue," said Christie sadly.

That earned her a sympathetic look. "Give your brother time, darlin'. It's a lot to get used to. He'll come around."

Come around to her living in a brothel? She doubted it. Blue's letter had been crystal clear. As long as she lived with whores she was no sister of his. As for Zee, he blamed the deputy for shaming Fred so publicly and for seducing his sister . . . though as to the latter, Christie wasn't at all sure it hadn't been the other way around.

Zee gave her shoulder a last comforting pat, then strode off to have a word with the driver. The Englishwoman, whose name Christie had learned was Vesta Galvin, noticed that Christie was now alone and came to join her.

"Does your companion always wear men's clothing?" Vesta's gaze followed Zee who was pulling down the brim of her hat against the glare. "Because I must say," she continued, apparently unaware she might be giving offense, "it makes her look fine, very fine." The praise came as a pleasant surprise to Christie, who had braced herself for the worst.

The desert breeze carried Zee's conversation to them in hot gusts. "The Gila Bandit . . . twice last month . . . any risk?"

"But she's still quite clearly a woman," continued Vesta, pursing her lips in consideration. "Pretending to be a man is not her intention, is it?"

Christie regarded her curiously. Maybe the unusual attitude was because she was English.

With a visible start, Vesta recollected herself. "I beg your pardon, Miss Hayes. How rude of me to make such an impertinent remark about your traveling companion! You must understand, my interest is professional."

"Oh. Are you a dressmaker?"

"My husband and I are on the Stage, my dear." At Christie's confused glance, she clarified, "Not this stage." She pointed to the coach. "*The* Stage." Realizing that Christie was still none the wiser, she continued, "We design and sew our own costumes."

Christie was about to ask whether the jovial little Englishman, whose name Vesta told her was Dan, could *really* sew, when Zee tipped her hat to the driver and turned. As it always did, the breath caught in Christie's throat when those remarkable blue eyes found her. With pleasure, she watched Zee stride toward her on long Levi-clad legs.

"Is everything all right?" She gazed up into Zee's tanned face and resisted the urge to reach up and smooth the creased brow.

"Not sure," said Zee. "But don't worry, darlin'. I'll handle it." Her frown eased, and she smiled.

Zee's open endearment made Christie glance anxiously at Vesta, but the Englishwoman merely smiled at her and asked, "Who's the Gila Bandit?"

"Stagecoach robber," said Zee.

"Is he likely to attack us?"

"Targets gold shipments mostly, and Dusty says we ain't carrying any."

"Dusty?"

"The driver."

"Oh."

The fat banker was taking a covert interest in their conversation, noticed Christie. So was Colonel Gregg, who happened to be passing on his way back from answering Nature's call. The Colonel stopped beside the three women and puffed out his chest. "No need to worry about bandits, ladies. I'll protect you."

Zee's eyes narrowed and Christie could tell from the way her jaw clenched that she was about to say something rude. She reached for Zee's hand and squeezed it. Zee sucked in her breath and let it out again. Then she excused herself, grabbed the spade from the Colonel, and went off in search of a cactus and some privacy.

Christie turned back to the man in uniform. "Er, thank you, Colonel, but Zee's a deputy sheriff. She can more than take care of any bandit herself."

"Fascinating!" said Vesta.

Gregg's mouth dropped open. "But she's a wom . . ." He trailed off.

"Yes, she is," said Christie dryly. "You may have heard of her. Deputy Zee Brodie? She and Sheriff Hogan brought in the Cody Gang last month."

"That murdering bunch of train robbers?" His eyes widened. "Then why isn't she wearing a badge?"

"It's in her vest pocket. She only wears it in Cochise County."

He frowned. "Isn't she rather a long way from her jurisdiction?"

But Zee was returning, spade in hand, and before Christie could answer, Colonel Gregg excused himself and walked away.

"Something I said?" asked Zee.

Christie chuckled. "I just told him about you capturing the Cody Gang."

"Ah." Zee held out the latrine spade. "Better hurry. It's another three hours before the dinner stop and we're due to leave in five minutes."

"Oh," said Christie. "Give me that, then, and be quick about it."

Chapter 2

IT WAS JUST after noon when the stage pulled into the adobe relay station where they were to have dinner. For the past hour and a half, Zee had been riding up on the box with the driver. The blistering heat hadn't bothered her any, she was used to it, but she'd had to pull her bandanna up over her mouth and nose against the dust. Now she knew where the driver's nickname came from.

Christie had pouted when Zee confessed that being cooped up with eight others in the muggy gloom of the stage was making her antsy, but reluctantly approved her solution. Zee smiled, recalling the passengers' bulging eyes as, while they were still traveling at full speed, she eased herself out of the door's open window, pulled herself up onto the roof, and snaked her way forward to join the surprised driver.

For something to do, Zee had persuaded Dusty to let her take the reins for a spell, only to hand them back soon after with the rueful admission that handling a team of six was harder than it looked. After that, she confined herself to daydreaming about what she would do with Christie once they got to Phoenix, staring through the shimmering heat haze at the Catalina Mountains, or pretending to shoot the jackrabbits flushed from cover by the thump of hooves and rumble of wheels. She was whistling—Angie's whores had brainwashed her with their damned player piano tunes—when the relay station came into view. As Dusty brought the stage to a halt directly outside the entrance, she jumped down, pulled down her bandanna, and went to open the stage door.

Her arms were suddenly full of mischievous blonde. A grinning Christie disentangled herself and stepped aside to let the other passengers off.

"Ooh." Christie stretched, emphasizing the curves beneath the green dress, and Zee eyed her appreciatively. "I swear every muscle in my body aches, Zee. Was it any better for you up on the box?"

"Some." She removed her hat and banged it against her thigh, sending up a cloud of red dust.

Christie tried not to cough. "Maybe we should call you Dusty too."

"Sorry." Zee took Christie's arm and guided her into the welcome cool of the dining room. "C'mon. We don't have long here."

"I missed you," said Christie as they chose seats at a creaky trestle table whose place settings consisted of bent cutlery and dented tin cups. "And that's not just because Mrs. Grummond took your seat."

Zee gave her an affectionate glance. "Did she? Sorry 'bout that."

A fat Mexican woman bustled in and began placing platters of food in front of each traveler. Zee inspected the tough piece of steak thrust between two soggy soda biscuits and sighed. Well, all right . . . as long as there was coffee to help it down. She looked around and relaxed when the woman returned carrying a pot of steaming black sludge and poured some into Zee's tin cup.

Christie eyed her own food and took a dubious bite. "It's not too bad," she said, as though trying to convince herself.

"We'll make up for it in Phoenix," promised Zee, chewing hard then helping the gristly lump down with a gulp of bitter coffee.

When Hogan had asked Zee to go to Phoenix and help Sheriff Coogan identify a prisoner—Johnny Cactus's description wasn't on record but Zee had ridden with the outlaw in her Hellcat days—she had intended going alone, on horseback. Then Christie had asked her persuasively (so persuasively, in fact, that they had almost broken the bed) if she could come too. That was when the idea had come to Zee to treat this jaunt as a kind of honeymoon. So she had wired ahead, booking them a room in Tucson and another in Phoenix, at what Angie assured her was the best hotel.

Well, Christie deserved it for putting up with that tiny room at Angie's Palace and the suggestive sounds coming through the walls night after night. Angie and her girls had been good to Zee, and the brothel was the first place in a long while she had even come close to calling home. But now she had someone else's needs and feelings to consider, and it was time to move on.

She pictured Christie's face when she told her the news.

"What are you smirking at?"

"Nothing."

Green eyes regarded her suspiciously. "Zee?"

"All aboard," came the driver's voice.

Relieved at the interruption, Zee kicked back her chair and stood up.

"C'mon, darlin'. Our carriage awaits."

Chapter 3

CHRISTIE WAS GLAD Zee had chosen to ride inside the stage with her for the next portion of the journey. Being squeezed between Mrs. Grummond and the flabby-bellied banker (whose name, she had learned was Walter Bonney) was not an experience she wished to repeat. It had taken another of Zee's glares to make the sour matron resume her place on the middle seat.

Zee's presence had also nipped in the bud another unpleasant development. Colonel Gregg had taken to eyeing Christie with open admiration and to making overly flattering remarks. Fortunately, a glare from Zee had soon returned his attention to the passing landscape. Now if only Zee could do something about the preacher.

Ignoring his fish-eyed stare, Christie rested her head on Zee's shoulder and stared out at the clumps of cacti and desert paintbrush, wondering what Phoenix would be like, and what Zee was being so secretive about.

She must have dozed off, because she woke disoriented to find the stage slowing and Dusty's voice calling, "Rest stop. Everybody out."

"Thank heavens!" cried the girl in the pink dress, whose name Christie had learned was Annie Stenhouse. She scrambled for the door, and the other passengers weren't far behind her.

"Have a nice nap?" asked Zee, as she handed Christie out.

She stifled a yawn. "What time is it?"

Zee pulled out her pocket watch. "Three o'clock."

Christie groaned and shook her head. When the driver passed round a full canteen, she took it eagerly and eased her parched throat with a few mouthfuls of tepid water. Then the call of Nature came, so she grabbed the spade and went off behind a cactus to answer it. When she returned, the preacher was standing in her path. She sidestepped, but the man in black did likewise.

"Something I can do for you, Reverend?"

"My dear," he said, "your soul is in grave danger."

Christie blinked at him. "I beg your pardon?"

He glanced at Zee who was being talked to by the English couple. "That woman is the spawn of Satan. If you allow her to corrupt you, you will go straight to Hell."

"How dare you!" Christie tried to walk around him, but once more he placed himself in her way. Then came the Bible quotations, giving chapter and verse, on which he based his condemnation of the two women. Christie became aware she was gripping the spade handle so tightly her knuckles had gone white. She resisted the temptation to hit him over the head with it.

The litany of hate continued but eventually he was forced to pause for breath. She seized her chance.

"Why, you narrow-minded, hate-filled, unchristian—"

His eyes widened as she advanced on him. Giving the spade a nervous glance, he stepped back. Then something made him look down. He screamed.

Shocked by his reaction, Christie halted. In the sudden silence—conversation had stopped and all heads had turned their way—she heard what the preacher must have heard scant seconds earlier: a dry rattle.

Heart pounding, she scanned their surroundings. Then she saw it, the diamond-backed snake lying coiled beside his boot, the tip of its tail vibrating in warning. And as she watched, the deadly reptile began to uncoil itself. A broad triangular head reared, and a forked tongue flickered.

"Don't move," she told him.

Then something flashed past her, making her flinch; a gunshot rang out; horses whinnied and began to rear in their traces; and the preacher cried out, clutched his leg, and began rolling on the ground.

Christie was dimly aware of Dusty rushing to calm the panicked horses, and of Zee's voice raised in anger, but her attention was on the snake. A small knife had pinned it through the neck to the dirt, and it was in its death throes. *Where did that come from?*

She looked round and saw Zee and the colonel glaring at one another. Smoke curled from the muzzle of Gregg's revolver.

"Did no one ever tell you not to fire guns around untrained horses?" yelled Zee. The colonel's reply was lost as the preacher reclaimed Christie's attention.

"I'm dying," he moaned. "I can feel the poison spreading."

She knelt next to him and tried to pry his hands away from his calf. Weren't you supposed to cut the wound open and suck out the poison? Zee would know. "Let me look." But he only hung on tighter.

When Zee didn't join Christie as expected, she looked round to see what was keeping her and blinked in astonishment. Zee was murmuring in one of the horses' ears and patting its neck.

"Zee." The deputy looked round at her shout. "The Reverend's been bitten. We don't have much time."

"No he ain't." But Zee gave the horse a last pat and came over to join Christie anyway. She squatted on her heels next to her.

"What are you talking about?" Christie suppressed an urge to slap some sense into Zee. "Look, there's blood." The preacher had at last released his grip, and his trouser leg and palm were indeed bloody.

"Gregg's bullet must have nicked him," said Zee calmly, "because I knifed that snake 'fore it had chance to bite anyone." She batted away his hands, tore his trouser leg open along its seam, and examined the wound. "See. No puncture. No swelling. Just a graze from a bullet. Almost stopped bleeding already."

While Zee pulled her knife free of the dead rattler, wiped the blade clean on its carcass, and shoved it back in her boot, Christie peered at the supposed snake bite. *She's right*. She sighed and stood up.

"Hey," came Zee's voice. "You all right?" Her hand rubbed Christie's back.

Christie nodded. As the panic of the last few minutes receded, tiredness and anger replaced it. She turned to stare down at the man with the long whiskers, who was examining his calf and torn trousers, his face the picture of disbelief.

"This woman you called a 'spawn of Satan' just saved your miserable life."

The preacher's head remained bent, but a telltale flush spread to the tips of his ears. Afraid of what she might do to him with the latrine spade, Christie let Zee take it from her and guide her toward the stage.

"Spawn of Satan, huh?" Zee seemed amused. "That's another term for Hellcat, right?"

Christie sighed. "Maybe." She tried to snap out of her sour mood. "Nice throw, by the way."

"Thanks." Zee held her gaze for a long moment, then squeezed her hand. "There'll always be jerks like the Reverend, darlin'. Best just to ignore 'em."

"Easier said than done."

"You'll do all right."

Zee's confidence put new heart into her and she returned the squeeze.

"All right, folks. Rest break is over," yelled Dusty, breaking the moment of quiet intimacy. "All aboard."

Chapter 4

THE NEXT HOUR passed without incident and Zee rode on the box with Dusty again. They were swapping scurrilous stories when the trail began to deteriorate and he was forced to concentrate on his driving.

This particular stretch, she saw, had suffered from erosion. Up ahead was a deep dry wash where torrential rain from a summer storm had washed the trail away. As the horses thundered toward it, Dusty tried to rein them in to a more reasonable speed. They had the bits between their teeth, though, and were slow to respond. He cursed and reached for the brake lever, but by then the stage was careering into the wash and beginning to skew.

Zee grabbed for the handrail and hung on.

The horses were back under control and the stage straightening up when, halfway down the slope, the vehicle checked sharply. Zee's jaws clapped together, and she was flung forward, almost losing her grip. She barely had time to register that the near back wheel had struck a rock buried in the dirt, when the stage began to tilt.

"We're going over," yelled Dusty.

She let go and jumped for it, hitting the ground in a roll and coming to her feet just in time to see the side of the stage hit the ground with a sickening *crunch*. A glance reassured her that Dusty was picking himself up and dusting himself off. Zee's thoughts turned to Christie.

The wheels were still spinning and startled cries and curses were coming from inside the stage when Zee tugged open its upper door. Seconds later, a fair head popped into view and Zee pulled Christie to her and held her tight, heart pounding at the thought of what might have happened.

"I'm fine," soothed Christie. "Shaken up but fine. See?" She flexed her elbows and wrists in demonstration, but Zee wasn't convinced until she had checked her over for herself.

She made a protesting Christie sit quietly in the shade of the downed vehicle, then began to help the dazed passengers out one by one. Both Mrs. Grummond and the preacher spurned her hand so she shrugged and let them climb out as best they could. Amazingly, all except the flabby banker had escaped with bumps and bruises. Mr. Bonney, however, was cradling his right arm and whimpering.

Zee checked it. "Broken," she said.

"Driver, this is an outrage!" Mrs. Grummond's hands were on her hips.

"Sorry, ma'am," said Dusty. "The horses must have still been a mite unsettled from that gunshot." Colonel Gregg flushed and looked at his boots.

But the apology made no difference to Mrs. Grummond. "Wells Fargo will be hearing from me. Your incompetence could have killed us all . . . And look what you've done to our luggage."

Boxes and suitcases, valises and bags had broken free of the leather boot and were strewn about the dry wash in all directions. The impact had burst open many of them—clothing and toilet articles lay in plain sight. Zee blinked at the corsets, dresses, and ladies' boots spilling from Dan Galvin's case.

The Colonel and Annie each began gathering their belongings and cramming them back into their bags. The other passengers, including Christie, joined them.

"My bags," said the clearly anxious banker. "I must see to my bags."

"Later," Zee told him. "Let's get this arm fixed first."

"I'll do them for you, Mr. Bonney," offered Christie. It had taken her only a moment to repack their few belongings (Zee believed in traveling light). She started examining baggage labels.

"This is gonna hurt," warned Zee. She braced the banker's shoulder with one hand, grabbed his wrist with the other, and pulled.

"Aargh!" Heads turned in their direction then hastily turned away again.

When the ends of the fractured bone had lined up to her satisfaction, she released her grip. "The worst is over." She patted him on the shoulder and looked up.

Christie was coming toward them. "Your bags are all intact, Mr. Bonney." She halted in front of him. "They must have very strong locks."

Some color came back into his cheeks at that, and Zee wondered what he hadn't wanted the other passengers to see. But she had other things on her mind. What could she use for a splint? A comb, maybe? A hairbrush?

Her gaze wandered, then settled on something. *Ah*. With a "Be right back," she crossed to the kneeling Dan. "May I?" She whisked a corset out of his hand.

"Er . . . erm . . ." Startled brown eyes gazed up at her.

She grinned. "I'll take that as a yes."

Christie was tending to the banker when Zee resumed her place by his side. The smaller woman's hands were nimbler than her own, so she handed her the corset.

"What on earth?" Christie's eyebrows climbed.

"Wrap it round his arm, good and tight. The stays should keep it stable."

"Ah." She set to work with a will . . . or would have, but Bonney had recovered himself sufficiently to see what she intended and jerked his forearm away.

"Are you crazy?" he cried. "No decent person would be seen in such a thing."

"Don't be silly!" Christie reached for him, but once more he resisted, though every movement added more beads of sweat to his brow.

Zee grew tired of this. If he kept moving his arm around, the fracture would need resetting.

"Now listen and listen good." She pinned him with her glare. "Stay still, shut up, and let my friend help you . . . or I'll break your other arm."

After that, he was meekness itself, and not only allowed Christie to wrap the corset around his right arm but thanked her profusely. Only trouble was, it wouldn't stay put.

Christie snapped her fingers. "Your bandanna, please, Zee."

"Good thinking." Zee untied the red neckerchief and handed it over.

As Christie clearly had Bonney and his injury under control, Zee straightened and went to join Dusty who was examining the toppled stage.

"At least the wheel's still in one piece," he said. "Seasoned white oak. Strong as iron."

Zee pursed her lips. "We could do with some kind of lever."

"Yeah. Ain't got one though." He turned and surveyed the male passengers. "And they don't look up to the task."

Zee followed his gaze to the injured banker, gaunt preacher, short Englishman, and over-zealous army officer. "We'll manage," she said. "Hook up the team and I'll organize the manpower."

By the time Zee had marshaled all the able-bodied passengers (including the women—she rebuffed all squawks of objection and outrage with the quiet question: "Do you want to *walk* to Phoenix?") Dusty had strung a line round the coach and attached the team to it.

"Ready?" he called.

Zee nodded.

"Hi." He cracked his whip above the horses' heads, and they strained forward. As instructed, the passengers hooked their fingers under the edge of the coach and pulled, or got their shoulders under it and pushed. Twice they tried, and each time it lifted very slightly, then fell back to its original position.

"All right. Let's take a break," called Zee. She stood back and flexed shoulders that a moment ago had felt as if they were being pulled out of their sockets. The other passengers followed her example while Dusty instructed the horses to rest.

"What was that you said about walking to Phoenix?" asked a dispirited Christie, examining scraped hands.

"Don't worry, darlin'. One more try ought to do it." Privately, Zee wasn't so sure.

She let everyone catch their breath, then resumed her position. Reluctantly, the others did the same. "Right," she yelled. "This time, put your backs into it." She signaled to the waiting Dusty. "Now."

He cracked his whip and shouted, "Hi, Blaze. Hi, Mustard," and, with a jangling of harnesses and creak of leather, the horses began to pull.

Zee heaved with all her might, and beside her Christie did the same. With a reluctant groan and creak of tortured wood, the coach began to lift . . . one inch, two inches, three . . .

"That's it," panted Zee. "Keep going."

Already the stage was higher off the ground than it had been on the previous attempts. Dusty cracked his whip again, and the horses surged forward, putting their full strength into it.

"Give it everything you've got." Zee's arms were aching from the strain, but then came a lurch, and suddenly, miraculously, the backbreaking weight on them was gone.

A loud cheer went up as the stage rolled upright and settled onto its wheels with a satisfying *crunch*. It was still bouncing on its thoroughbraces when the grinning passengers turned to congratulate one another.

Christie gave Zee a hug. "Is life with you *always* this eventful?"

"Yeah," said Zee. "'Fraid you're just gonna have to get used to it."

Chapter 5

DUSK WAS GATHERING, and in the distance a coyote had started to howl, when the battered stage rolled into the relay station.

Zee had warned Christie not to expect much. "It'll just be somewhere to eat and sleep." *Just as well*, she thought, staring out of the window at the rambling complex of old buildings and ramshackle stables. There were even some chickens wandering around the yard.

"Is this it?" asked Mrs. Grummond. "Well! I just hope they don't have fleas."

For once, Christie found herself in agreement with the woman.

"You'll be able to get some proper treatment for that arm of yours, Mr. Bonney," said Gregg, eyeing the corset immobilizing the banker's arm. Bonney grunted and shifted in his seat.

"All right, darlin'?"

Christie turned to smile at Zee who had taken to sitting inside again and was discreetly holding her hand. She suspected Zee was more shaken up by the spill than she cared to admit. "Just wishing it was our hotel in Phoenix," she murmured.

Zee smiled. "It's only for one night. Think you can manage?"

"I can if you can."

That earned her an approving squeeze of the fingers. Then the stage door opened, and a plump little man with a huge mustache welcomed them all to his "humble abode."

Zee got out first, and Christie let her help her down since she ached all over. They retrieved their luggage, then allowed themselves to be corralled by their affable host. Dusty, meanwhile, was unhitching the horses with an ostler's help and leading them away toward the stable block.

When all five women were gathered together in a group, their host said, "Follow me, ladies," and led them at a brisk trot along the dusty path to the women's sleeping quarters.

From the outside, it looked like a huge barn. Inside, it was better than expected, but not by much. Off a long corridor were ten identical rooms, all tiny and all containing a bed and a water jug and washbasin. Their host allocated Zee and Christie the one at the far end.

As the other women were assigned their billets, Zee and Christie escaped to their room and scanned their surroundings.

"Hardly the lap of luxury," said Christie, "but at least that bed's big enough to sleep two."

Zee nodded. "Sure is. During busy periods, complete strangers are expected to double up."

"Surely not?"

"Luckily," Zee winked at her, "we ain't strangers."

Christie sat on the mattress, which had seen better days, and watched Zee wander over to the partition separating them from next door. Zee rapped it with her knuckles.

"Walls are wafer thin," she concluded.

Christie sighed. Though she was tired and sore, she had been looking forward to Zee bedding her. "Guess we'll have to stick to snuggling then."

"Yeah?" Zee kicked the door shut and advanced on Christie, a predatory gleam in her eye.

"Mmfph!" Christie let herself be kissed, then remembered the thickness of the walls and persuaded Zee to simply hold her. It felt good to be alone with her at last, to relax against the lean, muscular body and feel safe and cherished. But then Zee's kisses resumed and became more urgent—

"First sitting, ladies, if you please." Two raps at the door accompanied their host's voice.

"Damn!" Zee released Christie and sat up. "Just when things were getting interesting."

While they both got their breath back, Christie busied herself refastening her buttons and straightening her dress.

"First sitting," came the host's voice again, a little fainter this time, as he progressed along the corridor.

"We *should* eat something." Zee stood and allowed Christie to run a comb through her hair.

"As long as it's not another gristle sandwich. There." Christie stood back and assessed the result. "You'll do." That remark earned her a kiss, then Zee turned toward the door.

"Well. Only one way to find out about the food."

As they set off along the corridor, the door of the room next to theirs opened and Vesta Galvin came out. She smiled at them. "May I join you two for supper?"

"Please do," said Christie politely, ignoring an elbow in the ribs from Zee.

As they walked across the graveled yard to the dining room, they passed a makeshift sign saying "Saloon" and an arrow. Zee darted off to investigate and came back grinning.

"It's a shed with a dirt floor and whitewashed walls, but it'll do," was her verdict.

In the dining room, the three of them sat together. Then Vesta's husband came in, saw them, and hurried over. The remaining passengers took their places at the other tables. Once they were settled, the host's wife bustled in carrying platters of food.

Supper was a welcome surprise. The stewed chicken melted in the mouth, the fried eggs were newly laid, and the bread had been baked that morning. Christie wolfed down her food until the platter could have been licked clean, earning herself an amused glance from Zee. Then came cups of freshly brewed coffee, which bore no relation to the sludge they had been served at dinner.

Conversation proceeded in fits and starts. The day's excitement was the primary topic—the Galvins were full of praise for the way both Zee and Christie had handled things—then came talk of their plans for Phoenix.

"We'll be working, of course," said Vesta. "Two performances a day and three on Saturdays . . . The rest of the Company are already there," she explained, in response to Christie's enquiry. "Yes, we usually do travel with them, but we made an exception this time. Mr. Galvin," she turned to regard her husband fondly, "has distant relatives in Tucson, so we took time off to visit them. Didn't we, dear?"

The little man nodded, seeming content, like Zee, to merely listen to the conversation.

"And what are your plans, Miss Hayes?" Vesta turned to regard Christie.

"Oh . . . er, Deputy Brodie has some sheriff's business to take care of. But after that . . . Well, I've never been to Phoenix before, so she's promised to show me around. Haven't you, Zee?"

Zee, who had just taken a gulp of coffee, merely winked at her. Christie blushed and changed the subject.

The day's traumas were catching up on her with a vengeance and she found herself more and more trying not to yawn. The third time this happened, Zee reached over and pushed a strand of hair out of Christie's eyes.

"Go to bed," she ordered.

"It's still early."

Zee shrugged. "It don't matter."

The Galvins grinned as their gazes tracked between the two of them.

"Very well," said Christie. "Are you coming to bed too?"

"Think I'll have me a smoke and maybe a whiskey and a hand of cards or two first." She grinned at Dan and Vesta. "Anyone care to join me in the saloon?"

Christie tried not to be annoyed. It was she, after all, who had decreed they should merely snuggle. And it *was* early.

"I'll take you up on that smoke," said Dan. "Then it's bed for me too." He turned to his wife. "'The long day's task is done, and we must sleep,' eh, my dear?"

Vesta nodded. "Too long. I think I'll turn in too." She yawned, then apologized.

"Well, don't be long," Christie told Zee, rising and giving her shoulder a pat.

"I won't."

Vesta rose too. "Good night, dear," she told Dan. "Sleep well."

His brown eyes gleamed as he blew her an extravagant kiss. "Good night, sweet lady."

Leaving Zee and Dan chatting about Five Card Stud (Christie resisted the urge to roll her eyes), she and Vesta walked back across the yard to their quarters. They were nearly there when Vesta sighed.

"Is something wrong?" asked Christie.

"Silly of me, I know," said Vesta, "but this is going to be the first time in months that I've slept in a different bed from my husband." She glanced sidelong at Christie. "At least these quarters won't keep you and the deputy apart."

Christie was sure that even the tips of her ears must have turned pink. "Mm." She kept her voice neutral.

Vesta laughed. "You must never be ashamed of what you and Deputy Brodie share, Miss Hayes. Love, wherever it is found, is to be cherished." She became melancholy again. "But I shall miss my Dan."

They reached Vesta's room, and she said goodnight, leaving a thoughtful Christie to proceed on alone.

In her own room, she poured cold water from the jug into the basin and washed herself. Then she pulled on her nightdress, climbed beneath the rough sheets, and dozed off. Some time later, she was dreaming of Zee, when the faint click of the door latch was followed by a sagging of the mattress. A warm, familiar presence snuggled up behind her, bringing with it the scent of tobacco, and whiskey, and Zee herself.

"You asleep, darlin'?" Hot breath tickled Christie's ear.

"Mm," she murmured, caught between sleep and wakefulness.

A hand fondled her breasts through her nightdress. "Still feeling sleepy?"

"Zee!" Every nerve in her body now tingling, Christie rolled over onto her back. "Not now I'm not."

She gazed up into eyes glinting in the moonlight, then the silhouetted head leaned closer and warm lips pressed against hers. She gave herself up to Zee's knowing caresses, whimpering as her nightdress was removed and tender spots were licked and sucked. Then she remembered the thinness of the partition separating their room from Vesta's.

"The noise, Zee."

"Pretend you're a coyote."

Christie struggled to free herself. "I'm serious. We mustn't."

The pleasurable sensations stopped and the pillow was whisked from under her head. She was wondering where it had gone when Zee presented it to her.

"Scream into this."

"What?" But then she could barely think as once more Zee's lips and strong fingers were moving over her, and a fierce trembling overtook her. "Oh, my Lord! Zee!"

Hastily she pressed the pillow to her mouth.

Chapter 6

ZEE FINISHED UP the salt pork and potatoes that constituted breakfast. Not quite up to the ham and eggs that Christie liked to cook for her whenever she got the chance, but not bad. She reached for her coffee and, as she drank, thought about the little blonde's needs.

Sharing the brothel kitchen with Angie's cook wasn't ideal. And sharing a tiny bedroom definitely wasn't the same as having a place of their own. Christie needed to be able to entertain friends when she felt like it (and that would include her stupid brother when he saw sense), and she couldn't ask respectable folk to a brothel.

Christie hadn't complained once, of course, but Zee wasn't blind. Christie deserved more, and she was going to get it. Fortunately, the capture of the Cody Gang had netted Zee a tidy sum in reward money. Enough to purchase the Cooper house.

Sure it needed a bit of renovation and decoration—that was why it was so cheap—but Angie and her girls had promised to help her take care of that. And the garden, if you could call it that . . . well. Old Coop had worked hard on that vegetable plot, so Christie should have no trouble growing whatever she wanted.

Zee grinned, remembering their first meeting, when her horses had eaten Christie's flowers, and, their second, when Zee had presented her with a sack of bulbs. Christie seemed to bring out the pussycat side of the Hellcat, and Zee was glad of it. Not that you'd know it from last night, she thought guiltily. She feared she had worn poor Christie out.

The dining room door opened and the Galvins came in with Colonel Gregg. Gregg's black eye had developed nicely during the night, and a reflective Zee flexed her knuckles. He blenched when he noticed her and chose a table as far from her as possible, to the English couple's evident chagrin.

Next to enter was Dusty. The stage's driver had matched Zee drink for drink but looked none the worse for it. He tipped his hat to her then took a seat and dug into his breakfast with a gusto that matched Christie at her hungriest. Moments later, having cleared his platter and gulped his coffee down, he was on his feet and heading for the door.

Christie appeared in the doorway, her gaze darting over the diners. It settled on Zee, and a smile replaced the slight frown. Zee's heart swelled with affection and she watched Christie appreciatively as she made a beeline for her.

"Why didn't you wake me?" Christie took her seat opposite Zee.

"Thought you could use the rest."

"Very funny," grumbled Christie, but she brightened when the host's wife placed a breakfast platter in front of her. "Thank you."

For the next minute, Christie concentrated on shoveling down her salt pork and potatoes, then she paused, fork halfway to her lips, and said accusingly, "Your knuckles are skinned."

"Are they?" Zee's gaze wandered to where Gregg was wiping his lips on a napkin.

"Were you in a fight last night?"

She shrugged. "A minor disagreement."

"About me?"

"Your name might have come up."

Christie sighed. "Is it always going to be like this?"

"A pretty woman, a group of those who *like* pretty women, and plenty of whiskey? Yeah, I guess so."

Christie chuckled. "I love you."

"Me too." Zee reached across the table and took her hand.

At the next table, Mrs. Grummond was complaining to Annie about the racket the coyotes had made last night. Zee gave Christie a sly glance.

"You sound a bit hoarse this morning, darlin'. Think you may be getting a head cold?" A sharp kick on the ankle was her reward for that impudence.

"Just you wait," muttered Christie.

"Promise, promises."

Then Dusty appeared in the dining room doorway and yelled, "Stage for Phoenix is ready to leave. All aboard."

They followed him out into the early morning light where a fresh team of horses had been hitched to the stage, and the luggage, which the passengers had piled there before going for their breakfasts, had been loaded into its boot.

Zee took her seat next to Christie, and then they were off. While the stage swayed and jolted toward Phoenix, Christie rested her head against Zee's shoulder and stared out of the window. Zee amused herself by watching her fellow passengers out of the corner of her eye.

Bonney was snoring. Must be laudanum in that silver flask of his. A regulation splint and bandage had replaced the corset that had so offended the fat banker. Zee wondered if he had returned the undergarment to its rightful, if rather unlikely, owner. The Galvins, meanwhile, were telling anecdotes about their life in England, much to Mrs. Grummond's disdain. Annie seemed to appreciate the amusing stories though. Her braying laughter was threatening to get on Zee's nerves and she took a deep breath.

"You all right?" murmured Christie.

"Sure." She forced a smile.

Gregg was busy too. Thwarted of Christie, the colonel had switched his attentions to the only other eligible woman available. His flowery compliments made Annie blush and toss her head. It was all for show, though. Even while he was praising the girl his gaze kept straying to Christie's ankles or the curves that filled out her dress so nicely. Zee fought down the impulse to give him another black eye.

As for the black-garbed preacher—since the rattler incident, he had avoided both Zee and Christie, and now he refused to meet her gaze. Being ignored by a bigot was one step up from being preached at, she decided, and she turned her gaze to the passing landscape.

An hour into their journey, heavy clouds darkened the sky, and moments later came the pounding of rain on the roof. The noise woke a dozing Christie and she looked round, disoriented.

"Summer storm," said Zee. "Be over any minute." And indeed it was, leaving a welcome feeling of freshness behind, having damped down the ever-present dust.

She pulled out the pocket watch Molly had given her (funny how Christie's presence had eased the pain of Molly's death), and flicked open the case. *Hmmm. Shouldn't be far now to the Gila River.*

People said it was uncanny how the Gila Bandit knew when there was gold on the Tucson-Phoenix stage. But Zee knew from her own stage-robbing days that the supernatural had nothing to do with it. Most likely, there was an inside man at Bonney's bank. She had a strong hunch that Bonney was carrying gold in his personal luggage, hoping to sneak it through unremarked. But if even one other person at his bank knew about it, then so would the Gila Bandit.

She thought about that for a while.

After the next rest stop, when the passengers were about to retake their seats for the final stretch of their journey, Zee told Christie she would be traveling up on the box for a spell. Then she took Dusty to one side and told him her plan.

At first he was resistant. If the Bandit tried to ambush them, he argued, he'd rather go hell for leather for the river. The horses were reasonably fresh . . . they could outdistance the Bandit.

Zee shook her head and showed him her tin star. "No. He ain't gone too far down the road to ruin yet, but he will. It's time to bring him in."

In her Hellcat days she'd had nightmares about gunning down some innocent bystander by mistake. She'd been caught and sent to Yuma before it came to that, though. It was the first piece of luck to come her way in quite a while, even if at the time it had seemed just the opposite.

Dusty shrugged. "All right, Deputy. You know best."

Zee only hoped he was right.

When all the passengers were aboard and the doors shut, she slipped down from the box and round to the back of the stage, then crawled into the leather-covered boot.

"IS THAT THE Gila River?" asked Annie.

Christie followed the girl's pointing finger, expecting to see something spectacular but finding only the same old desert landscape. Then she noticed the wavering line of trees and shrubs on the horizon and knew they could only exist near a water source. She leaned back in her seat and wondered how Zee was faring up on the box.

"I believe it *is* the river, my dear," said the preacher. "And once we cross, it should be plain sailing to Phoenix."

"What about the Gila Bandit?" continued an eager Annie. "Do you think he'll attack us?" The girl seemed unaware she might be frightening her fellow passengers; the banker, for one, had gone pale.

"No need to fear him while *I'm* on board, Miss Stenhouse." Colonel Gregg patted the holster at his hip.

Just then, a volley of loud gunshots made everyone jump. The stage checked violently, throwing them forward in their seats. "Whoa, boys," came Dusty's voice. "Whoa."

"What's going on?" asked Vesta as the stage slowed to a stop.

"I don't know." Christie strained to see out of the window. "Those shots sounded as though they came from nearby."

The door opened and a sheepish looking Dusty stood there. "Nothing I could do, folks. He got the drop on me. You'd better get out nice and quiet now."

He stood back. Only then did Christie spy the gray horse and its hooded rider, and the two cocked six-guns pointing straight at them.

"Out here where I can see you," came the gruff voice.

As Christie stepped down from the stage, she looked round for Zee, her heart sinking when she saw no sign of her. *But she can more than look after herself,* she reminded herself. Vesta and Dan stepped down next, followed by the other passengers. Last to emerge was Gregg, gun in hand, knuckles white as he pulled the trigger.

Two gunshots rang out in quick succession, and he cried out, dropped his revolver, and cradled his hand—the fleshy part of his palm was bleeding copiously. With a cry, Annie rushed to offer him her handkerchief as a bandage.

"Stupid move," said the Bandit, who appeared unharmed. "Next one to try it ends up dead."

Vesta and Dan moved closer to one another and held hands. The preacher began to pray under his breath.

"This is an outrage!" said Mrs. Grummond, her ample bosom heaving.

The Bandit ignored her. "No one need get hurt," he said. "I only want the gold."

"There *is* no gold," protested Bonney. "Your information must be wrong." But even Christie could tell that the banker was lying. He was trembling and sweating even more than usual.

"Damned if it is!" said the figure in the black hood. He waved a gun muzzle at Dusty. "Get the banker's luggage out of the boot . . . You too, shorty."

Dan's brown eyes were terrified. "Me?"

"And you, Reverend," continued the Bandit. "Unless unloading luggage is 'gainst your religion."

The preacher opened his mouth then shut it again. Torn trouser leg flapping, he limped round to the back of the stage where Dan and Dusty were waiting. The driver hopped up and undid the straps holding the boot closed then handed down Bonney's bags. Judging by all three men's expressions, the bags were much heavier than expected. They placed them on the ground and awaited further instructions.

"Stand clear." The Bandit aimed and fired.

Christie's ears were still ringing, and the scent of gunpowder was acrid in her nostrils, when she registered that a bullet had shattered the lock on one of the bags.

"Open it," ordered the Bandit.

Dan crouched and flipped open the bag. Inside were several small pouches. The drawstring of one had come loose and gold dust was spilling out. Christie gulped. It was more wealth than she had seen in her entire life.

"No gold, huh?" The Bandit relaxed his guard. As he did so something emerged from under the stage, barreled past Christie, and leaped at him. The horse reared, and the startled bandit, who had dropped one gun in his attempts to stay in his saddle, fell as Zee bore him to earth with a *thud*.

Christie gathered her wits and rushed forward. Her help was unnecessary though. By the time she reached Zee, the deputy was kneeling astride the dazed bandit, who was face down in the dust.

As Zee pulled his gloved hands behind his back and lashed them together with his suspenders, the stunned passengers watched her, mouths open. Only Dusty was composed enough to offer assistance. Zee waved him away and winked at Christie.

"Told you I'd handle it." She rolled her captive over onto his back. "Now let's see what we've got." She pulled off the black hood with a flourish . . . to reveal auburn curls, long lashes over eyes so dark they were almost black, a pert nose, and a Cupid's bow mouth.

"Oh my!" said Annie into the shocked silence. "He's a she."

The Gila Bandit's mouth worked then she spat. "Nice." Zee wiped the spittle from her cheek. "Very nice." She hauled the woman to her feet and gave her a little shake. "No need for that."

A loud *crump* made Christie turn. Walter Bonney was lying flat on his back in the dirt, like a beached whale.

"He's fainted!" cried Mrs. Grummond.

As the passengers gathered round the unconscious banker and watched Dusty wet a neckerchief with water from his canteen and mop Bonney's forehead, Christie looked at Zee.

"Where *were* you?"

"In the boot." Zee's answer brought an intake of breath from her prisoner.

"The boot?"

"Sure. Passengers have even been known to take a nap in there." Zee looked smug. "It's kinda cramped, but not bad."

Christie folded her arms. "So you *knew* we were going to be attacked?"

"No. Had a hunch though."

A faint spluttering proved to be Bonney recovering consciousness and refusing a mouthful of water.

"And you didn't bother to tell me?"

"Coulda been a false alarm. Didn't want to worry you for nothing, darlin'."

The endearment brought a snort from the Gila Bandit. Zee turned an icy gaze on her. "That's enough outta you."

"But you didn't know it was a woman?" persisted Christie.

"Fooled me like everyone else. Must bind her breasts or something." Zee glanced at the banker, who was being helped shakily to his feet. "What's wrong with him, swooning like that?"

"Always was lily-livered," muttered the Gila Bandit.

Christie blinked at her. "You *know* him?"

"Should do. Been married to the windbag for fifteen years."

Zee guffawed.

"He's your husband?" Christie couldn't take it in.

"That explains how she always knew when his gold was on board," said the still chuckling Zee. She shoved her prisoner toward the stage.

"Why, Jane?" came Bonney's pained voice as they approached.

His wife brushed past him with barely a glance. "Why not? All that money, Walter. Yet you never spent any of it on me."

"But Jane—"

"Show's over, folks," called Dusty, who with Dan's help had stowed Bonney's heavy bags in the boot once more. "All aboard."

While the relieved and chattering passengers boarded, Christie watched Zee use the driver's spare set of reins to lash her prisoner to the roof—putting her inside the stage with her husband would be asking for trouble, as would sitting her next to Dusty. When Zee at last climbed down, Christie greeted her with the hug she had been wanting to give her since they were held up.

"When I got out and couldn't see you," she whispered in Zee's ear, "I feared something terrible had happened. I thought I'd lost you." She felt suddenly tearful.

"It takes a lot more'n that to get rid of the Hellcat." Zee gave her a squeeze then released her and held her gaze. "Don't you know that by now?"

Christie sniffled and fumbled for her handkerchief. "I'm beginning to."

Chapter 7

THE RECENT RAINFALL had swollen the Gila River above its normal level but Dusty assured Zee that the ford was still manageable with care. It was either that or wait, and with a schedule to stick to and the passengers champing at the bit, he was reluctant to delay.

Zee shrugged. "You know best."

He turned back to his lines. "Hang on." He cracked his whip above the two leaders' heads, and the team plunged down the bank, the stage rumbling hard on their heels, the tethered gray stallion that was the Gila Bandit's mount bringing up the rear.

Zee hung onto the handrail, watching the water level climb above the horses' fetlocks, then their knees. Their ears went back as twigs and other debris swirled round them.

"Hey, you with the blue eyes," came a woman's voice.

"The name's Brodie." Zee turned to find Jane Bonney frowning at her.

"Promise me something?"

"What?"

"If we get swept away, you'll cut me loose. Least that way I stand a fighting chance."

A large branch *kerranged* off the near forward wheel then floated off downstream. The horses were chest deep now, snorting and showing signs of wanting to turn back. A judicious crack of the whip strengthened their resolve.

"It won't come to that." Zee became aware of the driver's gritted jaw. "Right, Dusty?"

To her alarm, he ignored her and shook the reins, encouraging the wheelers—the largest and most dependable members of the team—to put their backs into it. "Yah."

The horses were almost swimming. It couldn't get much deeper could it?

Zee craned her neck and peered over the side. The water hadn't yet reached the bottom of the door but it wasn't far off. Noses were pressed against windows, and there was a concerned edge to the muffled voices.

Once the river started seeping inside the stage, the passengers would panic. She crossed her fingers.

The horses were swimming in earnest now, straining in their traces, veins popping and tendons standing out in their arching necks. The stage passed the ford's halfway mark, and Zee shot the grim-faced man beside her another glance. Shouldn't the water level be dropping by now? She gritted her teeth and hung on.

It was imperceptible at first, then slowly but surely, the level began to fall. Then the horses were no longer swimming but wading, pulling the stage more and more strongly toward the bank.

Zee let out her breath. "That was close."

Dusty's jaw worked, then he nodded. "Thought for a moment I'd misjudged it."

She laughed, releasing the tension of the last few minutes. "Glad you kept that to yourself."

They powered up the bank in a shower of grit and sand.

An hour later, they had reached the outskirts of Phoenix and were heading for Central Avenue. Dusty reined in his team and halted the stage outside the Wells Fargo office then jumped down and began unloading the bags ready for the passengers.

Zee cut the Gila Bandit loose from the roof and helped her down, then felt a familiar presence behind her. Holding her prisoner's arm with one hand, she turned and smiled down into green eyes. "Hey."

"Hey," returned Christie, giving her a fond look.

"We made it," said Zee unnecessarily.

Christie nodded, taking in their bustling surroundings before turning back to her.

"I have to get her," Zee indicated Jane Bonney, "over to the sheriff's office, and then take care of that Johnny Cactus business. Think you can find our hotel all right?"

"It's the Republic, isn't it?"

Zee nodded. "Best hotel in Phoenix."

"All right for some," muttered Jane.

"I'll find it," said Christie.

The urge to touch her was too much for Zee, and she stroked a soft cheek. Eyelids fluttered closed in response.

"Deputy Brodie. Miss Hayes." Loud voices shattered the quiet moment, and they turned to find a jovial Vesta and Dan Galvin bearing down on them. The Englishwoman was holding something in her gloved fingers.

"We're in a hurry, so we can't stop. But we had to come and say good bye."

"Indeed, sweet ladies. 'Parting is such sweet sorrow.'" Dan smiled and gave a gallant bow that made Zee want to laugh.

"But by way of a thank you," continued Vesta, ignoring Dan's antics, "for the good care you've both taken of us all these last couple of days, we thought you might like these." She pressed two small pieces of card into Christie's hands since Zee's were occupied with her prisoner.

"Oh!" said a clearly delighted Christie. "Tickets to the theater. Thank you so much."

Probably some Shakespeare play. Zee hoped Christie wouldn't expect her to go.

Dan tapped his pocket watch and Vesta grimaced. "We must rush," she said. "We've got a matinee this afternoon, then an evening performance, and we have to get our costumes cleaned and pressed first." She sighed. "And after this journey, heaven only knows what state they're in."

With a last smile and wave of the hand, they retrieved their bags from Dusty and headed off down the street. Zee tipped back her hat and watched them go.

"We gonna stand here forever in all this glare?" asked Jane, jostling Zee with an elbow. "I'm parched."

"Quiet, you." She tightened her grip and gave Christie an apologetic glance. "Gotta get going, darlin'. Got one prisoner to deliver and another to identify."

"Well, don't take too long."

"What's the rush? Got some entertainment in mind?" Zee leered at Christie. Jane rolled her eyes and pretended to puke.

"Yes, but it's not what you think." Christie smiled and patted Zee's arm. "I'm taking you to the theater."

Chapter 8

CHRISTIE PACED HER hotel room for the umpteenth time. Where *was* that aggravating woman? She had last seen Zee heading up Central Avenue toward the town jail, argumentative prisoner in tow. That was two hours ago. Since then, Christie had had a snack, a long soak in the capacious bath, and a refreshing nap.

She glanced at her pocket watch. If Zee didn't hurry, they were going to be late. The sound of the door handle turning brought her to a halt, and she swiveled on one heel.

Zee stood in the doorway, hat in one hand. "Sorry I'm late, darlin'." She threw her Stetson unerringly at the hat stand and kicked the door closed behind her. "Sheriff Coogan sure likes to talk." She appraised their surroundings. "Nice room."

She crossed to the large bed, sat on it with a groan of relief and, after giving it an experimental bounce, began to pull off her boots.

"What are you doing?"

Zee froze, her boot half off, and looked up. "Huh?"

Christie put her hands on her hips. "The Theater. The matinee. Vesta and Dan's guests. Remember?"

"Oh, that." Zee finished taking off the boot and started on the right one. "Thought you were joking. 'Fraid I just ain't in the mood for Shakespeare, darlin'."

"Who said anything about Shakespeare?" asked a surprised Christie. "It's Vaudeville."

In other circumstances, the expression on Zee's face might have been funny, but Christie was too busy getting her to wipe her boots with a damp cloth, brushing the worst of the dust off her Levi's and vest, and running a wet comb through her glossy black hair to think about that.

At last she stood back. "You'll do." She reached for her drawstring bag. "Now let's go. We'll just about make it."

"But I was planning to take a nap," protested Zee, still fighting a rearguard action even as Christie shooed her down the stairs, into the lobby, and out of the hotel's double doors. "You know. You, me, a nice soft bed . . ."

Her smile filled Christie's stomach with butterflies, and for a moment she was tempted to turn round, head back to their room, and spend the rest of the day ravishing Zee. She took a deep breath and steeled herself. How often did they get free tickets to the Vaudeville?

"Later," she promised.

"I'm counting on it."

ZEE STARED AT the spotlit figure on the tiny stage and tried not to fidget. She'd much rather be in bed with her girl than sitting here listening to a coarse comedian tell an endless series of *double entendres*. She glanced at Christie who was holding a gloved hand to her open mouth and seemed torn between shock and enjoyment.

A program lay open on Christie's lap. Zee squinted at it. Garish red type proclaimed: "Ferdy Leybourne's Company of American and European Novelties." So far, they had seen four comic acrobats who rolled round the stage like tumbleweed, and two Irish lasses who sang plaintive ballads that didn't leave a dry eye in the house (except for Zee's). The plump comic currently regaling the guffawing audience with off-color humor was Ferdy Leybourne himself.

"I thought Dan and Vesta were supposed to be in this," she grumbled.

"Sh." Christie's gaze was riveted to the stage. "They are." A gurgle of laughter escaped her and her cheeks turned crimson. "Oh my! Did he really say what I think he did?"

Zee reached for the program and ran one forefinger down the list of acts. Next on was "The Incomparable Vesta Vance and the Ribtickling Dan Corri. All the way from England."

Guess those are their stage names.

A roll of drums from the band and a loud round of applause made her look up in time to see Ferdy Leybourne running into the wings.

Onto the stage in his place strutted a dandy wearing Eastern garb. He stopped center stage, stroked his beard, and lit up a cigar. There was something oddly familiar about the fellow. Maybe it was just that the checked trousers, high collar, and trimmed goatee reminded Zee of Fred Younger, Christie's ex-beau. Next onto the stage danced a plump little dairymaid, complete with apron, frilly bonnet, and milk pails. The face under the pigtails was instantly familiar.

She blinked. "Isn't that—?"

"Dan," confirmed Christie, as the little Englishman capered around the dandy, then curtseyed to him, provoking a ripple of laughter from the audience. "No wonder he doesn't even have sideburns." He struck a pose and broke into song.

The singing was all right, thought Zee, if you liked that kind of thing. Dan had a pleasant enough tenor voice. But his lyrics were all about a milkmaid's troubles with lustful farmers, and, though on the surface innocent, were couched in the most suggestive language Zee had ever heard (and she'd heard quite a bit). She was tempted to put her hands over Christie's ears, but far from being shocked, Christie seemed to be enjoying herself.

All the while the milkmaid sang and capered, the Eastern dandy continued smoking his cigar and regarding "her" with a supercilious air. The song ended, and the dandy made a "be off with you" gesture. The milkmaid thumbed "her" nose, curtseyed, and scampered off.

Alone on stage once more, the dandy crushed his cigar under his boot-heel, stepped forward, struck his own pose and began to sing. His posture, his manner, everything about him was masculine. It was only when a soprano voice rang round the auditorium that Zee realized he was a she, was in fact Vesta.

"Come into my arms," sang Vesta, launching into a romantic ballad and directing it at a pretty girl in the front row. Zee raised one eyebrow, then settled back in her seat and listened appreciatively.

The murmurs of shock had given way to delighted appreciation, as the audience realized how skillfully they had been taken in and happily colluded in the deception. When the song came to an end, and the dandy removed the yellow rose from "his" buttonhole and threw it to the young woman, now pink with delight and embarrassment, there was a spontaneous outburst of applause.

"So that's why," said Christie.

Zee turned to look at her. "Why what?"

"Why she was so interested in the way you dress."

"And why Dan's suitcase was full of women's clothing."

"Imagine what the Reverend would have said if he knew." They chuckled at the thought.

The dandy bowed and strolled offstage as Dan returned, dressed this time as a very short, stout, and unconvincing Red Indian woman. His song was about trying to make the woman's "brave" more amorous and was just as suggestive as his earlier number. Then Vesta came back on, dressed as an army officer with a more than passing resemblance to Colonel Gregg. Zee chuckled as the officer courted a pretty girl in the second row.

She was sorry when the Galvins' act came to an end and they took their bows and left the stage. She wasn't interested in the acts that followed, the dancers and comedians, the troupe of trained collie dogs who simulated rescuing a child from a burning house. When the curtain fell at last, Zee was glad to be able to stretch her legs—the theater seats hadn't been designed with her lanky frame in mind.

"Well," said Christie, as they made their way backstage to congratulate their former traveling companions before returning to the hotel. "That was a surprise."

"Mm," said Zee. "And much better than Shakespeare."

Chapter 9

"ARE YOU GONNA be much longer?" asked Zee.

Christie suppressed a grin, gave her hair a final stroke, and placed the hairbrush on the hotel dresser. She stood up and crossed to the big bed.

"You can help speed things up." She turned until her back was facing Zee. The creak of bedsprings signaled that Zee was sitting up. Moments later, she felt her stays loosening and breathed a sigh of relief.

"Thanks." She pulled the uncomfortable undergarment off and folded it, then placed it with her dress. Just because Zee tended to throw her clothes all over the floor didn't mean she was going to. She turned to find an appreciative gaze raking her from head to foot.

"Don't know why you decided to wear a corset again." Zee leaned back against the pillows, putting her hands behind her head and crossing her long legs at the ankles.

"You have to dress up for the Theater," said Christie. She stripped down to her drawers, conscious that Zee was watching her every move and slowing her disrobing deliberately.

"Get over here, you little tease," growled Zee at last.

Christie laughed, draped her stockings over a chair back and went to join her, giving Zee's big toe a tweak.

"What on earth do you *do* to your socks? They need darning again."

Zee dismissed the hole. "I'm a growing girl," she said. "Come here."

Christie was only too willing to be pulled into Zee's embrace. Playful wrestling escalated into heated kissing before the need to breathe made them pull back.

"Mm." Christie nestled into Zee's arms. "This is the perfect end to a very strange couple of days."

"Yeah. Who knew there were so many women pretending to be men out there?"

"And men pretending to be women," added Christie. She was pensive for a while. "Why do you think they do it?"

Zee shrugged. "It's a mighty fine disguise if you want to rob a stage."

"But Vesta and Dan . . ." She trailed off as she considered the English couple's act. Dan had made her laugh until she cried, but Vesta . . . well Vesta's act had both confused and intrigued her, and, she wouldn't mind betting, a lot of the audience felt the same. A nibble on her neck brought her out of her reverie.

"Does there have to be a reason?" asked Zee. "Maybe that's just who they are."

The nibble became a delicious suction, and Christie knew she would have to wear a scarf tomorrow. She pulled back her hair, revealing more of her neck for Zee's attentions, and mulled over her reply. Inescapably, her thoughts turned to her brother. *Will he ever accept that this is just who we are?* She sighed.

Zee stopped what she was doing. "You all right?"

Christie looked at her and brushed one tanned cheekbone with her forefinger. "Do you think Blue will ever come around?"

"Yeah." Zee took her hand and kissed its palm. "Wanna know why? I think he's angry, mostly. A lot at me, a little at you. A woman, an ex-outlaw, no less, seduced his sister, his friend's fiancée." She raised a sardonic eyebrow. "If I didn't know better I'd be shocked myself."

"But it wasn't like that," objected Christie.

"But that's how it seems to him, darlin'. And it's a lot to swallow."

Christie's shoulders slumped. "So there's no hope then?"

"Sure there is." Zee hugged her. "Once his anger wears off, he'll want to see his little sis. I guarantee it. You love each other, always have, always will. All those memories of your parents, all that shared history . . . that's a lot to ditch. He'll come to his senses, and sooner rather than later."

"But he said," Christie's throat was suddenly clogged with grief, "as long as I'm living in a brothel—" She stopped, taken aback by Zee's grin. "What?"

"I was saving this piece of news for when we get back, but now's as good a time as any." Zee released her, rolled over, grabbed her shirt from the hotel's plush green carpet, and began delving in one pocket.

"What news?"

Zee pressed a much folded, legal-looking document into Christie's hands. She opened it and stared at its contents.

THE OLD BARN, SCHOOLHOUSE LANE, BENSON
Transfer of Title Deed
In consideration of four hundred dollars, the receipt whereof is hereby acknowledged, Raymond Cooper, now resident at 4, Glenn Street, Tucson, hereby transfers to Miss Zerelda Brodie, Deputy Sheriff of Cochise County, now resident at Angie's Palace, Benson, and Miss Christie Hayes, also now resident at Angie's Palace, Benson, the above property. Details are as follows . . .

Christie's vision blurred. "Oh, Zee. Is this . . . ?" She put a hand to her mouth. "Have you . . . ?" She took a deep breath and tried again. "Does this mean what I think it means?"

The self-satisfied grin on Zee's face made Christie feel like both throttling and kissing her.

"Yeah."

"But how could you afford it?"

"Been putting aside some of the reward monies I've earned over the last year." Sudden doubt filled the blue eyes. "That's what you wanted, right? Our own place? There's even a garden for if you want to grow—"

Christie flung herself at Zee.

"Oof!"

She showered her with kisses and endearments.

"Darlin'," panted Zee, when Christie allowed her up for air at last. "You're gonna be the death of me."

"That could well be," agreed Christie happily. "But what a way to go."

PART THREE

Full House

Chapter 1

ZEE CAREERED ROUND the corner into Main Street, gambling that the heavy sacks in the back of the buckboard would keep it from turning over.

A whiskery old gent in worn britches and suspenders leaped out of the way. "Goldarn it, Brodie! Where're you off to in such a hurry?" he yelled after her.

"Sorry, Silas. My lady's waiting and I'm late."

Collecting the horses and wagon had been no problem—Zee had telegraphed the livery stable before she and Christie left Phoenix, and when she arrived, Bradley had the gelding and buckboard ready and waiting for her, along with her own mare. It was loading Taylor's supplies and selecting the surprise bolt of dress fabric that had taken the time, and Zee still had no idea if the color would be to Christie's taste or not.

She glanced back, checking that the mare tethered to the rear of the buckboard was keeping up. An indignant whinny greeted her, but the mare seemed fine. She faced front again and cracked the reins.

As she neared Benson's Wells Fargo office, she was relieved to see Christie wasn't pacing up and down and cursing (though the gentle Christie rarely cursed) but was talking to a mustachioed man in an embroidered waistcoat.

Zee brought the buckboard to a halt beside them. "Hands off, Hogan. She's spoken for."

Christie stopped talking and turned to smile at her—Zee never got tired of seeing that smile. "I've been telling Sheriff Hogan all about Phoenix," she said.

Zee winked. "Not *everything* I hope?"

Christie's cheeks pinked, and Zee laughed and jumped down from the buckboard.

"Brodie," said her boss. "Glad to have you back."

"Thanks. But I ain't *officially* back 'til tomorrow." She reached for the luggage Christie had been guarding and began stowing the bags in the back with the supplies.

"Can't blame a man for trying," said Hogan. "You and Miss Hayes have had your holiday, now *I* need one."

"Aw. Getting old?"

"Well, I am, and that's a fact." He chuckled. "But it wasn't looking after the jail all on my lonesome wore me out. It was listening to Angie going on and on about what it was taking to make your place even *remotely* habitable. Old Coop let that place go to rack and ruin."

Zee slapped him on the shoulder. "That's why it was dirt cheap." She turned to find Christie looking at the gelding and buckboard. "Will it do?"

Christie nodded.

She handed Christie up into the seat, then hopped up beside her. "You drive." She picked up the reins and handed them over.

Christie looked at her. "It's been some time since I drove one of these."

Hogan came to stand beside them. "Angie said there's enough water to tide you and the horses over for a couple of days. And she's fixed for the water wagon to call day after tomorrow."

Zee tipped her hat. "Tell her much obliged, will you?"

He grinned. "Oh, you'll be able to thank her in person." Zee wondered what he meant by that, but before she could inquire he stepped back, tipped his hat, and started to walk away.

The buckboard remained stationary, and she glanced at Christie who seemed to have been struck by paralysis. "We gonna sit here all day, darlin'? Got us a new home to go to and," she lowered her voice, "a new bed to christen."

That got Zee a startled look and a hasty "Sh." Chuckling, she made herself as comfortable as possible on the hard wooden seat, pulled down the brim of her Stetson against the noonday sun, and folded her gloved hands across her stomach. Then she waited.

Christie took a deep breath, exhaled, muttered what might have been a curse under her breath, then flicked the reins. The dozing gelding started to life and the buckboard jerked forward with a rumble.

By the time they reached Schoolhouse Lane, which was on the edge of town, Christie was handling the gelding and buckboard as though she had been doing so all her life and was even humming to herself. Zee gave her an amused glance and tipped her hat to a passer-by.

They had passed several of the townsfolk on the way. Zee knew them all, and most had called out a greeting or tipped their hats. One or two of the more upright citizens had pretended not to see her, but that was only to be expected given Zee's Hellcat past and the disreputable circles she moved in. Christie's acquaintances were as yet limited (unless you counted those who frequented Angie's Palace), but Zee hoped that would change now they had a home to which Christie could invite more respectable guests.

The buckboard trundled past the schoolhouse on the left then Curly Shaw's spread on the right. "Nearly there," said Zee as, up ahead, an odd-looking house came into view.

"Is that it?" Christie's voice was hoarse with excitement. She stared at the rundown vegetable garden and the rutted track leading round the side of the house, whose origins as a barn were all too obvious.

"Yeah." Zee gave her an affectionate glance. "Ain't much but it's all ours. Home sweet home."

At Zee's direction, Christie turned the buckboard up the track, which brought them round to the yard at the back of the house. Zee jumped down, opened the gate, and closed it again once Christie had driven through. Then she helped Christie down and watched her take in their surroundings.

"Needs work," she admitted, bashing her hat against her thigh to get the worst of the dust off. "Fence needs fixing. And there's a hole in the roof." She pointed at the ramshackle barn that the previous owner had built next to the house and where she intended to keep the horses and buckboard. "I asked Angie to focus on the kitchen and main bedroom. Anything else we can fix later."

She ran a hand through her hair then resettled her hat. "Not as grand as your place in Contention but . . ." She moved behind Christie and hugged her.

"It's fine." Christie relaxed against her, and Zee gave in to the urge to press her lips against fair hair. "Anyway, making this place spick-and-span will give me something to do while you're at work."

"Yeah." Reluctantly Zee relinquished her hold. "All right. First things first."

The water trough in the yard was dry, so she took off her hat and emptied her canteen into it. While the gelding drank, her mare nickered. "I'm getting to you . . . That's enough, boy." She pushed the gelding away and let the mare drink.

Christie meanwhile climbed into the back of the buckboard and investigated the supplies. "I hope you got everything I asked for," she called.

"Everything but the kitchen sink," muttered Zee, shaking the last water droplets out of her hat and putting it back on.

"Pardon?"

She turned to find Christie regarding her suspiciously. "Yeah," she said. "Taylor assured me everything on your list is there."

"Good." Christie resumed her excavations among the sacks of coffee and flour. "Wait a minute. I didn't order this." She was peering at the bolt of fabric.

Zee smiled. "That's a little something extra. Thought you might have a use for it."

Christie put her hands on her hips. "Anyone would think we had money to burn." She relaxed into a smile. "But it will make some lovely curtains. Thank you, Zee."

It's curtain material? Zee held her smile with an effort.

Christie gestured. "Help me down."

Zee grabbed Christie round the waist, but instead of helping her down, swept her up in her arms and headed for the back door.

"Hey!" Christie squirmed, her attempts to free herself sending pleasurable sensations straight to Zee's groin. "What are you doing? Put me down."

"Putting first things first, darlin'. Now keep still or I'll drop you."

Zee stopped on the doorstep, shifted Christie into a more secure grip, and clouted the door hard with a boot heel. It swung open in a spray of splinters.

"I'll mend it later," she told Christie, who had finally realized what she was up to and stopped struggling. Careful not to bang that precious head or those pretty ankles on the doorjamb, Zee carried Christie across the threshold.

Once inside, she set Christie on her feet again, and found herself on the receiving end of a kiss so intense her knees almost buckled.

"Phew," she said, when Christie allowed her back up for air. "You sure know how to kiss."

"I had a good teacher." Christie took her first look at her surroundings. "Oh! It's lovely."

Kitchen certainly looks different from the last time I was here, thought Zee, gazing round in amazement. Old Coop had lived like a pig in a pigsty, but Angie and the girls had transformed the place. The floorboards had been swept, the kitchen table scrubbed within an inch of its life, and the disreputable stove renovated and made ready for action.

Christie disappeared into the pantry. Zee put her hat on the table, then turned one of the four wooden chairs round and straddled it.

"Look. How thoughtful." Christie emerged bearing a jug full of cool lemonade and poured them both glasses.

Zee drank hers down in one, licked her lips, and considered. "Not as good as yours, darlin'." Christie beamed at her and sipped hers.

Zee let her gaze wander round the room, over the tinware hanging on the wall, and the zinc sink, which she was pleased to see, had a foot of water in it. She stopped at the lace-edged gingham curtains now framing the sparkling windowpanes and chuckled.

"Something amusing?"

"Just glad Angie didn't think to do this place up like the Palace," explained Zee. "Wouldn't have put it past her." A thought struck her. "Damn. The bedroom . . ." They exchanged horrified looks.

"She wouldn't have."

"She might."

Zee was out of her chair and out of the kitchen at the double, and took the stairs three at a time. Christie's dress hampered her but she wasn't far behind.

Thank God! No red wallpaper, velvet drapes, or mirrors, was Zee's first thought as she pushed open the door to the main bedroom. Her second was: *Now that's what I call a bed*.

A cough signaled that Christie was waiting and Zee stepped aside to allow her to enter.

"My goodness!" Christie blinked. "It's bigger than that bed at the Republic Hotel." She fingered the pillowcases. "Are these satin? Whatever possessed her to buy something so impractical?"

Zee strode across to the bed and flung herself down on it. "Good old Angie." She gave an exploratory bounce. "Must've oiled the springs." Another bounce. "Comfy too." She reached out a hand. "C'mere."

For a moment Christie looked as though she was considering joining her. Then she sighed and shook her head. "Later, Zee. Those supplies are in the sun. They'll spoil if we don't get them inside."

"Aw, darlin'." But Christie was no longer there to see Zee's pout. She listened to the footsteps descending the stairs, flopped back against the pillows, and frowned at the ceiling.

The horses in the yard outside nickered a greeting, then came a grunt that must be Christie trying to unload something heavy on her own. "Of all the stubborn—"

Zee was out of the bed, down the stairs, and out in the back yard in time to relieve the flushed Christie of a sack of meal.

"Thank you." Christie brushed hair out of her eyes and smiled down at her.

"All right, later," said Zee, slinging the sack over her shoulder. It was a concession and a promise.

IT TOOK AN hour and much toing and froing before they got all the supplies stowed to Christie's satisfaction (she had very decided opinions about what should go where) and the two horses fed and watered and stabled in the barn with the buckboard. Then Christie cut them both some well-earned slices of bread and ham.

They reduced the late dinner to crumbs, and were drinking lemonade and bantering about whether "now" had become "later" (Zee was of the opinion that it had and was having some success in talking Christie round to her way of thinking), when there came a loud knock at the back door.

"Are we expecting anyone?" asked Christie.

"Not that I'm aware of." Zee made no move to answer the door. Perhaps they would go away.

"Shall I see who's there?" Christie stood up.

Zee shrugged and took another gulp of her drink.

Christie returned with a plump, kind-faced woman in a brown dress, carrying a pie. "It's Mrs. Shaw. Our neighbor."

"Howdy, Ann," said Zee, smiling. There wasn't a nicer couple in all of Benson than Ann and Curly Shaw. That they were to be neighbors had been another point in the Old Barn's favor. "Take a seat." She shoved a chair forward with her foot.

"I'm not stopping, Zee. And please, Christie, call me Ann . . . I know the two of you must be very busy—just back from Phoenix, your first day in a new house and so on. And I thought you might not have time to cook. So I brought you this."

She thrust the pie at Christie who accepted it with a smile and placed it on the table.

"How considerate."

"It was no trouble . . . I'm sure you'd have done the same had our positions been reversed . . . My. What a nice kitchen." Ann was looking around. "I didn't dare come in here when Cooper owned the place." She grimaced. "I was afraid I might catch something."

"It is nice, isn't it?" agreed Christie. "Some . . . er, friends of ours organized it while we were away. Of course there's still a lot of work needs doing on the rest of the house. And I want some more shelves put up here and here . . ."

While their attention was elsewhere, Zee pulled the pie dish toward her and sniffed it. Mm. She poked two fingers through the pastry crust and licked the juices off them. As she had thought. Peach. She helped herself to more.

The buzz of conversation had stopped, she realized, and she looked up. Two pairs of outraged eyes, one green, one gray, were looking at her.

She stopped sucking her fingers. "What?"

Christie opened her mouth then closed it again. "I see you've started without me," she said dryly.

"But, darlin'. It's peach pie."

Christie's lips twitched. She reached out and reordered a strand of Zee's hair. "All right. Go on. As long as you don't forget . . . half of it is mine."

At that, Ann began to laugh. In fact, when she left, five minutes later, to walk back to her own house, she was still smiling.

"Alone at last." Zee pulled Christie onto her lap for a quick kiss and cuddle, which escalated into something more. *Was that a horse whinnying?* she wondered hazily. And where were the voices and laughter coming from? Christie's renewed assault on her mouth banished every thought except taking her to bed. Still kissing, she grasped her and stood up. She was half way up the stairs—

Bang. Bang. Bang.

Zee broke the kiss. "Damn it!" Christie sighed and disentangled herself from Zee's embrace.

This time it was Zee who answered the door. (*Must get that latch fixed,* she reminded herself.)

"Surprise!" A beaming Angie Tucker was standing on the doorstep. Behind her were Clubfoot Liz, Rowdy Molly, and Lazy Alice. At any other time Zee would have been glad to see her friends, but right now . . .

"Who is it?" yelled Christie.

Zee noticed the champagne bottles clutched in each hand and that the women were all wearing their Sunday best. This wasn't just a quick visit by the looks of things.

"The Welcome Wagon," she yelled back.

"What a thing to say!" Angie poked Zee in the ribs with her fan. "Are you going to invite us in?"

A hand grabbed the back of Zee's shirt and yanked her out of the way. "Yes she is." Christie beamed at Angie and her whores. "It's lovely to see you. Come on in."

The giggling women stepped past Zee into the kitchen and a round of hugging and kissing and noisy chattering ensued. Zee sighed, threw an envious glance toward the quiet yard, then closed the door and went to join her guests.

ZEE STRETCHED. "I like this bed," she announced. "It's roomy. A person can spread out." She suited the action to the deed then curled herself back around Christie.

"It's certainly an improvement on that cramped bed at the Palace." Christie yawned. "What a day!"

Zee smiled, thinking of Rowdy Molly's expression just before the lanky blonde passed out from too much champagne and had to be carried to the wagon waiting to take them back to the brothel. "I thought they'd never leave."

"I could tell," came the response. "You had that glint in your eye all evening. The girls were ribbing me about it."

Zee frowned. "What glint?"

"You know. That 'I can't wait to take you to bed' one."

"Oh." She smiled and rubbed her thumb over the soft skin of Christie's belly, eliciting a hum of pleasure. "That glint."

She pressed her lips against fragrant-smelling hair and thought about the woman in her arms, the house that was now theirs, the life that lay ahead of them. Before, it had been a dream; now . . . the reality of it was a little overwhelming.

"Bed's been well and truly christened," she said instead.

"Mmmm." Christie gave a sleepy sigh. "Well and truly." From the look of her, their recent traveling, plus the day's excitement, followed by lovemaking had taken their toll on Christie. She was fighting hard to stay awake and keep Zee company, but losing the battle.

"'S alright, darlin'," said Zee. "I'll be here when you wake up. Sleep now." Once more she pressed her lips to Christie's hair. "Sweet dreams."

Christie snuggled back against her and captured her hand, pressing it against her belly. "'Morrow, love," she slurred. Then there was only the sound of her breathing.

Chapter 2

IF CHRISTIE COULD have whistled while she worked, she would have. But since, even with Zee's tutelage, she had still not quite got the hang of it, she contented herself with humming instead.

As she stoked the stove then put her loaf in to bake, she hummed a few bars of "Beautiful Dreamer." And as she washed and dried the breakfast dishes and cutlery and put them in their appointed places, she hummed some more.

Her thoughts were only half on her work, however. She was preoccupied with a certain deputy. After feeding Zee a large helping of ham and eggs and extracting a promise that she be home for dinner at noon, she had sent her off to work with a loving kiss that still made her lips tingle.

I'm happy, she realized. She laughed and resumed her humming.

It was odd keeping house again. Christie had kept house for her brother for years of course, but with Zee it was . . . "different" was the best description she could manage. And after the cramped and noisy confines of the brothel, this kitchen, the bedroom, that bed . . . why, they were heavenly.

She stood in the middle of the kitchen, stretched out her arms, and spun round until she was giddy, then stopped and took herself to task. There was work to be done—so much that she didn't know quite where to start. So she had better get on with it.

She smoothed down her apron, tied back her hair in a scarf, and fetched a broom from the closet. Then she ventured into the front room Zee had ruefully shown her yesterday. It was to be the parlor, but at present it was a cobweb-festooned health hazard.

Whatever the previous occupant had believed, it wasn't that cleanliness was next to godliness. Clouds of dust billowed up all around Christie and set her coughing. She laid aside the broom, ran upstairs, and helped herself to one of Zee's red bandannas, then caught her reflection in the mirror. Her masked nose and mouth made her look rather rakish, she decided. "I'm Hellcat Hayes," she drawled, trying to arch her eyebrow the way Zee did. "The terror of Benson." She shook her head at herself, then ran downstairs laughing and resumed her sweeping.

When the worst of the dust had been brushed into the yard, she fetched a mop and a pail of their precious water (thank heavens the water wagon was coming tomorrow) and started washing down the walls. As she worked, she hummed and thought about the future.

It would be nice to have a proper parlor in which to receive guests. The kitchen was all very well for informal occasions, but . . . She appraised the windows, which needed a clean. That bolt of sky blue calico Zee had bought would not only do for curtains but matching tablecloths too. Of course they'd need some tables first. The furniture in this room had been beyond saving, so they would have to start from scratch.

Maybe it would be cheaper for Zee to make the tables herself, she mused. Zee was good at carpentry and they had spent an awful lot of Zee's savings on the house already. Though Zee said she'd have no difficulty providing Christie with the weekly allowance she'd asked for, they would still have to be careful. It was up to Christie to be frugal and make economies where she could.

She finished washing down the wall and stood back to admire the result, rubbing her itchy nose until she realized she was coating it with more dirt. What was one more blob, though, when she was already covered from head to foot in the stuff? She emptied the dirty water over the vegetable patch out front, then put away the pail and mop.

Sponging her face and hands clean and brushing her hair made her feel human again. She put on a fresh apron, poured herself a glass of lemonade, and sank into a kitchen chair.

She had been resting for ten minutes when a knock at the back door dragged her from a very pleasant daydream involving Zee and the huge bed upstairs. The unexpected visitor turned out to be their neighbor, Curly Shaw. The big man, whose real name was Cornelius, owed his nickname to his riot of curly black hair. He was bearing another of his wife's peach pies.

"Truth be told, I'm glad to get rid of it," he confessed, waving aside Christie's thanks. "I'm mighty sick of peaches, but don't tell my wife I said so."

He crushed his hat against his expanding belly (the result of too many peach pies?) and glanced at his surroundings. The kitchen seemed to meet with his approval.

Then he took a breath and exhaled, his words coming out in a rush. "Main reason I'm here, Miss Hayes, er, I mean, Christie, is . . . Well, it's this way." His face reddened and Christie wondered what on earth was coming next. "Seeing as how there's no man about the place, and seeing as how there's bound to be heavy work: chopping wood, fixing things that get broke and the like . . . Well, it occurred to Ann and me that you might, er . . . well, might be in need of some male assistance now and then."

Christie considered this rather garbled speech. "Oh, you're offering to be our handyman if we need you?"

"That's it exactly." He gave her a relieved glance. "It was Ann's idea. She said, seeing as we're your closest neighbors and all."

"Quite." Christie nodded. "And how very kind of you to offer. We really do appreciate it." She smiled. "But Zee is more than capable of taking care of all the things that need doing around the place. She's strong and very good with her hands."

A memory of last night's bed-christening activities surfaced and she tried not to blush. Fortunately, Curly didn't seem to notice. He was nodding, clearly at ease once again.

"Thought that's what you'd say. But I had to go through the motions. Once Ann's got an idea in that head of hers—" He gave her a conspiratorial grin. "She forgot that one of the two women in question is Zee, I reckon."

He crammed his hat on his head. "Well, I'll be on my way then, Miss Hay . . . erm, Christie." He tipped the brim of his hat. "The offer still stands, should you two ever need it."

"Thank you. That's very kind."

CHRISTIE WAS SITTING on the parlor floor, surrounded by lengths of sky blue cloth marked with tailor's chalk, when an odd sound caught her attention. She stopped cutting and cocked her head.

Squeak . . . Creak.

It seemed to be coming from the front. She put down her dressmaking shears, got to her feet, and approached the now sparkling windows.

A boy of about ten, clad in clean but patched dungarees, was swinging on the front gate.

Squeak.

"Well!" She supposed he must belong to their other neighbors, the Rikers, since the Shaws' two children had grown up and left home long ago, according to Zee.

Creak.

Zee had told her not to expect any neighborly treatment from the Rikers. "Hymn-singing hypocrites the pair of 'em. Adah's one of them Temperance Union busybodies. I ain't exactly their flavor of the month since I stopped 'em smashing up the Last Chance Saloon." She grimaced. "Ernie's just as bad. He's president of the bank."

"Banking's not necessarily a bad thing," said Christie.

"It is if you call in the loans of folks who are desperate and steal their homes off 'em."

"That doesn't sound very Christian."

"It ain't." Zee hugged her. "There's more charity in your little fingernail, darlin', than in their whole sorry carcasses. My guess is they'll give us a wide berth, which suits me just fine."

Zee hadn't mentioned the Rikers had a son.

Squeak.

Christie tucked a wayward strand of hair behind her ear, smoothed her apron, and went out to talk to him.

Creak.

"Hello, young man. Would you please stop swinging on our gate? You'll have it off its hinges."

The stare he gave her was disconcerting. "No."

Squeak.

She blinked at him. "I beg your pardon."

"No."

Creak.

She frowned and considered what to do next. "Do your parents know you are not in school?"

Squeak.

"You're the Rikers' boy, aren't you?" She folded her arms and waited.

Creak.

"I said you're the Rikers' boy, aren't you?"

"And you're the Hellcat's whore."

She sucked in her breath. For a child to even know such a word . . . "Don't speak to me like that."

The boy stopped swinging and stepped down from the gate. He fixed that unnerving gaze on her again. "Why not? It's true. You're the Hellcat's whore," he repeated. "And everyone knows it."

Her face felt hot. "I'll thank you to keep a civil tongue in your head, young man, or I'll put you across my knee."

He smiled and she was suddenly reminded of boys who pull the wings off flies. He was trying to goad her, she realized. Sticks and stones, she told herself. Sticks and stones. She kept her breathing slow and steady.

"A killer and her whore, living as man and wife," continued the boy, watching her closely. "It's disgusting."

Now Christie's dander was well and truly up. *Where's a broom when you need it? A good swift smack will have to do.* She marched toward him, raising her hand, but he stepped back and darted off.

He had run barely ten yards before he turned and yelled at her, "Why don't you go back to the brothel where you belong? You're both going to Hell anyway."

Still boiling with anger—an unfamiliar sensation and one she could do without—she shaded her eyes and watched him hare off down the road.

Christie marched indoors and headed for the kitchen. There, she shucked her apron and grabbed her bonnet. She had barely finished tying the ribbons under her chin before she was outside again and on her way to the Rikers' place.

It was smaller than the Shaws' rambling old spread, but larger than the Old Barn. Its inhabitants clearly had money—a nice porch ran across the front of the house, which was painted white with a green trim, and the roof was shingled. As she crunched up the stony path toward the front door, between the tubs that someone had planted up with bay trees, she could hear dogs barking.

She knocked at the ornate front door and waited. The parlor's lace curtain twitched. Moments later, a stout woman was standing in the doorway, staring down her prominent nose at her.

"Mrs. Riker?" Since the boy was about ten years old, Christie supposed his mother couldn't be more than thirty, but the staid dress of black broadcloth added ten years to her age.

"Yes."

"I'm Christie Hayes, your new neighbor. Pleased to meet you."

Adah Riker stepped back and began to close the door.

"Hey, wait a minute!" said an indignant Christie. "It's about your son."

The door paused, seemed to think about what it should do next, then opened again.

"Joe?"

"Is that his name? Small boy, about ten years old, curly hair, brown eyes, freckles, wearing dungarees."

"What about him?" Adah's tone was stiff.

"He's been round at my house, damaging my front gate and insulting me."

"When was this?"

"Just now."

"Can't be our Joe. He's in school."

"He *should* be in school but he isn't. He insulted me and Deputy Brodie."

Mention of Zee made Adah blink. "What did Joe say?"

Christie's cheeks grew hot. "I . . . it's too upsetting to repeat."

"If he said you should be in a brothel and the deputy should be in the jail not running it, then it was the simple truth."

"I beg your pardon?"

"You heard me. If that's all, I have better things to do than talk to the Hellcat's whore." Adah stepped back and shut the door in her face.

Shock rooted Christie to the spot. She stared at the door, finding the wood's grain oddly fascinating and noticing that a fly had been caught in the paint.

"Told you." The hateful voice jolted Christie out of her paralysis. She twisted and saw Joe Riker peering round the corner of the porch at her. Then the parlor curtain twitched, and the boy ducked out of sight again.

She didn't remember walking back to the Old Barn, but somehow she found herself back in her own kitchen. She tore off her bonnet, hung it up, pulled out a chair, and sat down. Leaning one elbow on the table, she rested her chin in her palm and stared unseeing at the wall. If everyone felt as the Rikers did, her dreams for a normal life with Zee were only so much smoke and mirrors.

The ticking of the clock seemed deafening in the silence, and she could hear the logs crackling and shifting inside the stove. She felt oddly detached. The numbness would wear off soon, she supposed, and then would come some other emotion—hurt, anger, sadness . . . maybe all three?

A little while later—ten minutes by the clock—Christie realized with a start that she had better begin preparing Zee's dinner or Zee would go hungry. Mechanically, she peeled some potatoes and put them on to boil, then she got out the salt pork from the pantry and began to slice.

Chapter 3

ZEE WHISTLED AS she strode along the boardwalk toward the Wells Fargo office. She had been in the jail, leafing through the bundle of bulletins and Wanted posters that had come in during her absence, when she heard the hoofbeats and rumble of wheels that meant the stagecoach was here. With a little luck the package she had ordered should be on it.

A crowd of passengers and passers-by had gathered next to the stage. She broke into a run as she realized that they were watching two men fight.

"Out of the way." She elbowed her way to the front, took in the situation at a glance, then grabbed Jim Marlin by the back of his collar and hauled him off the stage driver, Cal Unger, who was half his size.

"What in tarnation's going on, Jim?" She gave the big man a shake that clapped his jaws together before releasing her grip on his collar.

He glowered at her from beneath bushy eyebrows. "No call to treat me that way, Deputy. I'm within my rights." He kicked a wooden crate that lay on the ground behind the stagecoach, and she heard the tinkling of broken glass. "This ain't no use to me."

Blood had spattered the front of Unger's shirt. Zee pulled off her bandanna and shoved it at him. He gaped at her then accepted it and pressed it to his bleeding nose.

"Says I damaged his glassware." The cloth muffled the driver's voice. "But it was like that when I took possession."

Unger had always been honest in his dealings with her, so she was inclined to believe him. She turned to Marlin. "Reckon your beef's with the Stage line, Jim, not Cal here."

Unger nodded carefully, so as not to exacerbate his nosebleed. Marlin cursed under his breath, but his shoulders slumped and Zee knew the fight had gone out of him. Sensing the fun was over, the bystanders began to disperse.

She watched the big man pick up his crate and carry it inside the office with the green painted shutters. Moments later came the sound of raised voices. Zee sighed and hoped she wouldn't be called on to break up yet another fight.

Unger fingered his nose and decided it had stopped bleeding. "Thanks, Deputy." He offered Zee the sodden bandanna.

She grimaced and declined it with a quick shake of the head. "Just doing my job. 'Course, I might have to whup you myself if I find you've given the same treatment to *my* package."

He blinked at her. "No, no, your stuff is just fine and dandy." He hurried round to the stage's boot and pulled out a burlap sack. "Here it is, safe and sound." His hands, she was amused to see, were shaking.

She took the sack from him, hefted it to assess its weight, then loosened the drawstring around its neck and peeked inside. The contents looked unprepossessing, but then, she was expecting that. She tipped her hat at him and grinned. "Looks all present and correct, Cal. Thanks."

While he breathed a sigh of relief and turned back to his unloading, she swiveled on her heel and headed back to the jail, jiggling the sack as she walked and whistling the chorus from "Come into the Garden, Maud." *Hope Christie likes 'em.*

"Hey, Brodie." The familiar voice made her stop whistling and glance round. Red Mary was across the street waving at her, her breasts threatening to spill over the top of her low cut pink dress. "You coming to the Palace for a bite to eat?"

Zee shook her head. "Thanks for the invite, Mary, but Christie's making me dinner," she called. "I'm on my way home now." *Home.* She tasted the word and found it good.

The whore wasn't quite quick enough to hide the scowl that mention of Christie provoked and Zee covered her grin with a cough. It did a body good, she decided, to have two women fighting over 'em. Not that there was any contest, of course. Christie had won her heart and the sooner Red Mary accepted that the better. She tipped her hat to the disgruntled whore and resumed her progress.

Her mare was tethered to the shady hitching post outside the jail. She tucked the burlap sack into a saddlebag and patted the horse's neck. "Won't be long, girl," she murmured in one twitching ear—the cells were empty today so no prisoners needed feeding. "Just got to leave a note."

Zee took the steps up to the jail two at a time and flung open the door to the office. It took her only moments to find some paper and scrawl: "Gone Home For Dinner. Back in One Hour." She was halfway out the office door, when a thought made her smile, and she went back and struck out "One" and scribbled "Two" in its place. There. That should provide enough time for after-dinner plans involving Christie and a bed.

Outside, she mounted up and kneed the horse into a trot. As she headed up Main Street, she pulled down the broad brim of her hat against the sun's glare and pondered a puzzle. Why was it that, as soon as she returned to work, things always got interesting?

Hogan's logbook said things had been as quiet as the grave while she was away. Oh, there'd been a fistfight or two, and minor fires at the Golden Slipper and the Last Chance Saloon, oh and the arrival of that gambler from New Orleans which had provoked the sheriff into sending a telegram to check up on him, but that had been it. Her first morning back, and *already* she'd had to separate two of Angie's girls (they'd been trying to knife one another over a handsome client), and a pair of silver miners, lifelong friends, had taken it into their heads to brain one another with shovels, all because one had called the other's new shirt "puke-colored." Then there had been the scuffle outside the Wells Fargo Office . . .

She waved at the boy playing marbles on the boardwalk and turned the mare off Main Street.

She'd assess the gambler herself this afternoon, she decided, as she cantered past McGillivray's, where a loud hammering indicated the undertaker was hard at work. Americus Millain might be an honest cardplayer, he might also be the biggest cardsharp this side of the Mississippi. Hogan had noted that Millain had a pretty little octoroon in tow; Zee was curious to see her too.

Her stomach rumbled. *Wonder what Christie's got for dinner. Whatever it is, it'll sure be welcome.*

The Old Barn came into sight, and impulsively she kicked the mare into a gallop. She pounded up the track alongside the house, jumped the back gate, and pulled up in the back yard. The horse whinnied and tossed her head.

"Thanks, girl." She dismounted, gave the mare a pat, and led her to the trough. Seconds later, burlap sack in hand she was lifting the latch and pushing open the back door with an enthusiastic *thump.*

Christie was standing with her back to her, serving up an appetizing smelling dinner. Zee admired the shapely rump for a brief moment then strode toward her.

"Miss me, darlin'?" She flung her hat at the hat stand, discarded the sack and her gloves on the table, and pulled Christie into a bear hug. To her surprise, the other woman let out a sob, turned in the circle of her arms, and grabbed hold of her, pressing herself into Zee.

"Hey!" Zee was in danger of toppling backward. She steered them both over to a chair and sat down. "What's wrong?" She pulled Christie onto her lap. *Damn!* "Is it something I did?"

But Christie was crying so hard, it was impossible to make out what she was saying in between the sniffles and sobs and hiccups.

First she had to get Christie calmed down. Zee rocked her, pressed her lips to hair and cheek, stroked her back, all the while whispering the soothing stream of nonsense that worked when her horse got skittish. After a while, the sobbing lessened and the death grip round her neck eased.

The fair head lifted and puffy eyes regarded her blearily.

"What's wrong?" repeated Zee.

Christie's nose was congested and her lips were swollen, but Zee caught the mumbled words "Rikers" and "whore" and "Hell." Her lips tightened.

"Tell me again," she ordered. "Slowly." When the whole sorry mess had been laid out for her inspection, she disentangled herself from Christie and stood up.

Christie looked at her in alarm. "Where are you going?"

She reached for her gloves. "To teach those Rikers a lesson." A cold rage was pulsing through her. Those sanctimonious lumps of horse dung! How dare they treat Christie like that! She flexed her hands, anticipating the satisfying feel of fists thudding into flesh.

Christie grabbed hold of Zee's arm. "No."

"Darlin'." Zee tried to shake loose the hand restraining her.

"No." Christie's voice was urgent. "Listen to me. You're not the Hellcat anymore. You're the law and you can't go taking it into your own hands."

She growled. "Just watch me."

"What the Rikers said was just words, Zee. Horrible, hurtful words, it's true, but I should have been thick-skinned enough to ignore them."

"Words can cause as much harm as bullets," she objected. But Christie's impassioned plea had reached her, and already her anger was ebbing, and from Christie's relieved look, she could sense it.

"Damn." Zee flopped down, feeling as though she had just wrestled a bear. One finger at a time, she pulled off her gloves. "Why can't I whup someone when I feel like it?" she complained, only half in jest.

"Because then you'd be little better than a savage." Christie sat on Zee's lap again, as though she belonged there by right, and, the way it felt to Zee, she did.

"The Rikers are the savages." She slipped an arm round Christie's waist. "They had no call to speak to you that way."

Christie sighed. "A lot of people seem to feel the way they do. Blue does." The sadness in her voice almost broke Zee's heart.

"Your brother does *not* think you're a whore," she protested. "He thinks you keep bad company . . . and that bit's true." She gave Christie a rakish grin.

Wistful green eyes regarded her. "Maybe I was foolish to think we could set up house like a normal couple, Zee. Maybe we should go back to the Palace and—"

"Damn it!" Zee grabbed Christie by the shoulders, earning herself a startled glance. "Just because the Rikers think we should live a certain way, it don't mean we should. Hell, the way I see it, their disapproval is a point in our favor."

"But—"

"No buts. I ain't gonna apologize for who I am and neither are you."

"But respectable fo—"

"Respectable folk ain't worth a plugged nickel. It's folk like Ann and Curly who matter. Kind folk, decent folk. Got me?" Christie winced, and Zee released her grip as though burned. "I'm sorry, I didn't mean to hurt—"

"It's all right." Christie smiled at her, then ran a knuckle tenderly over Zee's cheek. "I understand." She snuggled against Zee and sighed. "You're right, of course. I know it. It's just . . . I don't *feel* it . . . here," she thumped her own chest, "yet."

Zee held her close. "You will, darlin'. Give it time."

Zee's grumbling stomach broke the companionable silence.

"Oh." Christie sat up, a hand to her mouth. "Your dinner. It must be stone cold by now. Maybe I can reheat—" She tried to get up, but Zee held her in place.

"Stay put." Zee stretched across the table and pulled one of the plates toward her. She sprinkled salt on a cold potato and held it to Christie's lips. Small white teeth took a tentative bite. While Christie chewed contentedly, Zee popped a potato in her own mouth and reached for a slice of salt pork.

"There are knives and forks, you know," chided Christie, but she didn't seem to mind when Zee tore up the meat with her fingers and fed her. Soon both plates were empty.

"Somehow, eating food like this tastes better," said Christie, licking crystals of salt from Zee's palm, the sensation sending a pleasant jolt through her. Zee grabbed Christie's hand and returned the favor, and got a wide-eyed look in response.

"When do you have to go back?" Christie's voice was a mere husk.

Zee glanced at the kitchen clock. "Half an hour." She gave a sly smile. "Got something in mind?"

Christie slid off her lap and held out a hand. Zee took it and stood up.

"I think that bed needs rechristening, don't you, darlin'?"

"My thoughts exactly."

Chapter 4

ZEE LOOPED THE mare's reins over the rail outside the Golden Slipper and pushed her way through the swinging doors. The chatter, laughter, and clink of glasses lessened as every head in the place swung toward her, and that meant quite a few.

She tipped back her hat and grinned. "Afternoon, gents," she called. "And ladies," she added, causing a ripple of laughter—there were plenty of women in the crowded gambling den, but few of them were "ladies." The conversation and slap of playing cards on baize resumed.

A beautiful young woman in a lemon-yellow dress, sitting on her own by the bar, was a class apart from the usual hostesses, whose job was to siphon the customers' surplus money into the gambling den's pockets by serving drinks at the tables and whoring. Unlike them, her dress flattered her figure but kept it discreetly under wraps, her flawless complexion required no face paint, and her manner was demure.

Zee gave her a closer look, and decided she was in fact little more than sixteen. Her dark chestnut hair was slightly wavy and Zee would have bet that her tanned complexion owed little to the sun.

Guess she's the octoroon Hogan mentioned.

Zee crossed to the bar, then positioned herself so she could see the girl clearly in the mirror.

She seemed to be on edge. When she wasn't fiddling with her gloves, her eyes, which were so dark as to be almost black, were fixed on a man in a small-brimmed hat, striped silk shirt, and embroidered vest, who was sitting at one of the poker tables. In that get-up, he certainly wasn't one of the Golden Slipper's regulars.

Must be Americus Millain.

The chief hostess, Kitty Lee, came over and fluttered long eyelashes at Zee. When Zee politely but firmly declined her invitation to buy some house champagne and go upstairs with her, Kitty shook her head sadly, ringlets dancing, but left her in peace.

Zee rested a boot on the foot rail. "Whiskey, Jack." She felt in her vest pocket for a coin and flipped it toward the barkeep.

He caught it. "Sure thing, Deputy." He reached below the counter for a bottle. When he'd finished pouring she took it off him and examined the label.

"This the best you've got?"

"Yeah. Been a run on the good stuff—that new fellow mostly. Won't be getting another delivery 'til next week."

"Guess it'll have to do then." She took a sip of the rough liquor and shuddered. "By new fellow d'you mean Millain?"

Her words carried, and the girl sitting further along the bar stiffened at the name.

"That's him. Got a winning streak going."

Winning streak, huh? Zee knocked back her shot glass in one, then turned and leaned back against the bar. Millain's pointed beard disguised a weak chin, she decided, just as he glanced up. His eyes widened as she caught and held his gaze, but he recovered his poise quickly, flashed her a charming smile that set her teeth on edge, and resumed his game of cards.

Zee turned her back on him. "'Nother whiskey, Jack," she called, slapping another coin on the counter and shifting so she could see both the girl and Millain in the mirror.

"Tell me about this winning streak." She took a gulp. Either the liquor was improving or her taste buds had died.

"Already cleaned out Luke Howells." The barkeep polished the bar with a cloth. "And it looks like he's just done the same to Horace Beecher."

Zee glanced in the mirror. Horace's gleaming bald head was cradled in his hands, and his friends were trying to comfort him. A smirking Millain, meanwhile, was raking in the contents of the pot.

"Remarkable luck," she said dryly.

Zee smiled her thanks at the barkeep, then turned and strode over to Millain's table. She eased past a white-faced Horace, who was now being helped from the room, and grabbed the chair he had vacated, swiveling it round and straddling it.

The players looked at her in surprise.

"Howdy, Brodie." Bob Lewis mopped his balding head with a handkerchief. "You thinking of sitting in for a spell? I should warn you, Millain here is in form."

Silas Ward glowered at the depleted pile of coins in front of him and grunted agreement.

"No," said Zee. "Just came over to introduce myself." She held out a gloved hand to the gambler from New Orleans. "Deputy Zee Brodie."

He shook it. "Americus Millain. At your service, ma'am."

"Deputy or Brodie will do fine, thanks. So what brings you and your lady friend to Benson?" She glanced meaningfully at the girl in lemon-yellow who was watching them.

He shrugged, unwrapped a fresh deck of cards, and began to shuffle them. "Oh, you know how it is, Deputy. A man gets tired of staying in one place all the time." He smiled. "I had a hankering to travel."

She raised an eyebrow. "Yeah?"

He knocked back the contents of the glass of whiskey sitting by his elbow. Almost as soon as he put it down, a hostess brought the bottle and refilled it. He smiled at her and tossed her a dollar, then looked at the other players. "Ready to win back some of your money, gentlemen?"

"Count me in," said Bob.

Silas nodded and twanged a suspender.

"Sure you won't sit in, Deputy?"

She shook her head.

"All right, gentlemen. Ante up." Millain tossed a dollar in the pot and waited for the others to add their token bets.

As he dealt, Zee rested her chin on the chair back and followed his every move with an eagle eye. He handled the cards like an expert. He glanced up, saw the direction of her stare and smiled. She pursed her lips. Either he wasn't cheating or he was damned good at it.

When everyone had their cards (they were playing Five Card Stud), Millain placed the remainder of the deck in the middle of the table and reached for his own cards.

He was the type to wear out his welcome everywhere he went, she guessed, watching the players examining the hands they had been dealt. The sooner the reply to Hogan's telegram came, the better.

Bob was sitting to the left of the dealer, so it fell to him to open the betting. He tossed in a dollar.

"See your dollar and raise you five," said Silas, suiting the action to the words.

Zee considered the silver miner's dwindling pile of coins. *Risky play, Silas. What've you got, a Full House?*

Millain hesitated then reached for some bills. "See your five," he said, tossing them into the center of the table.

As the game unfolded, it became clear that the New Orleans gambler's winning streak had deserted him.

Guess he couldn't risk cheating with me around.

He placed his cards face down on the table. "Gentlemen, regretfully, I fold."

Bob grunted. "Me too." He laid down his cards. "Let's see what you got, Silas."

"No yer don't. Didn't pay to see 'em, did yer?" A cackling Silas mixed his cards back into the deck, then began to rake in the pot's contents. "You've brought me luck, Brodie." He gave her a gap-toothed smile.

"Reckon we're even," she said, "seeing as how I nearly ran you down with the buckboard the other day."

Millain appeared to take his change in fortunes philosophically. "Lady Luck is renowned for her fickleness. She deserted me today," he shrugged, "but there's always tomorrow." He stood up. "And now, if you'll excuse me, gentlemen. Deputy. I have more pleasurable activities to pursue." He gave them a knowing wink and zigzagged his way through the tables toward the girl in yellow.

Zee watched him grab the pretty octoroon by the wrist and guide her (though it verged on dragging) toward the Golden Slipper's exit. It was almost imperceptible, but she was sure the girl had flinched when Millain reached for her. She frowned. If the girl was as terrified of Millain as she seemed, why stay with him? Something wasn't right about those two.

"Know anything about her?" she asked.

Bob snickered, noting the direction of her gaze. "Thought you'd already got your hands full with that little blonde of yours, Brodie." She glared at him and he held up his hands defensively. "Hey, only joking."

"Her name's Julie," piped up Silas. "That's all I know, 'cepting that he's got her wrapped round his little finger. Millain says 'Jump,' and she says 'How high?'" He looked wistful. "Wish my missus was like that." He jingled his winnings and a smile split his craggy features. "At least I ain't gonna catch it in the neck this time."

Zee rolled her eyes. "You mean you were betting Fannie's housekeeping money *again*?"

"Hey, I'm the one as earned it," protested Silas.

Still shaking her head at the silver miner's antics, Zee made her way out of the crowded den. Outside the Golden Slipper, she paused beside her mare and glanced up the street.

Millain and the girl were walking toward Mrs. Sandridge's boarding house. He still had hold of her arm. The conversation between them seemed to be all one way—she was listening and nodding. As though sensing Zee's gaze, he glanced back at her. She pretended to tighten her horse's girth, and by the time she looked up again, the pair had vanished inside the boarding house.

Zee put her foot in the stirrup and mounted up. As she rode toward the railroad station, she pondered Millain's treatment of Julie. Slavery had never taken off in Benson, and it was now illegal anyway, but she couldn't help wondering . . . She sighed. All she had was hints and suspicions, nothing to grab hold of.

The stomping of her boots on the station telegraph office's floorboards brought old Henry, the clerk, to the window. He pushed up his wire-framed spectacles and peered at her.

"What can I do for you, Deputy? Want to send a telegram?"

"No. Just wondering if there's been any reply to Hogan's telegram yet."

"The one to New Orleans?"

She nodded.

"It came in five minutes ago. Now where did I put it?" He blinked at his surroundings then brightened. "Ah, I know."

Moments later, telegram folded neatly in one pocket, Zee stepped out of the telegraph office and headed for her horse.

Chapter 5

IT WAS ONLY after Zee had ridden off back into town that Christie noticed the burlap sack lying forgotten on the kitchen table.

She opened the drawstring and tipped out the wizened contents onto the scrubbed wood, then laughed out loud. Buying flower bulbs for her was getting to be a habit for Zee. Who'd have guessed the former Hellcat was such a romantic? She sorted through the bulbs and corms with a fingertip, then replaced them in the sack for later.

Humming softly to herself and feeling much happier than she had before Zee came home, Christie finished making the parlor curtains and hung them. She cocked her head first to one side then the other as she viewed them from all angles, and felt quietly pleased with the results.

After that, she made some more lemonade, then found a scrap of paper and stub of pencil and sat down to make a list of all the things they would need in order to turn this house into a home.

The whores had ferried Zee and Christie's possessions over from the brothel, but they didn't amount to much. Christie glanced round the kitchen then bent her head and wrote.

Cutlery. Crockery. Tinware. Theirs was on loan from the brothel but they would need their own—just the essentials first, of course.

Bed linen. She had discovered (with mixed feelings—they felt wonderful on the skin but were hard to launder) that the satin sheets were only on loan too.

Material for shirts and some new Levi's for Zee. The deputy was rough on her clothes . . . and on Christie's too. She had lost count of the number of buttons that needed replacing and seams that needed restitching due to Zee's impatience. She chuckled fondly and sucked the end of the pencil.

Whitewash. Matches. Kerosene for the lamps. Soap . . .

Time passed, and almost before Christie knew it, Zee was riding into the back yard and tying up the horse. She put down her pencil and hurried to put the food on the table.

After Zee had devoured boiled beef and canned vegetables, and eaten more than her fair share of that second peach pie Ann Shaw had sent over (Christie was unable to resist ribbing her about it, but Zee merely grinned, unrepentant) Christie asked Zee about her day. Zee's interest in the gambler from New Orleans and the girl in yellow intrigued her.

"Is she his mistress?"

"No." Zee stretched like a cat then relaxed. "His ward. Name of Julie Fontenot."

Christie blinked. "But I thought you said . . ."

Zee patted her lap and Christie slid onto it. One hand curled round her waist, the other settled on her knee. "Yeah, I did," continued Zee. "And I've a feeling he's a mite more friendly with Miss Julie than a guardian oughtta be."

Christie made a face.

"They ain't blood relatives, if that's what you're thinking."

She twisted and looked at Zee. "Oh. So what exactly *are* they?"

"It's quite a story." Zee smiled, her eyes crinkling at the corners. "Want to hear it?"

Christie poked her in the ribs.

Zee chuckled and squeezed her knee. "Few years back—'fore your time, darlin'—steamboats were all the rage. Well, it seems Americus Millain used to do his gambling on the Delta Queen, one of the stern-wheelers that sailed between New Orleans and St. Louis. Bit of a card sharp. Quick to defend himself against those accusing him of cheating. Too quick, if you get my drift."

"He killed people?"

"Twelve, all told."

The blue eyes were distant and Christie wondered if Zee was thinking about those she had killed in the line of duty.

Zee sighed and shook off her melancholy. "Anyway. The Delta Queen had a five-piece orchestra, the finest in wines and liqueurs, a restaurant filled with dee-lectable offerings, and," she glanced at Christie, "lots of beautiful women. Pretty much a floating bordello."

She felt her eyes widen. Zee chuckled and chucked her under her chin.

"Not like Angie's Palace, though. The Delta Queen girls were high-class whores. Spanish, French, some even had Haitian blood. *Filles de joie*, they called themselves. And they didn't come cheap."

Christie chewed her lower lip. "How do you know all this?"

"Knew a woman who worked on the Delta Queen." Zee shrugged. "Her looks were fading by the time I met her, but you could see she must once have been really something. She liked to talk about the good old days. You know, after we'd . . ." She trailed off.

"Oh." Christie stifled the pang that mention of Zee's previous conquests always brought. She became aware Zee was studying her and smiled brightly. "Go on."

"That's all in the past," murmured Zee.

"I know," said Christie just as quietly. "Go on about the riverboats."

It was a moment before Zee continued. "Well," she said. "One of the *filles de joie* was a quadroon named Marian Fontenot."

"Fontenot. Isn't that the same—"

"Yeah. She was very beautiful by all accounts. Tall, long-legged, graceful . . . and very popular. She could have had her pick of the beaux, but the poor woman fell in love with Americus Millain." Zee sighed. "She and him got intimate." She gave Christie a significant glance.

"She had a child?"

Zee nodded. "Died of it too."

"How tragic! So Julie's their daughter? But I thought you said—" Zee's hand clamped itself over her mouth.

"Are you gonna let me tell this story or not?" For answer, Christie licked Zee's palm. Zee smiled and withdrew her hand. "The child died," she went on. "The little octoroon is Marian's by a previous liaison—she was six when her mother died."

"Oh."

"Now, Marian knew she was fading fast, so she made Millain promise to look after Julie. Had the guardianship papers drawn up, all above board and legal like."

"He signed?"

"Yeah."

Christie didn't like the way this story was developing. "And you think—?"

"No matter how well intentioned he started out, somewhere along the trail he changed. Maybe when he saw how pretty she turned out, he decided not to look a gift horse in the mouth." Zee shrugged. "Who knows."

"So you think he's had," Christie searched for the right word, "relations with his ward?"

Zee nodded. "Think he's been hitting her too."

"That poor girl! He's supposed to protect her."

"Sure is, 'til she's married or turns twenty-one anyway." Zee stroked Christie's hair. "But he's in *my* jurisdiction now, darlin', and if I see him doing something he shouldn't . . ."

"You'll take him to task," finished Christie.

Zee nodded. "Damned right," she growled.

THEY WERE SITTING cuddling in the kitchen when Zee looked at the clock, gave a start, and stood up. The abruptness of her movement tipped Christie off her lap and onto the floor. Outraged, Christie stared up at her.

Zee chuckled and held out a hand. "Stop dawdling and get your glad rags on."

"What are you talking about?" A cross Christie allowed herself to be pulled up and set about dusting off her skirt.

"We're going over to Angie's." Zee grabbed her hat from the hook, reshaped the crown, and crammed it on her head. "Go on. Get changed. I'll get the buckboard ready."

"But I've been looking forward to spending time alone with you."

Zee paused in the doorway and looked back at her. "It'll do you good," she said seriously. "Besides, some of the girls are bound to have letters they need help with. We've been away a spell."

Christie threw up her hands and stomped up the stairs, grumbling. In the bedroom, she changed into her only good visiting dress and eyed her reflection in the mirror. She was still trying to fix her hair so it didn't look like a bird's nest when Zee's shout wafted up the stairs.

"Come *on.*"

Christie gave her reflection a last despairing glance, then stomped downstairs and through the kitchen, muttering about inconsiderate good-for-nothings who sprung unexpected and unwanted invitations on their better half. She grabbed her drawstring bag, bonnet, and shawl, then slammed the back door behind her and allowed herself to be helped up into the buckboard.

The corner of Zee's mouth quirked and Christie silently dared her to make just one, *just one,* smart-aleck comment. But Zee merely flicked the reins. The gelding pulled the buckboard forward, and they rattled out of the yard and down the track.

Christie glowered at the night sky. It was a full moon, and the stars were clear and bright. She tried to remember her constellations, sucking in a lungful of air and then exhaling, feeling her bad mood gradually evaporate.

A hand reached across and adjusted the shawl around her shoulders and she looked over at the silhouetted figure next to her.

"Sorry for being so bad tempered."

The shoulders shrugged. "I deserved it," came Zee's voice. "Shoulda told you earlier. Truth is, we were sitting so snug and cozy, I forgot all about Angie's invitation."

She turned to face Christie. "Told her this afternoon we'd go. Thought, what with the Riker lad and everything, being with folks who appreciate you for who you are might cheer you up." A pause. "And I know you've been missing playing the piano."

Christie reached over and patted Zee on the knee. "You're right," she said. "It *will* do me good. And I have missed playing the piano." She sighed.

"One day I'll buy you a piano," said Zee. "Not a player piano, a proper one."

Christie snorted. "With what?"

White teeth gleamed in the moonlight. "I'll think of something."

Chapter 6

FOUR HOURS LATER, Christie lay in the back of the buckboard, hands laced over her stomach, staring hazily up at the stars, and conceded that she'd enjoyed her evening.

The inhabitants of Angie's Palace had welcomed them like long lost friends—even Red Mary's face had cracked into a smile (though it was probably more for Zee's benefit than Christie's).

They spent the evening in the brothel's back room with Angie, who was wearing her trademark Turkish trousers and smoking her pipe. In between clients, the whores popped in, staying to tell them the latest gossip and funny stories about Zee that made her look rueful and curse under her breath and on one occasion—Christie had unfortunately been too far away to overhear the exchange—spray a mouthful of whiskey all over her cards.

Zee had played poker and complained about the chattering women gathered around her, but Christie could see that, despite protestations to the contrary, she loved the attention. As for Christie, she wrote some letters for Lazy Alice, played the player piano to her heart's content, laughed until her cheeks ached, sang until she was hoarse, and danced until her feet hurt. She also drank more champagne than she was used to.

"You all right back there?" came Zee's voice.

"Jush fine," said Christie. For some reason her tongue wouldn't work properly. "T'morrow," she said thickly, "I am going to see Miss Bartlett."

"The school teacher?"

"The very shame." Christie licked her lips and tried again. "Same . . . Aha!" She crowed in triumph.

"Why?"

"Eh?"

"Why are you going to see Miss Bartlett?"

"'Cause that'sh what Angie shuggested."

A long suffering sigh drifted back to her on the cool night air. "And why did Angie suggest that?"

"'Cause if anyone can shtop that little brute from playing hooky and teach him some mannersh, it'sh hish teacher." Why did so many words have the letter S in them?

"Ah. Good idea."

"My thoughtsh exackly."

"Doubt if she'll be able to help though."

The stars were spinning in a clockwise direction. *Fascinating.* "Of coursh she will. Anyway . . . better'n doing nothing."

Zee grunted.

A thought struck Christie. "Zee?"

"Hm?"

"What was it that Clubfoot Liz said that made you shpit out your whishkey?"

"Nothing."

"Must've been something. Standsh to reason."

"Sure you really want to know?"

"Would I ashk you otherwishe?"

There was a moment's silence, then Zee said, "According to Liz, things are a lot quieter since we got our own place."

"Ah, how shweet. You mean the girls miss ush?" Christie flexed her lips and tongue and tried again. "Us?"

"Not exactly."

"Then what?"

"Seems whenever I bedded you, you made such a racket it set off all the cats in the alley out back."

Christie tried to make sense of that. Then her cheeks grew hot, and so did the tips of her ears.

"Hey," came Zee's voice. "You all right back there?"

"Oh, shure. Just dying of embarrashment," muttered Christie, softly so not even Zee could hear.

"You *did* ask," chuckled Zee.

Not softly enough apparently.

"WHY'VE WE SHTOPPED?" Christie peered up at Zee. One minute the deputy had been carrying her up the stairs, making interesting threats involving a feather, the next she was standing frozen outside the bedroom door, an odd look on her face.

"Wait here." Zee set a disappointed Christie back on her own two feet. She drew one of her Colts, cocked it in one smooth movement, and with her free hand relieved Christie of the lamp.

"Wha—?" Christie blinked at the empty space that had held Zee only seconds before. *Next time, I'll avoid the champagne.*

Then Zee was back, and Christie was relieved to see that her gun was holstered. She didn't look happy though. "Window's broke," she said tersely.

"What broke it—a bird?"

"Must've been."

For a moment Christie had the impression Zee was going to say something else. She grimaced. "Blood and feathersh everywhere?"

"No. No sign of the bird now either. Must have flown away." Zee started down the stairs. "I'll get something to board up the window." She paused and looked back. "Stay clear of it, darlin'. There's glass on the floor."

"All right." Christie pushed open the bedroom door and lurched through it. The cold struck her instantly—it must have been that which had alerted Zee. She frowned at the shattered windowpane and the shards of glass glittering on the floorboards. *More money down the drain. Dratted pigeon!*

She was still struggling to undress when she heard booted feet clattering up the stairs. Zee took one look at her, grinned, then put down the hammer, planks, and broom she was carrying and came to help.

"My fingersh won't do what I tell them to," complained Christie.

"Mine will." In no time flat, Zee had stripped off the troublesome dress, followed by the impossible petticoats and undergarments. "See."

"That's only because you've had lots of practice undressing me." The night breeze from the window was raising goose pimples and she hugged herself to keep warm.

"Here." Zee had found Christie's nightdress and was holding it out to her. These days, Christie seldom wore one (Zee kept her warm at night), but tonight, she allowed Zee to help her into it.

"Get into bed," ordered Zee. "I'll fix the window. Won't take long."

Huddled beneath satin sheets, Christie watched Zee sweep the shattered glass into one corner then nail some boards over the broken pane. Almost at once, the room felt warmer.

"There." The hammer joined the broom in the corner with a *thud* that made Christie wince, then the mattress was sagging as Zee sat next to her and put an arm round her shoulders. "You all right?"

"Tired." Christie leaned into Zee. A huge yawn overtook her and Zee laughed.

"So I see. Still cold?"

"A little."

Zee grinned and started to pull her shirt off over her head. "Have to see what I can do about that."

Chapter 7

THE SOUND OF distant gunfire from the north made Zee look up. *Knew it was too good to last.*

She threw aside the *Police Gazette*, grabbed her Stetson from the hat stand, and left the jail at a run. Seconds later, she was in the saddle.

Outside the Golden Slipper, Jack the barkeep flagged her down. "In here, Deputy," he called. "Millain's gone and killed Polly."

Zee's lips thinned. She dismounted and handed him the reins. As she pushed open the swinging doors, faces turned toward her, and a nervous silence greeted her. The crowd drew back as she elbowed her way through. Then she saw the body sprawled on the floor, blood pooling around its head. Apollinar Juarez's disreputable, striped trousers and shabby leather vest were instantly recognizable.

Damn you, Polly! What were you thinking?

She squatted on her heels, reached for his skinny wrist, and confirmed what she already knew—the amiable little Mexican was dead as a doornail. She uncurled his fingers from the Smith and Wesson Schofield and sniffed the muzzle. It had been fired recently.

Zee pushed back her hat and scanned the faces peering down at her, seeking one in particular. Americus Millain's expression was unapologetic.

"It was self-defense. He drew on me." He gestured with his half-smoked cigar. "Ask anyone."

She straightened and looked him in the eye. "I will."

Bob Lewis was standing next to Millain. She raised an eyebrow at him. "Bob?"

He scratched his balding pate before answering. "Polly shot first. He called Millain a cheat and then he drew."

She caught sight of a familiar pair of whiskers. "That tally with your recollection, Silas?"

"Reckon so."

Millain's smile was smug. "See."

She chewed the inside of her cheek. She saw only too well. Polly had been no great shakes with a gun; he carried it mostly for show and wouldn't have drawn unless provoked. Millain probably feinted with his left hand, then drew with his right. But there was no way she could prove it. "I see all right . . . anyone sent for McGillivray?"

"He's on his way, Deputy," called out Kitty Lee.

"Better pass the hat then." Zee looked at Millain. "You first." She took off her Stetson, upturned it, and held it out.

The gambler's jaw dropped. "Damned if I'm going to contribute! I killed him fair and square."

She gave him a cold glare and was pleased when something—uncertainty, fear?—flickered in the depths of his brown eyes. "You took Polly's money and his life. Least you can do is give him a decent burial."

A murmur of approval greeted her words and he glanced uneasily at those standing nearby before meeting her gaze again. "Well," he said. "When you put it that way . . ."

He tossed a couple of silver dollars into the hat. Several of the onlookers gave money too. Zee reached a gloved hand in her pocket and pulled out a dollar; it jingled as it joined the others. Already there was a tidy sum—enough for the undertaker to give Polly one of his better quality coffins.

She emptied the contents of the hat into Bob Lewis's hands and put the Stetson back on. "Give that to McGillivray when he gets here." Bob nodded.

Satisfied she'd done the best she could, for now at least, she gave Millain a last considering look then spun on her heel and headed for the door.

As she passed the bar, a flash of jade green caught her eye. She turned and saw it was the pretty octoroon wearing yet another fashionable dress. As Millain settled down to another card game, Zee headed for his ward.

"Julie Fontenot?"

The girl looked startled at being addressed. She glanced to where her guardian was sitting, then ducked her head, eyes refusing to meet Zee's. "Yes." Her voice was barely audible above the rising hubbub.

"I'm Cochise County's Deputy Sheriff," said Zee. "You need any help, you come to me. Understand?" Julie fiddled with her gloves. "Understand?"

The girl smoothed her dress before replying. "Yes."

Zee sighed. If she was any judge of character, Julie was so scared she would have to be in mortal danger before she asked for help. Well. At least she'd tried.

Feeling in need of some fresh air, she pushed her way through the swinging doors and out onto the street.

ZEE HAD JUST looped her mare's reins over the jail's hitching post when a terrible clattering, clanging noise hurt her ears. She turned. Benson's fire wagon, its bell clanging, its mangy mule braying in protest, was heading along Main Street toward her. Straggling along behind the rusty old water tank and pump came a motley group of townsfolk, some still doing up their shoelaces or pulling on their coats.

"Hey, Marvin," she called to the fire chief, as the wagon passed. His usual job was distributing the water he hauled up from the nearby San Pedro River each day. "Where's the fire?"

"Angie's Palace."

No wonder there are so many volunteers. The madam had a longstanding arrangement with the fire service—a week's worth of free passes to the brothel for those who helped put out a fire.

Now Zee knew where to look, she could see the dark plume of smoke curling up into the sky. *Hope none of the girls are hurt.* She ran back inside the jail, grabbed a shovel, and set off after the fire wagon.

The whores were pacing up and down in front of Angie's Palace in varying states of soot-stained undress. Some of the townsfolk had gathered to watch the fun, and were whistling and calling out comments—the men appreciative, the women disparaging—earning themselves obscene gestures and replies for their pains. When Zee arrived, the onlookers rapidly developed interests elsewhere.

The fire was out back by the kitchen, so Zee made her way round there in time to see the fire crew (Marvin and three men pumping the lever, two more pointing the hose nozzle, the rest getting in the way) damping down the flames. It hadn't been a big blaze, just a very dirty one. Zee frowned. A strange scent underlay the overpowering smell of soot and wet wood. It reminded her of something.

She used her shovel to beat out some still glowing embers then became aware that Angie had joined her. "Anyone hurt?"

"Only their pride." The brothel owner surveyed the damage and sighed.

Marvin came over to join them; his shirt was soaked through, and his face was streaked with soot. "It's out, Angie. Looks like it started over there." He pointed to some singed timbers lying next to the kitchen.

"That's odd. I thought it must have started inside, a spark from Hattie's stove maybe." She shrugged. "Thanks, Marvin. Usual arrangement?"

He grinned and went to tell his men. Zee chuckled then became aware Angie was studying her, a small smile on her face.

"You're entitled to a free pass too, Deputy."

"Thanks, but no thanks. Christie's more'n enough for me."

Angie laughed. "I thought you'd say that." She frowned at the singed timbers again. "Whatever can have caused it?"

"Or *who*ever," said Zee. She had placed the scent at last. "Someone used kerosene."

Angie blinked. "Arson?"

"It's a good bet."

"But who would do such a thing?"

"There's plenty as has a motive. The Temperance Union biddies, the Benson Society for Improvement of Public Morals, not to mention a member of the fire crew eager to receive a week's free pass to bliss . . . Hey!" Zee sucked the knuckles that Angie had rapped with her pipe and gave her a reproachful glance. "But I'd say," she continued, "the likeliest is the person who set fire to the Golden Slipper and the Last Chance Saloon while I was in Phoenix."

Angie frowned. "And just who would *that* be?"

"Don't know yet." Zee grabbed her shovel and prepared to head back to the jail. "But I will."

Chapter 8

ZEE SMILED AS she rode past her front door. The neglected garden had been dug and watered—it looked as though Christie had planted the flower bulbs.

Christie herself wasn't home, though, she discovered as she dismounted and gave her horse a drink. The gelding and buckboard were missing from the barn, which meant Christie had either gone to visit the schoolteacher or gone shopping.

As she unstrapped the new pane of glass she had collected from the glasscutter's and carried it inside, Zee tried not to feel ill-used. It wasn't as if Christie was expecting her for dinner; earlier she had packed Zee's saddlebags with some fresh-baked bread, a slab of boiled ham, and, for a treat, some gingersnaps. But after such a frenetic morning—a killing and a fire was going some, even for Zee—things had quieted to such a degree that she'd been twiddling her thumbs. And since there was work to be done around the house . . .

Grumbling to herself, she sat in the kitchen, eating her bread and ham and listening to the loud ticking of the clock. For the first time in her life, she realized, she felt . . . *Lonely, damn it.*

She carried her cookies out back and leaned against the trough while she crunched them, glad of her horse's company. The mare nosed her shoulder; Zee patted the animal's neck.

"Think yourself lucky you ain't romantically involved, girl," she mumbled round a gingersnap. "It ain't all sunshine." The mare nickered and Zee could have sworn the animal was laughing at her. "Pathetic, ain't I? Let's keep this our little secret, huh?"

When she'd finished eating, she brushed the crumbs off her shirt, swallowed a mouthful of water from her canteen, and headed back indoors, grabbing a hammer and some nails as she went. In the bedroom, she rolled up her shirtsleeves and set about removing the damaged pane of glass and fitting its replacement.

As she worked, she glanced out at the Rikers' house, which was only a stone's throw away. A boy was playing with a ball in the yard, but when he saw her glaring at him, he disappeared.

Stone's throw is right. She wondered whether she should have told Christie about the fist-sized rock she had found lying on the floorboards instead of just shoving it back out the way it had come.

No. It had been the right decision. Christie had been tipsy and tired and would only have been upset. She didn't need to know it hadn't been a bird crashing into their window but a rock thrown by the Riker kid. One thing was for sure, if Zee caught the varmint sneaking around their house again, she'd tan his hide so he couldn't sit down for a month.

She hammered in the last nail, stood back, and admired her handiwork. Then she swept up the glass and other debris and went downstairs.

The basket of wood beside the stove was running low, so while her mare tossed her head in annoyance at the noise, she split some logs in the yard, brought the pieces inside, and added them to the basket. That job done, she set about putting up the extra hooks and shelves Christie had hinted she would like added to the kitchen as soon as possible.

When she had finished, a glance at the clock showed it was time to head back to the jail. She stripped off her shirt and undershirt, dunked her head in a pail of cool water (more water had been delivered, she was glad to see), and sponged herself down, glad to be free of the accumulated grime and sweat at last.

Dressed in a clean shirt, hair slicked down, and the dust banged off her hat, she felt almost presentable as she mounted up and headed back into town. As she rode, she wondered whether things would be as quiet as they had been when she left. Knowing her luck, the Four Horsemen of the Apocalypse would be waiting for her.

CHRISTIE REINED IN the gelding outside Taylor's General Mercantile Store and put on the brake. She reached for her bag, then jumped down from the buckboard and went inside.

Ned Taylor was standing behind his counter, serving a woman with a huge bustle. As the apron-clad storekeeper smiled at Christie, his customer turned to see who had come in, sniffed her disapproval, and turned away again.

Christie sighed. *It would have to be Madame Clemence.*

Ever since the aborted appointment for a trousseau, the seamstress had kept her distance from Christie, even crossing the street to avoid her on one occasion. Christie couldn't blame her. When she'd eloped with Zee, her ex-fiancé had cancelled the trousseau. The seamstress had already spent time and effort on the measurements, but Fred flatly refused to pay her for it.

He always was tight-fisted, thought Christie, wandering round the store. *Hard to imagine I ever considered marrying him.*

When she had learned Madame Clemence was out of pocket, Christie got Zee to compensate her, but relations between her and the seamstress would always be frosty.

She picked up a skillet, hefted it, decided it was too heavy, and put it back on the shelf. A murmur of voices and faint footsteps signaled the presence of other customers. She rounded the shelf and came face to face with a woman in a black broadcloth dress and a fat man whose high collar looked as though it was cutting off his circulation.

Christie froze. *Oh dear!* "Good afternoon, Mrs. Riker. Mr. Riker."

Adah Riker remained mute and her husband frowned. "What's wrong, my dear?"

"This woman is the Hellcat's whore. How she has the *nerve* to show her face in here—" Her cheeks were now an angry red.

Christie pressed her lips together, trying to contain her anger. *Making a scene will only make things worse.*

"*Decent* people should frequent this establishment," Adah continued, "not the likes of—"

"I'll handle this, my dear." Riker pushed up his wire-framed spectacles and turned a stern gaze on Christie. "Take your custom elsewhere in future, Miss erm . . . whatever your name is. I'll not have my wife upset like this."

"I *beg* your pardon!"

The indignant voice made Christie jump and she turned to find Ned Taylor standing behind her, his cheeks flushed. He had finished serving Madame Clemence and come to be of assistance.

"*I'll* decide who I serve in my own store."

"Now look here." Riker puffed out his chest. "I shouldn't have to remind you, Taylor, that last year I approved a substantial loan for this store of yours."

"No, you shouldn't." Taylor's brows drew together. "But it was the *bank* loaned me the money not you. And nowhere in the paperwork, as far as I can recall, did it mention that I'd also signed over my say about who I will and won't serve."

Riker's jaw worked. Christie got the impression he wasn't used to having people talk back to him. *Serve him right.*

"Well!" said Adah, after a long pause. "If that woman," her eyes shot daggers at Christie, "isn't going to take her custom elsewhere, then I most certainly am."

"That's your prerogative, ma'am," said Taylor. "But you'll not find such good quality at these prices elsewhere."

"We'll see about that." With a toss of her head, she stormed toward the store exit. After a moment, her husband followed her.

"I'm so sorry, Mr. Taylor," said Christie. "I had no intention of causing any trouble."

"Of course not." He led her toward the counter. "And you didn't. They did. Not for the first time either. Sour-faced old hypocrites like the Rikers don't need rhyme or reason for making a fuss."

Even so. "But surely, you can't afford to lose such a good customer—"

"Truth be told, Miss Hayes, I'm glad to be rid of them. All I ever got was complaints about weevils in the flour or snags in the muslin." He smiled at her. "So, what is it you want from me this week?"

Christie remembered the shopping list. She fumbled with her bag's drawstrings, pulled the list out, and gave it to Taylor. He perused the piece of paper for a moment, then disappeared behind the counter. When he came back he was carrying kerosene and matches. He ticked off the items on the list then headed off to a different shelf. Companionably, she followed him.

"By the way, just so you know for future reference, there's no risk of me ever asking you to take your custom elsewhere," he added. "Deputy Brodie's a good friend of mine." He picked up the skillet she had rejected earlier, cast an assessing glance at her wrists, then put it back and selected a lighter one.

"Couple of years ago," he continued, "our boy Daniel got mixed up with a bad crowd. Drinking, gambling, women, all *kinds* of carryings-on. Hope I'm not shocking you by speaking about such things, Miss Hayes?"

"Not at all."

He grinned. "Guess you must be pretty unshockable, being with the deputy and all." He looked at the list and moved further along the shelf. "Ella and me thought Daniel was destined for the end of a rope." He picked up some knives, forks, and spoons and raised an eyebrow at Christie in query. She nodded.

"We were at our wits end," he continued. "Then, just over a year ago it must be, Brodie arrived. Hogan had hired her as his deputy without consulting anyone. What a ruckus *that* caused!" He rolled his eyes. "Anyway, she musta noticed I had something on my mind, and one fine day she asked me what it was. So I told her about Daniel." He smiled at the memory. "She said not to worry none, she'd straighten him out. Good as her word she was, too."

He selected some more items from her list then carried them back to the counter. Christie followed, eager to know more.

"What did she do?"

"Never did find out. Brodie wouldn't talk about it, neither would Daniel."

He grabbed a stub of pencil, jotted down the prices for the items now littering the countertop, and began to tot them up. When he'd finished he looked up.

"All I know is, one night he came home as white as a sheet. Said he was sorry for all the grief he'd caused his mother and me, and that it wouldn't happen again."

He rechecked his sums, drew a line under the total, and showed it to Christie, who sighed and nodded.

"The long and short of it is," he continued, "Daniel mended his ways. Took hisself off to Bisbee, found hisself a nice girl and settled down. They're married now, with a baby on the way." His proud smile became businesslike. "Will that be cash or credit, Miss Hayes?"

"Cash." She reached for her bag.

Chapter 9

THERE WAS SOMETHING odd about the garden, decided Christie, slowing the buckboard for a better look. When she had left the Old Barn, the garden out front looked neat and tidy, its soil, still dark from watering, had been level, but now . . . Clumps of soil lay everywhere.

Someone's dug up my bulbs. Jaw clamped against her anger, she turned the gelding up the track. *That dratted Riker boy. It has to be.*

Miss Bartlett had told her the boy wasn't in school that morning, and the silly young woman (she was Christie's age but you'd never have guessed) had seemed quite unconcerned about it.

"Oh, Joe is frequently ill, Miss Hayes," she said, as she distributed the textbooks for the next lesson while the school children played noisily outdoors. "He has a delicate constitution, you know. I had a letter from his parents about it."

Christie chewed her lip. *Delicate? That ruffian?* "Are you sure it was from his parents?"

That got her a wide-eyed stare. "Why ever should it not be?"

"You don't think . . . maybe Joe himself . . . ."

Dora Bartlett considered the suggestion for all of two seconds before emitting a peal of merry laughter. "Oh, Miss Hayes. You are so amusing. Why would any child *want* to miss school? They love it here. We have such fun."

Having faith in the children she taught was wonderful, but being willfully blind to their shortcomings was surely not to *anyone's* benefit. Resisting a strong urge to shake some sense into the dangerously naive schoolteacher, Christie left.

As she drove into the back yard, she saw the depleted log pile and her pulse quickened.

"Zee," she called, leaping down from the buckboard and dashing into the kitchen. "Are you here?" There was no answer, though, and she recalled there had been no sign of Zee's mare either. She sighed, sad to have missed her.

It took her an arduous half an hour to unload the buckboard, stable the gelding, and stack everything where she wanted it. She hung up the last of the tinware—the new hooks and shelves Zee had put up were perfect—then went upstairs to freshen up.

The windowpane was fixed, she saw as she entered the bedroom. She stared out of it, noticing how close the Rikers' house was to theirs and pursing her lips. Last night she had been too muddle-headed to think clearly, but now . . .

As she sponged herself down, changed into her housedress, and brushed her hair, she wondered if Zee had misled her about the real cause of the broken glass.

A knock at the back door jarred her out of her musings. *Who is it now?* She smoothed down her dress, and headed downstairs.

Ann Shaw was standing on her doorstep. Her smiling neighbor came in, admired the additions Zee had made to the kitchen, then got down to business.

"Curly and I are having a social tonight. And we were wondering if you and Zee would like to come."

Christie blinked—an invitation of this kind was the last thing she had expected. Socials had been common in Contention, the women sitting and sewing or crocheting while they talked (gossip was the main purpose of such get-togethers), or playing whatever puzzle games or card games were all the rage.

"The Meekers and Nortons have said they're coming," Ann continued, giving her an expectant look.

Was this the kind of evening that would appeal to Zee? "I don't think Zee—"

"She'll love it," said Ann. "And what better way to introduce the two of you into more respectable circles? It can only do Zee's standing in Benson good."

"We-ell. If you think so."

"I do."

"All right. We'll come." After all, what harm could it do?

Ann beamed at her. "Splendid." She turned to go. "We'll see you at eight."

ZEE LOOKED AT her cards again. Not bad. But was it enough?

Silas was absently rubbing his earlobe. That "tell" of his was a sure sign he didn't have much of a hand. She flipped another dollar into the pot. "Raise you."

"Mind if I sit in?" Americus Millain grinned down at the three players; behind him, looking cowed as always, stood Julie Fontenot.

Silas and Bob exchanged a wry look—this morning's killing of Polly had not endeared the New Orleans gambler to anyone—then shrugged.

"It's a free country." Silas scratched his whiskers.

"So they say," grumbled Bob.

Zee shoved the empty chair toward Millain with her booted foot. "Have a seat." One of the reasons she had come back to the Golden Slipper was to keep a close eye on him; this was as close as she could get.

"Thanks." He sat down, then twisted round in his chair, irritated to see that the hostesses were all currently occupied. "Get me a whiskey," he told Julie.

No please, no thank you, noted Zee. Julie nodded, her gaze once again refusing to meet Zee's, and headed toward the bar.

Zee watched the pretty octoroon go, then turned back to her game. She tossed in a couple more dollars. "And see you, Silas."

"Dang it. I'm gonna have to fold," said a glum Bob.

Silas frowned, then laid out his cards: Three Of A Kind. Zee bared her teeth at him and laid down hers: a Straight.

"Goldarn it, Brodie!" The old man's voice was exasperated. "The missus is gonna skin me alive."

She raked in her winnings. "Why d'you bet it if you can't afford to lose it, you old coot?"

Bob chuckled. "You tell him, Brodie." He gathered up the cards and began to shuffle them, then looked inquiringly at Millain and the others. "Five Card Draw?"

"Fine with me," said Zee.

Millain nodded and busied himself lighting up a cigar. His ward returned carrying a tray on which sat a full glass of whiskey and an unopened bottle (the rotgut kind, Zee was glad to see). She set it by his elbow. He grabbed the glass, drained it dry, then opened the bottle and refilled it.

"Make yourself scarce," he told Julie, without even looking at her. "I'm busy."

She scooted off toward the bar again. *Probably feels safe there*, thought Zee. The barkeep would fend off the worst of the predators, and it was a lot less crowded away from the gaming tables.

While Bob dealt the cards, she pushed back her hat and leaned back in her chair. Surreptitiously, she gave Millain the once over. He sported two revolvers low on his hips, but only the right holster was strapped down. The bulge in his coat pocket was probably a Derringer—deadly at close quarters but otherwise inaccurate.

She picked up her cards, saw at once they were useless and threw them down. "I fold."

The others grunted but decided to play on. Zee reached for her glass, winced at the cheap whiskey's bite, then let her gaze wander round the room before returning to the game at hand.

The bidding was fast and furious, and as far as she could tell no one was cheating. Silas started rubbing his earlobe once more, and it was Bob who won the contents of the pot with a measly Two Pair. Then it was Silas's turn to cut the cards and deal—which he did, muttering under his breath the while—and Zee was back in the game.

Over the next five hands, the winnings were spread fairly evenly—money ebbed and flowed first one way then another. As the level of whiskey in Millain's bottle dropped, his play became more aggressive. He bet early and high, forcing the other players out of their comfort zones and betting the limit more and more. Finally, his style of play began to pay off and the pile of winnings on the green baize in front of him grew.

Zee poked the meager heap of coins in front of her with a forefinger. This was Christie's money as well as hers; did she have the right to risk it?

"Too rich for your blood, Deputy?" Millain's smile was smug. She restrained herself to a grunt. He signaled to a hostess, who brought him a fresh bottle of whiskey.

Her next hand was a much better one—Four of a Kind, practically unbeatable—and Zee bid up to her limit, only to be beaten at the last minute by Millain's Straight Flush, its highest card a King. She pursed her lips. She had suspected he was cheating, now she was sure of it.

Two can play at that game.

In her Hellcat days, she had ridden for a while with Poker Bill. The Mechanic's Grip, the Peek, Second and Bottom Dealing, False Shuffling, Palming, Shifting the Cut . . . her fellow outlaw had taught her all those skills and more. These days, Zee played fair and only used her skills for party tricks or games of strip poker involving Christie. But someone needed to give Millain a taste of his own medicine, and it might as well be her.

Over the next half an hour, Millain's fortunes slowly but surely went into reverse, the tide sweeping his money in Zee's direction stemmed only when it was his turn to deal. At first, his brown eyes held puzzlement, then disbelief, then a growing anger. She could see from his expression that he knew he was getting taken at his own game—he just couldn't work out how.

She suppressed a grin as she placed her cards on the baize—Four Of A Kind. "Mine I think."

Silas snorted and Bob cursed, but Millain's face paled. He had bet his last buck on this hand . . . and lost.

Zee pulled the money toward her. "Guess that's you out of the game, Millain."

His eyes glittered and his hand moved toward his inside coat pocket. She rested her fingers on the butt of her Colt then paused. Was he trying to make her draw first? But when his hand emerged, it was clutching a folded piece of paper rather than the Derringer she had been expecting.

"Guess again, Deputy. This should keep me in the game." He tossed the paper onto the table, and Bob reached for it and unfolded what looked to Zee like a legal document.

"What is it?" asked Silas. "Title deeds? To a silver mine? Your ranch?"

"No. To the ride of your life, boys." Millain leered at Zee. "Might interest the deputy here too. Heard she likes fillies."

Zee frowned. "I ain't interested in your horse."

Bob had been reading the document, mouthing each word. "Who's this Ju . . . Julie Font . . . Fonten—"

"Give me that." She snatched the document off him, read it quickly, then frowned at Millain. "You'd bet your ward in a poker game?"

"She's my property, isn't she?"

Zee resisted the urge to shove the guardianship papers down his gullet. This was going too far, even for him. Then it dawned on her . . . he had no intention of losing Julie. It was his turn to deal—the odds would be in his favor.

News of the unusual nature of Millain's proposed bet spread through the Golden Slipper and a chattering crowd soon gathered around their table. Any hope Zee might have had that Julie didn't know what was going on was dashed when she saw the girl among them. Her face was a frozen mask.

I wouldn't treat my dog like that.

Zee considered and discarded possibilities. It would be tough to pull off in a single hand, especially with Millain dealing, but she still had a few tricks up her sleeve—literally—and if she played her cards right, this could solve the girl's problems at a stroke. She tossed a mental coin. *All right, then.*

"I've no objection if no one else has." Silas and Bob gawped at her. "How about it, boys?"

"What if I win?" complained Silas. "Fannie won't let me take another woman home, 'specially a young and pretty one." A burst of laughter greeted his remark.

"Yeah." Bob wiped the sweat off his forehead. "That goes for me too."

"Don't worry. If you win, I'll take her off your hands."

"Won't Miss Hayes mind?" called out someone in the crowd. Zee ignored them and resettled her hat. "So. Who's dealer?" She glanced at Millain.

He gave her a wet lipped smile. "I am."

She feigned a wince, earning herself a curious look from Silas. "Then deal, damn you." A mutter of consternation ran through the watchers and she suppressed a smile.

As the cards were dealt, Zee could have heard a pin drop. Breaths were bated, eyes eager, as the onlookers watched the progress of the game. Zee concentrated on Millain's hands. *That one came off the bottom. And that.* She picked up her cards and glanced at Silas. He was rubbing his earlobe.

Discarding two cards, she asked for replacements, which came once more from the bottom of the pack. She regarded her new hand with interest. He'd given her a single pair of nines. No doubt his own hand was more valuable.

So. A pair of nines, a six, a ten, and a Jack. What Millain didn't know was that she had two more tens up her sleeve from earlier. When his attention was elsewhere, she swapped them over. Keeping her actions hidden from the bystanders as well as the players was difficult, but she managed it.

Silas folded. So did Bob. Now only Zee and Millain were in the game. At last, with an air of triumph, he placed his cards, all hearts, face up on the green baize.

A sharp intake of breath was followed by murmurs. "It's a Flush. He's got a Flush."

"Mine, I think." He reached forward to gather in the pot.

"Not so fast," said Zee.

His head jerked up, and he stared at her. Card by card she laid out the two nines and three tens.

Millain came to his feet in a rush. "A Full House? But you can't . . ." She could see the realization dawning. "You cheated, damn you!"

At once people began backing away, clearing a space around the table.

"Prove it." She reached for her winnings.

He feinted with his left hand; she let him. "Damn your yellow hide, Brodie," he hissed. "Go for your gun."

She shook her head and stood up, taking a third of the money for herself and pushing the rest toward a startled Silas and Bob. "Split that between you." She tucked the guardianship papers in her pocket. "Anyone draws first, it'll have to be you." She gave Millain a cold glance. "And it'll be the last thing you do."

She rested her hand on her gun butt and waited. Millain lowered his gaze, and for a moment she assumed he had seen sense and was going to accept the situation. She nodded and turned, scanning the room for Julie and finding her trembling in a far corner. She took a step toward her.

"Brodie." Millain's voice halted her in her tracks. She sighed and turned to face him. *So.*

A vein in his temple was bulging and his face was red. "You're a cheating, lowdown, double-crossing, lily-livered bitch." His hand hovered above his six-gun but once more he refused to draw.

Impatient to get this matter over with, Zee feinted and, as she'd known he would, he fell for it. In front of witnesses, he drew first—pulling the gun on his right hip.

Americus Millain was fast, but Zee was faster. A wisp of smoke was still curling up from the Colt in her right hand when he hit the floor with a crump. He looked startled by the bullet hole in the middle of his chest, as well he might.

Her right biceps stung and she glanced down and registered blood-soaked fabric. *My favorite shirt too.*

Dismissing the wound, which was only a scratch, she crossed to the dying man and squatted next to him. Then she leaned closer and dropped her voice so only he could hear. "That's for Polly." His eyes glazed over and he was gone.

Zee shrugged and straightened. Pulling the guardianship papers from her pocket, she went to collect her ward.

Chapter 10

CHRISTIE HEARD THE sound of hoofbeats in the yard and smiled. Supper was almost ready—as a treat, she had bought some fresh beef from the butcher and roasted it. And after she and Zee had eaten, they would head over to their neighbors' social and spend a pleasant, and for once civilized, evening.

Strange. Were those voices she could hear, and the rumble of a buckboard fading into the distance? She must be imagining it. She straightened her apron and turned just as the kitchen door swung open and Zee filled the doorway.

"Hey, darlin'. Something sure smells good." Two strides brought Zee to Christie's side, then Christie was in her arms. She was returning the kiss enthusiastically, when something caught the corner of her eye. Something jade green.

A pretty girl with wavy chestnut hair and dark eyes was standing in the doorway. Her dress could have walked straight off the pages of the latest *Godey's Lady's Book*.

"Mmmph!" Christie pushed Zee away and turned to face the intruder. "Who are you?"

Zee looped one arm around Christie's waist. "This is Julie."

"Ju-Julie?"

"Millain's ward. I told you 'bout her. Remember?" Zee smiled at the newcomer. "Julie, this is Christie."

"Good evening," said the octoroon.

"Good evening," managed Christie between gritted teeth. She shook Zee's arm off, earning herself a puzzled look.

"You all right, darlin'?"

"I'm fine. Only you should have warned me you were bringing someone home for supper. I'm not sure I've cooked enough for three."

"We'll manage." Zee pulled out a chair and straddled it, then beckoned to their guest to sit down. Julie did so rather gingerly, peering at Christie through lowered lashes.

"Julie's here for more'n supper, darlin'," continued Zee. "I've asked Mrs. Sandridge to send her bags over from the boarding house. She'll be staying with us for a spell."

Christie stared at her in disbelief. "*With us?* But won't her guardian be wondering where she is?"

"No. He's dead." Zee reached for the plate of freshly baked biscuits and helped herself. "I shot him . . . Besides," she continued, crunching her biscuit, "we've got room. And it'll make a change for you, having company about the place while I'm not here." She smiled at Christie. "Mm. Great biscuits."

"You *shot* him?"

"Drew on me." Zee's tone was unconcerned. "Got lucky and nicked me too." She indicated the red bandanna wrapped around her biceps, which Christie had been wondering about.

Christie's voice rose. "You were *wounded*?"

"Now don't get het up—it's only a scratch."

It took Christie all of two seconds to untie the bandanna and examine Zee's arm. When she saw the wound was indeed only a scratch, she felt unaccountably worse rather than better. "Why must you be so hard on your clothes?" she complained, knowing she was being unreasonable but unable to stop herself. "Now I'll have to mend that bullet hole."

Zee winked at Julie, who was watching their interaction curiously. The wink made Christie furious. To relieve some of her tension she crossed to the stove and began banging pots and pans about. It didn't help. She turned and glared at Zee, who blinked, then got up and came to join her.

"Look, I know I shoulda asked you first," she murmured, "but she ain't got no place else to go."

"She could have stayed at Mrs. Sandridge's."

"On her own? She's only sixteen. Besides," Zee looked sheepish, "I felt kinda obligated."

"Because you killed her guardian?"

"No." Zee rubbed her jaw. "'Cause I won her in a poker game."

"You did what?" Christie stared at her. "How could you even *consider* using a person as a poker stake?"

"I didn't. Millain did."

"But you accepted his bet." Christie was so angry, she didn't know what to do with herself.

Zee looked nettled. "Only 'cause I thought it would be a way to get her away from him."

Christie put her hands on her hips. "So now she's your property? Doesn't that make you as bad as Millain?"

Blue eyes filled with hurt. "Is that what you think?" Zee looked down at her hands then back up, her expression puzzled. "You ain't usually like this. What's got into you?"

Since Christie didn't know herself, the question was unanswerable. A sudden need to be on her own overtook her. She untied her apron.

"I have to go out." She marched across the kitchen, grabbed her bonnet, and put it on.

Zee stared at her. "What about supper?"

She wrapped a shawl round her shoulders and pulled on her gloves. "The roast beef's nearly ready. Give it five more minutes then you can serve yourself and Julie. There should be plenty for two."

"Aren't you gonna eat with us?"

"No. I'm going over to Ann and Curly's." She picked up her bag. "They invited us both to a social, but since you'll be too busy entertaining our new houseguest," her mouth twisted on the word, "I'll make your excuses."

"Darlin'." Zee reached for her, her gaze pleading.

Christie evaded the hand and headed for the door. She was on the verge of tears and she didn't want anyone to see.

"Don't wait up," she managed. Then she walked out into the night.

THE SHORT WALK round to the Shaws' house did Christie good. The cool air cleared her head a little and dried the angry tears that had welled up as soon as the door latch closed behind her.

She should have asked me first. She opened the gate to Ann and Curly's spread, went through, and closed it behind her. *A poker game, for heaven's sake!* She trudged up the path to the front door. *That girl is lovely, suppose Zee and her—*

Pushing away that distressing thought, she rapped gloved knuckles on the door and waited.

Curly was still tying his tie when he answered the door. "Christie! You're a mite early." He remembered his manners and stepped back. "But always most welcome. Come on in." He peered past her into the night. "Zee not with you?"

She stepped inside, easing herself past him. "No. She's busy." A tear spilled over onto her cheek, and she wiped it away. Curly's brows drew together. He seemed about to speak, but was forestalled by the appearance of his wife.

"Christie," said Ann warmly. "No Zee?"

"She's busy," put in Curly, saving Christie the trouble of repeating herself.

"Oh. What a pity." Ann looked disappointed for a moment then she brightened. "Still, it'll do you two good to get out of one another's pockets for an evening. And I'm sure we'll still have fun. I thought we could play Charades."

Ann ushered Christie through to the parlor and gave her a stack of *Harper's* to keep her occupied while she finished getting ready. Christie turned the pages of the magazines, not really taking in the articles or illustrations.

Probably laughing and chatting. Haven't even noticed I've gone. I hope the roast beef chokes them.

A tear dampened the page, and she blotted it with her handkerchief. She heard movement outside. When Ann and Curly bustled into the parlor, Christie had assumed a cheerful mask.

The evening passed pleasantly enough, though it lacked the zest of the socials she had attended in Contention. She pondered that for a while then came to a startling conclusion: the evening's ingredients were the same; it was her taste that had changed.

Life at the brothel had always been lively, full of music and laughter and dancing. She had never known what was going to happen next. Catfights between whores were frequent, and involved much name-calling, hair pulling, and dress ripping. Then there was that time a drunk fired his guns into the ceiling, the bullets bringing down the chandelier, ricocheting round the salon, smashing mirrors and sending glass everywhere. Not to mention the games of strip poker in the back room, which, when Zee was dealing, always seemed to end with Christie stripped down to her drawers. Compared to all that, an evening of polite conversation, sewing, and Charades seemed, well, dull.

"—shot a man in the Golden Slipper, but he deserved it."

The snippet of conversation jerked Christie out of her reverie. "I beg your pardon? Were you talking about Zee?"

"Of course we were, dear." Ann Shaw looked up from her crocheting. "Who else gets herself into constant trouble? Go on, John."

"Happy to," said John Meeker, "but perhaps Miss Hayes would care to tell us Deputy Brodie's version of events?"

All heads turned to regard her and she blushed. "I didn't have time to ask her the details," she stammered. *I didn't give her the chance.*

"Oh?" Meeker seemed disappointed. "Well, then. By all accounts, the man she shot was that gambler who arrived last week from New Orleans, what was his name . . ."

"Americus Millain," supplied Virginia Meeker.

He nodded. "Thanks, Ginny. That's him. Anyway, it was Millain who killed Polly this morning."

"Polly?" asked a puzzled Christie.

"Apollinar Juarez," explained Meeker. "The talk's all over town, how Millain cheated Polly out of his money and suckered him into shooting first. Folks weren't pleased. They liked Polly." A grin spread over his bluff features. "But Brodie settled the score. Did to him what he did to Polly. Took his ward off him in the process too." He shook his head in admiration. "Got to hand it to her."

Christie sieved the nugget from Meeker's narrative. "Zee cheated?"

"No one would say so to her face, but it sure looks that way."

"Get her to show you her card tricks, Miss Hayes," broke in Maggie Norton. "She cheats so well you simply can't tell." Virginia Meeker nodded agreement.

Albert Norton took up the tale. "Way I hear it, Brodie didn't keep her winnings but split 'em three ways with the other players, Bob Lewis and Silas Ward." He stroked his bushy mustache and grinned. "They couldn't believe their luck."

"What about the octoroon?" asked Curly.

"Oh, her," said Norton. "Seems Brodie tore up the guardianship papers and set the girl free."

"Tore them up?" Christie blinked and stood up. The other people in the room were giving her odd looks, she realized. "Please excuse me. I have to go."

SOMEONE HAD TURNED down the lamp in the kitchen, and Christie blinked as she peered round the dimly lit room. The dirty pots and crockery had been washed and put away in all the wrong places, and a cot now stood beside the stove.

She crossed toward the portable bed and looked down at the girl nestling beneath the blankets. Sleep had brought serenity to Julie's anxious features, or perhaps it was feeling safe for the first time in years. *Poor thing*.

Christie turned, searching for Zee. The deputy was sitting in the corner with her feet resting on the kitchen table and her chair propped against the wall. Her hat was pulled low over her face, but the tension in her body showed she wasn't asleep.

"Zee," said Christie, keeping her voice low so as not to wake the sleeping girl.

A hand pushed the Stetson back, then pale eyes leached of color by the lamplight looked at her. A pang shot through Christie at the wariness in Zee's gaze. *I put that there*.

"Oh, Zee." She rushed toward her, crawled onto her lap (almost tipping the chair over in the process), and hugged her.

For a heartstopping moment, she thought Zee wasn't going to respond. Then strong arms wrapped round her and pulled her close. She buried her head in Zee's shoulder and from sheer relief started to cry.

"Hey. What's all this?" came Zee's voice. "The social can't have been *that* bad."

"No," she sniffed. "Though it was dull as ditch water without you. Oh, Zee. I'm sorry."

A hand brushed a lock of hair out of her eyes. "Me too, darlin'. I shoulda made it clear. I don't 'own' Julie."

Christie pressed two fingers to Zee's lips, silencing her. "I know. You tore up the guardianship papers." Zee kissed her fingers and she removed them.

"Yeah." Zee glanced at the sleeping girl. "But I couldn't leave her on her lonesome. She's never had to fend for herself before. Not sure she even knows how."

"That's why you brought her home?"

Zee nodded. "Pretty girl like her would be easy prey for some son-of-a-bitch. Probably end up in a whore house." She sighed. "It may still come to that."

Christie frowned. "There must be something more respectable she can do." Now she was safely in Zee's arms again, she felt compassionate toward the girl. (*Is that what the problem was? Jealousy?* It was an unflattering and salutary thing to learn about herself.)

She considered the problem of Julie's future. "Those fashionable dresses of hers. She made those herself, if I'm not mistaken. Which means she's a pretty fair needlewoman. Maybe she could get a job with Madame Clemence?"

Zee gave her a squeeze of approval. "Knew if I brought her home you'd think of something."

Christie pressed her face into a broad shoulder to hide her flush of shame. Zee had had faith in her; why had she not reciprocated?

"Hey now, none of that." Zee tucked a finger beneath her chin and raised it. Their gazes locked and held for a long moment, then Zee broke into a grin. "It's time to kiss and make up."

She bent her head and kissed Christie, a kiss so thorough it made Christie's heart race, her toes curl, her head spin . . . Except that the cause of the spinning turned out to be Zee standing up with Christie in her arms.

"Bed," growled Zee, elbowing the door open and heading for the stairs.

Christie had to clear her throat twice before she could speak. "Mm. Bed."

Chapter 11

ZEE STRODE UP to the telegraph office window, shook the handbell for service, and waited. The clerk appeared from the backroom, wiping his mouth on his sleeve and pushing up his spectacles.

"Morning, Deputy. What can I do fer you?"

"Sorry to disturb your breakfast, Henry." She reached in her vest pocket and pulled out the slip of paper she had worked hard on, paring the words to a minimum. "Need you to send this to New Orleans for me."

He accepted the message, and began to count the words. She slapped down the exact money. "That oughtta cover it."

He finished his mental arithmetic, looked at the coins, nodded, and scooped them up. "Pinkerton Detective Agency? You fixing to track down some bad guys?"

"No. Some good guys."

When no further explanation was forthcoming, he shrugged and wandered off to send the message. She leaned against the counter and waited, the uneven tapping of the Morse key punctuating her thoughts.

The idea had come to her this morning, when she was snuggling in bed with Christie, listening to the dawn chorus and the distant yapping of the Rikers' dogs as they fought over breakfast. Searching for Marion Fontenot's kin was a long shot—after all she had died a decade ago and assigned guardianship to her lover rather than a relative—but blood was thicker than water, and, if it paid off, it would be one more choice of futures to offer Julie.

More importantly, it would take the girl away from Benson and from Christie. The little blonde was trying hard to accommodate Julie, Zee knew, but she was struggling. Take this morning. On her way to feed and water the horses, Zee had tiptoed through the kitchen, expecting Julie to still be sleeping, only to find a delicious smell of frying ham and the girl up and dressed and preparing breakfast for three.

"Least I can do," said Julie, giving her a shy smile.

Zee had paused, her mouth watering in anticipation, and wondered whether to warn Julie that Christie might want to cook breakfast herself. Then the door opened and Christie came in.

In other circumstances it might have been funny, seeing Christie's wide smile vanish so abruptly.

Julie glanced round from serving out the portions. "I hope you don't mind, Miss Hayes." She ducked her head, the mannerism confirming Zee's suspicions that Millain used to hit the girl.

"Of course not." Christie managed a weak smile that made Zee want to hug her. "How very kind of you to take the trouble, Julie."

What made thing even worse, of course, was that the ham and eggs were delicious, and Julie's coffee was even better than Christie's. Zee enjoyed her breakfast, though Christie, she noticed, seemed to have lost her appetite.

When Julie rose to clear away the dirty dishes, Zee leaned toward Christie and said in a low voice, "She can dress make *and* cook. That should improve her prospects some."

Christie brightened. "It should, shouldn't it?"

When Zee was leaving for work, she grabbed Christie by the arm and urged her out into the yard. "Don't worry, darlin'," she said loyally if not entirely truthfully, "Your cooking's more to my taste." Then she kissed Christie until her knees gave way and gave her rump a slap. "And anyway, that ain't the reason I keep you around." Enjoying the flush that brought to Christie's cheeks, she mounted up and rode off.

The telegraph key stopped tapping out its dots and dashes and she looked up.

"It's sent," called the clerk.

"Thanks, Henry." Zee ran a hand through her hair and resettled her hat, then stepped outside and headed back toward Main Street.

Hogan's horse was tethered next to her mare, she saw, as she neared the jail. She pushed open the door to his office with a bang.

He looked up. "Morning, Brodie."

"Morning." She lassoed the hat stand with her hat and perched on the corner of the desk. "Nice break?"

"Fair to middling." He put down the logbook. "Looks like you've had a high old time while I've been away." He gave her a sly glance. "So now you're living with two pretty women? Hound dog."

"It ain't like that."

He laughed and gave her a shrewd glance. "How's Christie taking it?"

"Not well." She sighed. "It never occurred to me she'd feel so . . . proprietorial."

He fingered his mustache. "About you, or the house?"

"Both," said Zee. "I've only ever felt possessive about horses . . . and Christie, of course. It was different with Molly—her heart was mine, but her body . . ." She fiddled with a loose thread in her Levi's. "It's kind of flattering Christie feels that way." She looked up and caught his grin. "What?"

"Dang it, I do believe that little blonde's tamed the Hellcat. Never thought I'd see the day."

She felt herself blushing and changed the subject. "Yeah, well . . . So have you taken care of Granpappy Carpenter? I left him sobering up overnight." She grimaced. "He spends more time in the cell than he does at home."

Hogan nodded. "Gave him some coffee and beans and sent him packing."

"Good." She stood up and paced toward the window, watching the customers coming and going at the barbershop across the street. "Wonder what delights today holds in store."

"Temperance Union demonstration," said Hogan. "Outside the Last Chance Saloon at ten."

She turned and looked at him. "First I've heard of it."

He tapped his nose. "You don't have the right contacts."

"Ah, that pretty little widow over on Second Avenue?"

It was Hogan's turn to blush.

She gazed out the window again. "I dealt with those sour-faced old biddies last time."

"So? I'm the boss. I say who does what."

She folded her arms and looked at him.

Hogan pulled out a silver dollar. "All right. Toss you for it."

"Tails."

It spun through the air and landed on the battered desk . . . heads up.

Zee looked at it in dismay. "Damn it, Hogan. Is that thing double-headed?"

He laughed, pocketed the dollar, put his feet up on the desk, and crossed his ankles. "That would be telling."

ZEE COULD HEAR them a block away. They were singing "Rock of Ages" out of tune.

It was the usual culprits, she saw, as she drew nearer to the group of women huddled on the sidewalk outside the Last Chance Saloon—Adah Riker, Eliza Atkey, and their Temperance Union cronies.

One woman was rushing around handing out placards clearly made at the last minute. Zee read the slogans: "Down with the Demon Drink," "Woe to Whiskey," and her favorite "Outlaw Licker." She suppressed a bawdy laugh and approached the ringleaders.

The singing faltered as the women registered her presence, some undoubtedly remembering being picked up by the bustle and scruff of the neck and thrown into the street.

"You can't stand here, ladies." Frightened male eyes were watching them through the saloon's front window. *Wonder if their husbands are in there?*

"It's a peaceful protest, Deputy," protested the hatchet-faced Eliza Atkey, folding her arms.

"I sure hope it is, but you still can't stand here. You're blocking the way."

Grumbling and muttering, the women moved until they were half on the sidewalk and half in the street.

"Much obliged." Zee leaned back against a rail, folded her arms, and scrutinized the members of the Temperance Union one by one.

They shifted under her gaze. "Well, really!" said one. "Who does she think she is?" said another.

"Rock of Ages" came to an end, and after a short bout of chanting— "Say No to Liquor," "Save our Menfolk from Ruin"—the women switched to "There Is a Fountain."

Zee winced at the caterwauling. *I'll get you for this, Hogan.*

The protestors began to march up and down, waving their placards. A few interested bystanders were now watching, hoping for a brawl.

Sorry, folks, but there ain't gonna be a show tod—Wait a minute.

One of the women who'd caused trouble last time, Martha Curry, was having difficulty marching. Either her drawers had fallen round her fat ankles, or something under her petticoats was hampering her. Zee straightened and advanced on the plump woman, who froze and looked at Zee as if the deputy were the mongoose and she the snake.

"Want to hand it over?" Zee gestured.

Martha's abrupt halt had caused disarray as the marching women behind her bumped into one another. "What's going on?" asked someone. "What does she want with Martha?"

"Hand what over?" Martha tried to look down her nose, but since she was a foot shorter than Zee, it didn't work.

"I won't ask you again." Zee donned the menacing glare that had once cowed her fellow outlaws and Martha quailed. "Want me to turn you upside down and search under your petticoats?"

The women gasped and went pale. "I can't believe she said that!" "She's going to assault Martha." "Someone call the sheriff." "She *is* a sheriff."

Martha began to squirm and wriggle in a very odd manner. *What the hell is she doing? A rain dance?* Something thudded onto bare earth.

"Step back," ordered Zee.

Martha obeyed and her companions let out a shocked gasp. On the ground where she had stood lay a hatchet. Zee picked it up; it was still warm from its unusual hiding place. She looked at it then at the now blushing Martha.

"Peaceful protest?"

"Martha," hissed Adah Riker. "I thought we agreed—"

Zee tossed the hatchet from hand to hand. "Any more of these?" She regarded them each in turn. One by one, they shook their heads.

"Good," she growled. "Very good. 'Cause if there's even the hint of any trouble here today, you'll all—and I mean *all*—be spending the night in jail." She waited. "Got it?"

They nodded.

"All right." Satisfied that they would behave themselves this time, she turned and, hatchet in hand, headed back toward the jail.

Zee had gone only a few paces when she remembered something. She turned and shouted, "Oh, and by the way. It's spelled LIQUOR."

The women's mortified faces were enough to keep her guffawing all the way back.

Chapter 12

"HOW LONG HAVE you and Deputy Brodie lived together, Miss Hayes?"

Christie's rolling pin halted, and she considered the question. "Well, I've known her a little longer of course, but we've actually lived together for about two months. And please, call me Christie."

She smiled at Julie's surprise. "It isn't long, is it? Yet sometimes I feel as if I've known Zee all my life." She shrugged at the mystery of it and resumed rolling out her pastry.

Julie half-heartedly turned the pages of her magazine. Christie had selected it with care. *Every Saturday* was running an adventure serial about a heroine stranded on a desert island, and she hoped the exciting story would hold the girl's interest and encourage her to persist with her reading.

Christie had discovered that Julie's literacy skills were sadly lacking—Millain hadn't considered such things important in a ward—and she was taking steps to remedy that. Unfortunately, Julie seemed more interested in her hosts' personal lives than in fiction.

Julie peered at Christie from beneath lowered eyelashes. "Was it love at first sight?"

Christie snorted. "Hardly." She rested an inverted pie dish on top of her pastry, and cut around it. "The first time I met Zee, I was so frightened of her, I got her shot."

Julie's eyes widened. "Really?"

"Really." She lined the dish with the pastry and began to pile in the beef in gravy she had cooked earlier.

"But *then* you fell in love?"

"No, then I decided she was the most insufferable and impudent woman I had ever met . . . and also the most fascinating." She remembered her painful confusion. "I didn't know what was happening to me. That I could be in love with a woman like Zee was unthinkable."

"I see."

Christie had a feeling Julie didn't see at all. She knew nothing of love. How could she, given her life with Millain?

"But then you realized you loved her?"

The pie now ready for the oven, she cleared away her pastry making equipment and wiped down the table with a cloth. "No, then I got engaged to someone else."

By now Julie looked totally confused and Christie laughed. "You look the way I felt."

"But if you were engaged . . ." The girl fiddled with the corner of a page.

"I left my fiancé to follow Zee," explained Christie, still amazed in retrospect at her boldness.

"Just like that?"

"Just like that." She took off her apron and took the seat next to Julie. "We were supposed to be practicing your reading," she reminded. "Now." She pointed to the first paragraph on the page open in front of Julie. "Can you read that aloud for me?"

Julie sighed but began to read, stopping often to ask about a word. Christie offered suggestions and encouragement, pleased at the steady progress the girl was making—she had obviously been taught the rudiments, probably by her mother.

"Oh, I meant to mention . . . I saw a boy in the back yard earlier," remarked Julie, when they paused at the end of a chapter.

Christie gave her a sharp glance. "What was he doing?"

"Nothing . . . just staring in the window. When he saw me he ran away."

"It was probably the Riker boy. Horrid little brat!" She chewed her lip. What had he been doing in the yard? "Excuse me one moment."

She got up and went outside. But a cursory inspection revealed that the gelding was unharmed and nothing looked out of place. *Must have scared him off before he did anything.*

She went back indoors. Julie looked up. "Perhaps we should practice your writing for a while." Julie grimaced. "Don't you want to be able to sign your name instead of having to make your mark?"

"My name?" A slow smile transformed Julie's face.

Christie fetched a piece of paper and a pencil and sat next to her. "Watch what I do." She wrote the words "Julie Fontenot." "There. Now you try it."

While Julie busied herself tracing out her name over and over, the tip of her tongue poking out in concentration, Christie fetched some vegetables from the pantry and began to peel them. As she stared out of the kitchen window, she pondered again what Joe Riker had been doing in their back yard.

"Deputy Brodie is very strong, isn't she?" came Julie's voice.

Back to that topic, are we? Christie rolled her eyes, glad the girl couldn't see. "Yes. She is."

"Does she hit you?"

"Pardon?" A shocked Christie spun on her heel and stared at Julie.

"When you won't do what she wants you to," clarified Julie, stopping writing and looking up at her.

"When I won't . . . Zee has *never* raised her hand to me."

"Oh . . . Well, perhaps she will, when you've been together longer." She bowed her head and began to write once more.

"She would never hit me. She loves me. People who love you don't hurt you or force you to do things you don't want to. Surely you know that?" Silence met that remark. "Did he . . . did your guardian hit you, Julie?"

Julie rolled up one of the long sleeves of her dress. Christie's hand flew to her mouth as she saw the vivid bruises on the thin arm. "Oh!"

"He told me it was for my own good. And he was always careful to make sure they wouldn't show." Julie shrugged and rolled down her sleeve.

Christie blinked. Could the girl really be as stoic as she seemed or were her feelings merely dammed, waiting to burst? Christie suspected the latter. Perhaps given the chance and a sympathetic ear, Julie might be able to release some of the pent up hurt and anguish of her long, lonely painful years with Americus Millain.

For the next hour, Christie told funny anecdotes about her adventures with Zee, trying to show Julie there was another way to live and to build up her trust. Then, there came a moment when she sensed the girl was waiting for her, expecting her even, to ask the question that had been hanging over them unspoken. She crossed her fingers that her instincts were sound, took a deep breath, and obliged.

"Julie. Did Millain make you do things with him . . . intimate things," she asked as delicately as possible, "which you would rather not have done?"

The silence stretched, then a teardrop plunked onto the table, startling them both. "Yes." Julie's voice was a mere whisper.

"Oh, my dear." Christie swept her into a hug, rocking the now openly crying girl, stroking her hair and making soothing noises. It was probably the first time since her mother died, Christie reflected sadly, that anyone had held her this way.

Over the next hour, which was characterized by long tearful silences followed by confessional outbursts, Julie told her the pitiful story.

At first, Millain had been kind to her. She never went hungry, and he bought her pretty fabrics and pattern books so she could make herself fashionable dresses. (It reflected badly on him, he told her, if she looked old-fashioned and shabby.) But as the gambling fever and the drinking took hold of him, he changed.

Getting to this point had taken a lot out of Julie. They both needed the brief respite that came when Christie got up to put the pie in the oven and the vegetables on to boil. Then she resumed her seat, invited Julie back onto her lap and into her arms, and the story continued.

The worst had come when Julie turned twelve and became a woman at last. One night soon after, her guardian came home the worse for drink, remarked how much like her mother she looked, and took her to his bed. She tried to fight him off, but he gave her a black eye and nearly broke her arm. She had quickly learned not to resist. He had praised her then, and called her his "good girl." The comments her appearance caused the next morning also taught him a lesson—to make sure any bruises were hidden.

Bedding Julie had become a regular occurrence, and caused her much distress and, to Christie's surprise, guilt. "I'm going to go to Hell, aren't I?" she said, in between sniffles.

"No, Julie, you're not." *But Americus Millain certainly is.* She smoothed Julie's hair and thought how lucky she had been to escape having Millain's child. A faint smell of smoke made her glance at the stove, but the meat pie and vegetables were cooking as normal so she shrugged and dismissed it as her imagination.

She found a clean handkerchief and handed it over. "Here."

Julie accepted it and blew her nose. "I'm glad he's dead." She gave Christie a sideways glance, as though she expected disagreement.

"So am I."

That got her a pleased grin. "You are?"

Christie nodded. "He hurt you. He tried to kill Zee." She rocked Julie some more. "Oh, yes," she said grimly. "I'm very glad he's dead."

Chapter 13

ZEE WAS SWEEPING out the cells when the sound of the fire bell made her set aside her broom and go outside to investigate.

The faint clanging was coming and going on the gusting breeze, and it was hard to judge either direction or distance. Zee checked the sky for telltale signs of smoke. There was dark smudge to the northwest.

Loud hoofbeats made her turn just as Hogan reined in his mount in front of the jail steps. "It's your place, Brodie," he shouted. "It's on fire."

She was in the mare's saddle before he finished speaking. Urging it into a gallop, she headed northwest toward Schoolhouse Lane.

If anything's happened to her . . . Or Julie . . .

At last the Old Barn came into view. The odd looking house appeared untouched. Wisps of smoke were still rising from the rear though. *Must be the barn.*

She rode full tilt up the track alongside the house, scanning half hopefully, half fearfully for signs of Christie. What color dress had she been wearing? Zee's mind was a blank and she cursed under her breath. She turned the blowing mare into the crowded yard, managing just barely to avoid riding down the members of the fire crew, slid out of the saddle, and took in her surroundings in one appalled glance.

The barn was a smoking ruin, still dripping with the water that the soot-stained fire fighters had pumped onto it. The buckboard was a pile of cinders, as was the water trough and log pile. There was no sign of the gelding.

She turned toward the house. It looked as if the fire hadn't spread that far, thank God.

"It's out," said Marvin, who had spotted her and come to report.

"Anyone hurt?" She had yet to spy either Christie or Julie. The leader of the fire crew shook his head, and she felt almost dizzy with relief.

"Sent the women over to the Shaws' place," he told her. "Your gelding's there too. Miss Hayes managed to get him clear of the barn before the roof collapsed . . . Just as well she had the sense to send for help as soon as she did, Brodie. Fire could've spread to the house."

Zee slapped him on the shoulder. "I'm obliged to you." She assessed her surroundings again and shook her head. "Any notion what started it?"

"Thought I caught a whiff of kerosene."

"Arson?" She chewed her lip.

"It could be." He tipped his hat then and went back to join his crew.

She took one last look around the ruined yard, then set off to the Shaws' house, taking the most direct route and vaulting the boundary fence. She was just raising one gloved hand to knock on the front door when it opened.

"She's fine, Zee," were Curly's first words. "Absolutely fine."

"I'll be the judge of that," growled Zee. "Where is she?"

"In the parlor. It's through—"

But Zee knew where the parlor was and had already pushed past him. Ann Shaw came out of the kitchen, took one look at her, and stood back.

"When there's a stampede," Zee heard Ann telling her husband, "it's best to get out of the way." Then her attention was fixed elsewhere, for the parlor door had swung open and a soot-smudged whirlwind was flying toward her crying, "Zee!"

Zee braced herself just in time, as Christie flung herself into her arms, threatening to overbalance them both. Christie looked like a drowned rat and reeked of wood smoke but to Zee she had never looked more beautiful. She returned Christie's enthusiastic embrace and tried to speak, but couldn't for the lump in her throat. Instead, she simply gazed at her, grazing her thumb over soft cheeks, drinking in the sight of her.

Zee had an overwhelming urge to kiss those soft lips and gave in to it. Time passed, then a soft clearing of the throat made her remember her surroundings. She broke the kiss (to a murmur of protest from Christie) and looked up, blinking.

Familiar dark eyes were regarding the two of them.

"You all right, Julie?" asked Zee.

The girl nodded. "Thanks to Miss Hayes. She made sure I got to safety."

"Good girl." Zee gave Christie an approving squeeze, and got one in return.

Now she had Christie in her arms, she could relax and take in her surroundings. Julie didn't look much better than Christie did. The two women were in one piece, but their dresses were surely beyond salvage.

"The fire crew made us leave," said Christie. "Is it bad?" From her expression, she was bracing herself for the worst.

"Barn's gone. Yard's a mess." Zee shrugged. "But we can fix 'em both."

"Thank the Lord!"

Christie released herself then laced her fingers through Zee's and led her into the parlor. Still holding hands, they sat on the settee, pressed together along their length, though there was room and to spare. Julie chose a chair.

Zee found herself wanting to do nothing except gaze at Christie and grin. Julie's lips twitched, and she picked up a magazine and pretended to read.

"Er." A wary looking Curly stood in the doorway. "Ann sent me to see if anyone would like some lemonade."

"I'd love some," said Christie, smiling at him. She touched her throat. "The smoke, you know." Julie nodded.

"Me too," said Zee. After he'd gone, she placed her hat in her lap, took off her gloves, and ran her free hand through her hair. "So," she said. "How did it start?"

"We think the boy did it," said Julie.

"Boy?" Zee sat forward. "The Riker boy?"

"It must have been him," agreed Christie. "Julie saw him earlier . . . in the yard. He ran away then, but he must have come back."

Zee let go of Christie's hand and surged to her feet. "Why, that little—"

"We don't know it was him for certain, though," cautioned Christie.

Zee crammed her hat back on and picked up her gloves. "I'd bet those odds. Anyway, whoever did it'll have left tracks."

Christie stood up. "I'm coming with you."

"Not this time, darlin'." She ignored the look of outrage. "You'll only slow me down." She raised a hand to forestall Christie's protest. "And 'sides, if you don't mind me saying so, the two of you could do with a wash and brush up and a change of clothes."

Christie glanced down at herself. "What does that matter when—"

"It matters to me," said Zee. "Tracking the culprit may take a while, and I want you to be comfortable." Christie's expression softened and Zee followed up her advantage. "Besides, it's my job and I'm damned good at it. Let me do this, darlin'. I'll meet you back at the house later."

Christie sighed. "All right."

Zee gave her a last loving look, then strode toward the door. It opened just as she reached it. There was a clatter and clink—a startled Curly had almost dropped the tray.

"Well, are you coming in or going out?" asked Zee.

He blinked at her. "Coming in."

She stepped aside to let him past, grabbing one of the glasses of lemonade and draining it in one as he did so. He gaped at her as she put the empty glass back.

"Thanks."

With a wink at Christie, and a tip of her hat at Julie, Zee headed for the front door.

THE FIRE CREW had packed up their water wagon and gone home by the time Zee returned to the charred wreckage of her back yard. Her mare whinnied a greeting then nosed at where the water trough used to be. Zee took the hint, poured some water from her canteen into a palm, and let the horse drink. As she patted the broad neck with her free hand and whispered encouraging words in a twitching ear, her eyes scanned her surroundings.

Marvin's crew, their fire appliance, the mule, the water, her own horse . . . all had contributed to the churned up muddy mess. All traces of any boy who might have been lurking about had been well and truly obliterated. Perhaps if she started looking *outside* the yard, where the ground was still dry . . .

The mare lipped up the final drops of water, and Zee gave the animal one last pat. Then she slung her canteen over one shoulder, the rope she kept coiled round her saddle horn over the other, and set off.

It took her five minutes' scrutiny of the track alongside the Old Barn and the lane out front before she found it—half of a footprint: a right shoe, its heel worn down on one side, and so small it must belong to a child. She crouched and rubbed her thumb in the dirt, comparing the color and texture of the disturbed patch against that of the print.

Recent, very recent.

Satisfied she would know the footprint again, she straightened and looked toward the Riker residence. The print was leading away from the large, white house with the green trim not toward it. Much as she would have liked to go over there and accuse the boy, as Christie had once pointed out she was the law and couldn't take things into her own hands just because she felt like it. She needed proof, and she was going to get it.

The hard packed earth didn't hold tracks well, but a fragment of footprint here, a broken grass stem there was enough. As always, the skills Indian Jim had taught her ten years ago (the outlaw had been half Apache on his mother's side) served her well.

She followed the tracks across Schoolhouse Lane, along the boundary fence between two properties, then east toward the San Pedro River. Once away from Benson, they became easier to follow—the trail was obviously well used.

Determined not to spook her quarry, she kept a low profile, taking cover where it was offered, be it a lone saguaro standing guard over its surroundings, or, as the river drew nearer and the terrain changed, a thicket at the base of a stand of cottonwoods.

Zee paused to catch her breath and gulp lukewarm water from the canteen. In the distance a coyote yipped. She wiped her mouth with the back of her hand and considered what to do with the boy when she caught him. Was he a lost cause, or could he still be turned around? Slinging the canteen over her shoulder, she picked up the trail once more.

She had been tracking for an hour when the trail led her toward what had once been a coyote's den. Human hands had enlarged the entrance in the soft earth. She tiptoed forward and peered in.

Her senses told her the hideout was empty, and she eased herself inside the cramped quarters. Someone had left a stub of candle just inside the entrance, and she lit it and examined her surroundings. The occupant clearly didn't believe in tidiness.

Some of the items littering the den were typical of a boy's possessions: a stack of yellowing dime novels of the detective variety; a knife worn thin with honing, its bone handle snapped off; a pack of playing cards; a gunny sack containing cigars and matches; and several pieces of string.

Other things were more surprising: a grimy shot glass and empty bottle of whiskey; a lady's spangled garter. Zee twanged the garter and grinned. The grin vanished when she spotted the delicate necklace of turquoise beads she had given Christie. There were also a surprising number of containers of kerosene given there was no lamp in sight.

She replaced each item as she had found it. *Catching him surrounded by this stuff oughtta do it.*

The coast was still clear when Zee vacated the hideout. She hunkered down in a nearby thicket to wait.

It was dark and the temperature had dropped considerably when something brought her back to alertness. Her subconscious had tuned out the yipping coyotes and the call of a nighthawk hunting insects, so it must be something else. She sat up and pushed back her hat, which had fallen forward while she dozed. Footsteps, she decided, hearing the faint rhythmic crunch and feeling the slight vibration accompanying them. Coming her way.

Movement caught her eye. A small figure, silhouetted by the rising moon, was heading toward the hideout. This was no innocent bystander; whoever it was knew exactly where he was going. She held her breath and waited. He should reach the entrance to the hideout about . . . now.

The silhouette disappeared from view.

Zee gave a savage grin and waited a couple of minutes more then crept toward the den. The entrance was now illuminated by the faint, flickering glow of the candle. She stationed herself just outside.

"Didn't your parents tell you it's wrong to steal?"

Joe Riker barely had time to look up from his dime novel and turn wide eyes in her direction before she was lunging into the hideout, grabbing him by his collar and belt, and hauling him out into the open.

"Wha—? Let me go, you bitch."

Arms and legs flailed, and a heel thunked into her left shin, while a fist came too close to her eyes for comfort. She plonked the thrashing boy face down in the dirt, pressed her knee into his back to keep him pinned, grabbed the coil of rope, and hog-tied him.

"Whatever it is, I didn't do it."

She straightened and dusted herself off. "You're caught; might as well get used to it."

Since his struggles were only succeeding in bringing him mouthfuls of dirt, he subsided. "But Deputy Brodie." She noted the belated politeness with a wry smile. "It wasn't me. Honest."

"Got you fair and square for theft and arson, Joe. No use protesting." She shrugged. "You played with fire and you got burned."

Ignoring her prisoner's further squawks, she ducked back inside the hideout, emptied the cigars from the gunny sack (then reconsidered and stuffed a couple of them in her pocket, along with Christie's bead necklace) and refilled it with incriminating evidence. She took one last look and blew out the candle.

Zee emerged from the hole, stretched, and inhaled an appreciative breath of cool night air. She turned to her now silent prisoner.

"On your feet, son." She yanked Joe up by his collar, then with a grunt of effort heaved him over her shoulder. "Now let's see what your parents have to say."

Chapter 14

BAM. BAM. BAM.

Somewhere out back, dogs started barking, and inside the house a man's voice bellowed, "Adah, will you see to those dogs?"

Zee raised her fist again. *Bam, bam.*

"All right, all right. I'm coming."

The door swung open and Ernie Riker stood in the doorway, hair tousled, collar unbuttoned. His look of annoyance intensified when he saw who had disturbed him. "Oh, it's you." He pushed up his spectacles. "What do *you* want?"

Zee shifted the weight draped over her shoulder into a more comfortable position. "It's about your boy."

"Our Joe?" Adah's voice came from behind her husband. "Tell her to come back tomorrow. He's in bed and I won't have him disturbed."

"No he ain't." Zee heaved the hog-tied bundle off her shoulder and lowered it, letting it drop the final foot.

"Oof!"

Riker's eyes widened as the light spilling out the door illuminated his son's face. "Joe?"

Zee straightened, glad to be free of the boy's weight. "Found him in his hideout near the river. Spends more time there than he does in school, I bet. But you wouldn't know about that, would you? You let your son run wild. No wonder he's gone to the bad."

"How dare you!" Adah pushed past her husband and crouched next to Joe. "Are you all right, son? Did she hurt you?"

"Mama, she attacked me. She tied me up and slung me over her shoulder."

Adah's lips thinned. "Disgraceful! I shall be complaining to Sheriff Hogan—"

"Be thankful that's all I did," interrupted Zee. "By rights Joe should be in jail, since he's the one been setting all these fires. But him being so young and all, I decided to act lenient. Besides, I don't think he's the only one to blame."

"The fires? You must be mistaken." Adah looked at her son. "She is, isn't she, Joe?"

He opened his mouth then closed it again. Adah gave him a puzzled look and set about untying the rope, giving Zee a challenging glare as she did so.

Zee shrugged and let her get on with it. "Got the evidence right here." She reached for the gunny sack hanging from her belt. "Found these in Joe's hideout."

She pulled out the items one by one. First, the playing cards. "See these?" She flipped one over to display the design on the reverse—a yellow lady's slipper. "Only place you can get these is the Golden Slipper." She arched an eyebrow. "Had a fire there the other day."

"Anyone could have given him those." The final knot came undone, and Adah helped Joe to his feet and hugged him. He grimaced but submitted to her embrace.

Zee pulled out the grimy shot glass. She tapped it with a fingernail, the sound ringing clear as a bell in the night air. "This is from the Last Chance Saloon. Got this lettering L C S on the base here—see?" She held out the glass for inspection but Adah ignored it. "Had a fire there too."

Riker came out to stand with his wife and son, putting a burly arm round their shoulders. "So what?"

Zee displayed the spangled garter. "And this. Only one person I know wears these—Diamond Dust Kate." She saw no recognition in their eyes. "Kate works down at Angie's Palace. Had a fire there too. See a pattern yet?"

Joe's parents exchanged perturbed glances.

Zee pulled the delicate necklace of turquoise beads from her pocket. "He had this too. Came from my place. Had a fire there today. You'll have seen the smoke from your window, Mrs. Riker." Her lips twisted. "Shame you were too busy to help. Fire caused a lot of damage. Christie and the sixteen-year-old girl we've got staying with us coulda been killed."

Adah had the grace to look uncomfortable.

"What does any of that prove?" challenged Riker. "Our son has accumulated a few souvenirs. That doesn't prove he started the fires."

"When you take into account his stash of kerosene, it does."

"Kerosene?" Adah blinked.

"Even if he *did* have such a stash, as you call it," persisted Riker. "*Why* would our son want to set those fires?"

Zee folded her arms. "That puzzled me too," she admitted. "But I reckon I've figured it out. The kind of places and people targeted—your son did what you told him to."

Adah blinked. "How *dare* you! I have never, *never* told Joe to burn anywhere down."

"Not directly, perhaps. But every time you said the saloon and gambling den and whorehouse are a disgrace, every time you told him certain folks were headed straight for Hell, that's the message he got." Zee eyed the boy. "Ain't that right, Joe?"

He scuffed the dirt with his toe, and for a moment, she thought he wasn't going to answer. Maybe she'd chosen the wrong punishment. Maybe a spell in jail would have been better for him after all.

Then he looked up and stared her straight in the eye. "They deserved it," he said. "They'll all burn in Hell anyway—whores and gamblers and heathens the lot of them."

Adah put a hand to her mouth. "Joe!"

Zee nodded. "See? This is where all that hate talk has got you. Way he's heading, he'll end up with a noose around his neck for sure. But he's young, there's still time to turn him around . . ."

The glance Riker shot her was full of hatred, and she sighed. What chance did the boy have with parents like these?

"This would never have happened," he said, "if you hadn't bought that old house. When your kind move in, trouble is never far behind."

Zee ignored the jibe and gave the sullen-faced boy a stern look. "Now listen, Joe, and listen good. I'm letting you off, but things are gonna change from now on."

Adah opened her mouth but a glare from Zee silenced her.

"If I hear you've been skipping school again," she said, "I'm taking you into custody. Any more fires, you're the first name on my list. First sign of trouble at my place," she continued, "I'll come looking for you . . . Got it?"

Joe looked up at his parents. Adah avoided his anxious gaze, and Riker's face was so suffused with rage he couldn't speak.

Zee tried one last time. "Just so we're clear as crystal. This don't happen again or you'll all have me to answer to. And believe me, I ain't called the Hellcat for nothing." She put on her fiercest glare and at last saw the fear she had been looking for appear in their eyes.

Then she turned and walked away.

CHRISTIE WOKE UP to find herself in her favorite position—wrapped round Zee. She snuggled even closer.

"Comfy?" came an amused voice.

She gave a sleepy smile. "Very."

Her reward was a gentle squeeze, then a hand began to draw lazy circles on her back. For a while she basked in a blissful haze, enjoying Zee's touch, then it dawned on her . . . something was different.

"What?" asked Zee.

"I was just thinking how quiet it is. What's happened to the Rikers' dogs? At this hour they're usually barking." Christie twisted in Zee's arms and stared up at her. "Or did we oversleep?"

"No." Zee bent her head and pressed a gentle kiss on Christie's mouth. She pulled back and grinned. "Morning."

Christie returned the grin. "Good morning, my love." Her mind returned to the puzzle. "So why aren't they barking?"

"'Cause they're gone."

"Gone?"

"Not just the dogs, the whole damned lot of 'em." Zee brushed a lock of hair out of Christie's eyes. "Left a few hours ago—while you were snoring. Don't know how you managed to sleep through it, the din they were making loading up their wagon." She stretched, the play of muscles under skin distracting Christie.

"I do *not* snore." She poked Zee in the ribs. "They left? Just like that? I don't believe it." Releasing her hold on Zee, she rolled over and got out of bed. She padded over to the window, drew the curtains, and stared out at the Riker place.

No smoke curled from the chimney, and the open porch door was banging in the morning breeze. There were no curtains at the windows. She turned to look at Zee. The dark-haired woman was sitting up and leaning back against the headboard, hands clasped behind her head showing off her naked breasts in all their glory.

"You're right," said Christie. "The place looks deserted."

"Just as well," drawled Zee. "'Cause otherwise they'd've had a mighty fine eyeful."

Christie frowned, looked down at herself, and realized what Zee meant. "Oh!" Crossing her arms over her own naked breasts, she scuttled back to bed and pulled the sheets over herself.

"No." Zee pulled the sheets down. "I was enjoying the view."

Christie let herself be pulled into Zee's lap. Then strong fingers caressed her belly and ribs, and a warmth whose source was not embarrassment began to spread through her.

She tried to focus on the topic under discussion. "Why did they go? You didn't run them out of town, did you? I thought you said you were trying to turn the boy around."

Zee shifted her attention higher. "Looks like Riker put his own needs first. I thought, maybe, just this once . . . But no."

By now Christie was finding it hard to catch her breath let alone concentrate on the Rikers. "Uh?"

"Knew his standing would plummet when news about Joe's fire-raising got out," clarified Zee. "Couldn't face it. Skedaddled. Plain and simple. Good riddance, I say." She eased Christie onto her back and straddled her, a predatory gleam in her eye. "Now, darlin'. Less talk, more action."

Christie laughed and obeyed Zee's instruction.

A DELICIOUS SMELL of frying ham and eggs wafted up as Christie descended the stairs. She sighed. Julie must be cooking again. She couldn't begrudge the girl—this was her way of recompensing them for putting her up, and she was an excellent cook—it was just that . . . She chewed her lip and analyzed her feelings. Just that the girl made her feel like a guest in her own home.

Pushing such mean-spirited thoughts aside, she plastered a smile on her face and pushed open the kitchen door.

Julie was standing at the stove, spatula in hand. "Good morning, Christie."

"Good morning. Did you sleep well?"

Julie nodded.

A clatter of boots on the stairs, the sound of whistling, followed by the crash of the door flying open and hitting the wall, made Christie roll her eyes at Julie (who covered her smile with one hand) and swing round.

"Mmmm, smells good." Zee draped her gun belt over the back of a chair. "I'll just take care of the horses." She sauntered past Christie, giving her a slap on the rump as she did so and escaping out into the yard before Christie could react.

"She's in a good mood," commented Julie. Christie crossed to the window and gazed out at Zee, who was giving the mare and gelding water and hay, and, as she always did, talking to them as though they were people.

"Mm." She smiled and turned back. "Can I do anything to help?"

"No, thank you. It's nearly ready."

Christie sat down and passed the time admiring Julie's dress, which was the height of fashion and made of scarlet velveteen if she wasn't mistaken. She fingered her own much more modest outfit, made of shabby gray calico, and suppressed a sigh.

Julie had just finished doling out breakfast when Zee returned. She washed her hands, wiped them on the front of her check shirt (Christie tried not to grimace), and tucked into her ham and eggs. Julie's indulgent glance at Zee was not lost on Christie.

"So," she said, taking a sip of the excellent coffee. "What are your plans for today, Zee?"

Zee swallowed before speaking. "Need a new buckboard. Got to order some lumber too." She forked more ham into her mouth then registered Christie's puzzled look. "For the new barn," she said indistinctly.

"Ah."

"You?" Zee arched an eyebrow.

Christie mopped up her egg yolk with some bread. "Laundry and mending." She sighed. "Though I think the dresses Julie and I were wearing yesterday are beyond saving."

Zee reached in her pocket. "Get yourself some fabric. Make yourselves some new ones." She slapped some dollars down on the table and pushed them toward Christie. "That oughtta cover it."

Christie looked first at the coins then at Zee. "Can we afford it?"

Zee nodded. "Won 'em off Millain. Won't be needing 'em where he's gone."

Julie had stiffened at the mention of her guardian, but now her face broke into a smile. It was that which decided Christie. She scooped up the dollars and put them in her pocket. "Thank you."

"You're welcome." Zee drained her coffee cup, wiped her mouth on the back of her hand, and stood up. "Better get going." She buckled on her gun belt, settled it more comfortably on her hips, and reached for her hat.

Christie stood up and went to her side. "Are you going to tell Hogan about the Rikers?"

"Yeah, I'll tell him. One good thing, darlin', now the Rikers have skedaddled, you should have no more trouble from Joe."

"Thank heavens!" A thought struck Christie. "It's a long walk into town, and rolls of dress material are heavy."

"Hint taken." Zee draped an arm round Christie's shoulders and kissed her on the cheek. "I'll get Bradley's boy to bring the replacement buckboard out to you. All right?"

She smiled. "All right."

Chapter 15

THE HOOFBEATS AND Zee's whistling had faded into the distance when Julie started on the washing up and Christie went to assist her. After that, Julie practiced her reading for an hour, then they started on the laundry.

As Christie had feared, the singed dresses came to pieces in her hands. She sighed, set the material aside for rags, and got on with the rest of the wash. She had just finished draping a petticoat over a bush to dry when the boy from the livery stable drove up in a buckboard.

"Miss Hayes," he called, reining in and tipping his hat to her. "Your buckboard, with Deputy Brodie's compliments." He climbed down and unhitched the horse, then mounted up and rode off.

Christie inspected the wagon with a pleased smile then popped her head round the kitchen door. "Get yourself ready to go to town, Julie," she called. "The buckboard's arrived."

She fetched the gelding from its temporary home beneath the makeshift canvas awning Zee had erected, hitched it, then went back inside for her bonnet, shawl, and drawstring bag. When Julie hurried out to join her, Christie was waiting in the driving seat. That velveteen red dress was magnificent.

Julie saw the direction of her gaze. "Do you like it?"

"It's very fine," said a wistful Christie. "But I suppose not very practical."

"We'll find you something practical *and* pretty," promised the girl, with a smile.

The promise was soon made good. With Julie to advise on taste and the latest fashion, and Ned Taylor to caution the women about cost and important laundering considerations, they were soon home again with two rolls of very serviceable fabric. Christie had found a turquoise cotton faille that matched the anniversary necklace Zee had returned to her last night (much to Christie's surprise, since she hadn't noticed it was gone from her jewelry case), and Julie had clapped her hands when she sighted a deep gold silk that would complement her skin tone.

Hoofbeats in the yard made both women look up from the lengths of material strewn all around them, and they glanced at the kitchen clock then regarded one another curiously.

"Sounds like Zee," said Christie. "Wonder why she's home early."

The door banged open and the deputy filled the doorway. She was clutching a piece of paper in one gloved hand. It looked like a telegram.

"Hey, Julie," said Zee. "Good news." She strode across the kitchen and stopped in front of Julie, who stared up at her. "Found your kin. They want you to go and live with them."

For a moment, the girl looked stunned, then her face crumpled and she burst into tears.

A disconcerted Zee gaped at Christie, who stood up and snatched the piece of paper from her. "Give me that." She put her arms round the weeping Julie and gave Zee a furious look. *Of all the ham fisted—* "Haven't you got horses to water or something?"

Zee's expression reminded Christie of a kicked puppy, then her stoic mask dropped into place and she turned and went out into the yard, cursing under her breath. Christie sighed. She had handled Zee all wrong, but she would have to fix it later. Right now, Julie was her main concern.

"How could she play such a cruel joke on me?" sobbed Julie. "She knows I have no one in the world to care about me, except you two."

Christie opened the piece of paper, which was from New Orleans, from the Pinkerton Detective Agency. She read its contents through once, then again more slowly.

"It's no joke," she told Julie. "It seems you have an Aunt Sarah and Uncle William, and they are very much alive." The sniffles stopped and Julie blinked at her from red-rimmed eyes. "Do you remember them?"

A long silence followed and Julie's gaze turned inward. "There was a man, with a big, soft beard," she said at last. "And a woman who smelled of lavender. I don't know who they were. My mother took me to see them. I had ice cream."

Christie could see the child Julie had been as she spoke. "You must have been very young." She tapped the telegram with a fingernail. "According to this, they wanted to bring you up themselves, but Millain wouldn't relinquish custody—he said it was your mother's last wish, which it was. Later, he told them you were dead."

"Dead?" Julie's eyes widened. "But—"

"They also say you can have a home with them in New Orleans if you want it. They loved your mother very much and they have no children of their own."

"Oh."

"You don't have to make up your mind now," continued Christie. "You can live with your real family or stay here with me and Zee while we get something else sorted out. There's always that dressmaker's job with Madame Clemence we talked about. I'm sure Zee could convince her to take you on . . . or—"

But Julie still appeared overwhelmed by the news and Christie knew it would take some time for her to digest this information, let alone decide about her future. So she stopped talking and rocked the still tearful girl in her arms for a while.

"Think about it. Take as long as you like."

When she was confident Julie was sufficiently recovered from her shock to be left, she went in search of Zee. Dusk had fallen, and the stars were coming out. She followed the smell of tobacco smoke to the far corner of the yard and there found Zee leaning against the fence, looking up at the night sky.

"Julie all right?" asked Zee, her voice gruff.

Christie eased herself under Zee's arm and was relieved when Zee pulled her close. "She will be."

"What about you?" The cigar tip glowed red in the darkness.

"Yes." Christie turned to look up at the strong profile. "Zee, I'm sorry about earlier—"

"You did the right thing," interrupted Zee. "I forgot she's only sixteen. Direct ain't always best."

"It usually is," said Christie. "And your directness is one of the things I love about you."

"Is it?" Amusement colored Zee's voice.

"Yes . . . Since when did you start smoking cigars?"

"Since I found some cigars in Joe Riker's hideout."

"Joe smoked?"

"Yeah."

"Well I wish you wouldn't. I didn't say so before, but it's not half so pleasant kissing you."

Teeth gleamed in the moonlight. "Can't have that, now, can we?" Zee crushed the cigar butt under her heel, moved round behind Christie, and draped her arms around her.

"Thank you."

"My pleasure." Zee rested her chin on the crown of Christie's head. "So. What do you think she'll do?"

"Julie? I honestly don't know." Christie sighed. "I hope she chooses to go back to her family though. Is that mean of me? Wanting to keep our home just for us?"

"No, darlin'. That ain't mean, that's natural. You ain't got a mean bone in your body."

Christie winced at Zee's faith in her, especially considering how she had treated her earlier. "I wouldn't be too sure about that."

"I would." She felt a kiss pressed into her hair and relaxed back into Zee's embrace.

"Anyway, if she decides not to go," Zee's voice vibrated through her, "well, we'll cross that bridge when we come to it."

Chapter 16

". . . WILLCOX, LORDSBURG, DEMING, El Paso, Alpine, Sanderson, Del Rio . . ."

Zee barged her way through the huddle of passengers waiting to board a car and headed for one further down the train. A glance satisfied her that Christie and Julie were following in her wake. Both looked wonderful in their new dresses, and it felt good to be seen in the company of two such pretty women.

It had been a fraught week, with Julie unable to decide about her future, swinging first this way then that, her tears never far beneath the surface. At least Zee could escape from the emotional storm by going to work each day. Christie had no such relief.

"Suppose my aunt and uncle mistreat me the way my guardian did?" Julie wailed one evening.

"Just get on the train and come straight back here," said Zee.

But the look Christie threw her told her that practical answers weren't what the girl needed at present, so she shrugged and left them to have yet another convoluted talk.

They had had an awful lot of those it seemed to her, involving much crying and "what if" ing on Julie's part, much hugging, "there, there" ing, and hair stroking on Christie's, and, inevitably, more tears. She was glad to be out of it. The first few evenings she had occupied herself making furniture for the parlor. Then the lumber for the barn arrived, and she had another perfect excuse.

She was admiring the posts she had just sunk for the new barn, when a tired-looking Christie came out into the back yard to join her.

"She's going," was all Christie said.

Zee arched an eyebrow. They had been here before, twice. "Definite?"

"Definite."

She draped an arm around Christie. "I'll wire the Fontenots tomorrow. Get them to meet her train."

And that had been that.

There were some empty seats in the next car, Zee saw. She dumped the luggage at the bottom of the steps and waited for Julie and Christie to catch up. "This should do," she told them, handing them up, then grabbing the bags and following them inside.

While Christie selected a bench and helped Julie get settled, Zee stowed the cases. She also had a word with the porter, asking him to make sure no one bothered Julie, slipping him three dollars for his trouble.

When she rejoined the others, Christie was asking the girl for the umpteenth time, "Are you sure you'll be all right?"

"I'm used to trains. Millain traveled a lot."

Zee ran a soothing hand down Christie's back. "She'll be fine. The porter's agreed to keep an eye on her," she said. "And her aunt and uncle are meeting her at the other end."

Christie sighed. "I'm acting like a mother hen, aren't I?"

Zee knew better than to agree or disagree. Just then, the train whistle sounded: two long blasts. "Darlin', we'd better go. Sounds like the train's about ready to leave."

Christie leaned over and gave the girl a hug, then turned, hand pressed to a trembling mouth, and hurried toward the exit.

"Good luck to you, Julie," said Zee, meaning it. "And if you should ever be back this way again . . ."

Julie's eyes were brimming with tears and she wiped them away with a gloved hand. "Thank you for everything."

"You're welcome."

Then the car lurched and started into motion, and Zee tipped her hat and ran for it, almost falling off the bottom step and having to grab Christie's outstretched hand to steady herself.

"Thanks."

She turned to watch the train pulling out of Benson on the first stage of its long journey east. A forlorn, gold clad figure looked back at them through a grimy window.

Christie raised a hand in farewell. Zee took off her hat and waved it, and draped an arm round Christie's waist.

"She'll be fine, you know."

Christie forced a smile. "I know."

Together they watched the train recede into the distance.

"C'mon," said Zee at last. "Nothing more for us here." She put her hat back on and they walked arm in arm to where the buckboard was. Christie was uncharacteristically silent.

"You all right?"

"Just thinking."

"About Julie?" asked Zee.

"About how strange it's going to be to have the house to ourselves again."

"Good strange or bad strange?"

Christie gave her a wry look. "Good, of course. It's nice to have visitors, but it's also nice when they go home."

"Amen!"

Zee handed Christie up into the buckboard driving seat, then climbed up next to her. She took the reins before Christie could. "I'll drive. You look beat."

"I am," said Christie. "I could sleep for a week."

Zee flicked the gelding's reins and the buckboard lurched into motion. "Know what you mean," she said, when they'd traveled a few yards. "When it comes to weeping women or a gunfight, I'll take the gunfight any day . . . Hey!" She rubbed the rib that Christie's elbow had poked and gave her an unrepentant grin.

They were passing Angie's Palace, and Zee slowed as Angie herself appeared, spotted them, and hurried over.

"Hey, you two," called Angie. "Some new player piano rolls have arrived. Why don't you come over tonight and we can have some fun."

Zee was about to accept but she caught herself and looked at Christie. They had their signals down pat these days. Her raised eyebrow was answered by a slight moue.

"Sorry, Angie. Not tonight. Been a tough week. Me and Christie are planning a quiet night in, just the two of us. You know?" A grin showed that Angie did indeed know. "Maybe tomorrow?" added Zee.

Angie smiled and stepped back. "We're not going anywhere, Brodie. Come over when you feel like it. We can have a game of strip poker."

Zee was careful not to look at Christie. The other night they had had a heated discussion about strip poker. Zee had a feeling Christie was only *pretending* to be angry about the cheating that ensured she always ended up clad only in her drawers, but she still wasn't completely sure. She nodded at Angie and flicked the reins again. The buckboard moved forward.

"Thank you," said Christie, when they had moved out of earshot. "I really do want some quiet time alone with you."

"My pleasure." Zee reached over and took her hand. "Home?"

Christie smiled at her, a smile that didn't just light up her eyes but her entire being. "Home," she agreed.

PART FOUR

In-laws for an Outlaw

Chapter 1

ZEE SHADED HER eyes against the noonday sun and peered through the grimy windowpane.

It's a pigsty.

Stacks of dirty crockery marred the crumb-strewn kitchen table, and that dishcloth was a disgrace even to Zee's unfussy gaze. Christie would have a fit if she knew how her brother was living now that she wasn't here to keep house for him.

She scanned the interior again, its emptiness explaining why no one had answered her knock at the back door. *Blue must be having his dinner at the store.*

Cramming her Stetson back on, she stepped down off the back porch and made for the gate. What a pity her mare wasn't tethered outside instead of back in Benson. *Still. The walk won't kill me.*

Zee strolled into town, tipping her hat to passers-by and ignoring the looks coming her way. The stares would be for the usual reasons: the Levi's, the guns. Civilized folks tended to think women shouldn't wear either.

"Hang on, Brodie," came a familiar voice from behind. "To what do we owe this honor?"

She stopped and turned, smiling as the town marshal hurried across the street to join her. "Howdy, Milligan."

Pat Milligan's clothes bore knife-sharp creases, and his boots and badge of office shone. His blue linen shirt and serge trousers were snugger across his belly than they used to be. *Ain't nothing quite like the loving attentions of a new spouse.* She looked down at her own gun belt, which she had had to let out another notch last week. *Hm.*

"How's Kathy?"

"Never better." He stroked his mustache. "Christie?"

"She's well."

"Good."

"It's not official business, Milligan." They resumed walking. "I'm here to talk to Bluford Hayes. Know where his store is?"

"Commercial Street. I'll show you." Milligan's brows creased. "Haven't those two patched things up between them yet?"

"No. But I aim to change that—Christie's been fretting. Plus, Blue's got a piano belonged to their parents. He don't play and Christie could sure use it."

"Piano?" Milligan guffawed. "Watch out, Brodie! She'll be holding musical soirées next."

Zee pretended not to hear.

They were walking past a clapboard building with an elegant false front, bearing the calligraphed legend "The Cactus Club." The social club was frequented by Contention's wealthier businessmen, some of whom were clustered in the large bay window, smoking expensive cigars after a no doubt excellent dinner. One profile was instantly familiar, causing Zee to check her stride before continuing.

That ridiculous beard. Last time she had seen its owner, he had been considering calling her out.

Fred Younger turned toward her. His eyes widened and his jaw dropped.

Just my luck!

The creak of the Cactus Club's front door opening was followed by the sudden murmur of male voices. Her nape hairs prickled, and she glanced in a nearby window and saw the reflections of the men now gathered on the sidewalk staring after her. Fred's face looked like thunder, and Zee's hand dropped to her gun butt. Unless she missed her guess, he was the type to shoot someone in the back.

Millain saw the gesture and glanced back. Fred eyed him for a long moment, muttered something to his friends, then retreated back inside the social club. Zee relaxed and blew out a breath.

"So," said Milligan, resuming their conversation as though nothing had happened. "Christie wants a reconciliation with her brother, huh?"

"Yeah."

"Well, I wouldn't get your hopes up. Blue may not be very . . . approachable right now." They turned the corner into Commercial Street.

"Damn!" Zee glanced at him. "I know I ain't top of his popularity list, but—"

"It ain't that. Your timing's bad, that's all. His business is going down the drain."

As she digested that fact, she scanned the storefronts up ahead. There it was, on the left, a little way past the undertaker's. Large black letters spelled out "Bluford Hayes, Dry Goods."

"And that's the reason." Milligan pointed at the brand new storefront directly opposite Blue's faded store. The contrast could not have been starker. "Younger's Fabric Emporium," proclaimed fresh crimson letters. "We sell it Cheaper."

Zee chewed the inside of her cheek. "Younger's?"

"Alexander Younger put up the money, but I'm betting it was his son's idea. Fred's had a burr under his saddle ever since Christie jilted him."

"Strictly speaking, it was Fred jilted Christie."

Milligan shrugged. "Makes no difference. He's bound and determined to ruin anyone named Hayes. And he's succeeding."

Zee sighed. She had come to Contention to solve problems not add them to her list. When Christie heard about this . . .

"Well, I've errands to run, so I'll be off." Milligan tipped his hat to her. "Give my regards to your other half, and to Hogan when you see him."

"Sure thing." She gestured at Blue's store. "Much obliged for the directions."

"You're welcome."

"OH, IT'S YOU." The apron-clad man behind the counter slumped back onto his stool, the light dying from eyes the same green as his sister's.

"Yeah." Zee busied herself closing the door, eliciting another tinkle from the bell above it. In spite of his house being a pigsty and Milligan's warning, the state of the store's interior and of its owner came as something of a shock. She donned her poker face and removed her hat.

"Sorry to hear things aren't going well, Blue." She placed her hat on the counter and began to remove her gloves finger by finger.

He snorted. "Where did you get that idea?" He gestured at his empty store. "Can't you see I'm rushed off my feet?" He had lost weight since their last encounter, and there was a gray cast to his complexion. He also needed a haircut and shave.

Zee placed her gloves inside her hat and glanced at her surroundings. The cotton reels, boxes of pins, and pattern books needed dusting and the bolts of fabric straightening, but Blue didn't seem to notice or care. Bad sign that. Best to change the subject maybe. "Christie sends her love."

Mention of his sister seemed to perk him up a bit. "Is she with you?" He looked around.

"No."

His shoulders slumped again. But his reaction had given Zee hope that her journey hadn't been wasted after all.

"But she's well. She was hoping for a reply to her letter."

For a moment, Blue looked puzzled, then he flushed. "Oh, that. I meant to answer it. Got things on my mind."

"She thinks you're still mad at her."

Blue shook his head. "I was, but . . . that doesn't seem important now. Besides, it wasn't her fault." A flash of his old spirit returned. "What chance did she have?" He glared at Zee. "You stole her right out from under our noses."

"I did?"

"Christie was well-brought up, respectable, until she met you. Now she's mixing with outlaws and whores."

Zee rubbed her chin. "That's how you need to see it, be my guest. But given how he's behaving now, would you really rather she'd married Fred?"

Blue dropped his head in his hands and groaned. "I don't know. I don't know anything anymore."

"Christie'll be mighty glad to hear you don't bear her a grudge. She's been fretting."

He doodled in the dust on the countertop. "Tell her I'm sorry."

"Why don't you tell her yourself? We've got our own place now; your sister's done it up real nice too. She'd love it if you paid us a visit." He stared at Zee as if she was crazy, and she stifled an urge to shake a sense of proportion into him. "Look. Everyone has setbacks from time to time."

He let out a hysterical laugh. "My life is in ruins, and you call it a setback?"

All this drama just because his store was going broke? Something didn't add up. "There's more to it than the store, isn't there?" He didn't answer. "Look, don't make me force it out of you." His eyes widened as he remembered who he was dealing with.

There was a long, tense silence, then he murmured, "It's Jenny."

"Jenny?"

"The blacksmith's daughter."

Zee leaned against the counter and folded her arms. "All right. Tell me all about Jenny."

It was a tortuous job, prizing the details out of him, but eventually she managed. For nearly a year, Blue had been courting Tom Farnham's youngest girl. More than that, he had got her pregnant. Such things weren't a scandal these days as long as the boy married the girl. And that's what Blue had wanted to do. But his dreams had turned to dust when he asked Farnham for permission . . . and was refused.

"Why in blazes?"

"Seems I'm not good enough. Oh, Farnham didn't object when I started seeing Jenny—my business was in fine fettle, then, and my name had just been put forward for the Cactus Club. But after Christie took up with you . . ." Blue's voice trailed off.

Zee could imagine what had happened next. Still stinging from his treatment at Zee and Christie's hands, Fred Younger had blackballed Blue and set out to ruin him. That didn't necessarily mean an end to his prospects as Farnham's son-in-law though. Especially since the girl was pregnant.

"Why didn't you two just elope?"

"I was thinking about it, but then Jenny up and left." Blue's voice wavered and he turned away, but not before she saw his eyes were glistening.

"She left?"

"To have the baby and get rid of it. And after that, well, she's to marry Andrew LeRoy. He owns the hotel; it's doing well and—" His voice broke and he stopped.

Zee filled in the blanks. Jenny's family must have applied pressure to the girl somehow and she'd given in. They'd spirited her away somewhere, to spare the family the shame that was becoming more obvious by the day. They'd also arranged to give away the baby, when it was born, so nothing would stand in the way of Jenny's marriage to LeRoy.

Blue, poor sap, stood to lose not only his prospective wife but also his child. And his business was following hard on their heels. No wonder he was going to pieces.

This called for action. "I'll fetch her back for you," said Zee, wondering, even as she spoke, whether she was doing the right thing. *But Hell, he's Christie's brother. I can't just stand by and watch him fall apart.* "Then you two can get hitched."

He stared at her from red-rimmed eyes. "Aren't you listening to me? Jenny left me. She doesn't want me. And who can blame her?" He gestured at himself and his surroundings. "Some catch!"

His spineless attitude infuriated her. "She told you that herself?"

"No. But her father said—"

"And you *believed* him?"

"Well—" He folded his arms defensively.

"A man should fight for the woman he loves, Blue, not just let himself be trampled on like some gutless—" She stopped as a glint appeared in his eyes. *I may have pushed him too far.*

He placed his hands flat on the counter-top and leaned forward. "You have the nerve to come here and insult me after all you've done?" His voice rose. "This is *your* fault. If it hadn't been for you, Fred Younger wouldn't be trying to ruin me and my business wouldn't be on the rocks, I'd be a member of the Cactus Club and Farnham would think I was perfect for Jenny. What's more, so would she." He reached beneath the counter and produced a shotgun.

"Easy, now." Zee held up her hands, palms out. "You don't wanna be firing that thing by mistake."

"Don't I?"

The barrel was pointing at her belly. It was shaking, and the knuckle of his trigger finger was white. Her mouth went dry.

"Think, Blue, before you do something you'll regret." She reached for her hat and gloves. "How will Christie feel if you ventilate me?" She pulled on her gloves. "And killing a deputy," she tapped the tin star pinned to her vest, "ain't something you should do lightly."

His eyes were glazed, his forehead clammy.

"I'm gonna walk out of here, nice and easy. No sudden moves. See?" She kept her voice even, as though she were talking to a skittish colt. "We'll talk about this some more in a few days. All right?"

She walked toward the door, the shotgun barrel following her all the way. By the time she reached for the handle, her shirt was sticking to the small of her back. The doorbell's tinkle was deafening in the fraught silence, and she braced herself for a shotgun blast. It didn't come. She looked back. Blue was regarding the shotgun with appalled astonishment. He released his grip, and it clattered to the counter top. Then he bowed his head and began to sob.

Should she stay and comfort him, or would that just make matters worse? Zee flipped a mental coin, shrugged, and closed the door behind her.

Man has some spunk after all. Shoulda figured that; he's Christie's brother.

It was only as she was walking away that she remembered the second errand that had brought her to Contention. *Damn! Forgot to ask him about the piano.*

Chapter 2

THE MOURNFUL SOUND of a train whistle came from just up ahead. Zee quickened her pace.

She had passed her spare time until the train was due playing cards in one of the saloons. There wasn't much else to do in this town if you excluded the red light district, and she had no hankering to visit that. It was seedier than its Benson equivalent, the whores as different from the girls at Angie's Palace as alley cats from Siamese.

But, preoccupied as she was with some good drinking whiskey and a winning hand, time had slipped away from her. She took a shortcut to the station, relying on her sense of direction to get her there, and was beginning to recognize her surroundings. *Just a right, then a left, and the depot should be—*

A lariat dropped round her shoulders.

"What the . . .?"

The whiskey had dulled Zee's edge, and before she could react, the rope was biting into her arms, pinning them to her sides and preventing her from drawing her guns.

A leg scythed her feet out from under her, and she fell, unable to cushion her fall. She rolled over, and saw there were three men, two tall and one short, all with bandannas masking the lower halves of their faces. They halted a yard from her, laughing at her attempts to free herself.

The tall man in the blue bandanna drew back his foot. The toe of his boot caught her in the ribs, and pain flared, causing bright spots before her eyes.

"That's it," said the short man, evidently the leader, his voice muffled. "Give the bitch what she deserves."

The third attacker crouched next to her, studied her, and pulled back a meaty fist. She jerked back, and the punch meant for her eye glanced off her cheekbone instead. It stung.

Zee brought her knees up toward her chest and tucked her feet in, providing herself with a measure of protection and bringing the knife she kept in her boot within reach. Before she could reach for it though, the short man came over and kicked her in the side with enough force to bring tears to her eyes.

For a moment she wondered where she was. The sound of a train whistle tooting twice pulled her back. *Leaving without me.*

"Think she's had enough?" asked the man in the blue bandanna.

"Don't be stupid," said the short man. "We've only just started."

She blinked away the blurriness and stretched out her right hand. Her gloved fingertips brushed against the handle of the knife. *Almost.*

Movement warned her, and just in time, she dodged the kick aimed at her head. While the foot drew back for another go, she reached for the razor-sharp knife once more.

Got it.

Zee pulled it free of its sheath, flipped it point upwards, and sawed at the lariat. Once, twice . . . With a *twang*, the last strand parted and her arms were free. She came to her feet in one smooth movement, knife in one hand, the other drawing a revolver.

"Look out!" yelled one of the men, as the bullet zoomed through the space his head had occupied a second ago and plowed into a wall.

Zee cursed as the pins and needles of her returning circulation threw off her aim.

Her attackers didn't wait for her to recover. They turned and ran for it.

CHRISTIE HUNG THE skillet from its hook more vigorously than was necessary. "Where *is* she?"

She didn't know whether to be angry or concerned or both. She did know that banging breakfast utensils and crockery together as she washed them up and put them away wasn't helping.

She needed to make her feelings known, at full volume, to that good-for-nothing woman of hers. But that was just the problem. Zee wasn't here. She had promised to return last night, but the train from Contention had come and gone and there was still no sign of her. Christie checked the clock for the second time in as many minutes—nearly eight-thirty.

It didn't help that she hadn't slept well. She had tossed and turned all night in a bed that felt far too large, cold, and empty without Zee in it, radiating body heat and providing other comforts.

"What in heaven's name are you up to? And why haven't you sent a telegram?"

She was stacking the crockery so noisily, she didn't hear the back door opening and closing. But it must have, because suddenly there was an unmistakable sense of presence behind her. She spun on her heel and gaped at the tall figure standing there, turning her hat in gloved hands.

"Zee!"

The cutting phrases Christie had rehearsed evaporated, and she launched herself across the kitchen. Her bear hug brought a grunt of pained protest and she released Zee and stood back. Only then did she register the bruised face and torn clothes. "You're hurt!" She put a hand to her mouth.

Zee gave her a rueful smile. "Got bushwhacked in Contention. Feel as if a herd of beeves ran me down." She flinched as Christie reached for the sore cheekbone and the puffy eyelid above it, but Christie kept her touch feather-light.

"Let me look at you."

Christie tugged an unresisting Zee over to a chair and sat her down. Zee placed her hat on the table and took off her gloves then allowed Christie to unbutton her shirt and ease it off over her shoulders and down around her waist. A clean white bandage had been neatly wrapped round her ribs.

"You didn't put this on yourself. Who did?"

"Kathy Milligan." Zee ran a hand through cropped hair. "Missed the last train back. Spent the night on a cot at their place."

Christie undid the knots and eased the bandage off, wincing at the black and blue bruises revealed. She palpated Zee's skin to assess the damage. The worst of it seemed to be on her right side.

Zee grunted. "Careful, darlin'. Reckon a couple of ribs got cracked."

"Sorry." Christie sighed, rewrapped the bandage, and stood back. Zee rebuttoned her shirt and gestured, and Christie accepted the invitation to sit on her lap.

"I wish you had let me know what was going on." She snuggled closer, careful to avoid the damaged ribs. "I was worried." Zee's hand curled itself around her waist.

"Knew I'd get home before any telegram." A bloodshot eye considered her. "Anyway, I thought you'd worry more if you knew about the beating."

"You're probably right." A horrible thought occurred to Christie. "Did Blue do this to you?" She'd never forgive herself if her brother—

"No. Three sons-of-bitches got a lariat over me just outside the station depot. I'd had a couple of drinks, which slowed me down some. Took me a while to cut myself free."

"But then who—"

"Don't know for sure. They were wearing masks, and once I could fight back, they skedaddled." She gestured ruefully at herself. "They got in a few punches and kicks before that happened though."

Christie backtracked. "For sure? Could you make a guess?"

Zee nodded. "The leader, the one who cracked my ribs, was wearing shoes."

Christie picked up on the significance of that at once. "Not boots?"

"No. Custom-made, shiny shoes with higher than usual heels. He was short, darlin'. Dapper, wearing checked trousers." Her gaze was keen. "Remind you of anyone?"

Surely not? "Fred isn't violent. He wouldn't do anything like that."

"He's not the man you knew, darlin'. He's turned feral, and he hates my guts."

Zee's long fingers began to unbutton her bodice and tried to slip inside. Christie slapped them. "Stop that, Zee. You should be taking things easy."

"Are you prescribing bed rest, Doc Hayes?" The blue eyes had a knowing glint, and Christie's pulse rate picked up. It *was* tempting.

"What about your ribs?"

Zee pushed Christie off her lap, stood up, and held out a hand. "Long as we're careful," she said. "C'mon. Bed's awaiting."

Christie held her bodice closed with one hand, and with the other took Zee's hand. "Deputy Brodie," she said. "You're incorrigible."

"And that's the way you like it."

Chapter 3

"SO, DID YOU see Blue?"

Christie was feeling drowsy and relaxed, enjoying the feel of Zee's skin against her bare back, the arm draped around her waist. The sore ribs had cramped their style a bit, but they had managed surprisingly well.

"Yeah," came Zee's drawl. "He meant to reply to your letter, but he's had other things on his mind."

Christie turned over. "Does that mean—?" She tried not to get her hopes up, but her heart was hammering.

"Things are all right between you? Yeah, it does." Zee ran a fingertip down Christie's nose. "But he's still sore at me."

Christie bit the finger then released it, earning herself a grin. "That's wonderful. About him and me, I mean." She had hated being estranged from her brother. Blue was all the family she had left in this world . . . besides Zee of course. It felt as though a great weight had rolled off her shoulders. She hummed a few bars of "Beautiful Dreamer."

"Guess that's what you wanted to hear, huh?" Zee was smirking at her but she didn't mind.

"Yes." She made herself comfortable against Zee again. "How is he?"

The long pause alerted her that something was up and she twisted round until she could see Zee's face. "What is it?" Zee grimaced, and apprehension washed over Christie.

"Well, you know I said he had other things on his mind?"

She nodded.

"He has problems, big problems. And most of them are down to Fred."

Christie blinked. "What do you mean?"

So Zee told her, the whole sorry story, from the opening of the rival establishment opposite Blue's store to the ruin of his hopes for Jenny and the baby.

Indignation became shock then turned to anger. One fact in particular stuck in Christie's mind. "Jenny's *pregnant*?" That her straitlaced brother could have done the deed, and with that little chit of a girl . . . well!

Zee was laughing at her and she frowned. "What?"

"Guess he's as partial to bed sports as his sister. Must be a family trait."

She hit Zee a playful blow in the ribs, then spent the next five minutes apologizing and trying to rub it better. When Zee opined that *kissing* it better might be nicer, Christie knew Zee had recovered, and turned her roiling thoughts back to the subject at hand.

"The point is," continued Christie, "that Blue's in a bad way and needs our help. With the store and with Jenny."

"Well, he won't accept it from me, darlin'. I offered and got turned down flat. He thinks I'm to blame for all this." Zee's tone was neutral, but Christie could tell she was offended.

She stroked a muscled biceps. "Since when did the Hellcat take no for an answer?"

Zee blinked at her. "You want me to track down Jenny?"

"Do you think it might help?"

Zee's gaze turned inward, then she nodded. "Got a hunch it might."

"Well, then . . . As for Blue himself, and his store, well, I'm his sister. He'll *have* to accept help from me."

Zee grimaced. "Wouldn't bet on it. Besides, your presence there might make things worse."

"How so?"

"Way I figure it, most of Blue's troubles stem from Fred. That skunk is mad at us but he's taking it out on your brother. You go to Contention to help him, and it'll be like waving a red rag at a bull—" Christie tried to interrupt but Zee held up a hand. "No, darlin'. Hear me out. Fred's dangerous." She gestured at her cheek and her bandaged ribs. "And he's got friends. Someone could get hurt. And if it was you, I'd never . . ." She trailed off.

Zee was right, Christie realized with a feeling of frustration. She wanted to make Blue's life better not worse. But how . . . An idea came to her.

"Suppose Fred didn't feel the need to punish Blue anymore? Suppose he was able to crow about me, instead. To gloat and say 'I told you so' to my face?"

"I don't like the sound of—"

"You've had your turn, let me finish. Suppose he thinks he's won? That might defuse his anger, mightn't it? Make him leave Blue alone?"

"It might." Zee's gaze was somber. "But I wouldn't count on it. Anyway, just how are you gonna do that?"

Christie was quite taken with the simplicity of her solution. "I'm going to break up with you."

Zee's jaw dropped. It was the perfect opportunity to kiss her, and Christie took it.

THE WAITING TRAIN vented steam and whistled, a mournful sound reflecting Zee's mood.

"Maybe this wasn't such a good idea after all," said Christie suddenly.

Zee breathed a sigh of relief. From the first, she had thought the plan half-baked. If Zee was any judge of character, the only way to persuade Fred to back off was to find some hold over him.

"It's not too late to change your mind," she told Christie, who was looking very fetching in the turquoise traveling dress Julie Fontenot had helped her make.

"And do what instead?" The green eyes were reproachful. "I can't just sit around doing nothing, Zee. I have to help Blue somehow. And your way will take time."

Zee shrugged. "Go to Contention then, if you must. But you know what I think of the idea."

"I do. But humor me anyway." Zee gave her a wry smile and Christie wrinkled her nose delightfully at her. "Thank you." A thoughtful silence fell, then Christie continued, "Suppose there's nothing to find on Fred."

"Man like him, there's bound to be something."

"Well all right. But how will you find it?"

"I won't." Zee tapped the side of her nose. "But I know someone else who will."

"Oh . . . It won't be for long, anyway." Christie gave her hand a squeeze.

"Better not. Gonna be tough not having you around to kiss and cuddle."

"It certainly is." Christie heaved a gloomy sigh.

"Wish I was coming with you."

"So do I. But you have things to do. And I'm sure Fred won't hurt me, Zee."

Wish I was. "Not physically, perhaps, but he's gonna say things. 'Bout you and me. Things I'd tear his tongue out for if I was there."

"I can take it."

"'Course you can. You got spunk, I know that." Zee smiled at Christie. "Just you remember, darlin', no matter how hard he tries to, he can't dirty what's between you and me. I'm yours for good, and I ain't ashamed of that." She squeezed Christie's hand for emphasis. "And when I'm through finding Jenny, I'm coming to get you."

"Just take care of yourself."

Zee gave a frustrated sigh. *If only*— But it couldn't be helped. She couldn't go with Christie, and that was an end of it. The thought made her pull out her pocket watch and check it. Plenty of time before her appointment.

The train whistle blew again, louder and more impatient this time. Then again.

"She's getting set to depart. Let's get you on board." Zee helped Christie up the steps into the carriage, then returned for the cases. When Christie was installed in a good window seat, her luggage stowed nearby, she turned to say goodbye.

What Zee wanted, more than anything, was to kiss Christie. But some of the other passengers eyeing her would be getting off at Contention too. She couldn't risk revealing Christie's play this early in the game.

She drew herself up to her full height. "Safe journey, Miss Hayes. Give my regards to your brother."

Christie's startled disappointment gave way to comprehension. "Thank you, Deputy Brodie," she said, equally formal. "I will."

Back on the station platform, Zee gazed up at the lovely face behind the soot-streaked glass. Christie glanced to either side, then mouthed, "I love you."

Zee stifled a grin. "Me too," she mouthed back. The train lurched forward. The two women locked gazes and Zee kept pace with Christie for as long as she could, but soon the train left her behind.

Chapter 4

HE WAS WAITING for her as arranged, sitting in the far corner of the Last Chance Saloon, chair pressed against the wall, gaze trained on the street door.

If Hogan hadn't told her about Charlie Judkins' background, she would have dismissed him. "Nondescript" was the word, she decided. He could be anyone, go anywhere without attracting attention. *Good.*

She nodded a greeting and noted that the shot glass on the stained table in front of him was empty. She appropriated another glass and some whiskey from the bartender, then made her way over.

"Judkins?" He nodded. "Brodie."

She put the bottle and glass on the table, placed her hat next to them, then sat down. His clothes were clean but well worn and slightly old-fashioned, and his graying hair and mustache needed a trim. Though he wasn't small, his self-effacing manner gave the impression that he was. The ex-Pinkerton detective had been giving Zee the once-over too, his gaze lingering on her tin star before returning to her bruised cheek and eye.

He'll do.

She poured whiskey into the two glasses and pushed his toward him. "Thanks for coming." She downed her drink in one, wincing as the cheap whiskey found a cut on the inside of her lip, then wiping her mouth on the back of her gloved hand. He cocked his head to one side, inviting her to get down to business.

"All right. Here's what I need." She outlined what she wanted, and he listened until she had finished.

"Just the one man?" He took a gulp of whiskey.

"That's right. But I want to know his every move, no matter how small. He so much as *looks* at someone, I want to know the when and the where. Round the clock. That clear?" He nodded and she topped up his glass then her own. "So. Think you can do it?"

"Anything to be found, I'll find it, Deputy." Calculation filled his gaze. "For a price."

He named a figure that made her wince. Hogan had warned her good detectives came expensive, but still . . . They'd have to put off buying that couch for the parlor that Christie had her eye on.

"Got yourself a deal." She pulled off her glove, spat in her palm and held out her hand. He did the same and they shook.

"Half in advance."

Zee pulled the little leather pouch from her vest pocket, and threw it to him. It contained slightly more than he'd asked for. "That do?" He caught it, undid the tie, and gazed at the half eagles nestling inside.

"Pleasure doing business with you, Deputy." He pocketed the pouch, eased himself out of his seat, and stood up. "I'll be in touch." He tipped his hat.

"I'm counting on it."

After Judkins had left, Zee topped up her glass and gazed into it for a while. If he didn't find anything on Fred Younger, she'd have squandered their money for nothing. It was a gamble. But she had a hunch about Christie's ex-fiancé, and Zee always bet on her hunches.

She drained the shot glass, kicked back her chair, and stood up. It was time to get moving on the next item on her list.

MADAM ANGIE WAS in her office doing her accounts. "Brodie." She smiled and pushed away the thick ledger with undisguised relief. "Is this a social call?" She reached for her pipe. "Is Christie with you?"

"No to both." Zee took the seat offered.

Angie tamped tobacco into the bowl and cocked her head. "From the state of your face, I'd say you've been brawling."

Zee grunted but didn't enlighten her. "I need a favor."

"Oh?"

"Concerning The Sisters of Charity."

Angie's eyebrows crawled skywards. "You won't find any of them *here*."

"Reckon I knew that."

They both chuckled, then Angie leaned forward. "It concerns Sister Florence's establishment, I take it?"

"If she's the one who runs that place just outside Fairbank, yeah."

"The Willows. It's an Orphanage."

"More 'n that, from what I hear."

Angie lit up her pipe before answering. "True. The Sisters also take in fallen women, until their babies are born. A good proportion of the children in their care come from that source." She gestured toward the door, through which Zee caught a glimpse of several of the whores taking a break in various states of undress. "Occupational hazard."

"I also heard tell you and one of the Sisters have been," she cast around for the words, "close friends for a while."

Angie crossed her Turkish-trouser-clad ankles and laughed. "My my, you *have* done your homework, haven't you. Yes, Florence and I are friends. Not in the way you mean though."

"No?"

"I wasn't always a madam, you know. There was a time in my life when things were very . . . bad." Angie's gaze clouded. "Florence wasn't in charge of the orphanage then, of course. That's a recent development. But she always was kind-hearted. Found me and took me in when no one else would. For that I will always count her my dear friend." She forced a smile and Zee knew she wasn't going to hear any more on that particular topic. "So, are you going to tell me what this mysterious favor is?"

"A letter of introduction. Figured the Sisters ain't gonna take too kindly to someone like me," she gestured at herself, "nosing around. Thought if you could vouch for me, it might prevent them having the vapors."

Angie's eyes gleamed. "But why on earth would you want to—?"

Zee held up a hand. "Let's just say I've a hunch one of their current charges is in need of my help, and leave it at that. I'll tell you 'bout it once it's over and done with. All right?"

Angie sighed and sat back. "All right." She opened the desk drawer, pulled out a blank sheet of paper and reached for a pen. While the pen scratched across the page, Zee got up, crossed to the door, folded her arms and leaned against the doorframe. Whistles and catcalls greeted her appearance.

"Enjoying the view, Deputy?" asked Nellie the Fox, in between puffs on a cheroot.

"Mighty fine, thanks." Zee winked.

Rowdy Mollie straightened her petticoats. "Where's Christie?"

"Gone to Contention."

Red Mary's face lit up. "Does that mean you'll be requiring our services while she's away?"

Zee was about to set her to rights when Angie's voice came from behind her. "There. It's done."

She stepped back into the office and took the envelope Angie was holding out. "But this is sealed." The red blob of wax bore the imprint of Angie's signet ring.

"Of course it is."

"Wanted to read what you wrote," grumbled Zee. "What did you say about me?"

"None of your damned business."

"But—"

Angie laughed. "It's confidential. Between Florence and me."

Zee knew when she was beaten. She sighed and tucked the envelope in her vest pocket. "All right. But if Sister Florence comes after me with a shotgun—"

Angie wagged a finger at her. "Have a little faith, Brodie."

"I'll try."

Chapter 5

THE RIDE WAS a long and dusty one, and by the time Zee arrived at the clump of willows that had given its name to the orphanage she was hot and in need of some shade. It didn't help that her ribs were aching. She moistened her bandanna with water from her canteen and retied it, enjoying the coolness on the nape of her neck.

A dozen children, of varying ages but all energetic and grubby, were playing in the fenced-off yard next to the smaller of the two clapboard buildings—the school presumably. After the silence of the last couple of hours, their shrieks were piercing, and Zee's mare tossed her mane and nickered; she couldn't help but agree.

She dismounted and tethered her horse. By now, the shrieks had subsided and the children were crowding the fence, staring at her.

"Howdy, varmints." She tipped her hat and winked. Eyes widened and mouths dropped open. A gangly boy hared off indoors to fetch an adult.

"It's a woman," said a freckled girl in a much-patched, pink dress.

"Don't be stupid." The speaker was a boy with ginger hair. "Women don't wear trousers."

"That's quite enough of that," boomed a female voice. The large woman coming toward them was dressed in a black habit, veil, and pleated cape, and a white collar and coif. Behind her trailed the gangly boy. "Playtime is over. Indoors now, all of you, and leave our visitor alone." She clapped her hands twice. "I said now. Sister Euphrasia is waiting." She cast a sharp glance at a fair-haired boy about to pinch the girl next to him. "That includes *you*, Sam."

There were a few protests and whines, but a frown from the sister soon had the children disappearing indoors. That done, the nun turned her attention to Zee. Her mouth curled in disapproval though her greeting was polite enough. "May I help you?"

Zee took off her hat. "Sister Florence?"

"No. I'm Sister Agnes." Hands chapped by housework worked a rosary with a *click, click, click* of beads. "You wish to see Sister Florence?"

She nodded.

"Very well. Wait here and I will see if she is receiving visitors." Sister Agnes turned to go then paused and turned back. "Who shall I say is calling?"

"Deputy Zee Brodie." Zee fished the envelope from her pocket, still sealed, though temptation had almost got the better of her. "Got a letter of introduction here."

Sister Agnes took it and gave it a cursory inspection. Then she headed toward the other building, a two-story structure that must be the orphanage proper.

Zee put her hat back on and went to join her horse in the shade. She filled her palm with water from the canteen and let it drink. That chore done, there was still no sign of either Sister Agnes or the mysterious Sister Florence.

Wonder what Angie put in that letter? She squatted on her heels and whistled under her breath, then pulled out her pocket watch and flipped it open. *Christie should be in Contention by now.*

Somewhere, a door creaked open and Zee looked up. A large black crow was heading toward her. She blinked and straightened, pulling the brim of her Stetson down against the glare. The crow resolved itself into Sister Agnes, habit flapping.

"Deputy Brodie," called the sister, beckoning. "Sister Florence will see you. Please come with me."

ZEE BANGED HER hat against her thigh, to get the worst of the dust off, and followed Sister Agnes into the hallway. It was a welcome relief to get out of the heat.

Her eyes adjusted to the relative gloom of the interior and she allowed the Sister of Charity to lead her through into a small room labeled "Vestry." One wall was lined with closets. Furniture consisted of a small table and four uncomfortable-looking chairs. On the table was a brass handbell.

"Someone will be with you shortly." Sister Agnes left Zee alone.

Moments later, a different sister entered, bearing a glass of lemonade on a tray. Zee drained it in two swallows and handed it back with her thanks. Shortsighted gray eyes, already wide at her appearance (must be the battered face, she supposed), widened even further. Then the nun, who was short and thin and wore wire-framed spectacles, recollected herself and exited as silently as she had entered.

"Guess she wasn't Sister Florence either." Zee wandered over to the window and stared out at the windmill turning in the breeze, pumping up the water from the underground spring that was the reason the Sisters of Charity had chosen this site. In the distance a lesson bell rang.

"No. But I am."

She swung round in surprise.

"It's not often we are paid a visit by the notorious Hellcat." Like the other sisters, the new arrival was wearing a black habit, veil, and pleated cape, and a white collar and coif.

"The Hellcat don't exist no more, Sister. I'm . . ." Zee trailed off as she registered the twinkle in the gray eyes and the opened letter clutched in the nun's hand.

"Deputy Zee Brodie," completed Sister Florence. "I know. But allow an old woman a moment of excitement. It'll have to last me several years."

Zee snorted. "Old" was pushing it, she decided, taking an instant liking to Angie Tucker's friend. More like in her fifties. She'd also hazard a guess that Sister Florence had once been quite a looker, before time and the elements had coarsened her complexion.

"Please." Sister Florence gestured with a work-worn hand. "Sit." Zee did so. The sister did likewise and clasped her hands in her lap. "Now. Tell me what brings you to my establishment. As far as I am aware, none of the sisters are wanted by the law. Nor are any of our charges come to that. Though with scamps like Sam Baker, it's surely only a matter of time." She gave a rueful smile.

Zee started to lean forward, but her sore ribs made her think twice. "You take in fallen women here. That right?"

"If you mean desperate and wronged young women in need of our help," corrected Sister Florence, "then yes, we do. We care for them during their confinement, until they are well enough to pick up the pieces of their lives. Some take their babies with them, some entrust them to our care."

"I'm looking for one in particular."

Sister Florence's expression became watchful. "I cannot divulge the identities of the women here. It is a matter of trust and confidentiality."

Zee thought for a moment. "Suppose you don't tell me anything, but I tell you?"

"Very well."

"Her name's Jenny Farnham." Sister Florence's poker face was perfect. *Damn!* "The baby's father wants to marry her, but her parents have other ideas."

"I see."

"That all you can say? She's here against her will."

"No one is here against their will," said Sister Florence. "I am certain of that. Perhaps the parents have their daughter's best interests at heart. Or did that not occur to you?"

Her statement brought Zee up short. Could Blue have been right? Did Jenny agree with her parents' plans for her? Her mind raced. "Maybe it's just she's accepted her fate," she guessed. "Maybe she thinks she has no choice."

"That's a possibility," conceded Sister Florence. She got up, went to the window, and stared out.

Time stretched. Zee could hear the faint buzzing of a fly, the distant ticking of the clock in the hall . . . She picked at a loose thread on her Levi's and schooled herself to patience. At last she was rewarded.

"Deputy Brodie." Sister Florence turned to face her, her expression somber. "Partly because of the endorsement my old friend has given you," she lifted the letter she still held, "and partly because I myself have had some doubts about this particular young woman, I'm going to break my cardinal rule."

Zee let out a sigh of relief.

"Jenny Farnham *is* here . . . accompanied by her aunt, who rarely leaves her side."

Zee arched an eyebrow.

"Quite. Now it could of course just be that Jenny has been so upset by recent events she needs constant support. But," Sister Florence began to pace, her long skirts swishing as they brushed the floorboards, "as yet, none of us has made any serious effort to talk to the girl on her own." She shook her head. "A highly unsatisfactory state of affairs."

Zee nodded. "We need the facts, ma'am."

"The facts," repeated the nun, halting and nodding once. "I think I can arrange that." She reached for the handbell and rang it. The little sister in the spectacles who had brought the lemonade reappeared.

"Yes, Sister Florence?"

"Sister Mary. Will you please tell Miss Farnham that I wish to speak with her at once? Bring her to the vestry, will you?"

"Yes, Sister." Sister Mary bowed her head again and hurried away, but not before giving Zee another curious glance.

"But the aunt will come too," objected Zee.

"Indeed."

"She won't let Jenny speak to me."

"She'll let her speak to *me*, or I shall ask them both to leave the orphanage." Sister Florence looked at the closets lining the wall of the vestry then walked toward one and opened the door. "Hide in here, Deputy."

Inside the closet was a rail, from which hung black habits and other items of clothing. Zee grimaced but made space for herself amongst the nuns' apparel, which gave off the faint whiff of mothballs. Then the door closed with a click and she was in pitch blackness. *Good thing I'm not scared of the dark.*

She resigned herself to a lengthy, suffocating wait. But it wasn't long before she heard the sound of a door opening, followed by the murmur of voices. Turning awkwardly in the cramped space, she eased aside a clothes hanger that was digging into her back and pressed her ear to the door.

"—Jenny alone, if you don't mind, Mrs. Archer."

"I *do* mind," came a rather shrill voice. "I see no reason why anything you might have to say to my niece cannot be spoken in my presence. We keep no secrets from one another. Do we, dear?"

"No, Aunt." The reply was barely audible.

"Nevertheless," said Sister Florence, "I need to talk with Miss Farnham about certain . . . ahem . . . delicate, one might even say intimate, matters. Her health and the health of her baby, you understand, are my chief concern."

"Oh." There was an embarrassed silence. "Well, in that case . . . I shall wait outside."

There was a sound of the door opening and closing and Zee smiled in the darkness.

"Now, Miss Farnham. I have a favor to ask of you."

"Of m-me?"

"Yes. I want you to promise that, whatever happens in the next few minutes, you will keep it just between ourselves. Will you?"

"Yes, Sister Florence. But I don't understand."

"Thank you, child. It's quite simple. I have a visitor for you."

There was a click, then the closet door swung open. Zee took her cue and stepped out into the vestry, blinking.

Faun-like eyes gaped at her. Their owner, a pretty and very pregnant young woman of about Christie's height, who was wearing a shapeless gray dress, put a hand to her mouth. "But who are you? And why are you hiding in the closet?"

"Name's Deputy Zee Brodie."

Comprehension filled the dark eyes. "Oh! You're the one who seduced Blue's sister."

Fortunately Sister Florence seemed unperturbed by Jenny's revelation. *Angie must have told her in that letter.* "That's right."

Long lashes blinked at her. "How is Blue? Is he all right?"

Jenny's concern for Blue raised her a notch in Zee's estimation. "As well as can be expected," she said. "Considering his prospective wife and child left him."

Confusion filled Jenny's gaze. "Isn't that what he wanted? A fresh start back East, without me and the encumbrance of a baby?"

"No," said Zee. "And whoever told you it was is a damned liar . . . Pardon my language, Sister Florence." The nun waved the apology aside.

"But I don't understand," said Jenny.

"Hardly surprising as this situation appears to be rather . . . tangled." The sister gave the girl's hand a soothing pat. "Deputy Brodie has been trying to ascertain the facts." She turned to Zee. "Would you care to lay them out for us?"

"Thanks. Far as I can tell," said Zee, "Blue thinks Jenny wants to get rid of his baby and marry Andrew LeRoy. And Jenny thinks Blue wants nothing more to do with her."

"Concisely put," said Sister Florence.

Jenny was frowning. "But Papa said . . . Do you mean to tell me, Blue *does* want me after all?" A tear spilled down her cheek.

"That's right. In fact he's a broken man without you," said Zee.

"Oh!" The girl put her face in her hands and began to sob. Sister Florence produced a large handkerchief from somewhere and gave it to her.

There was a loud knock at the door.

"Sister Florence," came Mrs. Archer's voice. "Sister Florence. Is my niece all right? What in the world can be taking you so long?"

"She's fine," called Sister Florence, glancing at Zee then at the closet. "Nearly finished. One minute."

Zee nodded her understanding. "I have to go," she murmured in Jenny's ear. "But I'll be back to get you out of here." The girl's head came up and tearful eyes gaped at Zee. "You and Blue will be together again," she promised, giving the slender shoulder a squeeze. "Be ready to leave at a moment's notice. And whatever you do, don't tell your aunt anything. All right?"

Two spots of color appeared in Jenny's cheeks. She nodded, tentatively at first then more firmly.

"Good girl." Zee stepped back inside her hiding place, and the closet door swung closed behind her.

Chapter 6

IT WAS LUCKY the house was so close to the station depot, thought Christie, as she struggled along the road. She had forgotten Zee wouldn't be here to carry her luggage.

Maybe she should have wired Blue and asked him to meet her after all. But that would have given him the chance to say he didn't need her help.

She swapped the heavy cases over, redistributing the weight. It helped . . . for all of three paces. Her arms still felt as though they were being pulled from their sockets.

Will Zee still love me when my knuckles drag along the sidewalk?

Fortunately, the little clapboard house that had once been her home was just up ahead. Maybe if she took the last few yards at a brisk trot . . .

Her grip gave out two paces from the front porch. The cases fell to the ground with a *thud.*

A bewhiskered old man in a blue flannel shirt stopped at her muffled exclamation. "You all right, Miss?"

Christie turned, flexing her fingers. "Yes, thank you for asking."

He returned her smile, tipped his shabby hat to her, and continued on his way, whistling.

She shook her hands until the cramp eased, then turned and regarded what had once been her own front door. The roses around it were dying, she saw with some sadness. Blue must have stopped watering them.

Was her brother at home or still at the store? Only one way to find out.

She stepped up onto the porch, smoothed her dress over her hips, and retied her bonnet. It probably made little difference to her appearance. Train travel always left her feeling crumpled, sweaty, and smut-stained and the trip from Benson had been no exception. She took a deep breath, exhaled, and rapped the doorknocker twice.

For a long moment there was no response, then from inside came the sound of approaching footsteps. The door creaked open, and there stood her brother.

His jaw dropped. "Christie!"

"Blue." She flung herself at him and hugged him. After a moment, he returned her embrace. Then she stood back and looked at him.

Though Zee had prepared her for a change, his appearance shocked her. He had lost weight, she saw at once. And there were shadows under his eyes that hadn't been there before. He was also in need of a shave and haircut, and (she tried not to be too obvious as she sniffed) both he and his clothes could do with a wash.

"What are you doing here, Sis?"

A fat woman was coming down the street toward her—Mrs. James, their neighbor. Christie wasn't sure if she was in earshot yet, but, if she was, now was the perfect moment to put her plan into action.

"Oh, Blue," she cried. "Please don't turn me away. I made a terrible mistake. But I've come to my senses at last." She had been aiming for melancholy but suspected she had achieved merely melodrama. *I'm no Vesta Galvin.*

He stared at her.

"I've left Zee," she announced. "I've left her and I'm never going back."

CHRISTIE SHUT THE front door behind her. "I haven't really," she told the dumbfounded Blue. "That was just in case anyone was listening."

His brows knit and he stroked his mustache. "Are you feeling all right, Sis?"

"Perfectly well, thank you." She beamed at him, overjoyed to be reunited with the brother she had thought was permanently estranged from her. Her joy faded as she saw how red and puffy his eyes were. Had he been crying?

"But you're not well at all, are you? Zee told me all about it."

He stiffened. "Is that why you're here? Because if so—"

"Of course it is." She raised a hand to stifle further protest. "What kind of sister would I be if I didn't help my brother when he needs me?"

"I don't—"

"You most certainly do." She wagged a finger at him. "Look at the state of you! And of this house." A thin layer of dust covered everything, and there was a huge cobweb hanging in the corner by the stairs. "Mama would be horrified."

Blue blinked at his surroundings as though seeing them for the first time. "I suppose you're right. I've let things go a little."

Christie let raised eyebrows speak for her, and he flushed a delicate shade of pink that spread to the tips of his ears. With their coloring, the two siblings had always been susceptible to blushing. Seeing Blue's face now, she understood why Zee was always teasing her—it must be irresistible.

"Don't worry." She patted his arm. "I'll soon have this place . . . and you . . . spick-and-span again."

He sighed and changed the subject. "Shall I bring in your luggage?"

"Please."

She crossed to the banister and gazed up the stairs. It was peculiar being back here. It was still her home, and yet it wasn't. It made concrete something she had been beginning to suspect. Her place now was with Zee, in the house in Schoolhouse Lane.

"Thank you." She accepted the lightest of the cases from her brother. "Is my room still the small one at the back?"

Blue nodded. "It's just as you left it."

She started up the stairs. *But I'm not.*

THE FIRST THING Christie did, when she had unpacked, shaken the creases from her clothes, and put them away, was to prepare them both some supper. She was ravenous, but Blue's cupboard was almost bare. (She made a note to go shopping for supplies tomorrow.) Fortunately, she had come across some cold cooked potatoes during her search, and, with the aid of an egg, some milk, and sugar, was able to improvise.

While supper was cooking, she laid the kitchen table. Then she handed him the cutthroat razor and stood over him while he shaved. After that, she sharpened the scissors on a whetstone and trimmed his mustache, sideburns, and hair. That he allowed her to do so without a word of complaint worried her, though she tried not to show it. The brother she had known would have objected, but this new version of Blue couldn't seem to work up the energy.

By this time, an appetizing aroma of potato pudding had spread round the house and her stomach was rumbling. She removed the supper from the stove and served it, calling to her brother to wash his hands and come and eat. He did so, looking almost presentable if you overlooked his stale and crumpled clothes.

As she ate, she wondered what Zee was having for her supper. Then she noticed that Blue was only picking at his.

"Don't you like it?"

"It's fine. I'm just not hungry."

No wonder he was losing weight. "Well, try to eat a little," she urged. "You need the nourishment." He smiled at her and made an effort, but when she came to clear away their dishes, she saw that half his food remained. Luckily, potato pudding was excellent served cold, so she covered the plate and placed it in the pantry, in case he should feel hungry later.

After she had washed and dried the dishes, the day's exertions caught up with her, and though it was earlier than her usual bedtime, she said goodnight and made her way up to bed.

She gave herself a perfunctory wash, put on her nightdress, and slipped between the sheets. It was then that she made an unwelcome discovery. The bed that had once been cozy now felt cramped and yet at the same time empty. She was used to their huge double bed, she realized, and to having Zee's arms wrapped around her. Used to making love and whispering affectionate sweet nothings before falling asleep. Without these things, she found herself wide awake and lonely.

She sat up, plumped her pillows, then lay back once more and felt sorry for herself. Was Zee missing her as badly as she was missing Zee? She hoped so.

Christie snorted as anger and self-pity gave way to amusement, and she took herself to task. *If Zee could be here, she would, but she's off finding the blacksmith's daughter. So stop being selfish. After all, it won't be for long.*

After that, she found if she closed her eyes and pictured Zee lying on her bedroll beneath the stars somewhere and thinking of her, things didn't seem so bad. And somehow, before she knew it, she was dreaming of a dashing dark-haired outlaw, who held up her stagecoach and carried her off into the desert, there to have her wicked way with her.

Chapter 7

THE NEXT MORNING, Christie sent her brother off to work, his belly lined with cold potato pudding. She was glad he had managed to eat most of his breakfast, but less happy about his attire. There wasn't a clean shirt or pair of trousers in the house; she'd had to settle for the least offensive of his dirty ones.

The first chore on her list was obvious: laundry. Just to be on the safe side, she washed, rinsed, and put Blue's clothes through the wringer twice. Emptying the big iron kettle onto the parched back yard, she marveled at how grimy the wastewater now soaking away was. She was transferring the wet shirts from the laundry basket to the bushes, for the hot morning sun to dry, when she heard the sound of a door opening.

Her overweight neighbor appeared, carrying her own basket of laundry. Coincidence or was Mrs. James wanting to chat? She was a kind enough soul, but she did love a good gossip, Christie remembered.

The other woman smiled at her over the picket fence. "Good to have you back, Miss Hayes. Blue's house has been in need of a woman's touch."

She arranged the shirt to her liking before answering. "Thank you, Mrs. James. I'm pleased to be back." She wondered whether to add anything further then thought better of it. "Excuse me, won't you? I have a lot to do, so I'd better get on."

Mrs. James's face fell, but she nodded pleasantly enough and began to hang out her own washing. Christie grabbed the empty laundry basket and went back indoors.

After a brief rest and a glass of lemonade (she had also found some wizened lemons in the pantry), she tied a scarf around her hair to keep it out of the way and grabbed a broom and dust cloth. The house wasn't as filthy as the Old Barn had been when she and Zee first moved in, but it was getting there. After an hour of sweeping and dusting, she was tired and grimy. She looked at the clock in the parlor.

That time already? The rest will have to keep. I must go shopping.

Christie opened a window, leaned out, and shook the dust from her cloth, then stowed away her cleaning implements. She removed her clothes, poured some water into a basin, and had a quick wash.

The next problem was what to wear for her first jaunt into town. She must look respectable and repentant. Which meant a corset. With a sigh, she put one on and laced it, instantly missing the freedom of movement that had become second nature to her. *I hope you appreciate all this, Blue.*

She eyed the rack of dresses she had left behind when, acting on romantic impulse, she'd decided to remain with Zee in Benson. The dove-gray calico dress had once been her favorite but it now looked drab and too conservative. *I've been mixing with Angie's girls for too long.*

Nevertheless. She pulled it out, held it against her body, and gazed at herself in the mirror. Then she nodded.

Perfect.

AS CHRISTIE WALKED into town, she wasn't sure whether to be pleased or disappointed when few heads turned to follow her progress and those that did smiled and greeted her politely. *Strange how, when you want a rumor to spread, it won't.*

The sun was like a furnace, and she was relieved to step into the cool of McClellan's General Store. She pushed the door shut behind her, making the bell above it tinkle, then turned to see the big man in the starched white apron coming out from behind his counter.

"Welcome back, Miss Hayes." His smile was genuine. "Haven't seen you for a while."

"Thank you. No. I've been away." She pulled the list of supplies from her drawstring bag. "Will you arrange for these to be delivered as soon as is convenient, Mr. McClellan?"

His took the list from her and perused it, his smile broadening as he saw the extent of her order. "My my! Quite an order." He stroked his beard.

"Add it to Blue's account, if you please. I'll get him to settle up next week."

He pursed his lips, appraised her, then nodded. "Certainly, Miss Hayes."

His hesitation made her realize that she had no idea of her brother's current financial status. If the dry goods store was making a loss, he might be in trouble. Still, she could always dip into her own savings, which had remained untouched since she left Contention. (She had felt too awkward to ask Blue to send the money on while he was still angry with her.)

McClellan grabbed the pencil stub that hung from a string round his ample waist, licked it, and began to tick off the items. He paused. "End of the week before my next consignment of buckwheat flour comes in, I'm afraid. Would tomorrow be convenient for the rest?"

"Oh. I'd hoped to at least get the beef, butter, and apples this afternoon, if that's—"

He smiled. "No trouble at all. I'll send Malachi round with them."

"Thank you."

"Will that be all, Miss Hayes?"

She thought for a moment then nodded. "I believe it will. Good day to you, Mr. McClellan." Retying her bonnet strings, she headed out into the hot sun once more.

CHRISTIE WALKED PAST the Cactus Club, resisting the urge to tuck her head into her shoulders like a tortoise. So what if Fred was inside? Contention was a small town; she was bound to run into him sooner or later. But when her former fiancé didn't come running out of the club to confront her or jeer at her, she heaved a sigh of relief.

Her relief was short lived, however, when she saw the matronly figure in royal blue coming along the sidewalk toward her. Cora Chase's progress put Christie in mind of a steamboat at full paddle. The town's worst gossip must scent a juicy tidbit.

She was debating whether to cross the road, when Cora placed herself in her path.

"Miss Hayes. Well I never!" Black eyes gleamed. "So you've come back to look after your brother, have you? Very sisterly, I'm sure."

"Mrs. Chase."

"It's been distressing to us all to see on what hard times Bluford has fallen," continued Cora.

Christie was hard pressed not to make some angry retort. As far as she could make out, none of Blue's so-called friends had even *tried* to defend him from Fred's malice. They had, if anything, distanced themselves, afraid perhaps that the wrath of the Youngers might spill over on to them too. But she contented herself with, "I'm sure my brother will be very pleased to know of your concern."

She tried to edge past, but Cora blocked her once more.

"And your companion," continued Cora, a subtle emphasis adding quotation marks to the word. "Has she come with you?"

It dawned on Christie then that if she wanted her cover story to spread, this was the perfect opportunity. Everyone knew that you could drop a private word in Cora Chase's avid ear at breakfast and by sundown it would be common knowledge. She took a deep breath and plunged in.

"Deputy Brodie and I have . . . parted company."

Cora blinked at her. Clearly she had not expected Christie to surrender up such juicy information so easily. She recovered quickly though.

"Very wise, I'm sure. Did she try to," she licked her lips and leaned closer, "do something objectionable?"

"I . . . I'd rather not speak of it." Christie lowered her gaze as though mortified.

"How awful!" said Cora, with great relish. "Then it's just as well you separated yourself from her. Before your reputation was ruined entirely."

"Indeed." Christie had discovered, with Zee's help, that she didn't care a jot for reputation, but she kept her sentiments to herself.

"As I'm sure you have come to realize," continued the town gossip, oblivious, "your association with . . . that woman didn't show your brother in a good light, either, which can't have helped his present predicament."

Christie counted to ten.

"But all that is behind you now."

"Indeed it is." She forced a smile. "I have many chores to do, Mrs. Chase, so I really must be off." She edged around Cora, and this time the other woman let her pass.

"I do hope your brother is appreciative of your efforts," was her parting shot.

"Oh, he is, Mrs. Chase. Very." And with that Christie made her escape.

Chapter 8

ZEE PUSHED BACK her hat and watched the last of the sunset's lemon, peach, and coral tints disappear. Night fell in earnest.

About time.

She'd grown tired of twiddling her thumbs, waiting for it to get dark. But what she was about to do couldn't be attempted in daylight. At least not without attracting unwelcome attention.

She stretched the stiffness from her limbs, wincing as a twinge reminded her of her injured ribs. A ripe aroma wafted up to her nostrils and she grimaced.

These duds of Andy's smell like something died in 'em. The gelding tethered nearby nickered. "Yeah," she agreed. "Shoulda borrowed from someone who bathes regular, huh?"

Her own clothes were back in Benson, along with her tin star. She had decided it wouldn't do for a lawman to be seen abducting a pregnant woman from under the noses of her aunt and the Sisters of Charity. But a bandanna over her mouth and nose and buckskins borrowed from one of Angie's regulars should take care of the identification problem.

Trouble was, as well as stinking to high heaven, Andy Street's "second best" buckskins were too loose around the crotch and too tight under the arms. She wriggled, trying to ease the pinching. The gelding shifted in its traces.

"Easy, boy." She patted its neck. Normally the gelding pulled Christie's buckboard, but that would be too bumpy a ride for Jenny in her present condition, so tonight it was hauling the piano box buggy Zee had hired.

Pity she couldn't just throw the girl over her saddle and gallop off into the sunset. *But this ain't no dime novel. And besides, Christie might have something to say about that.* Zee grinned, picturing her reaction.

It was three days since Zee had seen Christie, and she was missing her. But, she consoled herself, if all went well tonight . . .

The stars were coming out in force now, a half moon rising. She sucked her teeth and hoped there'd be some cloud cover when it mattered.

Zee pulled out her pocket watch and peered at it in the moonlight. According to the schedule followed by those at the Willows, the children would be tucked up in their beds, and the adults would be finishing their supper before retiring for the night.

If all went to plan, the cup of after-supper coffee handed to Jenny's aunt would contain a little extra something that Zee had provided (courtesy of Doc Pellet in exchange for a bottle of good drinking whiskey).

Sister Florence had stared at the little phial of knockout drops in disbelief. "Is this really necessary, Deputy Brodie?"

"It's for her own good."

The nun's eyebrows rose.

"Jenny's aunt sees some masked desperado spiriting off her niece," explained Zee, "it'll be shoot first, ask questions later. I'd have to defend myself. Wouldn't *intend* hurting her, but . . ." She shrugged.

Sister Florence pursed her lips, then nodded. "Very well. If I have your assurance that these will not cause Mrs. Archer permanent harm?"

"Sure do."

The phial disappeared into a hidden pocket in her habit.

That had been yesterday and Zee had been on the go ever since, fetching the two-seater buggy, borrowing the buckskins, taking delivery of the canvas-and-leather contraption (a cross between a sling and a harness) that she had had made specially, and arranging a place for Jenny to stay while she waited for Blue to join her.

Zee checked her watch again then clicked the lid closed and repocketed it. It was time to get moving. She pulled the brim of her Stetson lower and tied the bandanna over her mouth and nose. Then she untethered the gelding and climbed up into the buggy's seat.

"Hi." She flicked the reins; the horse broke into a trot.

When the Willows came into view, Zee found some suitable cover and hopped out of the buggy. She tethered the gelding to a tree and gave it some of the feed she'd brought with her. Then she tossed the sling over her shoulder and headed toward the orphanage, the sound of contented munching receding behind her.

According to Sister Florence, the room Jenny shared with her aunt was on the second floor. Zee peered up at it. Had her ribs been in better shape, she would have thought nothing of clambering up the outside. As it was, she was glad she had persuaded the sister to leave the front door unlocked.

She slunk up to the door in question, and tried the handle with one gloved hand. It turned and she grinned in the darkness. She slipped inside and closed the door behind her. She wouldn't be coming back the same way.

A lamp was burning on a table in the hallway, and she paused to check that the coast was clear before continuing past the vestry. At the bottom of the stairs, she paused. It was the third and seventh treads that creaked on the first flight, wasn't it? She started up, stepping over the treads Sister Florence had warned her about. At the landing, she stopped to catch her breath. *So far so good.*

A murmur of voices made her freeze and peer through the banister rail. Two nuns came into view. Fortunately for Zee, they didn't look up. They were deep in conversation, about tomorrow's school lessons by the sound of it. The voices and footsteps receded into the distance and she let out her breath. That had been close. She resumed her stealthy progress, stepping over the fourth and sixth treads in the final flight of stairs as instructed.

As she tiptoed along the corridor, she thanked her lucky stars that, unlike the school children, the fallen women were allowed separate rooms. Plucking Jenny out of a dormitory unremarked would have been impossible. As it was, she only had to deal with the girl's aunt. She checked the number on the first door and moved on. Jenny and Mrs. Archer were in Number 8.

Zee had barely registered the loud snores issuing through the next door along when something else distracted her. More voices, this time getting louder. *Hell!* She had no choice but to open the door and slip round it, leaving it open the merest crack.

The snoring stopped.

Heart pounding, shoulders braced for the inevitable scream, Zee turned and squinted at her surroundings. From what she could make out, only one of the two beds in the little bedroom was occupied. The shape under the sheets moved—not to sit up though, but to roll over. Seconds later came a snuffle and a snort and the snoring resumed.

Zee slumped back against the wall and tried not to laugh. *Sonofabitch!* She shook her head, then turned back to the door and pressed her ear to the crack, trying to ignore the noises coming from the bed.

". . . you were right, Rose," came a woman's voice, muffled by the door. "That glass of milk did settle my stomach."

"Told you," said her companion. "Think you can get some rest now?"

"I'll try."

The voices moved past her. Moments later came the sound of a door opening and closing. Zee waited a little while longer, just to be sure, then slipped out into the corridor once more.

Number 8 was the last door but one, and no noise issued from its interior. She reached for the door handle, turned it, and slipped inside.

The occupants of the two beds were both asleep. Jenny's distended belly made her identity obvious. After checking that the occupant of the other bed was sleeping soundly—three pats on her cheek didn't wake her—Zee lit the oil lamp on the dresser and knelt beside Jenny's bed.

She pulled down her bandanna. *Don't want to shock her into having the baby on the spot.* "Jenny," she whispered.

The girl's brows drew together but she didn't wake up.

Zee tried a bit louder. "Jenny."

Eyelids fluttered open, revealing dazed eyes, then Jenny gasped and sat up. "What?" Comprehension dawned. "Oh, it's you. I didn't recognize you for a minute in those clothes." She yawned. "I was wondering when you'd come for me."

"Sorry it took so long." Zee helped Jenny out of bed. "Had one or two things to arrange. Get dressed."

The girl headed toward the clothes closet, then paused and turned to look at her aunt. Despite the disturbance, the older woman hadn't stirred. "What have you done to Aunt Archer?"

"Got someone to slip something in her drink."

"Oh." Jenny blinked then nodded and began to root through the closet. "I should wear something Blue likes, shouldn't I?"

"Just pick something comfortable."

Jenny made her selection quickly and began to dress. Zee busied herself with the sling and its attached rope.

"What's that?"

"Had it made specially. You step into it like so." She demonstrated. "Then buckle up these." The straps would spread the load evenly between hips and shoulders and avoid putting any pressure on the girl's belly.

Jenny's jaw dropped. "You're going to lower me out of the window?"

"Don't worry. It's strong enough to lift a horse." Zee noticed Jenny's shoes were still unbuttoned. "Here. Let me." Kneeling, she pulled off her gloves and buttoned them.

"Thank you. My aunt usually does them for me now that I can no longer bend." Jenny wrinkled her nose. "What's that smell?"

"My buckskins," said Zee. "Sorry." Pulling on her gloves again, she straightened and crossed to the sash window. She slid it open as quietly as she could and leaned out.

The moon had gone behind a bank of clouds. Nothing moved outside, and in the distance a lone coyote yipped. *Might just pull this off after all.* The night air, cool on her cheeks, reminded her to pull up her bandanna. She ducked back inside.

"C'mon. Let's get started."

When the reluctant Jenny had stepped into the sling, and Zee had fastened its straps and buckles, Zee placed a chair beside the window and lifted her up onto it.

Jenny's eyes widened. "You're as strong as Blue!"

Zee grunted and took up the slack of the sling's rope attachment by winding it around her waist.

"Are you sure this will hold me?"

"I'm sure." *Besides, if I drop you, Blue and Christie will both invite me to a necktie party.* She helped Jenny to sit on the window ledge, legs dangling outside.

"Don't look down. And remember. Be quiet. Sound carries further at night."

"I'll try."

"Good girl." Zee patted her shoulder. "All right. Let's go."

She took hold of the sling then eased it and Jenny out of the open window. Taking the weight on her forearms then spreading the load by leaning back and bracing her feet and knees against the wall, she began to pay out the rope. Hand over hand she lowered her precious burden, every now and then turning to release more of the rope wrapped around her waist.

Her knees hurt, the muscles in her arms and back burned, and the rope was slicing through her gloves, but she kept the ride as smooth she could make it. At intervals, she checked the girl's progress to make sure she wasn't swinging like a pendulum or spinning, and if she was to correct it. Jenny's frightened eyes stared up at her throughout, her lips pressed together.

Plucky kid.

At last Jenny's feet touched the ground, and the strain on Zee's arms vanished. She exchanged a triumphant wave with the girl, unwound the rope, and chucked the end down. With a last look at the aunt, who had slept throughout the whole enterprise, she eased herself out of the sash window, slid it closed behind her, then, ignoring her protesting ribs, half climbed, half slid down the clapboard.

Jenny was still struggling to unbuckle the straps when Zee landed next to her. She put a hand to her mouth.

"You startled me," she whispered.

"Sorry." Zee stripped off her ruined gloves and tucked them in her waistband, then took over the unbuckling. Jenny stepped out of the contraption and Zee picked it up, coiling the rope and slinging it over her shoulder.

"Come on. Buggy's this way." She held out her free hand to the girl, who took it.

The gelding snorted and tossed his head as they ran toward it. Zee calmed it with a soothing word and a pat before turning to help Jenny up into the buggy. Once the girl was settled in the seat, Zee draped a shawl around her shoulders and a rug around her legs.

"All set?"

Jenny yawned and nodded. "Where are we going now? Blue's house?"

Zee untethered the horse, hopped up next to Jenny, and picked up the reins. "No. Figure we should steer clear of Contention until you two are hitched."

Jenny blinked. "Oh, yes. I suppose that makes sense."

"Hi." Zee flicked the reins and the buggy lurched into motion. "Friend of mine in Benson has agreed to put you up for a spell."

They had gone only a few miles when the faint clanging of an alarm bell began to gust toward them on the cool night air.

"Oh no!" said Jenny. "That must be from the Willows. They've discovered I'm missing."

"Don't worry. It's too late for them to do anything about it." Zee flicked the reins and the gelding increased his pace. "Get some sleep. We've got a ways to go."

"At this speed?" The buggy was fairly rocketing along. "I don't think I can." Jenny pulled the shawl tighter around her shoulders.

"Try and rest then."

"All right." Jenny closed her eyes.

The scent of crushed sage wafted up to Zee as she concentrated on guiding the buggy around boulders and thickets of scrub. She was glad when the moon reappeared at last to illuminate the way.

A little while later, something slumped against her. She turned to find a sound asleep Jenny using her shoulder as a pillow. Jenny's condition, the excitement of her escape, the rhythm of hooves, and the rumbling of buggy wheels—all had probably contributed to Jenny's tiredness. Even so, this evidence of her trust touched Zee. She wondered if Jenny was dreaming of Blue.

Don't fret, Jenny. I'll get you to him safe and sound. Smiling, she drove into the darkness.

Chapter 9

ANGIE TUCKER ENTERED the back office where Zee was sitting twiddling her thumbs. "She's little more than a child herself." Her pointed glance made Zee take her booted feet off the desk and relinquish the chair.

Angie took her rightful place with a groan of relief and smoothed her housecoat over her knees. "Waking me up at this hour of the morning, Brodie. It's indecent." She reached for her pipe and tobacco pouch.

"How are they?"

"Fine, both of them. Strong as an ox, that girl. Just as well after all this excitement. Kidnapping her from the Willows! Whatever next?" Angie packed tobacco into the pipe bowl then looked up at Zee. "I've given her your old room."

"Thanks. I owe you one." Zee grabbed her hat from the desk.

"And you can be sure I'll collect . . . Now get some sleep, Brodie. You look done in."

"Could use a little shut-eye," she admitted. She glanced at the ornate clock that a pillar of Benson society had once awarded the madam for "services to the community." It had just turned five a.m. "Got a few hours before my next appointment. Think I'll go home."

"While you're at it, take a bath." Angie lit up and took a few puffs of her pipe. "Christie won't let you near her smelling like a skunk."

"That's Andy's duds not me," protested Zee. "You coulda warned me he stinks."

Angie chuckled. "Sorry."

Zee crammed her hat on her head and pulled on her battered gloves, then yawned again. "Ain't gonna see Christie till tonight anyhow. First I've got to see a man about a weasel."

THEY HAD AGREED to meet in Canisteo. The little railroad town was close to Contention but enough out of Fred Younger's way to make running into him unlikely.

Zee headed for the saloon with the cracked window and pushed open the door. Charlie Judkins was ensconced in a corner seat, his back to the wall. She strolled over, her footsteps muffled by the sawdust underfoot, and put a bottle of whiskey on the table next to his empty glass.

"Howdy." She took the chair opposite him. "You got something for me?"

The ex-Pinkerton detective smirked and took his time pouring himself a drink. Zee sighed and let him have his fun.

"Reckon I do," he said at last.

He pulled a battered old notebook from his pocket, flipped it open to a dog-eared page, placed it on the table, and pushed it toward her with a forefinger. She squinted at the pencil scrawl that passed for handwriting, then pulled the notebook closer for a better look.

Well, well! So Fred was trying to make himself some easy money, was he?

"You're sure about this? The ore was taken from his pa's stamp mill? And the worked-out mine belonged to a friend of his?"

Judkins nodded. "Seen the title deeds. And got an eyewitness who saw Younger grab the lumps of ore before they reached the crusher. No one tried to stop him." He shrugged. "Boss's son and all that."

"High grade?"

"Yeah. Lord Camborne's in for one helluva shock if he thinks his new silver mine's gonna produce more of the same."

"What a ninny! Fred certainly saw *him* coming." Zee drummed her fingers on the table and thought about Fred's mine-salting activities. "Figure his pa is involved?"

Judkins shook his head. "Stake my reputation he ain't."

She leaned back in her chair and allowed herself a smile.

"Reckon you were right." She pulled out the pouch containing the balance of his fee and tossed it to him. "You did have something for me."

Chapter 10

CHRISTIE PUT DOWN the rolling pin, smoothed her apron, and went to open the back door. A man was standing on her porch, his shirt and trousers pressed, his tin star polished to a dazzle. It was Pat Milligan. He took off his hat.

"Afternoon, Miss Hayes."

"Marshal."

"I've just heard the news. Is it true?"

She glanced over the fence—no sign of Mrs. James. "I take it you're referring to Deputy Brodie?"

His hands were crushing his hat, but he didn't seem to notice. "I can't believe she'd do something like this. Why, just the other day—"

"You'd better come in." She stood back to allow him over the threshold and closed the door behind him. Her decision was instinctive. This was one of Zee's friends and his distress was obvious. "No, it's not true."

Milligan blew out his breath. "Doggone it!" He pulled out one of the chairs and sat down, absentmindedly resting his hat in a sprinkling of flour on the kitchen table. "I knew it. Kathy thought the same." He cocked his head to one side. "You two still together then?"

"Yes. We concocted the story to keep Fred from hurting Blue any more than he already has." She took a chair opposite him and folded her hands in her lap. "I'm afraid it was my idea," she added.

Milligan shook his head. "And I'm not sure it was a wise one. These days, Fred's a wild one. Partly the company he's been keeping, partly . . ." He shrugged.

Christie sighed. "I know. And I'm sorry for my part in his transformation. I didn't intend to hurt him. Things just . . . turned out that way. But he's hurting my brother, Marshal. I can't allow him to do that. And though there's a risk, I don't believe Fred will injure me, for all that he tried to hurt Zee."

"Took quite a beating, didn't she? Kathy was shocked." He grimaced. "Pity we can't prove Fred did it."

He gave her an anxious glance. "He shows any sign of crossing the line with you, Miss Hayes, you come and get me, lickety-split. Understand?"

She nodded. "And remember, if you need to see a friendly face, come round to our place. Kathy and me will always be glad to see you, no matter what."

"Thank you. I appreciate that."

Milligan sighed. "As for Blue's store, it's a bad business, but my hands are tied. Younger's within his rights to open up his own store."

"I know," said Christie. "But coming on top of losing Jenny . . . well, it's the final straw."

"Jenny Farnham?" Milligan looked thoughtful. "I knew she and Blue were walking out together, but I thought that was all over. She's to marry LeRoy, so they say."

"That's her father's idea." Christie tried to gauge his likely reaction to what she was about to reveal, but couldn't. With a mental shrug, she dove in. "She's carrying Blue's child."

Milligan whistled. "So *that's* why they got her out of town double quick. Visiting relatives back East? Hah!" He leaned back in his chair and regarded her. "What's Brodie's part in all this, Miss Hayes? And don't tell me she isn't up to something, because I know her too well. You're here on your own, which means she's on the loose."

Christie gave him a rueful smile. "I'm not certain I should tell you, Marshal. It's not exactly . . . lawful."

He sighed. "Why am I not surprised?"

She chose her words with care. "What I *can* say is that, if everything goes to plan, Blue and Jenny will be back together again very soon."

He stroked his mustache while he thought, then came to his decision. "Then I guess that's all I need to know." He stood up and banged the worst of the flour from his hat.

Christie escorted him to the back door, where he paused as if struck by something. "So the Hellcat is playing Cupid? If that don't beat all! Must be your influence, Miss Hayes."

She thought about all Zee's loving gestures: the sack of bulbs brought back from Yuma, the turquoise bead necklace, the plush hotel suite in Phoenix where they had celebrated their "honeymoon," not to mention buying The Old Barn . . .

"No, Marshal. That's where you're wrong. Zee always had a romantic streak. She just never had much opportunity to show it."

THE APPLE PIE was baking in the stove, the beef roasting on the shelf beneath it, when her next caller arrived. The rail-thin woman at the front door was dressed in a black, buttoned-to-the-neck dress that couldn't by any stretch of the imagination be considered becoming.

"Mrs. Fair." Christie stared at the wife of the Presbyterian minister.

"I came as soon as I heard the news, Miss Hayes. Now you have broken with that woman," Christie could almost hear the quotation marks, "there is hope of redemption. You were bound for the fires and agonies of Hell, but if you repent, Almighty God in all his mercy will forgive you."

"Um—"

"Come with me now. My husband is waiting at the church." She reached out a gloved hand.

Christie took a step back. She had once had the misfortune to sit through one of Reverend Fair's sermons, and she had no intention of repeating the experience. It had been neither instructional nor edifying, indeed the minister seemed to have an unhealthy obsession with applesauce that was beginning to ferment—"a temptation of Satan," he called it.

"This is your chance to turn the page, to start a new chapter, Miss Hayes," urged Mrs. Fair. "To turn your back on the sins of the flesh, on drunkenness and debauchery . . ."

Christie's eyebrows rose. Just what kind of life did this woman imagine she had been living? "No thank you."

Mrs. Fair gaped at her. "Have you no care for your immortal soul?"

"Of course I have. But if I need to make my peace with God, I will do it in my own way and time. Please, thank your husband for his concern. Now, I am sorry, but I am busy." And with that Christie closed the door in her face.

CHRISTIE DIDN'T MENTION her visitors to her brother at supper that night. He'd had another disastrous day at the store, and the conversation, such as it was, was punctuated by gloomy silences.

"It'll be all right in the end, Blue, you'll see," she reassured him for the umpteenth time, hoping to God she was right. "Zee will get Jenny back, and then, if you want, you can leave Contention and start again elsewhere."

He grunted and pushed his half-eaten meal round the plate. She resisted the urge to shake some sense into that stubborn head of his. It must be difficult for him to be other than pessimistic. He didn't know Zee like she did.

Talking of which, if only the deputy would send her a telegram to let her know how things were going. It would be no easy thing spiriting off a pregnant girl.

The fact that Blue had a baby on the way still shocked Christie, though she was not quite sure why—perhaps it was just that a sister doesn't like to imagine her brother active in that way. That their relationship had progressed so swiftly, and that they had been so careless . . . It was understandable though. Perhaps passion had overwhelmed all good sense and reserve. She smiled, remembering how, shy and inexperienced as she was, she had practically flung herself at Zee in that noisy little bedroom in Angie's Palace.

Blue put down his knife and fork and stood up, the scrape of his chair jarring her back to the present.

"I'm tired, Sis. Think I'll go to bed."

"All right." She kissed him on a stubbly cheek and began to collect up the used cutlery and plates. As she washed and rinsed the dirty crockery, she realized something and her eyes widened.

My goodness! I'll be an aunt. And so will Zee.

CHRISTIE CLOSED THE door of the store behind her, hiding her brother's doleful countenance from view, and set off down Commercial Street. She had spent the morning at Kathy Milligan's, talking mostly about Zee, she realized with slightly mortified hindsight, and then on the way home had dropped by Blue's store, to check he had eaten all of the dinner she had packed for him.

She glanced at the bustling store opposite her brother's deserted establishment with something like hatred. *Was* it her fault that Fred had turned out to be so despicable? Or had he been that way all along and she had just not recognized it? The thought of what marriage to him could have been like made her blood run cold. Thank heavens Zee had come along when she did.

"Well, well," came a familiar voice. "If it isn't the Hellcat's little whore."

For a moment, she thought she had somehow conjured up the object of her ruminations, and she turned fearful of what she might find. It was a man not a demon, of course, but Fred's smile had a devilish edge to it.

"Good afternoon, Mr. Younger." There was no reason for her to forget her manners just because he had.

"So. You've come back to Contention with your tail between your legs." He fingered his beard and exchanged a sly glance with the two men accompanying him. "That's not all she's had between her legs, if I'm any judge."

His indelicate language shocked her; he had never treated her this way before. Her heart began to pound, and she took a deep breath to steady herself.

Several of the townsfolk had halted and were observing this encounter. And why not? They had heard the gossip, and Mrs. Chase and Mrs. Fair had no doubt embroidered it further. They would relish the treatment Fred was meting out. After all, Christie had broken the rules of propriety, first in eloping with a once notorious outlaw (and a woman at that), and second in returning home unrepentant. A public humiliation was her just dessert.

Stick and stones, she told herself. *I knew this would happen. And if it succeeds in turning his anger away from Blue . . .* "I've come back to look after my brother."

"Ah yes. How *is* Bluford?" His smile was malicious.

She bit her lip before replying. "As well as can be expected, given the circumstances."

"You have no idea how it has pained me, pained all of us," Fred exchanged another look with his friends, "to see him brought so low."

"You are wrong," she said. "I have a very clear idea."

Her cool rejoinder made him blink, then he frowned. "Your brother should close his store. There are plenty of other men, better men, who could make a go of such a business, even if he is incapable of it."

She wondered if he could hear her teeth grinding. "No one could tell, to hear you talk, that you once considered him your friend. But I have no wish to discuss my brother's affairs with you. Good afternoon, Mr. Younger." She turned and made to walk on. But somehow Fred was there, blocking her way. She halted.

"I'm to be married, you know," he said conversationally.

"Oh." She blinked at his abrupt change of manner. "Congratulations. Do I know your intended?"

"I shouldn't think so. Cecilia moves in quite different circles from those you frequent." His lip curled.

In spite of herself, she asked, "Cecilia?"

"The eldest daughter of Colonel Fremont." He preened himself. If the occasion hadn't been so fraught, she would have found his smugness amusing. "She is a much more suitable match," he continued, "than you would ever have been. She is beautiful, refined, wealthy—"

"Then I wish you both much joy and happiness." If this new attachment would heal the harm she had caused him, assuage the bitterness he so obviously still felt . . .

"And there is not the slightest likelihood," he continued, "that she will lose all sense of decency and decorum and elope with an unnatural she-devil who should be hanged from the nearest gallows."

"You tell her, Fred," shouted the leaner of his two companions. The other man guffawed.

Christie had had enough. She stepped forward, only to be blocked by Fred once more. "Please," she said, wishing Marshal Milligan was nearby. "Let me pass."

"My dear," came a woman's shout, startling both of them, "I can't wait here all day. You promised to give me directions. Will you come now or must I find my way alone?"

Christie turned to see who the voice belonged to. Fred did likewise. A horse and four-seater buggy had stopped nearby, and its owner, an impressive looking woman in a black habit, veil, and pleated cape, was leaning out of it. To Christie's surprise, the nun seemed to be addressing her.

"I beg your pardon?"

"Come, child." The woman beckoned.

Though Christie had no idea what the nun wanted, it was too good a chance to miss. She pushed her way past the discomfited Fred toward the buggy.

"Climb in." After a brief hesitation, Christie took the outstretched hand and let herself be helped up. "Walk on." The buggy lurched into motion.

As they left Fred and the goggling bystanders behind, Christie regarded her rescuer. "I think you must have mistaken me for someone else."

Kind, gray eyes looked back at her. "Unlikely. The woman I'm after is small, pretty, has long fair hair, green eyes, is likely to be in some trouble or other—"

Christie's indignant protest died when she saw the twinkle in the nun's eyes. A suspicion began to form.

"Answers to the name 'Christie Hayes.' Have I missed anything?"

"Who *are* you? Do you know Zee?"

"Sister Florence of the Willows Orphanage, Fairbank, at your service, Miss Hayes. And yes, I have had the pleasure of making Deputy Brodie's acquaintance." They came to a junction, and the sister reined the horse to a halt and looked about her. "But I really *do* need directions. I am unfamiliar with Contention. Which way is it to your brother's house?"

A dazed Christie pointed out the way.

Chapter 11

"ZEE SENT YOU?" Christie and Sister Florence were sitting in Blue's parlor, drinking a reviving cup of tea from the best china, and Christie's heartbeat had at last calmed to something near normal.

"No, child. I had to bring Jenny Farnham's aunt home. Mrs. Archer is distraught at having lost her charge. And so is Mr. Farnham. They blame my establishment for its lax security, and I fear they may be right. I shall have to refund their donation and say forty Hail Marys as penance." Sister Florence seemed surprisingly cheerful at the prospect.

"Lost?" Christie held her breath.

"It seems that Jenny went missing in the night. Mrs. Archer fears some demon bent on evil intent spirited the girl away, and she said as much to the Fairbank marshal." Gray eyes flicked to Christie's face then away again.

Her heart sank. "The marshal's involved?"

"Nominally. He's an old friend of mind. It is my opinion that the girl ran away, and I told him so. It happens, on occasion, when a girl is held against her will. I do not think the marshal will be pursuing the case with his usual vigor."

"I see." Christie breathed a sigh of relief. So Zee's plan had worked. But where was she now?

"I thought you might." The nun smiled. "And so, since I was already in Contention, I thought I might as well call on you."

"I'm very glad you did."

Sister Florence gave her a sympathetic glance. "That unpleasant little man was your ex-fiancé?"

"Yes and no." Christie sighed. "Fred's not the man I knew. He's become cruel. I don't *think* he would have hurt me, but I certainly wasn't enjoying our encounter. Thank you for rescuing me."

"You're welcome." Sister Florence finished her tea and stood up. "Well, time is getting on and I have a long way to travel. I must be off."

Christie nodded and accompanied her out front where the horse and buggy were waiting. Several bystanders had gathered to speculate about the vehicle's owner. When they saw the black habit and veil, their eyes bulged. Christie suppressed a laugh. More food for the gossips.

The horse had finished its water, so Christie retrieved her pail. She helped Sister Florence up into the driving seat.

"I'm sorry to have missed your brother, Miss Hayes." Sister Florence gathered the reins. "Will you tell him that, though I have no knowledge of her present whereabouts, when I last saw his Jenny, she was in good health and spirits? I am sure he will be hearing from her soon."

"I will." Christie paused and debated whether to ask about Zee. "And, er . . . Deputy Brodie?"

Sister Florence winked. "Better keep a lamp burning in your window tonight, Miss Hayes. If I'm any judge of character, you can expect a visit of the romantic kind . . . Walk on."

THE SASH WINDOW jammed. Zee froze; it wasn't much of a squeak, but in the midnight silence it had sounded deafening.

She waited, expecting the rhythm of soft breathing coming from inside to alter . . . it didn't.

Been creeping into too many women's bedrooms lately. Hope this is the last.

She eyed the gap between the partially raised window and the ledge. It would be a tight squeeze, but it would do. She took off her hat and threw it inside, then went through head first, wincing as the ledge pressed into her ribs. Taking her weight on her gloved hands she did a controlled roll, coming to her feet in one smooth movement and scanning her surroundings.

The single bed was against the small room's far wall. She crossed to it in two strides and knelt beside its head. Christie's face looked peaceful in repose, the hair fanning out around her on the pillow giving the impression of an angel.

Zee pulled off her gloves and leaned toward Christie. "Darlin'," she whispered, placing her hand over Christie's mouth and feeling the warm breath on her palm.

Eyelids fluttered open and wide eyes stared up at her. Lips moved against her palm; she withdrew it.

"Zee!" Christie sat up and threw her arms around her.

So much for keeping the noise down, thought Zee. Then Christie's lips pressed passionately against hers, a tongue sought entrance, and she couldn't think of anything much anymore.

The bedroom door crashed open. "Are you all right, Christie? I heard— What in God's name? Get the hell away from my sister, you sonofabitch!"

Zee and Christie broke their kiss and turned, still short of breath, to stare at the silhouette in the doorway. Even in the starlight, Zee could tell a shotgun was pointing straight at her.

"Blue?" croaked Christie. She cleared her throat and tried again. "It's all right, Blue. It's Zee."

"What?" He disappeared from view and reappeared moments later with a lantern. He shoved it forward so the light fell on Zee.

"Howdy." She shaded her eyes against the glare.

"Brodie." His voice was flat. "What are you doing with my sister?"

"What does it look like?"

A blush stole over his face. "Oh." They locked gazes, neither willing to be the first to look away, and Zee was aware of Christie's eyes tracking between the two of them.

"Will you stop pointing that thing at me?" said Zee at last. "It's getting to be a habit."

He looked at the shotgun as though wondering how it had got there, then placed it on the floor.

"Much obliged." She perched on the edge of Christie's bed. A hand slipped into hers; she squeezed it. "Didn't mean to wake the whole household, but since you're here." She reached her free hand inside her vest pocket, pulled out a folded piece of paper, and held it toward Blue.

He stepped forward and took it. "What's this?"

"Directions. To Angie's Palace in Benson. Jenny's waiting for you there."

"Jenny?"

She rolled her eyes. "The blacksmith's daughter. Attractive girl . . . Belly out to here?" At the last remark, a finger prodded her in the back. She ignored it.

"I know who she is." Blue flushed. "But she made it clear she doesn't want me. She's going to marry Andrew LeRoy."

Zee turned to Christie. "Was this slowpoke dropped on his head as a baby?"

The question got her another prod and a whispered, "Don't be mean."

"Look," she said, as patiently as she was able—the feel and scent of Christie was making her itch to do things she shouldn't while a brother was present. "Farnham hornswoggled the both of you real good. Told *you* Jenny wanted to marry someone else. Told *her* you didn't want a baby complicating your life."

Blue's jaw worked. "She thought I didn't want her?" His voice was barely audible and the lantern light reflected off unshed tears.

"That's right." Zee gentled her voice. "But she knows better now. And she's waiting for you, in Benson." When he still showed no inclination to move, she added, "Thought you might need a horse. It's in the back yard."

"But the . . . the store . . ." Blue reminded Zee of a man coming awake after a nightmare, unsure whether it was over.

"Forget about the store," came Christie's soft voice. "You have no customers anyway."

"Damned right," chimed in Zee. "Anyway, what's more important? The store or your happiness?"

"Go to her, Blue," urged his sister. "What are you waiting for?"

The transformation had continued while they spoke. Blue's shoulders no longer slumped; his eyes were bright. "She's in Benson and she wants me?" His voice was questioning, almost shy.

Zee nodded.

He reread the note again, twice, then beamed from ear to ear. "Sonofabitch! She's in Benson and she wants me."

Zee exchanged a wry glance with Christie. "Reckon he's got it."

"A horse, you said?"

"Yeah. A gray. In your yard." She gave Christie a sidelong glance. "Probably eating your flowers. Will you stop prodding me?" She rubbed her back and pouted.

A grinning Blue was already turning, almost tripping over the shotgun in his haste. The door slammed closed behind him.

Christie shook her head. "Where are his manners? On Blue's behalf, I'd like to say thank you, Zee."

"It's all right, darlin'. It's understood." She turned and pulled Christie toward her. "Now. Where were we?"

"Here, I believe."

While they kissed, Zee registered the sound of drawers opening and closing in the room next door, followed by footsteps thundering down the stairs. The back door crashed open and shut, and in the yard a horse whinnied.

A thought struck her and she broke the kiss. "And make sure you marry the girl," she yelled.

"I will," came Blue's faint reply.

As hoofbeats faded into the distance, eager lips reclaimed Zee's and she laughed and rolled onto her back, stretching out on the bed and pulling Christie on top of her.

ZEE YAWNED, SQUINTED against the bright sunlight, and listened to the sounds of Contention waking up. Through the still half-open window drifted the clip clop of a horse going past, the rumble of a buckboard's wheels, a shouted "Good Morning."

She stretched, careful not to disturb the naked woman draped over her—Christie's nightdress had ended up on the far side of the room, along with Zee's boots and most of her clothes. A fair head nestled against her breast. Zee's gaze traveled on, lingering on the curve of a shoulder, the tapered waist, the swelling buttocks—her own feet shattered the vision of loveliness. They were jutting over the end of the tiny bed.

Damn! Got another hole in my sock. She wiggled the offending big toe and yawned again.

It was long past their usual getting up time, but Zee felt no urge to rise. Her recent exertions had tuckered her out. They had made love twice, pent up passion making the first time fast and furious and causing them both to cry out—partly, in Zee's case, because she had aggravated her ribs. Later, they had taken things more slowly and tenderly, but still reached an intensity that left Zee shaking and a tearful Christie in need of cradling.

She drew a circle with her index finger on a downy back that begged to be touched, and Christie gave a contented sigh and snuggled closer.

"We should probably get up," came a muffled voice a little later.

Christie breath was warm on Zee's breast. "Hey, that tickles!"

"What does?" A tousled head rose and green eyes regarded her.

"Nothing."

A smile curved Christie's mouth as she took in her position. "This?" A pink tongue darted out.

Zee sucked in her breath and sat up, then pressed a rueful hand to her ribs.

Christie sat up too. "Still sore?" She nodded. "Your bandage needs changing." It was indeed coming adrift.

"Later," said Zee. "Got other things to do this morning."

"Such as?"

"Take care of Fred." Christie's face fell, and Zee studied her. "Want to tell me about it?"

She sighed. "I think the best thing Blue and I can do is leave Contention altogether. Fred is never going to forgive me."

"Figure it's time to drop that idea anyway, darlin'."

Christie's surprise gave way to curiosity and annoyance. "Do you mean to tell me that I've been letting Fred humiliate me and all the while you have something on him?"

"Only found the lever we need yesterday. Would have told you earlier, only we had other things on our minds." Zee leered.

Christie drummed her fingers on her thigh and gave Zee a pointed look. "I'm listening."

"All right. It seems Fred has set himself up in the mine salting business."

Christie's eyebrows shot up. "He's defrauded someone?"

"Yeah. Used high grade ore from his father's mill to make it look like a friend's clapped out silver mine is a going concern. Sold it to an English ninny with more money than sense."

Christie's eyes clouded. "What's the matter with him, Zee? He has everything he could want: friends, wealth, connections . . . And he's just got engaged to Colonel Fremont's daughter, Cecilia. Why would he risk all that?"

Zee kissed her on the nose. "Not *everything*," she corrected. "He ain't got you."

Chapter 12

CHRISTIE TIDIED AWAY the breakfast things and glanced at Zee. The deputy had her feet up on the kitchen table and was leafing through an illustrated "erotic handbook" that Christie had purchased via mail order last year and then been too apprehensive to open.

When Zee had found the racy book in Christie's underwear drawer (what she was doing in there, heaven knows) Christie's face had burned with embarrassment. But rather than being shocked or laughing at her, Zee had chucked her under the chin and settled down to read it. Christie suspected that Blue's reaction would have been considerably different.

Zee turned the book sideways. "Good Lord! Is that possible?" A dark eyebrow rose in mock astonishment. "The things you read, Miss Hayes. Are you sure this hasn't corrupted you?"

Christie flicked the tea towel at her. "Of course it has. Why else do you think I ran off with you?"

"Good looks and charm?" Zee turned another page. "Maybe we should try that?"

Curiosity got the better of Christie and she leaned over to check the illustration. Her cheeks heated. "Um. I'd rather not."

Zee laughed and winked. "Just teasing." She patted Christie on the rear. "Shame though. Looks rather pleasurable." Christie looked at her, and Zee threw up her hands. "All right, all right." She closed the slender volume and tossed it aside, then stood up and stretched, a wince crossing her face.

"Your ribs?" Christie took off her apron and folded it.

"They're fine. C'mon. Let's get you over to the store."

Christie sighed. She had wanted to accompany Zee when she confronted Fred's father, but Zee wasn't having it.

"You'd be walking into the lion's den, darlin'," she'd said. "You told me you weren't that popular with his folks when you were their prospective daughter-in-law. How do you think they feel about you now?"

"But—"

"And if Fred and his cronies are there . . ." Zee pulled the disappointed Christie close and stroked her hair. "It ain't safe. Let me handle this. Let me put a spoke in his wheel he can't pull out. If nothing else, I owe him for the whupping he gave me."

So she had sighed and agreed to mind Blue's store instead.

Zee reached for her boots and pulled them on, then appraised Christie. "You going into town like that?" She buckled her gun belt and settled it on her hips.

"What's wrong with it?"

"Not a thing. Can tell you left off your corset though."

Christie looked down at herself and blushed. Zee's arrival had upset her routine and she had automatically dressed the way she did while in Benson. "No one else will be looking at me the way you do."

"Don't bet on it."

She hesitated, then shrugged. People were going to be scandalized as it was; what did one more thing matter? Jutting her jaw a little, she grabbed her bonnet and tied the ribbons under her chin.

Zee crammed her own hat on her head and reached for her gloves. "Got everything you need?"

Christie draped her shawl round her shoulders, checked that the keys to the dry goods store were in her bag, and nodded.

WELL, THIS IS interesting, reflected Christie, *and an experience I am in no hurry to repeat.*

She was walking into town, head up and shoulders back, trying to ignore the shocked looks and frowns coming their way and to keep up with Zee's long-legged stride.

"Sorry," murmured Zee, slowing her pace. "That better?"

"Much. Thank you."

Being seen with Zee was certainly sorting out who Christie's real friends were. Mrs. McPherson stepped off the sidewalk and crossed the street. *That makes three.*

"Is it me they object to, or you, or that we are back together again?" she whispered.

"Does it matter?"

"Not really." But she regarded Zee with new eyes. Her Hellcat past meant she must encounter this kind of hostility all the time.

It was just their luck that the one person Christie *wanted* to ignore them made a beeline for them. Contention's chief gossip spoke when she was still a few yards away.

"Good morning, Miss Hayes." Black eyes gleamed as they turned toward Zee. "I don't believe we've been introduced. I'm Cora Chase."

"Deputy Brodie." Zee tipped her hat but kept on walking, her hand under Christie's elbow making sure she did the same. The plump woman in blue was forced to get out of their way or be mowed down. Wisely, she chose to step aside.

"Nice meeting you," called Zee.

Christie glanced back at the frustrated figure staring after them and snorted. "That was mean."

"Did you *want* to talk to her?"

"No."

"Well, then."

Up ahead, a scrawny woman in a buttoned-to-the-neck black dress appeared. She stopped dead in the middle of the sidewalk, put a hand to her mouth, then crossed herself and fled back the way she had come.

"Something I said?" asked Zee.

"Wife of the Presbyterian minister. She thinks you're the Devil incarnate."

Zee grinned. "I'm working on it."

"Hey, Brodie. Miss Hayes," came a man's voice from behind. "Hold up a minute."

Zee came to a halt and turned round. "Howdy, Milligan."

Christie turned in time to see Pat Milligan clasp Zee's hand. She smiled at him and he tipped his hat.

"Giving our sheltered townsfolk something to talk about?" He fell into step beside the two women as they picked up the pace once more and headed toward Commercial Street.

"Guess so." Zee glanced at Christie. "All we need for a Full House is a nun. But she went home. Ain't that right, darlin'?" Christie snorted.

Milligan gave them a baffled look. "Er . . . yes, well, so, where are you off to?"

"I'm minding the store," said Christie.

"Is Blue ill?"

"No, he's gone to Benson."

"And I'm off to see Fred's Pa," chipped in Zee. "To tell him a few home truths about his son."

The marshal's brow creased. "He ain't gonna like that, Brodie. Need any help?"

"No thanks." Zee patted the butt of one Colt. "Got all the help I need."

"If you're sure . . ." He turned to Christie. "What kind of business does your brother have in Benson, Miss Hayes?"

Zee beat her to the draw. "Gone to see a girl about a wedding."

For a moment Milligan looked puzzled then his brow cleared. "Jenny Farnham?"

Christie nodded.

"Last I heard she'd gone missing."

"Really?" Zee brushed a speck of something from her vest. "Last I heard, she'd turned up."

Milligan looked at her then at Christie. He stroked his mustache. "Had she now?"

"Seems so." Zee gave him her butter-wouldn't-melt smile and Christie stifled a laugh.

He opened his mouth to ask another question, then thought better of it. "Pass on my good wishes to the young couple when next you see them, will you?"

Christie nodded.

They reached Blue's store and halted outside it. Milligan tipped his hat to them and disappeared in the direction of the jail.

Christie pulled out the bunch of keys, selected one, and slid it into the lock. It turned stiffly, making a grating noise. She made a mental note to oil it then paused with her hand on the door handle and looked up at Zee.

"Are you coming in?"

Zee shook her head. "Sooner I deal with Younger, sooner we can go back to Benson."

"I'd like that too," said Christie, meaning it. "This town doesn't feel like home any more." The remark obviously pleased Zee though she didn't comment on it.

"Be back as soon as I can, darlin'."

"Are you sure I can't come with you?"

"Best not."

"I know, I know. I'm as popular with the Youngers as horse dung on Fred's high-heeled shoes."

"Such language!" Zee grinned. "You've been spending too much time with Angie's girls. At least *this* piece of dung," she indicated herself, "has information that'll guarantee her a hearing."

"You'll be careful?"

Zee raised Christie's hand to her mouth and pressed her lips to it. "Ain't I always?"

THE DOORBELL TINKLED and Christie looked up from the bolt of serge she was straightening. Milligan was standing in the doorway.

"Just checking you're all right, Miss Hayes."

"I'm fine." She blinked at him. "What time is it?"

"Eleven o'clock."

Where had the time gone? And why hadn't Zee returned yet?

He advanced further into the store. "I just took a walk past Younger's place. No sign of a disturbance."

What was Zee doing in there—playing checkers? "I suppose that's a good thing."

He nodded. "Well. Since you're all right." He tipped his hat. "I'll be on my way."

"Thanks, Marshal. It was kind of you to look in on me."

When he'd gone, Christie tried to picture Zee talking to the wealthy mill owner in the library—Fred had once told her his father had read none of the books on his shelves; he purchased them by the yard. A setting like that would make Zee feel ill at ease. She thought about that for a bit then corrected herself. No. Zee would feel at home anywhere. It was Christie herself who would feel ill at ease.

When Fred was still on his best behavior and trying to impress Christie, she had visited the Younger mansion several times. It wasn't a home, more a gloomy museum. Four times as large as the house she had shared with Blue, its numerous rooms were stuffed with high quality furniture from San Francisco. Every surface boasted crystal vases and fragile ornaments (Caroline Younger referred to them as *objets d'art*) which had been shipped over from Europe. Christie was always terrified she would break something.

It wasn't just her own feelings of inadequacy, she realized with hindsight, it was the supercilious way in which Fred's family treated her. Once, she asked if she might play their grand piano (hers was a little upright instrument, whose timbre couldn't compare), but his mother had flat out refused. Caroline Younger gave no reason, but Christie suspected she thought her future daughter-in-law's indelicate touch would force the instrument to go too quickly out of tune.

She ground her teeth as she remembered the countless humiliations, the nagging. Fred, his snobbish sister Julia, his mother . . . everyone except his father, always in the library discussing matters of business, kept offering her unwanted pieces of advice.

"You should wear something more fashionable, Christie. Here, have a look at the latest *Godey's Lady's Book*." "Your hair style is sadly behind the times, Miss Hayes. Why not try wearing a hairpiece? It would make all the difference." "It's best not to use such a common expression when referring to that, my dear. We always say . . ." "Christie, you are standing like a milkmaid. Stand up straight and try to look more refined."

If she was so beneath them, why on earth had Fred asked her to marry him in the first place?

Because he intended to mold me into something else.

It was a minor revelation and one that made her appreciate Zee all the more. Fred's family had never accepted her for who she was. Right from the start, Zee had.

Chapter 13

ZEE HALTED AT the end of the drive and stared. Christie hadn't warned her that Alexander Younger (or his architect) was an aficionado of the Gothic Revival style sweeping the West. Arched windows and doorways and a steeply gabled roof might suit a church, but on a residential house in an Arizona mining town they looked ridiculous.

It was surely no coincidence that Younger had built his house here in the wealthy part of Contention, as far from his silver mill as possible. No choking dust, no rumbling day and night from the huge presses grinding the ore, could be allowed to disturb *his* rest.

She continued up the drive. At one window a lace curtain twitched. *Someone's home.*

Zee mounted the step up to the front porch and reached for the brass knocker. Before she could grasp it, the solid oak door opened.

"May I help you?" The mousy young woman was wearing a black and white maid's uniform.

Zee took off her hat. "Mr. Younger, please. Mr. Alexander Younger. He at home?"

"Who is at the door, Nellie?" The voice was muffled but familiar.

The maid turned her head and spoke to someone in the hall. "A visitor for Mr. Younger, sir."

"I'll take care of it," said the voice.

Nellie's brows drew together, but she stood aside. A dapper little man with a Vandyke beard took her place.

"What the devil do *you* want?" asked Fred.

"With you? Nothing. With your father? Reckon that's between him and me."

"Clear off." Ignoring the protests from the shocked maid, Fred slammed the door in Zee's face . . . or tried to. She had stuck her booted foot in the gap. For a short and painful period, he continued to try to force the door closed, then he opened it again.

"Now that ain't what I call hospitable," chided Zee.

"Damned if I'm going to let the Hellcat into my house."

"*Your* house?" She pressed her palm flat against his chest and pushed him out of her way.

As she stepped into the hall, the maid looked at her with wide eyes. Zee plucked the note she had written earlier from her vest pocket and held it out.

"Be mighty obliged, Nellie, if you'd give this to your employer. It explains the business I'm here to discuss."

"Do no such thing," Fred told the maid. "This person is leaving, or I will have her thrown out."

Zee crossed to a chair and sat down. "Yeah? Just try it." She placed her upturned hat on the little table beside the chair, pulled off her gloves finger by finger, and dropped them into it.

The maid hadn't moved. Her gaze kept flicking between Zee, Fred, and the piece of paper in her fingers.

"Mr. Younger will agree to see me," said Zee, "once he reads my note."

"What *is* all this commotion?" A voice wafted down from the top of the stairs and all present turned to regard the woman descending. Her clothes looked expensive and were no doubt up-to-the-minute, and she frowned at Zee's male attire and the tin star pinned to her vest. "And who is *this*?"

She was too young to be Alexander Younger's wife. Must be his daughter, decided Zee.

"Name's Deputy Brodie. I'm here to see your father."

"Deputy Br— The one who stole that pathetic little fiancée of yours, Fred?" Zee bridled at this characterization of Christie but kept her thoughts to herself. "About what, may I ask?"

"As I was just telling your brother, that's between—" Zee paused as Fred suddenly noticed that the maid had taken advantage of the distraction to slip away and rushed after her.

"Come back, Nellie. I thought I told you—"

While Fred's sister gaped after him, Zee studied the paintings on the wall. Old Masters presumably; worth a few dollars, but far too dark and gloomy for her taste. She preferred landscapes or horses; Christie liked cheerful pictures—dogs, children, that kind of thing. Each to their own. Angie favored imported erotic prints. Zee had always preferred doing to watching; that little book of Christie's had given her a few ideas.

A shadow fell over her, and she looked up to find the sister frowning at her. "Yeah?"

"I think you should leave. Now."

"That's queer. So does your brother. But I'll leave when I've talked to your father."

"He won't talk to you. He knows who you are. *What* you are. And what you did to Fred, to our family. You are not welcome in this house."

Zee shrugged. "Let him tell me that himself and I'll go."

Somewhere in the interior, a door opened. Footsteps grew louder. Zee squinted through the gloom. A large, rather overweight man came into sight. Close behind him, gesturing and protesting, came Fred. Zee stood up and reached for her hat.

"Deputy Brodie?"

The new arrival stopped in front of her. Unlike his offspring, Younger senior was an imposing figure. His clothes were of the finest quality, conservatively cut, and he favored old-fashioned whiskers. His gaze was difficult to fathom—hostility and curiosity combined.

"That's me." She held out a hand; he looked at it for a moment then shook it. "Mr. Younger, I presume." A spluttering sound came from his daughter's direction. Zee ignored her.

"You presume correctly. Your note said you have some business to discuss?" She nodded. "Very well. Follow me." He turned back the way he had come.

Fred's face was beet red. "But father, she's the one—"

"I know very well who she is." Younger's eyes swiveled and found Zee again. "This way, Deputy." With a smirk at the fuming siblings, Zee followed.

He led her toward a door at the far end of the hall then gestured for her to enter. She found herself in a large room that reeked of tobacco; the shelves lining its walls groaned with leather-covered books. He closed the door behind them, shutting out the sound of heated conversation.

"Sit." Younger took an armchair in front of the unlit fireplace and gestured at the other chair. She took it.

On an adjacent occasional table lay a silver handbell and the note she had asked Nellie to give him, opened. He rang the bell. The door opened and the maid came in.

"Sir?"

"Some refreshments for our guest, Nellie." His gaze turned to Zee. "Tea? Coffee? Sherry? Lemonade?"

"Nothing, thanks." She flashed a smile at the maid then at her host. "But don't let me stop you."

"None for me. That will be all." The maid bobbed a curtsey and exited.

Alone once more, they regarded one another. The silence stretched.

Younger was the first to give in. He reached for the note lying on the table, and held it up. "Is this a threat?"

"It's a statement of fact."

His eyes narrowed. "This 'sensitive information' you say you have about my son . . . What makes you think I mind whether it is made public or not?"

"Reckon you're a man who cares about his hard-won reputation." She raised an eyebrow. "Am I right?"

There was another long pause. "Yes," he said finally. "I would take a very dim view of anyone who tried to tarnish my good name."

"And if the tarnisher was your own son?"

He stood up and began to pace in front of the fireplace. "Why should I believe your lies, Deputy Brodie? I know who you are. I know what you did, how you seduced Miss Hayes and corrupted her." Zee examined a fingernail. "For all I know," he continued, "this is just a continuation of your rivalry with Fred." He stopped pacing.

She looked up. "Mr. Younger. This ain't about rivalry. Frankly, I'd prefer to have nothing more to do with your son; the man's mean as a rattler, and his friends ain't no better. But he's set on hurting me and mine, and I can't allow that. Pardon my plain speaking."

Alexander Younger's cheeks had reddened, and she thought he was going to tell her to leave. But he got a grip on his temper and said, "I must confess, in recent times the boy has been a severe disappointment to me, as for his friends . . ." He trailed off and shook his head. "But he's still my son." He resumed his seat.

She leaned forward. "That's why I've come to you rather than to the town marshal."

His face paled. "Has Fred really done something to bring shame to my family?"

"Yeah."

"You can substantiate this accusation?"

"Sure can."

The fight seemed to go out of the old man, and he sighed and leaned back in his armchair. "Very well." He steepled his fingers. "You'd better tell me all about it."

So she did.

NELLIE PUT DOWN the tray of drinks, cast a curious glance at her now pale employer and scurried out. Alexander Younger picked up the half-full whiskey decanter and filled the two glasses on the tray. He pushed one toward Zee and drained the other himself.

While he refilled his glass, Zee sipped hers. It was hard to believe the smooth amber liquor bore the same name as that rotgut they served in the Golden Slipper.

The color had just about returned to his cheeks when he spoke. "What will it take for you not to go public with this?"

Triumph surged through her, but she kept her poker face in place. "First," she ticked off the points on her fingers, "Lord Camborne gets his money back. By now, he should realize the silver mine Fred and his friend sold him is worthless. Reckon he'll be feeling pretty foolish and more than willing to keep it quiet if the sale is declared null and void."

Younger grunted. "Go on."

"Second. Fred stays out of Contention and Benson." She considered for a moment then amended it. "Hell, out of the Territory entirely works better. Crux of the matter is, from now on he stays away from both Christie and Blue. He's caused the Hayes family enough grief."

"Fred's mother will object to not being able to see her son—"

"It's not negotiable." Zee's gaze was hard.

Anger flared behind Younger's eyes, then faded, replaced by thoughtfulness. "I had been wondering whether Fred might not benefit from some time in Europe. Many young men have their horizons broadened by a Grand Tour." He stroked his whiskers. "It won't suit Cecilia Fremont, of course. But that can't be helped." He nodded. "I'll talk to Caroline about it."

"Do that. Third. The Fabric Emporium Fred got you to open on Commercial Street, opposite Hayes's store. It closes, today."

Younger scratched his whiskers then shrugged. "All right. Is that it?"

"One final condition. But I don't think it'll be hard to fulfill. Put Blue Hayes up for membership of the Cactus Club. His name was proposed once before, but your son blackballed him." He had the grace to look shamefaced. "With you as his sponsor that shouldn't happen a second time."

Younger stood up and crossed to a bureau, from which he retrieved a box of cigars. He brought it back to his seat, flipped open the lid, and took one, then gestured to Zee to help herself.

She started to reach for one then remembered what Christie had said and shook her head. "No thanks."

He shrugged and busied himself clipping and lighting his cigar. She waited until thick smoke was curling toward the ceiling.

"Well. Is it a deal or ain't it?"

Younger blew out a smoke ring. "You've got yourself a deal."

Chapter 14

CHRISTIE WAS GAZING out of the window when an officious-looking man reined his horse to a halt outside the busy store across the street. She watched him dismount, tether his horse to the hitching rail, and barge his way inside.

She was just turning away, when the store's customers began to file out onto the sidewalk, some red-faced and gesticulating. A "closed" sign appeared in one of the windows. Then the rider emerged and rode away.

"Well!" she murmured, registering the tinkle of the doorbell. "Wonder what *that* was about."

"Ain't it obvious?"

She swung round. Zee was standing in her doorway, a smug grin on her face. Christie beamed at her. "What took you so long?"

As Zee advanced into the store, Christie threw herself at her and gave her a bear hug.

"Ribs, darlin'."

"Sorry." She relinquished her grip and stood back, scrutinizing Zee. "Are you all right? When you didn't come back . . ." But she could see no evidence of fresh injury.

"Took me a while to find the Younger place, that's all. Getting past his offspring slowed me up some too. Saw him in the end though." She took Christie's elbow and guided her back to the window. "Went like clockwork."

"He agreed to call Fred off?"

"See for yourself." Zee gestured, and Christie saw that shutters were going up on the store across the street.

That rider must've been Younger's messenger. "Blue will be very happy to get his customers back."

"Yeah." An arm circled Christie's shoulders and she leaned into it. "Looks like it's working already too. That couple is headed this way."

Two of the thwarted customers—a fat woman in a bustle and bonnet, and a beanpole of a man with a walrus mustache—were indeed crossing the street toward the dry goods store. Christie recognized the Munros.

"Oh." She shook off Zee's arm, tidied her hair as best she could, and straightened her apron.

"You could always put up the 'closed' sign," suggested Zee.

Christie ignored her, scuttled behind the counter, and tried to look nonchalant as the door opened, tinkling the bell.

"Good morning, Mrs. Munro, Mr. Munro." She smiled her best smile. "Nice to see you."

"Miss Hayes." The fat woman frowned. "Is your brother not here today?" Her husband's gaze slid over Zee, who was lounging against the counter, and then away again.

"No. He's not . . . What may I get for you?"

"Oh . . . er . . . Ten yards of dimity, please."

Christie ran her gaze along the shelves and grimaced. Blue kept the bolts of that particular corded-cotton material on the very top shelf. She would need the little stepladder from the back. "We have a good selection of stripes and checks, as you can see. Which one would you like?"

Mrs. Munro pursed her lips. "I'm not sure. Could I see that one," she pointed, "and that one."

Christie nodded and was turning to fetch the steps when a hand on her arm halted her. Zee eased past her.

"Allow me." Zee reached up and lifted down the bolts in question then placed the heavy rolls of fabric on the counter as though they weighed no more than thistledown.

Christie shot her a grateful smile and began to unroll the material for Mrs. Munro's inspection.

"So, Mrs. Munro." She spread out the pale-blue striped dimity. "What do you think?"

"Hm." A fat thumb and forefinger rubbed the material between them. "A good thickness," she said grudgingly. "But I don't know. That pink." She turned to her husband. "What do you think, dear? The blue or the pink?"

Munro shrugged and looked out the window. Choosing material was clearly women's work in his eyes. His wife turned back to Christie. "The blue," she said. "I'll have the blue."

"Ten yards you said?" Christie fetched Blue's dressmaking shears, measured the material against the gauge glued along the counter's edge, and cut off a length. While Zee restored the bolts to their rightful places on the top shelf, Christie folded the dimity, wrapped it in some brown paper, and tied it with string. *There.* She gave the parcel a satisfied glance. *Even Blue couldn't fault that.*

The price book was under the counter and she retrieved it and checked the cost. "That'll be three dollars, please."

"*How* much?" Mrs. Munro looked outraged. "They were selling dimity for twenty-five cents a yard across the street."

"Then perhaps you shoulda gone there," said Zee.

It was the first time she had addressed the woman, and Mrs. Munro started, like a horse on hearing a rattler. Mr. Munro turned from viewing the street outside—the other store's disgruntled customers had dispersed—and came to stand protectively beside his wife.

Christie shot Zee a quelling look. "I'm sorry if you think it's too much, Mrs. Munro. Blue costed it carefully, and I know my brother—he wouldn't set a price that isn't fair."

Mrs. Munro looked as though she was going to disagree, but a hard stare from Zee made her close her mouth and shuffle closer to her husband. "Very well." She opened her drawstring bag and counted out the exact money. "But I shall have to think twice before recommending your establishment to my friends."

Christie took the money and put it in the empty till. "I'm sorry to hear that."

Mrs. Munro sniffed, tucked her brown paper parcel under one arm, and marched out of the store, her husband giving Zee a wary look before following her.

As the door swung closed behind them, Zee called a sarcastic, "Pleasure doing business with you." Then she vaulted over the counter, locked the door, and flipped the sign in the window round to "Closed."

"What are you doing? It's not even dinnertime yet and—"

"Far as I'm concerned, it's time to go home." Zee strolled back toward Christie.

"What about the store?"

Zee leaned her elbows on the counter, bringing the two of them face to face. "We didn't come to Contention to run a store."

"But—" A sloppy kiss on the nose stopped Christie. "Zee!" She blushed and wiped her wet nose with one hand.

Zee grinned and straightened up. "I'll ask Milligan to keep an eye on the place until Blue gets back. If your brother wants to stay in Benson awhile longer, he'll have to find someone to run the store in his absence."

Christie pursed her lips and considered. The store *was* Blue's responsibility. She and Zee had their own lives to lead. And she very much wanted to get back to them.

"You're right." She undid her apron and hung it on a hook. "I'll close up."

"Atta girl."

Chapter 15

AS IS ALWAYS the way, it took far less time to pack for the return trip to Benson than it had for the trip out. There was no careful selecting of items that might be needed, it was just a case of spotting things that didn't belong in Blue's house and stowing them in the luggage. Even so, it took Christie longer than a fidgety Zee wanted.

"Will you stop pacing up and down?" asked Christie. "There's plenty of time before the train leaves."

Zee sighed and threw herself on the bed. "I know." She clasped her arms behind her head. "It's just that . . . the sooner we leave, the better."

Christie stopped her packing. "What's wrong?"

"Just a hunch."

"About?"

"Fred."

"But his father said—"

"I know." Zee pushed herself up off the bed and began to pace once more. "But if Fred's the hothead I think he is, he won't take kindly to his father making deals involving his future, even if it's aimed at keeping his sorry carcass out of jail. He'll come looking for me 'stead of thinking things through."

Christie considered that for a moment, compared the man she had known with the person he was now. Fred's pride had always been easily hurt, she remembered. Then he would lose his temper. She chewed her lower lip. "Maybe we should tell Milligan."

Zee stopped her pacing. "It's not my safety I'm worried about, darlin'."

Christie blinked in confusion. "I'm sorry, Zee, I don't quite—"

"What if he comes after me and I have to kill him?" Somber blue eyes regarded her. "How will you feel about me then?"

"How will I . . .?" Christie stepped forward and slipped her arms around Zee's waist. "Oh, sweetheart." She leaned her head against Zee's chest, felt strong arms come up to hold her. "Nothing could change the way I feel about you."

"Nothing?"

She thought for a long moment. "Well, if you were to bed Red Mary again . . ."

Zee chuckled. "You really don't like her, do you?"

She wrinkled her nose. "No."

Zee kissed her then drew back. "You don't have to worry about her, you know."

"I know." Christie smiled.

She stepped out of Zee's arms and continued her packing, thinking of what Zee had said. When she had folded the last item and closed up the case, she turned to the waiting deputy.

"Even so," she said, "if possible, I'd rather you didn't kill him."

Zee's brows drew together. "Why?"

"Because he's so far beneath you, he's not worth it. And anyway," Christie picked up one of the lighter cases and headed for the stairs, "you made a deal with his father."

THEY HAD ALMOST reached the station depot when, from nowhere, a lariat dropped round Christie's shoulders.

"Zee!"

Zee, who was one step behind her, let out an oath.

The rope tightened, pinning Christie's arms to her sides and pulling her off balance. She dropped the case she was carrying, dug in her heels, and squirmed, trying to see if Zee was all right but failing. All she could hear was scuffling, solid blows finding their target, a man swearing then shouting out a warning, the sound of gunfire.

"Zee," she called out again, afraid.

A hand clamped over Christie's mouth. "Quiet and you won't get hurt."
Fred!

He turned her so her back was toward him, and held her. She shuddered as his body pressed against hers, but at least now she could see what was going on.

The lariat meant for Zee had been sliced to ribbons. Zee herself was intent on taking down the last of three attackers. Two were already disabled—one was clutching his thigh, trying to staunch the flow of blood from a knife wound, the other was holding his privates, rocking and moaning high in his throat.

Smoke curled from Zee's Colts as she stalked toward the third man. His hand was bleeding, his own holster empty—Christie scanned the ground and spotted the revolver Zee must have shot out of his hand. As he backed, he tripped over one of the cases. Before he could regain his balance, Zee had darted forward and clipped his chin a resounding blow with a gun butt. His eyes rolled up in his head and he toppled over backward.

Fred swore and tightened his grip on Christie.

Zee straightened and turned to face him, eyes glacial. "Let her go." She hefted the revolver in her right hand.

"Or what?" He tried to sound defiant, but Christie could smell the fear on him, hear it in his voice. "You wouldn't risk hurting her." He pulled Christie even closer.

"Wouldn't I?" Zee raised the gun, cocked it, and took careful aim.

Christie's heart threatened to pound its way out of her chest, and she screwed her eyes tight shut. Then came a single deafening gunshot. Fred yelped; his grip on her disappeared; the lariat loosened and dropped away; and Christie realized she was still in the land of the living.

The first thing she saw when she opened her eyes was Zee's concerned face gazing at her. She stepped out of the lariat, which had pooled around her feet, and staggered toward Zee.

"You all right?" A gloved hand steadied her.

Christie nodded and turned to look at Fred. He was kneeling, clutching his right shoulder, his shirtsleeve soaked with blood. Zee gave her a comforting pat on the shoulder, then stalked over and looked down at him.

"Don't kill me." Fred looked terrified and close to tears.

"Don't intend to." Zee hauled him to his feet. "Up you get."

He gave her a confused look. "Why not? I would've killed you."

"Made a promise to someone." She winked at Christie, then reached for one of the sliced pieces of lariat and began to bind his hands. "Reckon you musta been missing the day they gave out brains, Younger," she continued. "Your pa and me made a deal to keep you out of the calaboose, but it seems you're bound and determined to end up there." Dismay warred with indignation on Fred's face. "It won't be for fraud—gave my word on that. But you can't expect to bushwhack me and my lady and get away with it."

Fred's shoulders slumped. He was plainly no longer a threat, so Christie dismissed him from her thoughts and set about collecting her bags.

Zee looked up from tying up the rest of Fred's friends and smiled at her. "We'll drop these packages off at Milligan's, darlin'. Then we've got a train to catch."

Chapter 16

ZEE RAN A finger round the inside of her collar. *This is gonna chafe.* "Why'd you have to use so much starch?"

Christie turned from her position in front of the mirror. "It's a wedding, Zee. You have to look dressy for a wedding." She turned back to the mirror, smoothed the dress Julie Fontenot had helped her make over her hips, and cocked her head first to one side then the other. "Hair up or hair down?"

The question was clearly rhetorical so Zee ignored it. "Dressy, huh? Don't see why," she grumbled. She undid the shirt's top two buttons, reached for a clean red bandanna, and tied it round her neck. *That should help.*

Christie gathered up her hair and did something complicated involving hairpins. Zee could never be bothered with stuff like that—it was one of the reasons she kept her own hair cropped—but she had to admit, the end result was worth it.

Christie jumped as Zee dipped her head and nibbled the enticing nape of her neck. "That tickles!"

"Ain't quite what I had in mind," mumbled Zee, reaching round and cupping Christie's breasts. She checked the blonde's reaction in the mirror. Christie's lips were parted, her eyelids closed, the long lashes pale against flushed skin. With a grin Zee continued her attentions, sucking a tender earlobe, stroking the generous curves she could feel beneath the fabric.

Christie recollected herself and shook Zee off. "Not now. We'll be late."

"Some things are worth being late for." But Christie avoided her reaching hands and wagged her finger at her. She sighed and backed off.

On the bed lay the embroidered waistcoat Hogan had lent Zee. She slipped it on and buttoned it up. It was a bit loose on her, and too fancy for her taste, but still . . .

"You look nice." Christie had finished with her hair and was regarding Zee with a critical eye. "There's a spot on the toe of your right boot."

She made to rub it off on the back of her Levi's.

"Not on your clean trousers!"

Zee rolled her eyes, reached for a dirty bandanna, and bent to remove the offending mud. "That better?" She straightened and let Christie circle her.

Christie finished her inspection, smiled, and nodded. "You'll do."

Zee let out a sigh of relief.

They had got back from Contention the day before, and, after dropping off their luggage at the Old Barn and retrieving their horses from the Shaws, headed over to Angie's Palace to see how Blue and Jenny were getting on. There, Angie greeted them with a broad smile, the news that Blue had managed to get a wedding license, and an embossed invitation to the happy couple's wedding on the morrow when the marrying squire was due.

Zee received the news tranquilly. She'd been to quite a few weddings in her time. The ceremonies were quickly over, and she always enjoyed the celebrations that followed. This state of happy anticipation lasted until Christie told her in no uncertain terms that she must dress for the occasion.

She sighed and looked for her hat, from which Christie had sponged the worst of the dirt. It was on the dresser. She crammed it on her head then looked at herself in the mirror.

"See," said Christie from behind her. "You can look quite presentable when you try."

Still not sure about the waistcoat, Zee grunted. A smack on her bottom startled her out of her introspection. "Hey!"

"Come on, handsome," said Christie. "Time to see my brother make an honest woman of Jenny."

ZEE SURVEYED HER surroundings with interest. Angie had closed up the Palace for the day and transformed her largest reception room for the wedding. The card tables had been stacked away or were lined up at the side, draped beneath pretty tablecloths and awaiting the arrival of the buffet Hattie was preparing in the kitchen. Most of the ornate gold mirrors had been covered. Which was more than could be said for the whores. Even done up in their Sunday best, their dresses were cut far too low.

She smirked at the sight of them mingling with more respectable folks. Their profession was all too obvious. As was that of the black habit-clad nuns. Sister Florence had brought a few of her Sisters of Charity with her—they were apparently looking forward to the day out. It was just as well Jenny's parents hadn't been invited to the wedding, mused Zee. (It was thought best to present them with a *fait accompli*.) They would have had a fit.

"Blue looks terrified." Christie was eyeing the forlorn figure standing at the front.

"Can't imagine why."

"Suppose Jenny changes her mind?" Christie was too agitated to register Zee's irony. "Suppose she jilts him at the altar?"

"Well, for one thing," said Zee, "there ain't no altar. And for another, in her condition? Ain't likely. I'm just hoping she don't give birth during the ceremony."

Christie put her hands on her hips and glared at Zee who chuckled. It was so much fun teasing her. "It'll be all right, darlin'," she soothed. "You'll see."

The entrance doors swung open and every head turned. Sheriff Hogan was wearing a fancy new waistcoat. With him was a bandy-legged little man wearing a black sombrero and shabby chaps. A murmur went round the room.

"Is that the marrying squire?" asked Christie.

Zee nodded. "Crutchfield's quite a character. But he's quick and he's legal."

"What do you mean?" Christie frowned as Crutchfield threaded his way toward the front of the throng. There, the little man smiled and shook hands with a wan-looking Blue, then took his place facing the guests. Hogan patted Blue on the back and stood next to him.

A stir to one side proved to be Serena, plonking her shapely bottom on the piano stool and pumping the player piano's pedals for all she was worth. As the first chords of "Here Comes the Bride" (Angie had come across the piece on one of the new piano rolls) boomed around the room, the guests craned their necks round toward the entrance doors. Zee was no exception.

In the open doorway stood the bride-to-be, cradling her belly. Beside her, looking magnificent in crimson Turkish trousers, stood Angie. (Since there was no father to give Jenny away, the madam, who had taken quite a shine to her, had offered to do the job instead.)

When Jenny saw all the faces looking at her, she froze, unable to take another step. But Angie whispered something in her ear, and she nodded, took a deep breath, and continued on. As she passed, people shouted out well wishes. The fear in her wide brown eyes made her look even more faun-like than ever, and Zee gave her an encouraging wink. Then Jenny saw Blue and had eyes for nobody else.

Zee watched the pregnant girl hurry toward her intended, stand next to him, and shyly take his hand. From beside her came a muffled sniffle. She pulled out a clean handkerchief and handed it to Christie. Zee had pegged her as the type to cry at weddings. Looked like she was right.

Crutchfield had been watching the proceedings with a wide smile. Now, he stepped forward, clasped his sombrero to his chest with one hand and raised the other for silence. With a discordant squawk, the player piano fell silent.

"Howdy, folks." A ripple of laughter met his informal greeting. "Reckon we all know why we're here this fine afternoon." He nodded at the nervous couple. "Blue Hayes and Jenny Farnham are here to get spliced . . . And by the looks of it," he eyed Jenny's belly, "not a moment too soon."

The couple tried not to look at one another, their cheeks a matching shade of pink. The wedding guests laughed louder, and Zee reached for Christie's hand and squeezed it.

"So," continued the marrying squire, "let's get the formalities over and done with and we can get on with what's important—celebrating."

He waited for the laughter to die away, assumed a solemn expression, then turned to Jenny. "Take him?" he asked.

She blinked, looked at Blue, looked back at Crutchfield, who was clearly waiting for an answer, then murmured a rather tentative, "Yes."

Crutchfield nodded and turned to face Blue. "Take her?"

By now the groom had got the hang of things, and he nodded and said, loud and clear, "Yes."

"Done." Crutchfield's face broke into a smile. "One dollar, please." When it became clear that the pockets Blue was patting were empty, Hogan produced a silver dollar and flipped it to the marrying squire. He tucked it in his pocket then asked, "What are you waiting for, son? Kiss your wife."

As Blue kissed his bride, a cheer went up and hats were thrown into the air. The hand holding Zee's tugged her round.

"Is that it?" Christie looked astonished.

"Told you he was quick."

A side door opened and Hattie appeared with a tray of full champagne glasses. She placed it on a table and disappeared, then returned seconds later with several more.

"C'mon," said Zee. "Let's mosey on over to the bride and groom and congratulate 'em."

They made their way between the other guests, Zee guiding Christie with a hand in the small of her back. The noise rose as trays of food appeared and the mood turned to one of post-nuptial celebration. By the time they reached Christie's brother and his new wife, they were having to shout to make themselves heard.

"Congratulations, Blue. Jenny," bellowed Christie. She hugged them both in turn. "I finally have a sister-in-law."

Jenny gave her a shy smile.

Blue put his arm round his wife. "Do you think our parents would have approved?"

Christie laughed. "Probably not at first, but they'd have come around. You know they only wanted us to be happy."

He grinned and squeezed Jenny who laughingly protested. "Well, Lord knows, I am happy," he said, kissing her on the cheek.

"Goodness only knows what they'd have made of Crutchfield, though!" Christie craned her head. "Where is he?"

A few inquiries by Zee elicited the fact that the little man had disappeared, saying he had another wedding to officiate at. Not before eating a whole peach pie and drinking three glasses of champagne though. Which reminded her . . .

A tray was passing within reaching distance, so Zee confiscated it, handed out the glasses of champagne, and took one for herself.

Christie's brow wrinkled. "Should Jenny be drinking?"

"A sip of champagne won't hurt her." Zee raised her glass. "A toast. To Blue and Jenny. May you both find as much happiness with each other as I've found with Christie."

Green eyes brimmed and a tear threatened to fall. Zee wound an arm round Christie's shoulders and pulled her close. "I mean it," she murmured. The tear fell.

"Sorry, Blue." Christie produced her handkerchief and blew her nose. "I always cry at weddings."

Zee dropped a fond kiss on her head. "To the happy couple," she said. Glasses clinked, and they drank.

Chapter 17

"WAISTCOAT LOOKS BETTER on you than it does on me." Hogan's voice came from beside Zee. "But not by much."

"Have to take your word for it." She gave her boss a wry smile. "Be glad to get back into my old duds. This collar's killing me."

She passed him the whiskey bottle, whose contents she had made a good-sized dent in. Champagne was all very well for special occasions, but it wasn't a *real* drink. She glanced across the room to where Christie was talking to a tall woman in a black habit, veil, and pleated cape.

Hogan followed her glance and laughed. "You don't need to worry, Brodie. I don't think she'll be joining the Sisters of Charity any time soon."

Zee grunted and took another sip of whiskey. "Better not. Though it wouldn't be the first time I had to kidnap a girl from them."

"I'll pretend I didn't hear that."

Her gaze traveled to Blue and Jenny, who were in animated conversation with Angie, then continued on to where some of the whores were huddled in conversation, sly gazes resting on the newlyweds. "Hm."

"What?"

"Reckon that lot are planning a chivaree."

Hogan's eyes swiveled to follow her gaze. He became thoughtful. "Reckon you're right. Want me to put a stop to it, case it gets out of hand?" It wasn't unknown for shots to be fired, or for grooms to be kidnapped and dunked in the river.

Zee considered. "No," she said at last. "Can't have a wedding without a chivaree. But I'll go along, keep an eye on things . . . Jenny being pregnant and all."

He nodded and took a gulp of whiskey. "Know where they're spending the honeymoon?"

She checked for eavesdroppers and leaned closer. "Got themselves a room at Mrs. Sandridge's."

Hogan winced. "Watch out for the rolling pin."

"WHAT WERE YOU and the sheriff talking about?" Christie had tracked Zee down beside the buffet table.

"Oh, you know." She spoke round a mouthful of apple pie. Not as good as Christie's, but it would mop up the whiskey. "Bit of this, bit of that."

Christie folded her arms and tapped one foot. "Zerelda Brodie," she said, her use of Zee's full name signaling her displeasure. "I know you're up to something. If it involves my brother and his *very* pregnant wife, then I'm entitled to know about it. So if you don't tell me, this minute . . ."

Zee held up her hands in mock surrender. "All right, all right." Aware of the glances coming their way, she took Christie by the elbow and guided her to a corner where they could talk without being overheard.

"We're pretty sure that Red Mary and the others are planning a chivaree."

Christie looked dismayed. "But is that wise in Jenny's condition?"

"That's why Hogan agreed to my going along."

"Oh." She looked thoughtful.

"I promise, no harm will come to Blue, Jenny, or the baby. I'll make sure of that."

"And so will I."

"But—"

Green eyes fixed her with a look. "You have some objection to my going too?"

Zee knew that tone and conceded defeat. "No, darlin'. It's a celebration. The more the merrier."

ZEE HALTED OUTSIDE Mrs. Sandridge's boarding house. Christie did too, setting off a domino chain of collisions amongst those crowding her heels. Each bump was accompanied by the rattle of a tambourine, the *bonk* of a drum, the *clang* of a tin pail, each in their turn followed by shushing noises and whispered apologies.

Zee rolled her eyes. *As though they can't hear us a mile away.*

She hadn't expected so many people to turn up. There were about thirty in all, mostly whores and their friends, but also a few old reprobates and hangers-on who had heard that there was fun and free drinks to be had tonight. Many were already the worse for liquor, which had made instructing them in the "dos and don'ts" more tedious than it should have been. In the end, she had threatened to throw them in jail if they so much as pulled out a gun let alone fired it. What's more, while Blue was fair game, his wife was out of bounds. Many had grumbled at that, but in the end all agreed to her conditions.

The revelers were dressed as was traditional for a chivaree. Some had blacked their faces or donned their clothes backwards, and others were wearing masks. Zee hadn't bothered—there was no way to disguise her height and pale blue eyes. Neither had Christie, who saw herself more as an observer than a participant.

Zee pointed up at a window on the top floor. "That's their room." The curtains were drawn, the room dark.

"They're probably asleep," said Christie.

"Won't be for long." She turned to the waiting crowd and signaled. A cheer went up, and suddenly every hand was brandishing a musical instrument.

Well, maybe not musical, amended Zee as the ensuing cacophony threatened the eardrums of everyone in the vicinity. Kettles and tin pails clanked, drums banged, a horn tooted, but the worst caterwauling by far came from a cracked fiddle that Silas Ward had brought along. Christie stuck her fingers in her ears and gave Zee an appalled look.

She laughed and returned her gaze to the window. A lamp had been lit, and as she watched, someone slid open the sash. Next minute, Blue was leaning out, gesticulating and mouthing something that Zee thought might have been, "Keep the noise down. My wife's asleep."

A hand on her shoulder pulled her down to Christie's level, and she felt warm breath against her ear. "Look at his face! He's furious."

"It's a chivaree. What did he expect?"

Zee straightened then made her way toward the front door. She raised her fist and was about to thump the door for admittance, when it opened of its own accord.

"What on earth's all this noise? Can't decent God-fearing people get any sleep in this town?"

A middle-aged woman stood there, her hair tied up in papers, her expression stormy. One hand held closed her dressing gown, whose vivid shade of fuchsia made Zee blink, the other clasped a rolling pin. "Deputy Brodie. Might have guessed *you'd* be involved in this tomfoolery." She raised her makeshift weapon.

Whoops! Zee held up her hands in a placating gesture. "Evening, Mrs. Sandridge. Sorry 'bout the ruckus. We're here to chivaree Blue Hayes and his new wife."

She darted past the landlady into the hall just as the rolling pin came down, missing her arm by inches. Laughing under her breath, she headed for the foot of the stairs and peered up. At least the concert was muffled in here.

"Hallo, Blue," she shouted. "The sooner you come down and take your medicine, the sooner we'll be off your hands."

Doors opened upstairs and startled faces peered down the stairwell at her.

"Well, *really!*" said Mrs. Sandridge, coming up behind her. "You're disturbing everyone in the place. Call yourself the law?"

Zee turned and gestured at the empty spot on her vest where her tin star was usually pinned. "No, ma'am. I'm off duty." A loud *harrumph* met that remark but the rolling pin kept its distance. Keeping a wary eye on it, Zee turned back to the stairwell. Blue's face had joined those peering down at her.

"Come on down, Blue. We promise to go easy on you."

After a moment he gave a reluctant nod. Mission accomplished, Zee eased her way back outside, past the still annoyed Mrs. Sandridge.

Lamps had gone on all along the street, and faces now peered from every open window and door as people watched the chivaree. A distant coyote had added its howling to the din. If anything, it improved it.

Zee was contemplating putting her fingers in her ears, when something made her cheek smart. She glanced up, puzzled. Something hit her on the forehead too. *Hailstones?*

She snatched one of the tiny missiles out of the air and examined it, then laughed and shook her head. Barred from using their guns, people were firing peashooters instead, peppering the windowpane of Blue's room with dried peas.

Christie came up beside Zee and pulled her down to her level. "Is he coming?"

She ducked another shower of peas. "On his way."

"Good. I can't take much more of this."

The "music" stopped, and a loud cheer erupted. They turned in time to see an apprehensive Blue standing in the boarding house doorway. He stepped outside, and the crowd surged forward, taking Zee and Christie with it.

When things settled again, several of the stronger men had heaved Blue up onto their shoulders and were parading him up and down in front of the boarding house. The chivaree participants yelled catcalls, cast aspersions on Blue's sexual prowess, sent well wishes to the happy couple, or demanded drink.

A glance up at Blue's open window showed an anxious Jenny looking down at the melee. Zee gave her a reassuring thumbs-up.

Blue gaped down at Zee from his perch and mouthed, "What do I do now?"

Reaching into her shirt pocket for the wad of bills she had crammed there earlier, she eased her way toward him. "Take this," she shouted, pressing the bills into his hand. "Tell them to buy drinks with it."

He nodded his understanding. Struggling upright, his supporters adjusting their grip to keep him from tumbling, he held up his hands for silence. It took a moment for everyone to notice, then the crowd quieted into an expectant hush.

"Thank you for all your good wishes, folks. I appreciate them. Now if you don't mind, my wife," he gestured toward the watching Jenny, "is waiting for me, and it *is* our honeymoon."

"What about us?" yelled someone.

"Yeah. What will you give us to leave you in peace?" shouted someone else.

"And by way of a thank you," Blue held up the money, eliciting a loud cheer, "the drinks are on me. Enjoy yourselves."

A big woman in a sparkly purple eye mask—Red Mary, if Zee was any judge—hurried to the front and snatched the bills from Blue's hand. "Follow me," she shouted. "The celebration's just beginning."

Those who wanted to go home and those who wanted to continue partying parted company. After a momentary confusion, Zee, Christie, and Blue found themselves alone on the sidewalk watching the procession wend its way toward the nearest saloon.

As the laughter and chatter, the *clank* and *bong* and *rattle* of instruments faded into the distance, Christie breathed a sigh of relief. The watching faces along the street disappeared and the doors and windows thudded closed.

"Jenny, you'll catch cold." Blue was gazing up at his wife. "Go back to bed. I'll be up soon." She nodded, ducked back out of sight, and seconds later the sash window slid shut.

"All right?" asked Zee. Christie nodded. "How about you, Blue?"

He gave her a rueful grin. "Thanks for the dollars. You saved my bacon."

She grinned and shook his outstretched hand. "Always glad to help out a brother-in-law."

Christie cuddled closer to Zee and asked plaintively, "Can we go home now?"

Zee yawned as the day's excitement caught up with her. "Reckon so." She winked at Blue. "What you still doing here? Your bride's awaiting."

"Oh . . . yes." Blushing, he turned on his heel and headed for the boarding house's front door. "Good night," he called, as he disappeared inside. "And thank you again."

"You're welcome," shouted Zee.

"What a day!" said Christie, as they strolled arm in arm to where they'd left the buckboard.

"Mm." Zee helped Christie up before untethering the horse. "But you know what, darlin'?" She hopped up on the seat beside her. "The best bit's yet to come."

Epilogue

CHRISTIE HURRIED INTO the kitchen, glad to leave the tobacco smoke and noisy hubbub behind for a short while. No wonder Zerelda had burst into tears.

She peered out the window. In the back yard, Zee was talking to their niece and bouncing her up and down. Christie tried to make out what she was saying. Something about the horsey? Whatever it was met with an enthusiastic wave of miniature hands and feet. Christie chuckled and turned away.

Glasses. I came for glasses.

She was kneeling, unearthing them from a bottom cupboard, when the door opened letting in the noise from the parlor. Someone was playing "Beautiful Dreamer" very badly. It couldn't be Blue or Jenny, Hogan or Angie, Ann or Curly, as none of them could play a note. Which left . . . Surely not Sister Florence? Well, she *had* had rather a lot to drink.

"Need any help, Christie?"

She smiled up at Ann Shaw. "You and Curly have already done more than your fair share. Those peach pies were wonderful."

Ann closed the kitchen door behind her, muffling the noise. "Blue ate one all by himself," she said. "He's putting on weight, isn't he?"

Christie straightened and carried the glasses to the sink where she proceeded to wash the dust from them. "Let's not mince words, Ann. My brother is getting fat. He is also boring. If he tells me one more longwinded story about what he and the other members of the Cactus Club have been up to . . ." She broke off. "He's happy though. That's the important thing."

Ann picked up a tea towel and began to dry the glasses. Christie smiled her thanks.

"And Jenny expecting again too," said Ann. "Already."

"I know. Poor girl. Someone should have a word with her and Blue about where babies come from."

Ann shot her a mischievous glance. "Sister Florence, perhaps?"

Christie snorted. "Now *that* I would pay to see."

She stacked the clean glasses on a tray then looked out the window once more. Zee appeared to be explaining the intricacies of saddles to her namesake. She chuckled. Ann turned to see what had amused her and smiled.

"Curly was the same, when our two were young. Soft as butter, he was, though he pretended otherwise."

Christie leaned forward and rapped her knuckle against the windowpane. Zee turned at the sound, saw her, and grinned.

"Everything all right?" mouthed Christie.

Zee nodded, bounced her niece up and down one last time, then rested her against her shoulder and walked toward the house. The back door opened.

"Peaceful out there," said Zee, coming in and closing the door behind her.

Christie sighed. "Remind me again whose idea this soirée was?"

"Yours, darlin'. All yours." Zee bent forward, careful not to jog the sleepy baby, and pressed a kiss on Christie's cheek. "What are you two doing in here? You had enough already? Evening's still young."

Christie gestured at the tray. "We ran out of glasses."

Zee pursed her lips. "The way Sister Florence and Angie are knocking back the hard stuff, we'll soon be out of whiskey."

"She's certainly not your run of the mill nun, is she?"

"She's Angie's friend," said Zee. "What did you expect? Hey, little one. Ready for a nap?" The baby yawned, opened tiny hands like starfish then curled them closed again.

Christie regarded the two Zees fondly. With her fair hair and faun-like eyes, her niece looked nothing like her namesake. But Jenny had insisted on naming her daughter after the deputy, and Zee hadn't had the heart to say no.

"Let's get her back to her mother." She picked up the tray and led the way.

FACES TURNED IN Christie's direction as she entered the parlor, and a loud cheer greeted the new arrivals. She placed the tray of glasses on the top of the piano. Sister Florence grinned up at her and continued her discordant *plinkety plink.*

Christie turned and watched Zee make her way toward Jenny. The young mother was sitting on the sofa next to her husband. She smiled, accepted the baby from Zee, exchanged a few words with her, then stood up.

"I'm just taking her upstairs," Jenny told Christie, as she came within earshot. "She'll sleep now, I think."

Christie nodded. The smoke had grown thicker and made her eyes smart. She crossed to the window and flung it wide open.

"You never did tell us what this little shindig is in honor of, Christie," said Angie, whose pipe was the primary source of the smoke. "Your new piano?"

The upright pianoforte had arrived by wagon just over a fortnight ago—unexpectedly as far as Christie was concerned, but it was clear from Zee's reaction that she and Blue had been hatching the plot to transport it to Benson for some time. Overjoyed at the instrument's arrival, Christie had at once arranged for the tuner to call.

She had missed being able to play Chopin and Beethoven sonatas whenever the mood took her—the whores favored popular songs. Now, she could play the classics to her heart's content, though she was happy to switch to something lighter whenever Zee was around. On occasion, Zee even accompanied her—she had revealed an unsuspected talent for the jew's-harp and the harmonica (all those long evenings spent sitting by a camp fire, she confessed).

"Partly the piano," said Christie. "But today is also a very special anniversary."

Sister Florence stopped playing. "Really?" Her eyes were bright. "Whose?" The abrupt cessation of the music made all heads turn toward them. Christie's cheeks grew warm, and she resisted the urge to flee.

"Exactly one year ago," she announced, as a quizzical-looking Zee came to stand beside her, "something happened to change the course of my life." The parlor door opened and Jenny returned minus the baby, to be met by shushing noises and nods in Christie's direction. She slid into her seat and looked expectantly at Christie.

A warm hand eased into Christie's and she gripped it. "A year ago today, someone came into my life who has since become indispensable to my happiness." She turned to regard the woman standing next to her. "Zee."

Zee's gaze turned inwards, and after a moment she nodded, her expression one of surprised pleasure. "To the very day," she confirmed, raising Christie's hand to her lips.

A chorus of *oohs* and *ahs* met this gesture, until Hogan spoiled the mood by shouting, "Anyone got a pail of cold water handy?"

"If they have," riposted Zee, "it's going over *your* head."

Christie gave Zee and her boss a quelling glance and waited for silence to return. "What's more," she continued, "it was my brother who brought us together."

"I did not," protested Blue.

Christie frowned at him. "Was it not because he'd had dealings with you in the past that Hogan told Zee to wait at our house for the train?"

"Dang right it was," shouted Hogan. "That and the fact your house was nearest to the depot."

Blue stroked his mustache then gave a grudging nod. "All right. I'll give you that."

"And didn't you *then* manage to get called away on business, so that I was left all alone and unprotected when the notorious Hellcat arrived?" She shot Zee a coy glance that made her grin.

"When you put it *that* way . . ." Blue smiled and put his arm round Jenny, who clapped her hands together in delight.

"Was it love at first sight?" she asked.

"No indeed," said Christie at once. "In fact I thought Zee was the most terrifying woman I had ever met."

"Ha! Terrifying," called out Hogan. "That's Brodie all right." Zee glared at him and he held up his hands. "Don't kill me, Deputy. I'll come peaceable."

Christie ignored this by-play. "I soon changed my mind though. I came to think she was merely the most impudent and forward woman I had ever met." Her words were greeted with catcalls and laughter. Zee arched an eyebrow in mock outrage.

The goodwill coming from their guests was palpable now, and Christie felt suddenly at ease. This was her home; she was among friends; the love of her life was standing beside her, holding her hand.

"But the *real* clincher," she continued, "was the flower bulbs she brought me all the way from Yuma. What could I do after such a romantic gesture but follow her to Benson?" She gave an eloquent shrug. "My goose was well and truly cooked."

Zee pulled Christie toward her and gave her a hug. "So was mine, darlin'," she murmured in her ear. "And I wouldn't change a thing."

"A toast," yelled Sister Florence. "Everyone, fill your glasses."

A mad scramble for bottles and glasses ensued, and when the chaos had turned to order once more, a sea of smiling faces and raised glasses met them. Christie and Zee exchanged a glance and reached for their own glasses, which someone had thoughtfully topped up.

"To Zee and Christie, Happy Anniversary," chorused their guests.

Reflected in Zee's eyes was a love and affection that more than matched Christie's own. Smiling, she clinked her glass against Zee's. "And many more to come."

Barbara Davies was born in Birmingham but now lives in the English Cotswolds. She worked for many years in IT, before becoming a freelance writer and book reviewer.

Barbara started out writing short specfic stories and was first published in 1994. Since then, more than fifty of her stories have appeared in various anthologies, ezines, and magazines. Three of her short story collections are available from Bedazzled Ink.

She now also writes longer fiction in assorted genres. Three of her books were shortlisted for a GCLS (Golden Crown Literary Society) Award, and *Bourn's Edge* won a Goldie for Speculative Fiction. All five of her novels are available from Bedazzled Ink.

Her website is: www.barbaradavies.co.uk